THE ROYAL MARINE SPACE COMMANDOS VOL 2

JON EVANS

JAMES EVANS

IMAGINARY BROTHER

Join the Imaginary Brother mailing list at
imaginarybrother.com/journeytothewest

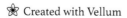 Created with Vellum

ASCENDANT

RMSC OMNIBUS - BOOK 3

PROLOGUE

Atticus shrugged. "I don't know, Colour Jenkins, I imagine Lieutenant Warden thought you'd make good use of an ogre clone, given your combat experience."

Colour Sergeant Stephanie Jenkins muttered something under her breath and Atticus stifled a smile. There wasn't much he could do. He could hardly haul Warden over the coals for his assignment of clone body types.

"We'll be able to reassign some clones shortly, so if you want to be redeployed into a different model, I'm sure we can do that for you."

"Thank you, sir, much appreciated," Jenkins replied, the basso voice her clone produced somehow fitting her usually gruff demeanour.

"Now, it looks like we're approaching the Deathless base. Let's see if we can't turn this place into something useful, hmm?" Atticus said.

The base loomed ahead, still huge and impressive despite the devastation caused by Warden and his assault team during the attack on the so-called 'mothership'. With more Marines being deployed, they now had the bodies to make use of the base and recover more of the potentially useful equipment the Deathless had been forced to abandon. That meant getting to the base with a team to properly catalogue whatever Warden and Marine X hadn't turned to rubble.

More importantly, Atticus wanted to garrison the base before the Deathless colonists, who had landed only eight hundred kilometres to the southwest, could retake the site and settle back in. Warden had offered to lead the group, of course, but Atticus had overruled him and now led the mission himself.

Lieutenant Warden was now extremely busy with his new task: overseeing clone redeployment, work assignments and logistics. Warden had winced visibly when Atticus had given him the good news, but he hadn't complained. The job had to be done, and handling councillors' complaints about deploying Marines ahead of colonists or arguing with politicians about what types of clones to grow was just an unfortunate part of it. Atticus couldn't help grinning at the thought of Warden getting involved in local politics and dealing with the 'personalities'.

"And it'll look good on your resume, Tom," Atticus had said. "The general likes to see his officers taking on these sorts of responsibilities and while you get stuck in here, I can take A Troop on a nice, easy road trip." Warden hadn't been keen but they had talked it over and, by the time Atticus had left, the lieutenant was elbows deep into the detailed plans.

Which left Atticus out in the field, doing the job he loved. HQ claimed he had been a captain for too long, but they respected his lack of interest in promotion. If he had gone much higher in the ranks, he would have been stuck behind a desk for the rest of his career. There just weren't any large scale wars in this day and age, so nobody above the rank of captain saw any interesting action at all.

The troop carrier ground to a halt and bumped him out of his daydream. He went to crack his knuckles, then realised it wasn't going to work with the fingers of his Deathless officer clone. He pulled on his armoured gauntlets and ran a diagnostic check to confirm the power armour was functional.

Around him, the Marines were piling out of the enormous Deathless troop carrier and deploying across the plain. Colour Sergeant

Jenkins was in the van, leading a section forward at double-time to secure the area and take control of the remains of the gatehouse.

Behind the Marines, the civilians pulled up, their rovers hauling sleds to take back to Fort Widley anything of value that wasn't required to get the base up and running.

<Movement ahead> sent Jenkins.

<Confirmed?> Atticus checked his rifle, suddenly wary.

<Hold for confirmation> sent Jenkins, then a moment later, <Confirmed. Drones have Deathless troops in sight. Advancing to cover>

Atticus paused, watching the Marines fan out as Jenkins and her team, about two hundred metres ahead, sprinted for cover.

He turned to the civilians and waved at them, contacting their lead vehicle by HUD.

<Pull back, there are Deathless on site>

He found Sergeant Millar.

"Get Section 3 back there in the APC to babysit the civilians, in case there are any Deathless out here. I don't want an ambush."

Then he gathered up Section 2 and moved out with them, sprinting to catch up with Jenkins.

∼

Atticus dove for cover as the head of the Marine next to him disintegrated under the impact of a railgun projectile.

"Railgun," he bellowed, and around him the Marines sought cover.

"Smoke out," he said, grabbing a grenade from his webbing and lobbing it forward. A cloud of concealing smoke spewed from the grenade, growing quickly as more grenades were thrown.

"Lance Corporal Mills, get me drone footage, I want to know where that sniper is," Atticus yelled as an enfilade clattered across the rocks they were sheltering behind.

Another railgun round boomed through the morning air, shattering a boulder and exposing the Marine who had taken shelter behind it. The trooper sprang forward, rifle returning fire as he bolted for cover. He almost made it but another round took him in the shoulder, spinning him around and separating his arm in a shower of blood.

"Bollocks to this — these rocks aren't as tough as they look. Jenkins, I need covering fire!" he shouted. "Keep moving."

<Sergeant Millar> sent Atticus, <get the cannon on the APC opened up around the gatehouse>

<Range is a bit extreme, sir, we pulled well back as ordered>

<I'm not interested in specifics, Sergeant, I only need to give them a reason to keep their heads down. Get it done>

<Roger that, sir> Sergeant Mills responded. The air was filled with fire from the Marines around Atticus, and then the cannon on the APC opened up too, rounds sparking off the foamcrete of the walls.

"Drone's up, sir," shouted Mills.

Atticus flipped to the drone's viewpoint, watching as the rounds suppressed the Deathless bastards. Time to move in three, two... one.

He sprinted out from behind the rock, rifle slung over his back as he wasn't planning to use it. Four hundred metres. Four hundred metres and the enemy had at least one railgun. If they kept their heads down, he might make it.

No such luck, he thought, as his leg went out from under him. Bugger. Damage reports flashed across his HUD, but he barely had time to register them as he crashed to the deck, throwing his arms out in front of him. He turned the dive into a forward roll and came up running, or at least stumbling quickly.

"You alright there, sir?" Jenkins asked.

"Just a scratch," Atticus replied jovially through gritted teeth, "but I wouldn't mind if someone could get those buggers to keep their heads down." He ran on, zig-zagging towards the wall.

"Roger that, sir. Come on, you lot — who wants to live forever?" Jenkins roared, rising to her feet and pounding after the captain. The enormous power armoured bulk of her ogre clone shook the ground as she sprinted forward, the shotgun in her hand pointed forward like a pistol. She fired at the top of the wall, where the enemy had to be, but the range was huge. The Deathless up there weren't immediately cowed and they returned a barrage of fire.

At two hundred metres, Atticus ordered an emergency cocktail of painkillers and stimulants from the suit's casualty support system. He put on a burst of speed as the pain lessened but the warning symbols were now blinking angrily in his HUD. He made it to a large rock and slid into cover, panting into his helmet for a few moments before righting himself.

The stimulants had kicked in now and he surged back to his feet, ignoring the alarms. Bullets ricocheted from the rock as he broke cover, sprinting forward as fire from his own team roared overhead. One hundred metres to go.

Atticus pulled a grapnel from his webbing as he ran and hooked the line to his harness as he drew closer to the wall. He switched direction again then took the shot as he fell under the shadow of the great wall. The grapnel looped over one of the foamcrete spikes that thrust out from the top of the wall and the winch yanked Atticus into the air even as he leapt at the wall.

He rose rapidly as the line was winched in. He pulled a flashbang from his webbing and lobbed it over the wall. It detonated as he neared the top of the wall. Then he dragged himself over the lip of the wall onto the parapet and unclipped from the line to free himself. As the grapnel swung free, Atticus unslung his rifle, shouldered it and fanned to the left.

Clear.

He turned right, rifle at the ready.

Contact.

Three rounds into the torso of a Deathless trooper still reeling from the grenade. Two more in the head of his mate.

Not his target though. He heard the railgun spit its lethal projectile again and wondered if he had lost another Marine to the brutal discharge. Fuck.

Where was the sniper? The bastard had to be here somewhere. Atticus pressed forward, his weapon kicking against his shoulder as he cut a bloody swathe through the Deathless troops.

Then he saw a flash from the roof of one of the buildings near the wall and heard the telltale sound of a railgun. He emptied his magazine towards the building and lobbed another grenade for good measure. He jogged back a few paces, swapped in a new magazine and slung his rifle. Then he turned to face the building, gritted his teeth and took a running jump.

Even as the power armour pushed him further than he could ever have jumped unaided, he knew he wasn't going to make it.

He wrapped his arms around his head and crashed through a window on a lower storey, rolling across the floor in a shower of glass and curses. Atticus staggered to his feet, shook himself free of the remains of the window then unslung his rifle and made for a staircase. The death knell of the railgun sang out again, and he yelled in frustration, taking the stairs four at a time.

The painkillers weren't doing much to suppress the punishment he was putting his leg through anymore and the 'scratch' burned like a red-hot poker. Well, like a bullet wound really, and he'd had lots of those. Never a red-hot poker, at least not to date, but it would surely be similar, wouldn't it?

The door to the roof was propped open, a sensible precaution if you wanted to get easily off the roof.

But not too smart if you're sniping at my Marines, you bastard, thought Atticus. He charged out onto the roof and ducked almost immediately as some cocky bugger tried to stab him with a glowing knife. Bloody hell, who gave these kids knives?

Atticus left the Deathless trooper with three ugly holes in his chest and throat, gurgling his last. The railgun fired again, revealing the sniper's location and Atticus crossed the roof as quickly as he could, one eye watching for any other jokers trying to stick things in his face.

He moved between two ventilation units and went left. The roof was clear, all along the wall. He swung quickly the other way, and saw the sniper was crouched near the wall.

But he wasn't aiming out over the wall — he was bringing his weapon to bear.

Atticus snarled and leapt. His rifle spat fire. The railgun boomed.

"Colour Jenkins, how goes it?" Atticus asked.

She crouched down, her power armoured bulk casting a welcome shadow over him. Reaching out, she helped him remove his helmet. There was blood around his mouth and his face was creased with pain.

"They retreated, sir. The lasses and lads gave them a good seeing-to and they backed off. We lost a few, though, even after you put the railgun out of action. These ones are putting up a better fight than the others. They're more cunning, more resilient," Jenkins said, offering him a canteen. He shook his head and spat blood onto the roof.

"Maybe more experienced," Atticus suggested. "Where did they go?"

Jenkins shrugged, the gesture incongruous in her huge ogre clone. "Not sure, sir, they legged it to a dropship and took off before we could catch up and put it out of action."

"A dropship? They must be from the ship Warden scuttled. They only captured three of their dropships; we thought the fourth had gone down with the ship."

"Looks like it survived, sir. And I think they've been stripping the base. Not just today either. Lots of stuff is conspicuous by its absence. They must have their own Fort Widley somewhere," Jenkins said.

Atticus nodded, or at least tried to.

"You look a bit peaky, sir, if you don't mind me saying. Not that it's easy to tell with these Rupert clones," Jenkins said with a grin that didn't really hide her concern, "they all look the same to me."

"Har de har har, Colour Jenkins," said Atticus, blood dribbling down his chin. He tried to wipe it away but his arm wasn't working properly. "I do feel a little under the weather. I think I'll just lie here for a bit and get my second wind."

"Pretty sure you're missing a large chunk of your lung, sir. I don't think you'll be getting your second wind any time soon."

"Figure of speech, Jenkins," he whispered, "figure of speech."

"Sorry, sir. Any preference when we redeploy you?"

"Marine standard, please, and tell them you can go up to HMS *Albion* and have your pick too," Atticus said, voice almost inaudible as he coughed and spat out more blood.

Jenkins shook her head. "Actually, sir, I think I'll stick with this one for a while. It has its advantages and it looks like we aren't done with the Deathless on New Bristol yet." He nodded.

"No, Colour Sergeant, I think they'll be a thorn in our side..." he coughed once more and his head lolled to one side.

Jenkins sighed. It wasn't the clone that made the captain tough. Atticus held the record for the most deaths of any serving officer in the Royal Marine Space Commandos. Not because he was bad at it, far from it, but because he led from the front and didn't ask his Marines to do anything that he wouldn't do himself. She reached out and closed his alien-seeming eyes, whispered a short 'Fuck you' to the Deathless and stood up.

The base needed tidying up and the captain wouldn't thank her when he was redeployed if they had stood around all day just wailing and whining. She walked over to the side of the roof and bellowed down at the troop. "Right, you lot. The captain's dead!"

"Again?" some joker remarked.

"Yes, again, and just for that you can detail all the Deathless bodies and gather them up to be taken back to Fort Widley for recycling. I want this place checked for boobytraps before we let the civilians move in to requisition equipment and supplies. Load anything the colonists need and we don't onto the transports and haul it back to Fort Widley," said Jenkins.

"Are we falling back, Colour?" someone asked.

"No, we're bloody not. We're going to turn this mess into a forward operating base," Jenkins said, "and I want it operational before the Deathless come back." She paused, looking over her troops. "Get ready, ladies and gents. When the captain is back on his feet, we're going to war."

1

"Is that another new clone, Edward?" said General Bonneville, leaning close to peer at the image of Atticus.

"Yes, sir, fresh and clean, although not the outfit I requested."

"What happened to the old one?"

"Railgun round to the abdomen, sir, bled out before there was a chance to receive medical attention."

"Nasty. Was it at that Deathless colony?"

"No, sir. We have that under surveillance, but the colonists appear to be civilians and we haven't approached them yet. They're too far away to get there easily on the ground and we don't know what their anti-air capabilities are like yet, so we've not tried dropships for scouting. This was at the military outpost the Deathless had set up while we were there foraging for supplies. Unfortunately, so were they."

"The colonists?" Bonneville asked, clearly confused.

"No, sir. We think these were some of the original Deathless troopers from the initial invasion. Warden captured three dropships when he destroyed their capital ship but the fourth was assumed to have gone down with the ship. It seems some Deathless troopers got off the ship and have been in hiding ever since. They used the drop-ship to retreat from the base, so we're pretty sure that's the scenario."

"I see. So you have one colony town that needs to be kept in check and a roving band of Deathless you need to find."

"That's about the size of it, sir. We're not done here yet."

"I had hoped you might have room for a breather, but it appears not." Bonneville nodded and looked at something off-camera. "We need to reinforce you as soon as possible. If the Deathless come back, I don't want us caught with our pants down. The Navy is sending reinforcements for Vice Admiral Staines and I'm sending a full battalion to New Bristol for deployment as quickly as you can grow new clones."

"Yes, sir, that will be helpful. Who will take command, if you don't mind my asking?"

"Take command?" said Bonneville, frowning. "I'm not changing my lead coach halfway through the game, Atticus. You'll remain in charge, Lieutenant Colonel, and stick with the mission until it's done."

There was a pause while Atticus processed that, then a look of mild panic rushed across his face.

"With respect, sir, I'm not qualified to be bumped up so many ranks," he said, desperately seeking a way to avoid the promotion.

"If it were with respect, Atticus, you wouldn't presume to lecture me on the rules of battlefield promotions. I checked, and you're more than qualified. You passed all the requisite courses years ago, you have the necessary experience, and you have served as a captain for, let me see," the general looked at something, apparently flicking at a data slate.

Atticus forestalled him, "I know how long I've been a captain, sir, thank you."

"Quite. If you don't want me to remind you of the exact number of years, perhaps we could simply agree that it has been far more than any captain still in active service? You've been allowed to pass up promotion opportunities several times because of your distinguished service record and because we had plenty of alternatives more interested in advancement. I'm afraid we're now long past the point of being able to indulge your preferences, Edward. This isn't a democracy, and we're in a real shooting war for the first time in years. You're the man on the ground, you're already familiar with the enemy, you have more experience than any of our serving lieutenant colonels, and you have a good relationship with local government. I've already discussed this with the governor and she described the idea as 'capital', reporting also that she found you good to work with. Sorry, Lieutenant Colonel Atticus, but I really don't have a choice here," Bonneville said with a shrug that was just the right side of mildly apologetic with a touch of rank-pulling 'get over it' for good measure.

Atticus sighed resignedly as the general concluded his monologue. He'd had a good run. In fact, he was pretty sure he held the record for longest serving Royal Marine Space Commando captain since the corps had been renamed. The rank bump had been something he had avoided because it would mean stepping away from the frontline.

"Yes, sir. I understand and thank you for holding it off this long. I'll miss being on the frontline, though."

"Atticus, I don't think you quite understand. Neither you nor I have ever been on a frontline like this. This is the first serious war in centuries. It was bad enough when we thought they were the first alien contact but now it turns out they're the deadliest species known to man, namely *homo sapiens*. That's worse, in my book. Plus, their ancestors sound like they could very well have been total crackpots, which is probably not a good thing. You're still going to be very much on the leading and bleeding edge of this war unless it shifts away from New Bristol," Bonneville said.

"Understood, sir." Atticus brightened a little. Maybe promotion wouldn't be as bad as he had feared.

"On the other hand, they do seem to be startlingly incompetent, don't you think?"

"Yes, sir. More experienced, maybe. We have some ideas about that but no real evidence so far. We're hoping that Warden and

Cohen's plan to visit the enemy at NewPet will yield the necessary intelligence."

There was a pause while Bonneville thought about this. Then he nodded.

"Speaking of Warden, he'll need a bump as well. He's ready to be a captain, wouldn't you say?"

"Undoubtedly, sir."

"Good, because the mission profile that he and Cohen drafted will need at least a full company. I'm going to be sending you the best-qualified people I can to form your new command. They will be full companies from existing units, of course, so they're familiar with each other. Governor Denmead will act as my proxy for the promotion ceremony."

"I'd like to keep my existing command team if I may, sir."

"That's fine. You'll need additional personnel, of course. A battalion commander gets a whole bevy of adjutants and other buggers to follow them around. You'll get used to it. Just remember to delegate everything and trust your people to do their jobs. Check your roster, promote whomever you feel is qualified then let me know which gaps I need to fill. I'll try to send people you've worked with before to fill any positions necessary."

"We'll need to promote Jenkins and Milton," Atticus mused.

"Fine, just send me the list and I'll rubber-stamp the promotions. Over."

"Yes, sir. Out."

The promotion ceremony had been brief, understated and yet somehow still excruciating for Atticus. Warden had practically fallen off his chair with laughter when he learned that Atticus was to be made up to lieutenant colonel. He had stopped laughing very quickly when Atticus had told him that he, too, was to be promoted.

They had then gone over the promotions for their teams. Colour Sergeant Jenkins was being made up to warrant officer and given the title of Colour Sergeant Major. Sergeant Milton would take Jenkin's spot as the new Colour Sergeant of Lympstone Company, which Warden was now taking over as captain.

Denmead had pushed the congratulations and back-slapping speech as far as she could without causing Atticus to blow his top. Her political acumen came to the fore as she expertly judged the fine line between embarrassing but entertaining pomp and a joke taken too far.

The crowd of colonists was suspiciously large, Atticus thought. He wondered which of his supposedly loyal troops had stitched him up there. There has been a lot of banners as well but nothing handmade, all good quality, professionally printed stuff.

The fireworks that went off at the end of the ceremony were evidently a surprise to Denmead as well as to everyone else. Atticus thought he sensed the hand of Marine X in that one.

The pièce de résistance had been the drone flyover by the children's militia pilots. The drones flew low, spewing red, white and blue smoke trails, and Atticus couldn't help but admire the ingenuity of it all, even as the prime suspects grinned uncontrollably and took photos.

After that, the embarrassed promotees were dragged off to a badly damaged but partly cleaned bar in Ashton for celebratory drinks.

∼

"I swear, Fletcher, there's a perfectly intact piano upstairs," said Goodwin, pointing to the mezzanine floor that protruded from the remains of the wall.

"Can't be – look at this place, it's a bloody mess. Never mind New Bristol, it looks like Old Bristol on a Saturday night. There're no windows, the bar is shot full of holes and look, half the optics are missing!"

"Well, it is a war zone, you know."

"Yeah, but my point is, you can't play a broken piano."

"I can't play the piano even if it were in perfect working order, but you can," Goodwin pointed out, reasonably.

"Yeah, come on, Fletcher, give us a tune," Milton joined in the cajoling.

"Look," Fletcher said, turning and almost losing half her pint with the vigorous motion, "Sergeant Milton, sorry – Colour Milton – it's hard enough to play the piano in a standard RMSC clone, but it'll be damn near impossible in this hulking great brute of a thing."

"She has a point," conceded Milton, "but what's the worst that could happen? Maybe you'll be able to play loud enough to drown out Ten's – what did he call it? Some word which apparently means singing along to ancient music, without being in tune."

"Carry okey dokey, I think," slurred Fletcher.

"Yeah, anything's got to be better than him singing about getting postcards from chimpanzees for the third time," grumbled Goodwin.

Fletcher shook her head in defeat and trudged upstairs, slightly wobbly on her feet, her clone's huge bulk shaking loose dust with every step. The mezzanine curved out over the stage below with the grand piano positioned so the pianist could look out over the audience while the singer strutted their stuff below.

She sat down on the large bench, gingerly applying her substantial rump to the seat. Fortunately, it had a strong but elegant frame, built in an imitation art deco style. It was easy to produce such furniture with modern 3D printing techniques, so even a piano wouldn't have been too hard to make, although this one was no masterpiece. Still, it should be perfectly functional if the bomb damage to the bar-come-nightclub hadn't been too extreme.

Fletcher gave the ivories an experimental tinkle then, satisfied that the keyboard was working as expected, began to hammer out a rendition of that perennial favourite, "Over the Hills and Far Away". It drew immediate cheers and applause from the Royal Marine and civilian audience alike. Ten's drunken signing was soon drowned out entirely by other drunken people joining in on the familiar tune.

Once she realised the crowd was backing her, Fletcher grew much more enthusiastic. She stood up, pushing the stool back so that she could really give the piano a bashing with her clone's enormous fingers.

"Amazing that it's still in tune," yelled Milton to Goodwin over the noise of the singing.

"I don't like tuna sandwiches," Goodwin shouted back.

Eventually, even Ten began to sing along with Fletcher's music, his brief irritation replaced by the drunk's unshakeable belief that he could carry any tune. There were many things that Ten did well and with great showmanship; drunken singing was not one of them.

But they carried on, nonetheless, belting their way through the popular verses and even a few that were familiar to the Marines and, it seemed, Governor Denmead, but not to most of the colonists. When the last verse was done and the last key tinkled, the crowd chanted Fletcher's name.

Abashed, she walked to the front of the balcony and bowed flamboyantly, accepting the applause with as much grace as she could manage and all the elegance that her huge frame allowed. The crowd clapped enthusiastically as Ten gave his most extravagant courtly bow.

An ominous creak momentarily quieted the crowd as Ten straightened.

And then, with an almighty crash, the balcony carrying Fletcher and the piano broke free from its brutalised supports and crashed down onto the stage, right on top of the unfortunate Ten.

There was a moment of stunned silence as dust rose from the massive pile of rubble. Then Fletcher staggered out of the cloud of muck and onto the floor, covered in filth but otherwise unharmed.

"Encore!" someone shouted, and the Marines all fell about laughing.

2

Aboard *Albion*, the cloning bay was running at full capacity. All three troops of Warden's company were redeploying into Deathless clones in preparation for the voyage to the NewPet system, releasing a steady stream of standard RMSC bodies to be returned to storage, some a little more heavily abused than others.

The techs had made some adjustments to *Albion*'s equipment in order to handle the very large ogre clones and the strange body shapes of the harpies, but both were being processed, now that the bodies had been shuttled across from their storage bays on *Ascendant*.

"Plenty of meat aboard *Ascendant*," Cohen had reported once the inventory was complete, "but the equipment is setup for standard deployment of stored personalities, not a redeployment from a living body."

And that had meant either killing the Marines still running standard RMSC bodies – not an option – or moving the Deathless clones to *Albion* and adjusting the cloning bays to handle the larger frames. It had taken a while to thrash out the details, not to mention the time required to setup and secure the encrypted backup links that would save the Marines' personalities back to *Ascendant* if their bodies were killed in action, but everything was now up and running.

"Do you know anything about this guy?" said Beaufort, staring at a monitor reporting progress on the download of Penal Marine X to his new body. "I heard he was some sort of criminal."

Petty Officer Brin, the other cloning tech, looked up from his own monitor and sniffed. His younger colleague was often more curious than was good for her; this was one of those times.

"His name is listed as 'Marine X'," said Brin, looking back at his own monitor, "and you don't lose your naming rights without having done something very wrong."

"So how come he's here, then? Why bother shipping him out when he should be chilling somewhere on a base doing punishment duties?"

Brin said nothing for a moment. Then there was a ping from the monitor.

"None of our business," he said eventually, fiddling with the controls. "Let's just get them up and running and let the captain worry about whom we're deploying, yes?"

"Just seems weird," muttered Beaufort, checking the controls on her monitor as Brin leant over the clone he was preparing. "I mean, I didn't get shipped out when I got done for that stuff back on base – not that I actually did any of it," she added quickly.

Brin had heard it all before and tuned out as Beaufort whined away about the injustices of her career and the long list of slights and grievances that had culminated in her posting to *Albion*, still an Able Rating despite her years of service.

Then Brin's clone coughed and tried to sit up and Beaufort finally stopped talking.

"There you go, sir," said Brin, helping the clone to sit and swing his legs down to the ground. "Bound to be a little confusion just after redeployment but you're okay. Do you remember where you are?"

The clone looked around, blinking and flexing his fingers. Then he nodded.

"Yes," said Captain Warden, staring at his new fingers and marvelling at the way they moved, "I know where I am and what we're doing. Any problems during the transfer?"

"No, sir, smooth and easy, nothing at all of interest."

"Good, that's exactly how I like these things to go."

Then there was a cough from across the room and the other clone, the one Beaufort had been monitoring, came round.

"What the fuck!" it said, clearly angry and scrabbling at the edges of the slab on which it lay. "I mean, what the actual fuck!"

Warden and Brin turned to see the clone flopping around as Beaufort hurried over to help him sit up.

"Er, Marine X," said Beaufort nervously, hands hovering over the clone's arms as the technician tried to decide how best to help, or even if it was safe to help at all, "you've been deployed after your, er, death."

There was a moment of silence as Marine X focused on the technician and frowned, still trying to work out where he was and what the hell was going on.

"You're aboard *Albion*, sir," said Beaufort, "you, er, you were in an accident, sir. With a piano."

"Wait, what? Sorry, the ears on this thing aren't working properly, I could have sworn you said 'piano'."

"It's a most amusing tale, Marine X," said Warden, striving manfully to keep the grin from his face, "and I'm sure Milton will be keen to walk you through the video."

Marine X looked around then glanced down at his fingers.

"Death? So this was a straight deployment?"

"Yes, sir," said Beaufort, "straight into a Deathless clone, no problems," she went on, checking her monitor, "clean and easy, complete transference."

Marine X heaved himself upright and frowned. He peered at Warden, who was at the same height, then glanced down at his hands again.

"This seems a bit small for an ogre," he muttered, looking over the rest of his body, "shouldn't I be a bit, you know, taller?" he stared meaningfully at the unfortunate technician, who swallowed nervously and glanced at Warden.

The captain nodded encouragingly, utterly refusing to help her explain.

"Er, well, it's not exactly an ogre, sir," said Beaufort. "We didn't have one to hand so, er." She stopped as the frown deepened on Marine X's face. "Sorry."

"Not an ogre," said Marine X testily, taking a tentative step on what seemed to be very long and thin limbs. "So what is it?"

He flexed his arms and there was a sudden rush of air. Beaufort jumped quickly back as Marine X turned, trying to see what was going on behind him.

"What the hell? Have I got wings? Are these wings? What sort of shitty nonsense clone have you stuck me in?" he asked, turning back to the technician. Everyone ducked as his wings swept around the room again.

"It's a harpy, Marine X," said Warden, "one of the winged clones the Deathless use for scouting and sniping." He jumped clear as X turned again, wings still outstretched. "Maybe you could fold away your wings? They do rather fill the room."

Marine X frowned again and paused, standing quite still as he concentrated. Then there was a snap and his wings folded away neatly onto his back. He looked again at his thin, graceful legs and arms, unnaturally narrow hips and slim chest.

"I really wanted to play with an ogre clone," he murmured, his disappointment obvious. "They look like such a lot of fun."

Beaufort smiled nervously.

"But you'll be able to fly, sir," she blurted, trying to put a positive spin on the situation. Marine X glared at her, an expression so angry and hostile that Beaufort took half a step back.

"Marines," said X slowly as if explaining a new concept to a child, "fight on land and water. That's it. The only purpose of height is to fall from it as quickly as possible."

"Beaufort is right, though, sir," said Brin, "and that clone is a remarkable piece of engineering. The ogres are big and tough and surprisingly quick but these harpies are entirely another thing." Marine X looked at him and raised an eyebrow, unconvinced. "The bones are super-lightweight but engineered with titanium, so they're ridiculously strong. And the flight muscles are, weight for weight, about three times as strong as an ogre's."

"Okay, right, yes, could be useful," conceded Marine X. "Anything else I should know?"

"The lungs look hyper-efficient as well, and the synapse tests suggest the reflexes should be off-the-chart fast," said Brin, enthusiastic now that Marine X's hostility had receded somewhat, "and I think, even on the ground, you'll find it moves very quickly indeed. But you might need to eat quite a lot; that clone burns calories at a very high rate."

"Hmm," said Marine X thoughtfully, strutting around the cloning bay and looking at himself in the reflective surfaces of the machines. He flicked out his wings again and gave them a flap. "Does this mean I can break a man's arm with one blow of my wings?" He flicked them back in again.

Brin frowned, not really wanting to think about why Marine X might need to be able to do that.

"Maybe, but you might want to take it easy for a few days, just while you get used to it."

Marine X looked back at the technician as he pulled on the cut-down uniform the Deathless harpies used.

"Easy? Yeah, sure," he said, flexing his arms and popping out his wings again to give them an experimental flap. He pulled them back in and fixed Beaufort with a steady gaze.

"I'll take it," he said finally, "but put me in an ogre next time, right?"

The technician nodded furiously as Marine X and Captain Warden left the cloning bay.

"They're growing more clones on *Ascendant* at the moment," said Brin after the door had slid shut. "Better let them know about Marine X's preferences." Beaufort nodded and sat down at a terminal to compose a message. "Wouldn't want to be in your shoes if he gets deployed to a lizardman next time," said Brin, grinning evilly behind his colleague's back.

3

The temporary council chamber in the depths of Fort Widley had become, over the last week, considerably more permanent-looking and was now seriously crowded as the councillors filed in for the meeting. Restoration of the cloning bays to full capacity had coincided with the end of the fighting, allowing the casualties to be deployed and the colony to return to near strength.

"Yes, yes, settle down," said Governor Denmead as the councillors jostled for space and squeezed themselves onto the benches arrayed around the walls of the chamber. "I know this isn't ideal and yes, it's on the list of things to fix, but, just for now, we all have to do the best we can with what we have."

Eventually they settled and Johnson, Denmead's assistant, was able to bring the meeting to order.

"You've all had briefing packs, and I'm sure you've all digested them," said Denmead, knowing for a fact that some of the councillors had only been deployed to new bodies that morning and so were now trying to catch up with several weeks' worth of updates, "so I'm going to leap straight into the main topic." She nodded at Johnson, who flicked at his data slate until an image appeared on the new display screen at the end of the room. The councillors shuffled and craned their necks until they could all see the screen.

"This is the Deathless base where Captain Warden and his troop engaged the enemy about ten days ago and where Lieutenant Colonel Atticus," said Johnson, nodding to Atticus where he sat in a quiet corner, "fought a second engagement that required him to deploy to another new clone. These are new images from the micro-drones deployed over the base to keep an eye on things."

"And we've now set the AI to watch for enemy movement," said Atticus, his voice hissing slightly through the alien mouthparts of the Death-less Rupert clone, "so that we won't be surprised again by any mischief the remaining Deathless are plotting." He frowned, not entirely happy to again be wearing a Deathless clone rather than the standard RMSC body he had requested. Some mix-up at the cloning bay, Warden had said.

"As you can see," said Denmead, highlighting a section of the base and zooming in using her own slate, "this part isn't a static building, it's actually a spacecraft." She paused to allow the murmur of disquiet to drift away as the newer councillors gazed in awe at the images before them. "It's now clear that the sole role of this craft is to land on a planet and construct the defensive walls and principle habitation and manufacturing structures of a military operating base. Then it moves to a new location and repeats the process."

"In other words, it's a fully-automated base-building machine," said Atticus, "and we think that it had almost finished its work when we stumbled across it."

"Fully automated?" said Grimes with a challenging eyebrow raised almost to his hairline. "So you're telling us that there might be more of these things, more bases out there, spread across the face of the planet, ready to deploy Deathless troopers?" There was another round of uncomfortable murmuring from the assembled councillors. These were clearly questions they hadn't considered.

"No," said Atticus firmly, leaning forward slightly to better engage, or maybe intimidate, his audience. "Examination of the logs and files of *Ascendant* show that this craft was launched only fairly shortly before we found it and so had time to build only one base, namely that one," he finished, pointing at the screen.

Grimes nodded, a flash of relief showing on his normally inscrutable face. "Well, that's the first piece of good news we've had in a long time."

Atticus smiled. It made a pleasant change to get a positive response from Grimes, for once, who was normally dour and pessimistic.

"Sorry, excuse my ignorance," said one of the newer councillors, "but for those of us only recently restored to active duty, can you please give us a quick update on what's going on? What is *Ascendant*, for starters?"

Denmead and Atticus shared a look then she sighed. "This is all in the briefing pack, Len, but I know you've only been up for a few hours. *Ascendant* is a captured enemy starship, renamed by Vice Admiral Staines, whose fleet is currently in orbit around New Bristol. The enemy is descended from one of the lost Arks, *Koschei*, a Russian vessel populated by body hackers and ultra-liberals intent on pushing cloning technology as far as it would go in their search for functional immortality."

"And that's why...?" said Len, gesturing at Atticus's unusual body and grinning weakly.

"Yes, Len, that's why Lieutenant Colonel Atticus is wearing such an unusual clone. This one was seized from the Deathless and is, we believe, the model used by their officer classes. Look, there's a ton of detail in the background files, and I don't want to spend much more time on the subject, except to say that we are at war with a force that seems to be very much stronger and better resourced than we are, here, on New Bristol."

"I might add," said Atticus, "that current projections based on new data from *Ascendant* suggest that the Deathless may be more widespread and more capable than we had previously thought. All of this information has been relayed to the Admiralty in Sol, of course, and we expect further guidance as soon as they have had a chance to digest it all. Marine reinforcements are arriving as we speak and will be deployed as resources allow."

"In the meantime, though, we're on our own," said the governor.

"Thank you, Governor," said Len, sitting back in his chair, "I'll go through the briefing pack," he added, waving his data slate, "and see if there's anything I can do to help. I have experience in first-contact theory and encounter simulation, if that's any use."

"We're a little past the point of first contact," said Atticus grimly, "but the techs are doing a deal of planning and could always use some help."

"If we could just return to the topic at hand," said Denmead testily, shooting a glance at Atticus before treating the councillors to a somewhat warmer smile, "we wish to discuss the mothership and the plans we are now making for it."

"Of course, Governor," said Atticus, pulling out his own data slate and flicking at it with his long, alien fingers, "in brief, ladies and gentlemen, we wish to repair the mothership, repair the base to some degree and then use both for our own purposes. Our circumstances, as you may have noticed," he waved his hand at their surroundings, "are somewhat reduced. This vessel's fabricators are considerably more sophisticated than our own and we plan to use them to both rebuild Ashton and then to extend our own resource extraction efforts."

"In other words, we're going to return this vessel to service as quickly as possible and use it to build our way back to the habitable, desirable and pleasant colony that we had achieved before the Deathless arrived," said Denmead.

"That works for me," said Grimes, showing an unusual amount of enthusiasm, "but what did you mean by 'considerably more sophisti-cated'? Are we talking bigger structures, faster mechanisms or better materials?"

"All three, as far as we can tell," said Denmead, flicking at her slate so that the display showed close-up images of the inside of the base. "The damage done during Captain Warden's attack was consid-erable but then so was the effort expended. You've all seen the videos,

I expect, and if you haven't, you really should watch the one of the truck hitting the base wall."

She pulled another image onto the display. "You can see here, in this shot of the edge of the wrecked wall that circled the base, exactly how the wall was put together. We know that this was built in less than a week. What does that tell you, Mr Grimes?"

Grimes examined the image, then sat back.

"I'd need to see a sample to be sure," he said cautiously, "but it looks like it might be some sort of carbon nanotube-reinforced foamcrete."

"Catch," said Johnson, tossing a lump of rock across the table to Grimes.

"Yes, look," Grimes said excitedly, "you can see the distinctive patterning caused by the addition of the nanotubes to the foam mixture. Very clever, very advanced. We've got stuff like this back home, but it isn't used much because of the time it takes to make it and the difficulty of getting it to work. Theoretically, though, you could form it into pretty much any shape you want by spraying layers on top of each other, like you would with an old 3D printer, which means you can build fantastically strong and elegant structures easily and quickly."

"And we don't do that because...?" prompted Denmead.

"We don't do it because it's overkill," said Grimes. "This stuff is tough, granted, and you can build incredible structures with it, but it's expensive and difficult, and there's just no need, most of the time."

"But if the Deathless have worked out how to do it quickly...?"

"Well, yes. The whole base is made of this stuff? Then I would very much want to get a look at their machines, as would Smith, I think, and we'd want to deploy them as widely as possible across both New Bristol and the rest of the Commonwealth. This could be a game-changer for new colonies, asteroid mining and space habitat fabrication. Why, with this material, if you can make it fast enough, you might be able to build orbital megastructures..."

Grimes tailed off, lost to the conversation in a daydream of vast, star-sized orbital megastructures.

"And that's why we want you to help with this effort," said Atticus
in an attempt to drag the conversation back, again, to the main topic.
"We have some technical resources amongst the Marines but this is
basically a civil engineering problem and it needs a civilian-led solution. That's where you come in," he said, looking at Grimes and
Smith, "since you're the two people best placed to handle the technology and bring it online."

"And while you're doing that," said Denmead, on the principle
that the best people to handle more work were those already loaded
down with tasks, "we also need to get the ship flying again and then
reprogram it to build useful villages, farms and outstations rather
than the rather useless military-style bases it normally constructs."

She paused to look around the room.

"That makes sense, people, doesn't it? We repair the ship, move it
to New Ashton, reconstruct what was destroyed and then deploy new
fabricators to extend and improve our infrastructure, our civic spaces
and our accommodation."

"And at the same time, we refurbish this base, which we're going
to name HMS *Sultan* in honour of long-closed facilities on Earth, and
set it up as a staging and training post for the Marines," said Atticus.
"In the event of another invasion, we will already have a ready-made,
fully militarised base of operations that should, with any luck, draw
focus from the civilian areas."

"HMS *Sultan*, eh?" said Smith, sharing a glance with Grimes.
"Well, I guess our first task is to get the local fabricators and manufac-
turing machines back on stream so that we can repair and rebuild.
After that, Governor, Lieutenant Colonel, it'll be over to you."

"Very good, Mr Smith," said Denmead, sitting back in her chair
and smiling benevolently at her councillors, "that will do very well
indeed."

4

Captain Warden stood on the bridge of *Ascendant*, watching the panoramic forward view monitors as the last shuttle from *Albion* departed after dropping off its cargo of supplies.

"Flight control, report," Lieutenant Commander Cohen said, in the distinctive, clipped intonation of a bridge officer.

"Status green, sir. All shuttles have now cleared our vicinity and *Ascendant* is ready to depart."

Cohen nodded. "Navigation, set course for NewPet."

"Course confirmed; navigation ready."

"Helm, engage hyperspace drive," said Cohen.

The transition to hyperspace was smooth and controlled, like diving into cool water; real warships didn't jerk, shudder or creak as they did in cheap holo-shows. Once the drive was engaged, space simply folded beneath the ship and it vanished from normal space, moving through hyperspace in much the same way that the conventional engines would manoeuvre the ship in normal space.

The difference, of course, was the vast distance that could be quickly travelled in hyperspace. Unlike a wormhole, which allowed near instantaneous transmission of information, movement through hyperspace took time. Travelling at sub-light speed, the ship moved through the folds of hyperspace before exiting back into normal space at a distance that should have required them to travel faster than light.

Warden didn't pretend to understand the physics. In fact, hardly anyone in the universe understood how it all worked. All he needed to know was that that the effective rate of travel was many times light-speed and that meant they could reach another system in weeks or even days, rather than centuries or millennia.

The fact that any wormhole larger than a pinprick would collapse without warning, at least with current technology, was both a blessing and a curse. Not being able to transfer ships meant that the Royal Navy couldn't deliver a ship instantly to a combat zone. The upside was that the enemy couldn't do that either, locking both sides into hyperspace or the slow vastness of real space.

Wormholes were still the arteries of modern life, allowing near instantaneous transmission of data across the vast reaches of spaces. Though the energy requirement was huge, any planet with sufficient power generation could easily allow its citizens to communicate through wormholes, sending messages to family or friends as if they were across the street rather than in another solar system.

"How long till we arrive?" asked Warden when the ship was comfortably underway.

"About two hundred and ten hours," said Cohen. Warden nodded thoughtfully. He was going to be busy. He now had a whole company to look after, and most of them were in fresh clones that were completely unfamiliar to them. They would need training if they were to use the clones to their full effect and they had fewer than nine days to get it done.

Warden excused himself from the bridge and went to see how Colour Milton was getting on with the setup of their training facilities.

∿

Warden entered the former mothership hangar from one of the upper balconies and looked out at the work Milton had done on their improvised training ground.

A wall of crates had been built on one side of the bay and bags of composite gel were being piled up as a backstop. That was the shooting range, positioned to ensure the rounds were not headed towards any of the access doors. You didn't want someone taking a shortcut through the range when they thought it wasn't in use; they couldn't afford to put more strain on the cloning bays.

The area to the side of the shooting range had been taped off to keep it clear of people and kit. On the other side of the hangar, mats had been laid out for unarmed combat practice, probably the most important training component for the newly deployed Marines. Martial arts, and even basic body movements such as throwing and catching a ball, were excellent ways to become accustomed to an unfamiliar clone model, and the RMSC had long experience in quickly getting their people ready for combat.

As Warden watched, a small flock of harpies flapped their way across the combat mats, gliding down from the balcony to land awkwardly on the floor. These were the clones that required the biggest adjustments. The different reflexes, muscle strength, even bone density, all played a part in throwing you off kilter.

The Marines seldom used winged troopers because they were just too specialised and while Ten had trained before in an RMSC clone with wings, it didn't compare favourably to this Deathless version. The harpy was lighter, faster and stronger than the RMSC equivalent, superior in every way, much though it pained Warden to admit it.

The practical difficulties of flight training, even in *Ascendant*'s immense hangar, were huge. About all they could do so far was climb up to a balcony and glide back down, flapping their wings a little to eke out as much distance as possible.

All the snipers and their spotters had been reassigned to harpies. With luck, deploying teams in winged bodies would help them reach otherwise inaccessible perches and allow them to target enemies they couldn't otherwise reach. The military advantages of being where the enemy didn't expect you were huge, since you could easily glide away from your perch once you were discovered.

"The problem will be food," Mueller had said when Warden had asked for his thoughts. "These clones are light and agile, but they have a high metabolic rate in order to deliver the energy required for the flight muscles. I estimate that they might chew, if you'll pardon the pun, through four to six thousand calories a day even if the wearer is only engaging in normal duties. If they fly, they might need six to eight thousand."

The other major downside was that the carrying capacity of the winged clones was much smaller than that of even the standard RMSC versions. Experiments had shown that a couple of days' food, a lightweight uniform and a primary weapon was about the limit that they could carry. The Deathless winged clones were superior and had lighter structures so they had a bit more leeway there, but they still needed calorie-dense food.

"And that means we're highly dependent on the lizardmen for any heavier weaponry," Marine X had said, "especially if we deploy our snipers for longer than a few hours. I recommend we use rail-guns, to conserve ammunition weight and increase effectiveness."

So deploying the harpies would require coordinated support from the lizardmen and, given their lack of armour, casualties were likely to be higher than amongst the beefier clones, if they were exposed to enemy fire. This meant they simply couldn't deploy them in forward roles in the same way they would usually do. The snipers and their spotters would have to restrict themselves to that function only, and stay off the front line.

Warden had asked Mueller to look at the available high-energy foodstuffs and try to come up with something better. He didn't want his sniper teams passing out on their perches from hunger and the standard chocolate protein bars still didn't add up to a pleasant meal. Despite the huge amount of sugar, they were more like chewing sweet cardboard than a chocolate bar.

Ten had sighed heavily during this conversation, looking somewhat miserable. Eventually, Warden had asked what was bothering him, and he'd confessed that the last time winged clones saw heavy use, there was a liquid diet that they were supplied. A pack of easily constituted energy supplements were added to their water supply and could be injected for a boost, should they need one in the field. He explained that this was particularly important when the wings were used to achieve lift, rather than just for gliding purposes.

"Why the long face then? That sounds like an easy solution. No pun intended," Warden had asked.

"Because the drink isn't like something you give kids or a soft drink you buy in a coffee shop. It tastes more like chemical plant runoff or essence of cabbage mixed in with dog food. It does not go down well and there's nothing you can add to it that will overpower the taste," Ten had replied.

"I've found it," Mueller said, excitedly, looking at his data slate. "Just as Marine X says, we can easily make enough of this with the food fabricators. Lots of supplementary vitamins and minerals, lots of energy and lots of electrolytes – which is probably what ruins the taste."

"Problem solved then," Warden said, though Ten didn't seem to agree.

In another area, Milton had a series of viewscreens and some chairs laid out as a classroom. She was going over HUD videos with the NCOs and lieutenants who now reported to Captain Warden.

Captain Warden. He still couldn't quite believe it. He hadn't expected a promotion for at least a couple of years but it seemed a shooting war had some career advantages. Nevertheless, professionally challenging and career-boosting though it was, he'd very much rather not be in a war against a group of Lost Ark malcontents with a fondness for genetic engineering and cutting-edge technology.

He moved to a ladder and slid down it, a handy trick he had taken the time to learn during his first posting aboard a Royal Navy ship. It saved a surprising amount of time but he'd seen more than one person cock it up and burn their hands or twist an ankle. Warden had taken the easy route to expertise; a conversation with a midshipman, a bottle of genuine gin from Earth and half an hour of supervised practice had given him the knack of it.

He smiled to himself as he remembered those simpler times aboard that first ship, back when his biggest concerns had been when he'd actually get to use his training in combat. Now that he had experienced combat, he was much more interested in ideas such as diplomacy and negotiation.

"Colour Milton, how are things going?"

"Fine, thank you, sir. I was just showing the replays from the attack on the base."

"Good, carry on, it looks like you're about to get to the good bits," said Warden.

Milton was showing the views from her own HUD and Warden's, not the mind-boggling video of Ten's exploits. Those files were kept strictly under wraps and even Lieutenant Colonel Atticus had avoided watching them.

"They're a bad example for impressionable boot-necks," Atticus had said, before comparing Ten's videos unfavourably to performance art made by adrenaline junkies whose only hobbies were ultra-extreme sports. "Just keep them out of the training programme." They would leak, of course, because these things always did, but the last thing anyone wanted was for young Marines to get the idea that Ten's behaviour was what was expected of them.

And so Milton had focused on the more normal videos so that the newly deployed Marines could see what the Deathless were like, how they responded under fire, how their weapons worked and how they moved and fought.

Warden stayed till the end of the base attack, through the distant music that signalled Ten's arrival, the enormous explosion of the dumper truck and the final assault on the mothership, which he supposed they should start calling a factory ship or something similar. He had wanted to bring it with them, in case they needed to deploy bases of their own, but the assessment of the civilian and Royal Navy teams had been that even with their combined efforts, it would take weeks to make the vessel space-worthy and even longer before it was fully operational again. It made more sense to leave it on New Bristol where, after only relatively minor repairs, it could do useful work while the techs laboured to bring it back to full capacity.

Instead, they would rely on the shuttles and dropships that *Ascendant* carried and hope none of the Deathless personnel at NewPet did a scan comprehensive enough to detect the absence of the enormous ship from its hangar. The jig would be up if they did, and they would have a devil of a time explaining the missing vessel if anyone got curious.

When Milton was done, Warden stood up to address the team.

"As you all know, this is an intelligence-gathering mission. We have no idea what we'll find when we get to NewPet. It could be an empty system, or it might be a convenient staging post on the way to more interesting places." He paused to look over the Marines. "But it could be a Naval base or even a civilian starbase. We're all in Deathless clones, and that's because we anticipate a need to infiltrate their facilities or to receive visitors to *Ascendant* in order to gather the kind of intelligence we need to support the Commonwealth."

There was a general murmur of surprise at that.

"Both those eventualities present significant challenges because, as you may have noticed from the signs around the ship, the Deathless speak their own language. It's not even Russian. They also have their own characters, presumably designed to be more efficient than either the Cyrillic or Latin character sets with which we're familiar. What we know about *Koschei* is that the founders of their group were all highly skilled academics, computer scientists, biologists, physicists and the like. They planned to improve on every aspect of their civilisation, and they didn't want to be constrained by any of the social mores or legal restrictions of the time.

"We don't know what we're going to find, so we're keeping our options open. If we find a target of opportunity, we may well launch an all-out assault, which could include a ground assault. If we were to find, for example, a vulnerable capital ship, we might attempt another capture, but havoc is not our primary objective. The goal is to gather as much intelligence as possible without giving much away in return.

"General Bonneville has sent some experts from the Puzzle Palace to join us, a team of language experts and lecturers from the staff training colleges on Earth. We will all receive some training on the rudiments of the Deathless language in case we have to bluff our way around their facilities on NewPet."

Hayes put her hand up. "Sir, won't we be using AI translation to handle most of this?"

"Yes, for ship-to-ship communication and anything over comms, that's the plan. If we have to go in person, though, and we think that's likely, the ability to take your helmet off and speak to someone could be the difference between success and failure. In addition, this is likely to be a long war, ladies and gentlemen, and even if a diplomatic solution is reached soon, we are going to need language skills in the long-term. We will be in the vanguard of that as the guinea pigs, which I'm sure you're all excited about."

"Will we be covering their written language as well?"

"Yes, that's part of the planned program, but time is short, so we'll focus on verbal skills. The HUD auto-translation of written language is automatic and the experts feel it's better than ninety per cent accurate, which should be good enough for our purposes."

"What's the balance going to be between combat training and this stuff?"

"You'll be pleased to hear that you'll be spending the bulk of your time on language skills, Lieutenant Hayes. You have two hours now to get in some concentrated physical training to familiarise yourselves with the clones. Those of you who have been using a Deathless clone for a while will be assisting with that until the first language classes start. I'm sending the training schedule to your HUD now. You will also note that we're going to be reviewing infiltration, stealth, sabotage and escape and evasion routines. I will be joining you for all this, so the pain will be shared. We have some excellent practical experts aboard for these aspects of mission prep."

"Who is doing the stealth training, Captain?" asked a suspicious Hayes.

"You will no doubt be delighted to hear that General Bonneville has decided that Marine X is best qualified to deliver a refresher course in creeping up on some poor sod and giving him the good news as quietly as possible." There was a chorus of groans until Warden raised his hand to quiet the audience. "Yes, I know he's a character, but he's also undeniably a Galaxy-class bastard when it comes to such matters, so you'd be wise to listen to his advice. I, for one, prefer to minimise the number of forced redeployments through which I have to go."

He paused to look around the team then nodded.

"Right, you all have PT to be getting on with. Try not to break anything; it won't get you out of language lessons."

5

"Coming up on NewPet, sir," came the message. Warden was in his quarters, reading again through his company's deployment list to commit to memory the details of which of his teams had been deployed into which clone types. Moving away from standard RMSC body designs brought a whole new set of challenges and opportunities.

"Very good, I'm on my way." He put down his data slate and swung himself off his bunk. Then he flicked the door controls and walked out, heading for the bridge.

"Sir," he said, nodding to Lieutenant Commander Cohen as he entered the bridge.

"Warden," acknowledged Cohen, nodding back, "we're close, re-entering normal space in," he paused to glance at the monitor and lick his lips, "forty-five seconds."

And then they would see what they would see. Nobody knew what sort of reception awaited them in NewPet. They didn't know what sort of forces might be arrayed against them or how the Deathless might react to their arrival. They didn't even know whether they would be noticed; it might be entirely normal for ships to make this journey or to arrive unannounced.

"I will confess to a certain, well, trepidation, Mr Warden," said Cohen as they watched the counter fall steadily towards zero, "there's a very real risk we'll give ourselves away in seconds and be shot to pieces before we achieve anything even vaguely useful."

It was ground they had covered several times during the voyage but without successfully formulating any plan more sophisticated than 'turn up, see what happens'. To Warden's mind, this was a somewhat lax approach, but he had reluctantly conceded that it was the best they could do with the information they had.

"There's a long naval tradition of formulating brilliant plans at the last minute," said Cohen, shifting uneasily in his seat, "although most of them also involved the commander losing some part of his anatomy, so I'm not keen to replicate the strategy entirely." He offered Warden a weak grin, then they both turned back to face the monitors as the countdown trickled towards zero.

"Three, two, one... and we're back to normal space," said Midshipman Martin from her unfamiliar lizardman clone.

For a few long minutes, nothing happened as the ship coasted towards the inner system where their nav-charts showed NewPet and the orbiting base it hosted.

Then a message flashed onto the monitor.

<<*Varpulis*. Proceed to dock bay six for refuelling and re-provisioning>>

The message was followed by a course that flashed up on the main display, a neat loop into the system to reach NewPet, which orbited its star at a little over a hundred and sixty million kilometres.

"At least the translation system is working," said Cohen with no small amount of relief, "acknowledge that, Midshipman Wood, and let's get that course laid in. No point hanging around."

"Yes, sir, acknowledging now."

"Course is laid in, sir, arrival in sixteen hours and thirty-seven minutes."

"Excellent, well done, everyone. Now, let's take a closer look at the planet, shall we? What can we see?"

The small science team had a well-equipped office and laboratory in the aft of the ship. They had rigged extra monitors on the bridge to provide video and audio feeds to Cohen and his team, just in case they found anything useful or interesting. It seemed that the architects of Deathless military vessels had made a serious effort to provide first-class research facilities to their scientists but hadn't thought it worthwhile to add a direct link to the bridge.

"The surface of the planet is rather green," came the voice of Chief Science Officer Mueller, who was down in what the crew had taken to calling 'the science pit', although it was really a very comfortable and well-equipped suite of rooms, "and we can see high concentrations of oxygen and nitrogen, so the atmosphere is probably breathable."

Warden frowned and shared a glance with Cohen.

"That sounds too good to be true, Mueller," he said. "What else can you tell us?"

"From this distance, not a great deal, I'm afraid. Once we're closer, I can give you a detailed breakdown of the composition of the atmosphere, thoughts on the florae and faunae, hi-res maps and topographical details of the surface and probably some indication of likely volcanic activity, but at the moment all we can really say is that it's likely to be wet in many places and that the gravity will be pretty similar to Earth's."

Warden nodded. All very interesting but it was clear that Mueller, whose normal posting was to lead a team of environmental and ecological research scientists based on *Albion*, had not been chosen for this mission because of his military background.

"And what about electromagnetic waves, Mueller?" asked Warden.

"Radios and such-like? Yes, plenty of those. Lots of activity all over the usual spectra and we can see lights on the night-side of the planet. All very normal." There was a pause. "I suppose that's the sort of thing you were interested in, Captain," said Mueller in a somewhat humbler voice. "Silly of me, sorry, I should have realised."

"Not to worry, Mr Mueller," said Warden, "but as soon as you know anything about the number of people on the planet, their locations, their technology..." he trailed off as Mueller nodded on the monitor, "anything you can tell us would be useful." Mueller nodded and killed the connection.

"I sometimes wonder if the Admiralty sends people like Mueller just to test the rest of us," Cohen mused, "but then we weren't really expecting this mission to be a shooting war."

The flight to the space station, which the crew had nicknamed 'Soyuz' for reasons that weren't entirely obvious to Warden, was uneventful to the point of extreme tedium. Warden slept a little, although his body didn't seem to need much rest, and checked his kit and armour. Then he found Cohen and Milton to talk about what they would do next.

"I'm not keen to dock with the space station," said Cohen, although they had known it might be necessary before they left New Bristol. "There are simply too many things that can go wrong, and once we're attached, breaking free may not be possible."

"We've already acknowledged the signal," pointed out Warden. "I'm not sure there's much else we can do."

"I know," said Cohen, "I know, but I don't have to like it. I'd just rather my first command didn't end with us all being captured by the enemy."

"Don't worry, you can always scuttle *Ascendant* if the worst comes to the worst," Warden said cheerfully.

Cohen glowered at him. "You Marines are always so bloody blasé about redeploying, aren't you?" Cohen said.

"Hazard of the job. You've got to look on the bright side of life, when you might step on a mine or take a railgun to the face at any moment," Warden said with a shrug. Cohen sighed and shook his head.

"How long will refuelling take?" Warden asked curiously.

"For a ship this size, we estimate that it might be anything from one to three hours," said Lieutenant Sierra, "but it's difficult to say for sure. Their documentation is unexpectedly lax in this area but from what we can tell, they mostly deliver fuel and raw materials through several high-pressure systems. That's one of the advantages of advanced fabricators; less need to load finished goods, although some of the weapon systems will be restocked by robots working on the outside of the ship."

"Lucky for us. If they had to bring everything in by hand they'd be sure to spot us."

"The bigger problem is the damage to the hull," said Cohen, bringing up an exterior shot of the hull that had been taken from *Albion* when they were re-supplying. "There's not a lot to see, thankfully, but if they do a close visual inspection or if dock six positions us in the wrong orientation –"

"They'll see the damage caused by the boarding pod," muttered Warden. "That hadn't occurred to me."

"Really? It's been causing me sleepless nights ever since we came up with this hare-brained scheme."

"But the hole was patched, wasn't it?" said Milton, nodding at the photo.

"It was, yes, but if their inspection is thorough, they'll probably spot the repairs and that might be enough for them to start asking awkward questions," said Sierra.

"And inspections are often very thorough and highly automated," said Cohen, "since nobody wants to fly in a ship whose hull has been dangerously ablated or where temporary repairs might not be able to handle combat stresses or that might be carrying space barnacles."

Warden thought about that for a moment. It did seem a reasonable fear. Then he frowned.

"Space barnacles?"

"Okay, no, I just made that up, but the point is that there are lots of things that could go wrong if the Deathless are any good as sailors."

Warden snorted. "Their soldiers haven't been much good so far. What's to say their sailors will be any different?"

Cohen raised an eyebrow at that but didn't have anything else to say on the matter. Milton also looked unconvinced, and rightly so; relying on an enemy's incompetence was a sure way to get caught out.

"Anyway," said Warden, moving swiftly onwards, "we need to worry about what we do while we're docked. If they notice the damage or realise we're not who we say we are, our only real option is to cut and run, right?"

Cohen nodded grimly. Nobody in the navy liked the idea of running from a fight, especially if it meant failing to complete their missions, and Warden could see that the thought sat poorly with the lieutenant commander.

"Let's work out what we're going to do with our sixty minutes," Warden said, skipping away from the idea of failure, "and how best to extract information from Soyuz while we're here."

"On that," said Lieutenant Sierra, "I have made some progress with our techs and we have have hacked together this." He pushed a small box across the surface of the table. "It's a backdoor, basically. You plug it into a network port like those ones," he pointed at the flat ports set into mouldings above the power outlets on the wall, "and that should give us a link into their systems."

Warden looked at the small box then raised an eyebrow and looked back at Sierra. "Just the one?"

"One should do the job, but we've got several. If we can install three, we'll have a reasonable chance of exfiltrating useful data." He saw Warden's skeptical expression and added, "We'll get a few more fabricated before you leave so you don't run out."

"What's the range?" asked Milton, picking up the box and waggling the cable. "And does it need power?"

"Battery powered, range about fifty metres, depending on what else is in the way. The best option is to use a data slate to dive straight in and rip out the files we need but if that's not possible, we'll try to pick up the signal from *Ascendant*, although that obviously only works while we're docked."

"Right," said Warden as Sierra passed over two more of the little boxes, "just walk us through the whole thing with that port over there," he said, gesturing at the wall, "and let's see if we can make it work."

~

And now they waited as the ship fired attitude thrusters to manoeuvre into the dock.

"Thirty seconds," said Midshipman Martin. Cohen and Sierra had retreated to the bridge leaving Warden and Milton just inside the main hatch with a full squad of armoured Marines waiting around the corner. They had raided *Ascendant*'s stores for Deathless uniforms that seemed appropriate for a space station, but the few images they had found in the computer or around the ship had been confusingly contradictory. They also had no clear understanding of the protocol for arrival at a space station.

"If there's an armed party waiting for us, sir," said Milton as the space station drifted gently closer, "then I'll see you on the other side and mine's a pint of stout."

"Really, Sergeant? I had you down as a fan of the old Port and lemon, if I'm honest."

"Only if it's a double, sir, or if Marine X is buying."

Warden frowned. "Marine X said something about a bet. I meant to ask earlier but..."

"Five seconds to dock," said Midshipman Martin.

"Maybe later, eh, sir?" said Milton, straightening her uniform.

There was a gentle clink and then a hiss of gas as the ship clamped itself to the space station and the cabin pressures equalised.

"Opening the doors," said Midshipman Martin, "and the best of luck to you all."

Warden stretched his neck, facing forward as the doors slid open, as tense as he'd ever been. Then the doors at the other end of the short corridor opened and he could finally see straight through into the station.

And there was nothing there. Nobody to greet them, no armed guards, no security that they could see of any type.

Warden stood there for a few moments. Then he sniffed and glanced at Milton. She shrugged and made an 'after you' gesture.

"Once more unto the breach," muttered Warden, stepping over the threshold and into the station. Milton followed and together they walked down the short corridor to a larger space, a reception room of some sort.

"Where is everybody?" murmured Milton as they turned into another corridor.

"Keep an eye out for a terminal," said Warden quietly, scanning everywhere for anything that might give them a clue as to what was going on, "or any sign of life."

At the end of the corridor, another door slid open and they suddenly stood in a huge space, a room at least a hundred metres across and full of Deathless soldiers. Milton twitched as if she wanted to draw a weapon. Warden frowned, eyes flicking as he counted, trying to estimate the number of troops that shuffled in lines from left to right, disappearing down a pair of corridors.

A minute later, most of the troops had gone and the room seemed even larger. It was scattered with chairs upon which a few soldiers lounged, kit bags at their feet. Most of the room was empty except for the eerie hum of the life-support systems.

"Staging post?" said Warden quietly. Milton nodded, not trusting herself to speak. "Those look like airport departure boards," said Warden, nodding towards the clusters of large monitors that were arranged above the doors that, now he came to look, were spaced at regular intervals along the walls.

"Feels like a military airport," observed Milton nervously, "and even less welcoming, if they work out who we are."

"You're right," said Warden, nodding as he glanced around. "Let's skirt the edges and see if we can find something useful, then get the hell out of here."

They strolled casually along the edge of the huge room, looking for an open terminal or an office where they could plug in to a network port. Fifty metres down, they found a quiet space with a dozen terminals.

"Perfect," muttered Warden as they slipped inside, "nobody around, network ports over there..." He pulled out one of Sierra's boxes and plugged it into a port. The techs had included self-adhesive tags on the back of the box, so Warden peeled away the releases and carefully stuck the box to the wall.

"Looks like it was meant to be there," said Milton as she fiddled with her data slate. "Yup, we're in. Translation system is mostly working, bit weird, but I can see some interesting things. Downloading now."

"More ports over here," said Warden, fitting a second box while Milton stared at her slate. "Right, that's done, let's try another room."

Warden followed Milton from the room only to see another officer clone walking towards them. The officer frowned, clearly confused to see someone leaving his office, then hurried on.

"Back, back," muttered Milton, turning to head back to *Ascendant*.

"Uh huh," said Warden, following. Behind them they heard the officer calling and moving quickly, hurrying after them.

"In here," hissed Milton, ducking into an empty side room. Warden followed, heart hammering and fingers twitching.

The room was long but only a few metres wide with a viewing port at the end. No other exits.

"Blades?" said Milton, fingering the handle of her dagger as she stood just inside the door. Warden looked around but couldn't see an alternative.

"Shit," he muttered. He hadn't planned to leave behind a pile of incriminating corpses.

Then the officer stepped into the room and looked at Warden, asking something that Warden's slate struggled to translate. The officer took another step forward, repeating his question, his hand falling to some sort of pistol at his waist.

Then Milton stepped forward and, with workmanlike calm, wrapped her arm around the Rupert's neck before neatly inserting her dagger into his throat. She stood there for a few seconds as the officer kicked, then dragged him into a corner and propped him against the wall.

"There, there," Milton said, patting his cheek. The corpse just sat there, eyes staring vacantly. "We'd better move, sir," she said. "If they track their officers, they'll already know something's wrong. We might only have seconds."

Warden nodded. He was fitting another of Sierra's boxes under the counter. "Almost done."

Milton looked around nervously, standing watch on the door. Her eyes were drawn to a monitor on one side which appeared to show a countdown and an external video feed.

"Looks like another incoming shuttle, sir," she hissed as Warden checked the box with his slate and triggered another download. "It's about to get really warm around here."

"Almost done, Sergeant," muttered Warden. Then he stood up and rammed the slate back into its case. "Right, let's go."

Milton slipped quickly through the door and Warden triggered the mechanism. The door slid closed behind him and they walked as nonchalantly as they could towards *Ascendant*'s corridor.

"This spy stuff is quite exciting," said Warden as the door to the departure lounge hissed closed. Milton just shook her head as she jogged down the corridor. She punched at the controls and the airlock door opened. Seconds later, she and Warden were back aboard *Ascendant*.

"Safe," she muttered, hands on her knees as she took deep, calming breaths.

"For some strange value of the word 'safe'," Warden said, "but a successful infiltration, I think."

~

"That was quick," said Cohen when Warden and Milton returned from their expedition. "I rather thought you'd be gone a lot longer."

"Things got a little sticky," said Warden, his post-infiltration high rapidly dissipating, "and we decided to make a quick exit."

Cohen raised quizzical eyebrows.

"A Rupert caught us, sir," elaborated Milton, "and we had to improvise."

"But we installed three boxes, and downloaded some things that might be interesting," said Warden, handing his slate to Sierra.

"I'll get these to the techs," said Sierra, taking Milton's slate as well, "and check on the comms links to the boxes." He disappeared and the others sat down.

"They're shuttling troops up from the planet," said Warden as the door closed behind Sierra, "and then shipping them out to other destinations. Looks like a staging post for troop deployments, which suggests that NewPet is a training ground as well as whatever else they're doing."

Cohen nodded thoughtfully. "We've seen flights to and from the surface and from the station to out of the system but no in-system traffic. I agree; it looks like a training location."

"But why here, sir?" asked Milton. "Why not train their troops at home and ship them out from there?"

Warden shrugged. "Deniability, maybe? Or something to do with space or terrain? Maybe their other planets are just too crowded." Then he frowned; that explanation was not at all appealing. "Either way, unless we learn something from our downloaded data, our next step is probably to visit the surface."

"I agree," said Cohen, standing up, "but let's give Sierra a few hours to see what he can find. You two look like you could do with a bit of time off."

⌇

"I'm sorry, Mr Mueller, but what are we looking at?" Cohen peered at the display at the end of the meeting room trying to work out why the Chief Science Officer had insisted on showing it to them.

"These are hi-res images of the planet's surface," said Mueller, speaking in the slow, calming tones of an indulgent father talking to a petulant child, "and we're looking at the northern hemisphere. As you can see, we have large islands and small continental masses, mostly covered with forest or jungle. The climate is predominantly damp and warm, which leads to what appear to be very large plant-like growths across all regions."

"Large plant-like growths?" asked Warden. "You mean the surface is covered in trees?"

"Not trees, no, because trees are a terrestrial species and won't have evolved here. And in any case, these florae are in excess of a hundred and fifty metres tall in some places, so are significantly taller than even the tallest trees on Earth."

"What else can you tell us, Mr Mueller?" asked Cohen, gently trying to prod the scientist back to the matter at hand.

"Well, the florae are very interesting, from a scientific perspective, but I suspect you'll be more concerned with the military bases and the trains."

There was a pause as if Mueller was waiting for confirmation to a question he hadn't really asked.

"Yes, Mr Mueller," said Warden eventually, "we would like to know about the military bases."

"Well, if we zoom in a little, the bases show up as clusters of dark spots in cleared areas surrounded by either desert or very low vegeta-tion." He flicked at his data slate so that the main display zoomed in to show something that could be a base but could just as easily have been a cluster of buildings sitting astride a road. "These areas you can see all around the 'base' appear to have been cleared of major florae so that there is at least a two hundred metre open space between the edge of the forest and the buildings."

"That makes sense," said Warden, nodding along. "You see it in fortresses on Earth as well. They would build the walls, dig an encircling moat and hack back the vegetation so they could see approaching enemies."

"But what enemies would attack here, I wonder?" said Mueller. "As far as we know, the Deathless are the only people in the system. Could they be attacking themselves?"

Cohen shrugged and looked at Warden. "It's possible," he conceded, "but I don't think it's likely. They appear to operate as a single political entity, so going to war makes little sense."

"Indeed. So why build bases with defensive walls? And why clear the forest from those walls?" asked Mueller. There was another pause as Mueller waited for feedback.

"What is your theory, Mr Mueller?" asked Warden eventually, keen to finish the briefing before his clone reached its expiry date.

"Megafauna," said Mueller, beaming at the conference room, "giant animals of some sort, possibly like dinosaurs and dangerous enough to require counter-measures." There was a moment of stunned silence from the officers, then Cohen sniffed and leant forward.

"What are these dark lines, Mr Mueller?" he asked, moving swiftly on and pointing at the image. "Could they be roads?"

"No," said Mueller, somewhat deflated by the utter lack of interest in his megafauna theory, "they appear to be high-speed rail tracks of some sort, possibly maglev lines or maybe even an enclosed vacuum system. Either technology would be ideal for transporting troops and supplies between bases, but they're not really interesting from a scientific perspective."

"How many bases, Mr Mueller, and how extensive is their rail network?"

"Ah, you have an incisive military mind, Captain Warden. We've found thirty-two bases so far, spread right across the globe, all linked by high-speed lines, although some of them appear to run through tunnels or across the sea. The bases seem to be distributed across all climatic zones and, generally, they each link to two or three other bases, depending on their isolation."

"Isolation?" asked Cohen.

"Many of the bases are separated by one to two thousand kilometres but a few are more than three thousand kilometres from their nearest neighbours, making them very isolated indeed. Even with the best technology, it's difficult to see them being reached by rail in less than three to four hours."

"What about airports or landing strips?" said Milton, "Where are they?"

"There's a spaceport here," said Mueller, highlighting an area where three bases sat at the corners of a triangle with sides twelve hundred kilometres long, "but there are no landing strips or runways of any sort, as far as we can tell."

"And why might that be?" asked Warden quickly, having grown used to Mueller's dramatic pauses.

"We thought initially that it might be an atmospheric problem of some sort but that doesn't seem to be the case. The air is slightly thicker than Earth's but not so much as to inhibit flight or render the process dangerous. At the moment, our best guess is that it's something to do with the indigenous florae and faunae but beyond that, I'm afraid we really can't say. And it could just be that the Deathless don't like flying or prefer trains."

"Hmm," said Warden, "well, thank you, Mr Mueller, you've given us a whole lot of information to process." He looked at Milton and Cohen. "And I suppose our next task is to work out where we go from here."

6

"This is one of *Ascendant*'s tech specialists, Midshipman Emma Cornwell," said Goodwin, Warden's own technical expert, "we've been working on the data packages exfiltrated from Soyuz and using the hacking boxes to search for more stuff."

The briefing room was full. Cohen and his senior officers were there, along with Warden and his command team. Marine X was skulking towards the rear of the room having sneaked his way in despite not being on the attendee list. Warden might have asked him to leave but the penal Marine had a surprisingly wide set of knowledge and it was difficult to know when he might make a useful contribution to any particular discussion, assuming his attention could be kept on the matter at hand.

"The bandwidth is restricted by the distance and the structure of the space station, so the transfer rate is very low," said Midshipman Cornwell, "but all three boxes are still working and we're getting useful amounts of information."

And everything they'd found so far suggested, as Warden and Milton had seen, that large numbers of troops were being trained on the planet then shipped out of the system through Soyuz.

"We've been looking for documents that might describe the

broader Deathless strategy but that information is proving difficult to find. There are several systems to which we don't have access," said Goodwin, "which is frustrating. It looks like the Deathless data security measures are effective and well-implemented once you get beyond the public sections."

"What are we doing about that?" asked Cohen. "Do we have any way around their precautions?"

"Not yet, sir," said Cornwell. "We don't know how they'll react if we try to brute-force our way into their systems, so we've concentrated on getting anything we can reach without arousing suspicion."

"Their security is good, but it still relies on people doing what they're supposed to do," said Goodwin, "and as we know, the weakest parts of any system are the operators."

"And we found an encrypted package on one of the slates that we can't access but whose file name and metadata strongly suggest that we should try to get into it," said Cornwell.

"If we've got the file, surely we can just send it back to the Puzzle Palace and let the teams there crack it," said Warden, frowning. "They've got plenty of power, after all."

"We thought about that, sir, but we think the package has a security system that relies on a biometric reading. It's really sophisticated, which is one of the things that made us pay attention to it. Somebody dropped it into an insecure folder on their slate, which was probably something they shouldn't have done, but the encryption is so strong we'll never be able to crack it, at least not quickly enough for the information still to be useful."

"So how does the biometric system work?" asked Cohen.

Goodwin glanced at Cornwell, who grimaced.

"We're not certain, sir, but our theory is that the package contains DNA identifiers of individuals, or possibly clone classes, who can be given access to the file. That fits with what we can see in *Ascendant*'s systems."

"You've seen the palm readers built into *Ascendant*'s computers?" said Goodwin, "The clones have different palm prints and DNA markers, much like identical twins have different fingerprints, although in this case the differences are deliberately engineered rather than emerging spontaneously in the womb, obviously. We think that if we load the file into *Ascendant*'s computers, we then only need someone from the approved list to provide a palm print and a DNA sample – the palm readers have built-in DNA scanners – and we'll get access to the file."

There was a moment of silence as the room digested this news.

"Would such a palm also allow us through the network security?" Warden asked, leaning forward.

"Maybe, but only if the person had appropriate clearance," said Cornwell, "and none of the clones we've tried so far has been able to gain access to the file or to the secure parts of the network."

"What do we know about the clones' DNA?" asked Cohen. "Could we manipulate it to fake a way through the security measures?"

Cornwell shrugged and looked at Goodwin. "I think that's a question for CSO Mueller, sir."

All eyes turned to Chief Science Officer Mueller, who was staring at his data slate and muttering under his breath.

"Mr Mueller?" said Cohen. "Are you still with us?"

"Hmm, what?" Mueller, looked up from his slate. "Sorry, I was miles away."

"We were asking about Deathless clone DNA and its use within the biometric security system. Can we hack it?"

Now it was Mueller's turn to grimace.

"The security system appears to be keyed to specific DNA sequences but, obviously, the DNA of the clones is the same within each class. They're clones, after all, genetically identical," said Mueller, flicking an image from his slate to the room's main display, "so biometric security doesn't just work with every individual. We think that the Deathless insert additional markers for certain individuals when their personalities are deployed, which allows clones to be uniquely identified and provides those individuals with enhanced access to facilities, systems or information. They've got some pretty advanced genetic manipulation technologies, so it isn't too much of a stretch to imagine such a system."

"But can we hack it?" Cohen persisted. "Could we use their techniques to insert the appropriate DNA sequences to one of our own clones?"

"Ah, interesting question," said Mueller, "and I think, given the level of sophistication we've seen in the Deathless cloning suites and their general approach to DNA, that yes, this should be possible using the technology aboard *Ascendant*."

"Excellent," said Warden, "how soon can we do it?"

"I suppose the answer to that," said Mueller, "is that it depends how long it will take to determine which DNA markers to insert and where they need to go in the strand. Do we have that information?"

All eyes turned to Goodwin and Cornwell.

"Er, no," said Cornwell, "I mean, obviously there's some sort of version of the key embedded in the data package, but it'll be hashed with a one-way code. If we have a DNA string, we can test it against the encryption, but we can't take the encrypted information and decipher or reverse it to discover the required DNA strand."

There was a disappointed pause.

"And that means our best option is...?" asked Warden to the room at large.

"It means our only option," said Goodwin apologetically, "is to find an individual who already has the necessary clearance and both a DNA strand and a palm print referenced within the encrypted data package."

7

"Do you think delivery will be a problem?" asked Warden as he reviewed the plans for the landing on NewPet. The science briefing had broken up and now Warden, Cohen and Milton were in the commander's meeting room to discuss the next stage of the mission.

"No, it shouldn't be, we can send you down in a shuttle, or maybe in the dropship if you plan to take a large team," Cohen replied.

"I think this looks like a good spot," said Warden, "at least to start with. There are buildings but not much movement around them, so with any luck, we can have a nose around without being rumbled."

"Who are you taking?" Cohen asked.

"Just Goodwin. She can do the hacking while I snoop and watch her back."

"I think I should go with you, sir," Milton offered.

"No, I want to keep this as small as possible. I don't want an entire troop down there; that would only create more chances for someone to give the game away."

"But you need backup, sir. Two Marines on their own in an enemy camp when their closest allies are what, two hundred kilometres away? We won't be able to get to you if there's a problem."

"I'll have backup, Colour Milton, don't worry. I'm going to have Marine X on overwatch to help with our exfiltration, just in case something goes wrong." Milton nodded slowly, although it was clear she wasn't entirely happy.

"Where do you want to rendezvous for extraction?" Cohen asked.

"I think this," said Warden, pointing at a spot on the map, "is probably a good point for both pickup and drop-off."

"And your fallback in case the first RV is compromised?"

"It would be a hard slog through the jungle, but this area looks okay, doesn't it?"

Milton sniffed, clearly not at all keen on the plan. Cohen seemed less concerned.

"Shouldn't be a problem," said Cohen breezily, "it's a standard gravity world, predictable weather patterns, can't see any reason we might have an issue landing a shuttle at either point."

"Sir, I really wish you'd let someone else go," Milton said.

"It has to be me, I've been getting the highest scores in the language classes. I've got the best chance of bluffing our way out of trouble," Warden said with an apologetic shrug, although 'best chance' didn't necessarily mean very much.

"So, to be clear, you'll land here under cover of darkness, proceed to this small base and find a way in. Once inside, you'll extract any information you can in the hope it will tell us where the departing troops are being sent. If things go smoothly, your extraction point is here and if everything goes pear-shaped, we'll pick you up here instead," Cohen said, gesturing to the highlighted locations on the map displayed on the screen as he did.

Warden nodded. "That's the long and the short of it. Any objections?"

Cohen shook his head and Milton followed suit, somewhat reluctantly, a moment later.

"Then it's settled, we'll present the plan to Vice Admiral Staines and Lieutenant Colonel Atticus. Milton, can you brief Marine X, please, and make sure Lieutenant Hayes has her troop standing by, just in case we need ground support as a last resort."

"Yes, sir," the veteran NCO said, snapping a salute before leaving the war room.

Cohen waited until she'd left then asked Warden, "She doesn't seem all that happy about this. What happens if you're captured?"

Warden sighed. "That's part of the reason I want Marine X backing me up. His role is more difficult than I let on to Milton and I'm not convinced she'd go through with it if I asked her to."

The Navy man looked at him for a moment before light dawned. "How will he do it?"

"He'll be taking a railgun. If I'm captured, or Goodwin, Ten will put out our lights."

Cohen shuddered at the thought. The grim necessities of war had never seemed quite so personal.

~

"Cohen, Warden, what's the news from NewPet?" asked Vice Admiral Staines.

"We are transmitting our data now, sir. To summarise, there is a sizeable Deathless presence in the NewPet system. Upwards of sixty thousand personnel, as far as we can tell so far."

Staines was visibly taken aback by that news. "Sixty thousand? What the hell are they doing there? Is it a colony world?"

"No, sir," said Warden. "It appears to be entirely run by their military."

"My word. It must be a naval base. With sixty thousand you could support an enormous fleet."

"There are some ships here, sir, but not very many, nor the infrastructure to support a large ongoing fleet presence. There's a space station in orbit around NewPet itself that operates as some kind of transport hub, but the bulk of the personnel are on the planet itself. We think they have large camps down there and they're training troops, thousands of 'em," Cohen said.

Atticus chimed in, "What else do you have for us? I see from the report you've been on the station but already left it behind."

"We believe the Deathless are sending troops from here to other systems, not just New Bristol. They have a massive embarkation area in the Soyuz space station and there are multiple destinations listed, but their names translate to 'Target 1', 'Target 2' and so on. We don't know what those names mean in terms of locations in space, but we assume they are separate systems," explained Warden.

"Understood," said Atticus. "So you need authorisation for a change of mission profile, I assume?"

"Yes, sir, we want to carry out missions on NewPet itself and change our focus from general intelligence gathering to trying to answer the question of where they're sending those troops."

"We expect that this will be the point where the mission will go hot and we'll be discovered by the Deathless," Cohen added.

Atticus and Staines were silent for a few minutes while they reviewed the plan and Warden found himself chewing his lip nervously, like a student waiting for his essay to be read.

Finally, Atticus looked up at the camera. "Whose plan is this?"

"It's mine and Captain Warden's, sir," answered Cohen.

"It's a bit thin, chaps," commented Staines. "Are you sure you've been through it thoroughly?"

"We think we've got the foreseeable areas covered, Vice Admiral," answered Warden.

"What happens if your team is discovered?"

"We have a secondary extraction point in case the primary is rendered unviable during the course of the mission, sir."

"All well and good," said Staines, "but if you are discovered on the surface, that will also throw *Ascendant*'s loyalties into question, won't it?"

Cohen coughed and Warden gritted his teeth as the two men exchanged glances. The Vice Admiral was right; as soon as the Deathless found intruders on their planet, they would check for anomalies in recent shipping movements to find out how they reached the surface. *Ascendant*'s surprise arrival would be an obvious discrepancy that they were bound to investigate.

"My apologies, Vice Admiral," said Cohen. "I will prepare a contingency plan in the event *Ascendant* is identified by the enemy during Captain Warden's mission."

"I also think we're missing an opportunity," said Atticus, flicking through the images that had been included in the data package. "If we're putting a team on the planet's surface, should we not also be gathering intelligence on the troop bases? That might be something that could be done while Warden is trying to locate an enemy officer who can open the encrypted files. There's a lot of activity on the planet and I, for one, want to know more about those troops and how they are being trained, not merely where they go once they finish their training."

Warden looked at the maps of the region and nodded.

"Yes, sir. I can add a second mission team to conduct surveillance on the Deathless troops while we infiltrate the target base and locate the information about their wider activities," Warden said, making notes on his data slate.

"Are you happy for us to proceed once we've made these changes, sirs?" Cohen asked hopefully.

Atticus and Staines muted their mics and had a short conversation before responding.

"We are agreed in principle that your mission should go ahead, gentlemen. That said, you need to make some changes to address the weaknesses we've discussed and although we recognise you are keen to get started, we want to see your revised plan before the mission is launched. We strongly suggest you sit down with your senior staff and that you take advice from the specialists and instructors that General Bonneville sent you. Present your plan as soon as you are ready and we will confirm authorisation if you've settled our doubts," said Vice Admiral Staines.

"Yes, sir, understood. We'll get right on it," Cohen confirmed.

"Remember," Staines leaned forward and wagged his finger to emphasise the point, "your priority is to find out where the Deathless are going and why, but bear in mind that a small amount of intelligence returned to HQ is a lot more useful than learning of a secret plan for galactic domination if you die before you can transmit the details. If at all possible, try to get out without them even knowing you were there."

"Yes, sir," said Cohen nodding, "we'll take every precaution."

"And we need to know more about the troops they're training, Warden," said Atticus, "so I want you to gather as much data as you can. If they've got tens of thousands of troops on NewPet, are they like the ones on New Bristol or are they from an entirely different batch? Make sure you record all unit insignia and get it to us for analysis."

"We'll include that in the mission profile, sir, and if we find anything actionable, we'll get it back to you. We won't let you down."

Cohen signed off and shut down the wormhole transmission.

"So, they didn't much like that, did they?"

"No, not one bit, but at least they supported the mission in principle, even if we did fuck up the first crack at the plan."

Cohen shrugged. "They were bound to find fault somewhere. I'm not happy about it but they have the experience and it's easy to criticise someone else's plan. Don't let it bother you, is my advice."

Warden grinned. "You're right, they are a lot older than us. They've probably done this to hundreds of junior officers. You reckon we can pull something workable out of this?"

Cohen shrugged. "No option, really. What's the worst that can happen?"

"Let's gather the team and see if we can't predict a few of the worst-case scenarios, eh?"

They went their separate ways, Cohen to gather his senior staff and Warden to go and find the Marines he wanted to hear from. Intelligence gathering operations were always tricky to plan, especially if you didn't know where to look.

An hour later they had re-worked the plan, thrashed out the details with the specialists and received at least grudging approval from Vice Admiral Staines. The plan was still thin but with so many unknowns, there wasn't much more they could do.

"You're sure about this?" asked Cohen as he watched the Marines prepping for their missions. "You don't want to take anyone else?" Warden was still taking only two people with him on the base infiltration mission: Goodwin to hack the Deathless computers and Marine X, who would be on overwatch to help them exfiltrate to one of the agreed rendezvous points.

The secondary mission would be led by Colour Sergeant Milton, who would take a small team to surveil the enemy training camps. They had found a location from which she could observe three camps that were placed close together.

"Or maybe it's just one large camp, slightly more spread out than the others," Milton had said. They had argued the point for a few minutes but nobody had been able to settle the question or even really explain why it was worth asking.

"What's the worst that can happen, sir?" said the irascible Marine X, grinning as he picked out weapons and supplies from *Ascendant*'s armoury.

Cohen glanced at the penal Marine but couldn't bring himself to answer. Milton did it for him, "You could come back with us, Ten?"

The criminal merely grinned, but Cohen thought the worst possible outcome was pretty obvious and he wasn't at all keen on Marine X's attitude, which smacked of the worst kind of amateur bravado. Why was a court-martialled Marine anywhere other than the brig anyway? He had never heard of such a deployment, but he'd checked the regulations and from what he could tell, it was above board, just very, very rare.

"I don't see an alternative," said Warden as he loaded magazines into his webbing. "I'm not all that keen on this plan myself, but do you see another way to get the information we need?"

Cohen shook his head. "It's a terrible risk," he said, "and not just to you."

Warden grinned and clapped him on the shoulder. "It'll be fine, you worry too much."

"And you don't worry enough," said Cohen, his face tight and grey, "but okay, yes." He held up his hands in resignation. "You're right, there's no other way. Just take care, will you?"

"Always. Don't worry, we'll be back before breakfast."

"Hah!" snorted Cohen. "Fine. We'll smoke you a kipper."

8

"This is shuttle *Gladstone*," said the pilot, Henry Smith. "Ready for launch."

"Acknowledged, *Gladstone*, thirty seconds."

The shuttle was small, designed for only a dozen passengers, but it still felt empty with only three Marines, even though both Warden and Goodwin were wearing power armour. Marine X sat opposite them, his thin frame dwarfed by his larger and more heavily armoured colleagues. Smith had volunteered for the mission and sat alone in the cockpit, the co-pilot's seat left vacant for this flight to reduce exposure.

<Another bet, Colour?> sent Marine X, head back and eyes closed as he relaxed in his seat.

<Why not? I'm on a winning streak. What did you have in mind?> she replied from the second shuttle, where she waited with her own small team.

<Weirdest alien encounter? It's a new planet, after all, and we've no idea what's down there. Could be some really freaky shit>

<Done, but if you lose, you pay up before the party starts, right? No more welching on your debts by getting yourself flattened>

Marine X grinned, his eyes still closed. It was a strange expression on his lightweight clone.

"Doors open," came the voice from *Ascendant*, "launch initiated."

"Acknowledged, *Ascendant*. Free-fall in ten seconds," said Smith over the internal comms system. "Right about now would be a good time to update your wills."

Ten snorted. "I'll leave it all to myself, can't imagine anyone else would want my stuff."

There was a bump as the shuttle was shunted to its launch point and then the artificial gravity disappeared as they moved free from *Ascendant*.

"Launched," said Smith needlessly, "firing attitude thrusters, nothing major, just some slow manoeuvring." They felt the slight jolt as the shuttle's engines fired briefly, shifting it away from *Ascendant* slowly at first but then more quickly as Smith tweaked their trajectory.

"How are we looking, *Ascendant*?"

"All good, *Gladstone*, no obvious signs of alarm, looks like you're in the clear."

"Acknowledged, *Ascendant*, and thanks. *Gladstone* out."

Warden, strapped securely into his seat, watched the video feed from Smith's monitors as they dropped quickly towards NewPet, heading for the nightside. Milton's shuttle followed just behind.

"Are you sure this will work, sir?" asked Goodwin nervously. "I mean, isn't it a bit risky?"

"Probably," said Warden, "but what other choice is there?"

They floated in silence for twenty minutes before Smith came back on the comms system.

"Re-entry begins," he said. "Hold on to your hats."

The shuttle bucked as NewPet's atmosphere began to make itself felt. Warden switched off the video feed and glanced at Goodwin, who looked somewhat uncomfortable. Warden grinned and Goodwin gave him a weak smile.

"Never really enjoyed this sort of thing, if I'm honest, sir," said the technician, hands clamped tight to the arms of her seat, "and I don't get how he does it."

Warden nodded and glanced at Marine X.

"I've given up trying to work out how he sleeps through these things. It's just a fact of life."

And Marine X snored lightly, utterly oblivious to everything around him.

~

"This is it," said Smith as the shuttle bumped down through the atmosphere. "Target forty kilometres ahead. The final approach will be bumpy and low, so get ready."

Even Marine X hadn't been able to sleep through the latter stages of their descent. They'd come down fast, much faster than a shuttle would have flown on a routine office transport flight, but now they were well within the atmosphere and dropping quickly, aiming for the relative safety of the hills.

"Two thousand metres," said Smith. "Sensors show nothing unusual, looking good so far."

The shuttle shot through the night sky, heading for the ground at a steep angle, aiming to get down and up again before the Soyuz was back overhead.

"One thousand metres, twenty kilometres out, still looking good."

"Just another walk in the park, sir," said Marine X, grinning. "Not sure what you were worried about."

Warden ignored him and focussed on the video feed from the front of the shuttle. The canopy was getting ever closer as Smith brought them down and began to level out in preparation for landing. Mueller had been right; the local plant-like organisms were huge, scraping into the sky like living towers, dwarfing anything he'd seen before.

"Four hundred metres," said Smith, "and I'll be looking for somewhere to land behind the hills over –" then he paused, and the shuttle lurched violently to one side then back the other way. Warden gripped the arms of his seat, all plans forgotten as the ship bucked violently.

"Are we hit?" he asked. "Is something shooting at us?"

"Negative," said Smith in a shocked voice, "not hit, but it was close. Shit, more of it, hold on."

The passengers watched the feed as Smith swerved violently, jinking the shuttle first one way then the other to avoid something that hung in the sky above the canopy.

"Taken some damage there, I'm afraid," said Smith as he brought the shuttle back to level flight. "Looks like there's some sort of nasty floating beastie out there."

"Is it serious? The damage?"

"Don't think so, sir, but I'll take a look when we're on the ground. Should have us down in a couple of minutes." The shuttle slowed further until it hovered just above the canopy. Then Smith took it gently down, easing it in amongst the giant plants and aiming for what looked like a clearing at ground level.

"Yeah, well, the ground's not quite as solid as I thought," conceded Smith as they stared at the shuttle.

All four of them were outside, standing on something that looked like a fallen tree trunk, staring at the shuttle as it sat in the mud, listing crazily.

"I think that's because you put it down in a fucking marsh," said Marine X, his sense of humour temporarily suppressed by having to slog through the muck with slimed wings to reach what passed for dry land around here. His thin uniform was soaked and covered in the stinking mess from the marsh, and he scraped ineffectually at his legs, trying to clean off the muck.

From here, they could see where the vines of the floating beasties, or 'gasbags' as Smith had christened them, had trailed over the port side of the shuttle. Whatever they were – and it wasn't at all clear – they had left blackened marks along the length of the hull.

"Let's get going," said Warden as Smith waded back to the shuttle and peered closely at the hull. "Anything you need, Smith?"

"No, sir, I think this is just surface damage, nothing serious. It looks like it's from an electrical discharge of some sort, though, so you might want to stay away from those gasbag things."

"Agreed. Good luck with the return flight, see you in a couple of days."

"Thanks, sir," said Smith, heading for the door. "Hope it goes well." And then he was gone, ducking into the shuttle and closing the door behind him. The three Marines watched as the shuttle lifted jerkily from the mud then crashed off through the foliage, climbing quickly out of sight.

Down here, beneath the canopy, the sudden quiet left by the shuttle's departure gradually filled with the chirrups and rustling noises of a rainforest. Not that anything sounded quite normal or familiar. The general oeuvre of a rainforest analogue was similar, though; the dank musk of the rotting vegetation, the close, humid atmosphere and the claustrophobic density of the canopy were strangely comforting.

"It's that way," said Warden, consulting his HUD and pointing, "about five kilometres. An hour, maybe, if we get moving."

Marine X picked up his kit, including the disassembled rail gun in the specially made carrying sack, and flicked out his wings. He gave an experimental flap, but the span was too great for flying in the dense jungle. He sighed, folded away his wings and slung his sack over his shoulder before following Warden and Goodwin.

Two hours of heavy slogging later, the three Marines lay on the ground at the edge of a low rise that overlooked their target base. The going had been tough, much tougher than they had expected, but they had eventually reached their target.

"There's not a lot going on down there," muttered Goodwin as she peered through her HUD, zoomed in so that she could scan the base, "hardly any lights, no movement that I can see."

"It's not exactly midday," said Marine X, who had sat up and was leaning against a tall plant-like thing, assembling the rail gun with his eyes closed, "maybe they're just asleep."

"Maybe," said Warden, fitting the suppressor to his rifle and checking the magazine, "but either way we need to get moving." His HUD had a countdown showing the time left until the sun began to rise. He glanced over at Marine X, who was running his hands over the rail gun, checking it over. "Ready, Marine X?"

"Yes, sir," he said, opening his eyes as he slotted a magazine into the gun, "good to go." Ten rolled over then arranged himself on the ground, gun trained on the base. The harpy's limbs fitted neatly around the rail gun's stock such that he was able to lie comfortably while cradling the weapon. "It's as if they were made for each other," Ten muttered as his hands rested naturally on the firing controls.

"Goodwin?"

"Yes, sir," said the tech, checking her own weapon then nodding in the gloom, "I'm ready."

"Here we go, then," said Warden, pushing himself upright and running in a low crouch across the open ground to the wall of the base. He stopped at the bottom as Goodwin joined him. The wall rose about them, ten metres high and topped with large spikes, just like the Deathless base on New Bristol.

"Familiar, eh?" said Warden, nodding at the spikes. Goodwin looked up and grinned in the dark. "And now we climb," said Warden, triggering the power armour's climbing feature. Spikes shot out of his fists and feet, and he kicked one foot into the foamcrete of the wall then levered himself up and rammed in his other foot. Goodwin followed suit and as Ten watched, the two Marines scaled the wall.

<What the hell do you think they put those spikes on their bases for? They're not much cop for stopping people getting in> Marine X sent, training his scope on the huge protrusions that curved out from the top of the wall.

<This really isn't the time> sent Warden, focusing on his climb.

<Maybe they're to keep out monsters> joked Goodwin as she heaved herself over the top of the wall and unslung her rifle.

<You're still clear> sent Marine X, <no sign of movement or alarm but I can't see beyond the wall>

<Acknowledged> sent Warden, unslinging his rifle as he joined Goodwin on the wall. And then they disappeared from sight as Marine X began scanning the walls and the roofs of the taller buildings, watching for anything that might present a threat to his commanding officer.

Warden and Goodwin crept along the wall, moving past cutouts that were obviously firing points. Warden paused a few times to snap images and shoot a little video for later analysis; he couldn't imagine why a base on a Deathless planet would need firing points on its walls but maybe someone else would be able to figure it out later.

"Just like the base on New Bristol," muttered Goodwin, clearly wondering about the same features. "Made no sense there either."

At the end of the wall, a door opened into a gatehouse tower. Warden signalled Goodwin, counting down from three, then jerked open the door. Goodwin swept inside, HUD showing her every detail of the room beyond, rifle leading the way. Nothing.

They went down the stairs, searching everywhere for a terminal they could hack, but the tower was bare and empty.

"Not even seats," muttered Warden as they descended through a large room and down to ground level. A door opened out into the base's courtyard and after a moment to check for guards, they ghosted across the open space to the closest building.

"You see anything?"

"No, sir," whispered Goodwin, "everything's quiet out here."

"Too quiet," hissed Warden, "I don't like it." He reached for the door control and Goodwin stepped back, rifle raised. The door slid open and the interior lights flickered on, bathing the courtyard in a fan of white light.

"Shit," muttered Warden as Goodwin moved quickly into the

room, checking for anything that might be an alarm. The door slid silently shut behind them, leaving them in what appeared to be a boot room of some sort, although the benches were covered in dust and lockers were empty, their doors hanging open.

"Where the fuck is everybody?" murmured Warden as they moved across the room to the next door. Goodwin touched the controls and the door slid open. Beyond, another room, much larger and festooned with monitors and control desks.

"Some sort of control centre?" asked Warden as they swept the room for enemy soldiers. Goodwin nodded, closing the door behind them before moving away to check the other side of the room.

"Clear," she said eventually, standing up from her crouch and lowering her weapon, "and these desks are covered in dust, sir. Looks like they haven't been touched in weeks."

"Or longer," agreed Warden, shouldering his weapon and peering at one of the dormant terminals, "but that works for us, right?"

"Indeed." Goodwin fished out one of Sierra's hacking boxes and plugged it into a network port. Then she pulled out a data slate, connected to the box and began to flick through the contents of the network. While she worked, Warden inspected the rest of the room. There was a staircase in the corner leading up to another floor, but the rooms above were as empty and forgotten as the rest of the base. He came back down and sat on a chair near where Goodwin was working.

<Anything moving?> he sent.

<There's something large crashing around in the jungle. Nothing near the base> sent Marine X.

<Nothing to see here> sent Warden <hacking now>

"I don't like this, Goodwin. It's unnatural."

Goodwin grunted but didn't look up from her work or answer, and Warden pulled out his own slate to check for messages or updates from Cohen. Nothing. Apart from the lack of Deathless at this base, it seemed that things were going to plan.

∾

"That's about it, sir," said Goodwin, pushing back from the desk and setting down her slate, "there's a load of information here but I don't think it's going to be very useful. If you want to know about leave protocols or the arrangements of supplies and local troop movements, we're sorted. For anything else, we still need access to the secure network." She paused to rub her eyes. "Or that encrypted file. I just have a feeling we might find something in that."

"Bugger," said Warden, stretching his neck, "I'd hoped to get some answers here."

"Sorry, sir, no answers," said Goodwin, packing away her kit, "but there is this." She flicked around on her slate until she brought up a map of the area, then she zoomed in until the screen showed their current location and the stretch of land to the west. She offered the slate to Warden.

"What am I looking at?"

"We're here," said Goodwin needlessly, pointing at the pale blue dot that pulsed gently on the map, "and this is the secondary target, the base of unknown use about fifteen kilometres to the west." She took the slate back and flicked over to a translated document. "And this is a list of the people currently in that base. I think we might find answers there," said Goodwin, returning the slate to Warden, "because all the guests on the roster are officers and there's a load of servants of some kind, civilians maybe, but basically cooks and masseurs and suchlike, plus a small garrison."

"Interesting," said Warden, flicking through the list, "and I think we've found a likely target," he said, tapping on a name to bring up a detailed profile of one of the current residents.

<Some... things are starting to stir out here> sent Marine X, intruding on Warden's musing, <it might be a really good idea to get moving>

<Acknowledged> sent Warden, <we're on our way>

"Right," said Warden, turning to Goodwin, "let's get out of here. I'm not sure I want to know what might be out there that could make Ten nervous, do you?"

9

Milton watched as the shuttle headed away from the bases, back the way they had come. The team had disembarked in a small river gully and they had a good ten kilometres to cover before they reached their observation point.

Fortunately, it was a clear night and, with the low light vision their HUDs provided, it felt almost like daylight. A night hike like this would be a nightmare without that level of visibility but the power armour also meant it was hard to twist an ankle. Nigh on impossible, really. They would be fine.

The only wrinkle they might reasonably encounter would be an enemy exercise. With three bases in their line of sight, the butte they were aiming for was an obvious landmark and Milton thought the probability that they might meet Deathless trainees on a night exercise was alarmingly high.

"Keep your eyes open," said Milton as her team arranged themselves. "I don't trust these Deathless bastards to be safely tucked up in their beds."

As they began their yomp to the top of the butte, she thought about options for falling back but there really weren't that many. And the bet with Ten about unusual wildlife was starting to look like it might have been a bad idea; there wasn't much of anything moving up here in this arid environment.

NewPet was turning out to be a planet of strange contrasts. This area was rocky with relatively little vegetation, so dry it bordered on being outright dessert. But less than two hundred kilometres to the north, where Warden had deployed with Ten and Goodwin, there was a lush forest that was the local equivalent of a jungle. A long mountain range ran east-west to separate the two zones, keeping the rain clouds from moving south into the arid regions.

Even at night, high up on the ridge, it was warm. Milton was soon grateful for the power armour's cooling systems as they trekked along the ridge that led to the butte where they planned to make their base for the next few days. Up here, there were only a few small shrub-like things and the occasional taller tree-like plant clinging to the lifeless rock or scraping a living from the dusty soil. During the day, this place would be battered by the sun and she had made sure that everyone had brought extra water rations. They would need to take care to avoid overheating or dehydrating, even with the automated water reclamation and cooling systems built into their suits.

The need to maintain secrecy and avoid prying eyes meant that their route was less than optimal. Even in the powered suits, it took almost three hours to cross the ten kilometres to the base of the butte and another half an hour to climb the cliff face. Once at the top, they had the luxury of a relatively flat plateau and several hours to make camp before dawn rolled around and the sun began baking the rock again.

Marine Cooke found a dip near the northern edge which must have been worn away by an ancient riverbed before the butte formed. It was deep and gently curved, and the tenacious plants of the region had established their dominion along the edges where fractures in the rock allowed them to put down roots.

"It's as good a spot as any," murmured Milton, looking around the ancient riverbed. "Let's get settled in."

The Marines moved swiftly to erect their campsite. The riverbed was covered with rolls of graphene-based, nano-weave camouflage supported by carbon-fibre rods and tied off to some of the larger shrubs. The favourable geography meant that the spot was much more spacious than some of the observation points Milton had set up in the past. Making sure their priorities were straight, she left her team to get a brew on while she and Marine Harrington went to check their views of each of the three camps.

During the night they would use passive night vision cameras to record the activity in each camp. They would continue during the day but would also use the Mark 1 eyeball and the binocular features of their HUDs to evaluate the enemy.

Milton and Marine Cooke identified three likely spots for the daytime observations and noted them on their HUD tactical maps before they returned to the camp for a brew. Then the whole team worked to place cameras and tiny passive sensors around the butte; some would warn if Deathless troopers approached on foot or in some sort of ground vehicle, some were designed to monitor air traffic. The rest of the equipment was aimed at the Deathless camps and the training grounds that surrounded them, recording everything they saw.

"It's a big camp," muttered Marine Cooke as they reviewed the feeds from the night vision cameras, "bigger than any I've ever seen."

Milton grunted her agreement. The camps were bigger than any she had seen as well but they still represented only a fraction of the troops on NewPet. Whatever the Deathless were doing here, it looked intensive and well-organised.

"Do you think they're copying our methods, Colour?" asked Cooke, chewing at his nails.

Milton looked sideways at him and frowned. The basic training for a new Commando was two full years and that only included normal operations with brief tasters of a range of specialisms to allow individual aptitudes to be assessed. The sheer variety of equipment and operational scenarios a Royal Marine could expect to encounter in their first five years of service meant that even this level of training wasn't always enough. And officers did a further year of intensive courses after earning their green beret.

"I certainly hope not," said Milton, worried by the idea now that Cooke had raised the possibility, "let's just focus on gathering information." Anything they could discover would be useful to the analysts on *Ascendant* but the material would also be sent back to the Puzzle Palace on Earth to be pored over in detail by experts who would extract every last morsel of intelligence from it.

Could the Deathless be replicating the Marines' own training programmes? It was a frightening thought.

The officers and the governor were certainly in awe of the Deathless' ability to produce bases, equipment and armaments far more rapidly than their own manufactories. The Deathless kit, including the power armour she was wearing, was excellent and often technologically superior to their own.

But to Milton, it seemed that only the Deathless' training and experience were letting them down. Maybe that was enough to explain the existence of NewPet and its camps. How long had the planet been in use? The Deathless were industrious bastards and she wouldn't have put it past them to have built all this in the last few months.

The best-case scenario was that the planet had long been settled and that the Deathless troops who had invaded New Bristol had been their best recruits, graduates of this training facility. If that were the case, whatever the Deathless were doing here probably wasn't all that effective.

But Milton didn't think that was likely.

Still, it would be dawn before they were able to get a proper look at the camps in action, and all Milton could do at the moment was speculate about their plans and capabilities. Time to finish their prep and get some shuteye before the Deathless surfaced in the morning.

Milton's few hours of restless sleep in the warm air of an alien planet were ended by an insistent haptic alarm that woke her just before dawn. An order to the suit's med suite furnished her with a cocktail of mild stimulants that cleared the last vestiges of sleep from her brain, like drinking the galaxy's strongest coffee. Harrington, who had been on sentry duty, returned to the campsite, gave a brief report, then took the reverse cocktail and fell immediately asleep.

Milton checked that each Marine was appropriately concealed under their individual camo nets, then joined Cooke to get an early look at the westerly base. There was a wide crevice in the cliff where it looked like a giant claw had gripped the edge of the butte and gouged out a notch as wide as three people, making it a great place for an observation point. A couple of shrubs used the shade of the notch to eke out a living, and all the Marines had done was sling another camouflage net over the top of the crevice to conceal their presence. It wasn't quite tall enough to stand up in but you could lay down and look through the shrubs or rise to a crouch to move about, and two people could fit easily side-by-side.

Cooke was already there, staring down at the base.

"What have I missed?" asked Milton as she wriggled into place, her armour grinding away at the ground. She wouldn't have fancied being here without power armour, especially as the Marines had nothing to use as padding between them and the rocks. The shrubs they were forced to squirm their way past to get a clear line of sight were covered in vicious spines that would not have made for a good day for an unsuspecting Marine in standard fatigues and body armour.

"Looks like they're just getting up," said Cooke, stretching his neck. "They're not the earliest of risers."

Milton grunted and settled down to watch.

Twenty minutes later, the sunrise was in full swing and it looked like it was going to be another day in paradise, if by paradise you meant a sun-drenched hell-hole a score of light years from the nearest gin and tonic.

A movement barely seen from the corner of Milton's eye caught her attention and she twisted her body to get a closer look. Something was crawling out from a crack in the rock, woken by the first rays of the sun. It made a beeline for a small shrub in front of her, where a fat little creature was happily chewing the leaves, itself an ugly cross between a slug and a beetle.

The thing that had drawn her attention had a long, sinuous body made of banded segments that made it look a little like a shower hose. Hundreds of tiny legs propelled it rapidly towards the bush and, when it reached its target, it reared up and slammed its head down into the abdomen of the slug bug. Milton and Cooke watched in horrified fascination as the creature's mandibles clamped down on the unfortunate prey.

"Ten won't have seen anything like this," she muttered, making sure she had good quality images of the thing as it fed, "no way he'll win this bet now." She'd call him later with the good news.

"Looks like a giant millipede," murmured Cooke, "if millipedes were the thickness of my, er," he paused and glanced at Milton, "my arm and grew to be two metres long. Fucking horrible, whatever it is."

Milton couldn't help agreeing, especially when the thing began to spew some kind of greenish liquid onto the slug bug, which writhed in agony as its flesh liquefied under the onslaught of the toxin the mega-millipede exuded.

"Gross," muttered Cooke, now thoroughly distracted from the job at hand.

Milton reached slowly across her webbing as the horror show went on. A moment later she sighted along the barrel of her pistol and put two rounds in the head and upper body of the millipede, sending it careening off the top of the plateau, dissolving dinner still twitching in its mouth.

Cooke gave her a startled look.

"What?" asked Milton, "That was disgusting to watch. And I had the suppressor on, so they won't have heard it down there. Besides," she added with a smug grin, "that's definitely going to win me my bet with Ten."

Marine Cooke nodded in agreement; the scene had been morbidly fascinating but it was enough to make you lose your lunch. That nasty wee beastie wasn't going to be missed.

'Down there', as Milton had put it, was Camp West, as the Marines had imaginatively named it, and it turned out to be for motorised ground vehicle training. Milton and Cooke watched, somewhat bored, as the troops rose, went through their morning ablutions and breakfast, then broke up into teams to practise vehicle drills.

The first couple of cycles were vaguely interesting. The Deathless would start behind a line, get into one of their enormous APCs, drive a hundred metres then pile out into a combat-ready defensive position. Rinse and repeat, ad nauseam while instructors strutted about shouting orders and berating anyone who moved too slowly or stood in the wrong position.

Milton didn't need to understand their language or even be able to hear them speak to know they were getting a bollocking. *Are your boots tied together? No? Then why aren't you running? You call that running? My sofa is faster on its feet! Did you mean to drop that rifle or was it improvisational theatre?* She grinned, glad that she was now firmly on the giving side of that relationship.

Then a message came in from Warden. She scanned through it in her HUD, the details flashing before her eyes.

"Looks like the captain hasn't found what he was looking for," muttered Milton. Cooke said nothing, still watching the enemy troopers training with their vehicles. "They're relocating to another base to try to kidnap an enemy officer."

That got Cooke's attention. He shifted a little to look at Milton. "That's a bit risky, isn't it, Colour?"

"Very," said Milton, grinding her teeth, "but if anyone can pull it off, it's those three."

"Three? I thought he was with Goodwin?"

"And Marine X. He's on overwatch, keeping the captain and Goodwin safe."

Cooke shuddered. "Rather them than me," he said with feeling, "that guy gives me the creeps."

Milton grunted and went back to reviewing Warden's message. Cooke's feelings about Ten could wait, although she made a mental note to find out if any of the other Marines had similar reservations.

Warden's message went on to say that their secondary target had a maglev station so the backup extraction plan should still work. Milton digested that then composed an update on the situation on the butte, which was luxurious by comparison since all they had to do was sit around all day and look at things, not yomp through dense jungle.

After two hours of watching vehicles drive back and forth, though, she had to admit that even 'luxury' could get boring and that she needed to move on. At least she was able to move around and get a little variety; Cooke had to stay here and watch this base all day. Maybe she'd swap the whole team around in a couple of hours so that they took turns observing different camps. It might help them to stay fresh, and there was no need to tell them she was just helping them cope with the boredom of the duty.

The second observation point overlooking Camp North was not nearly so comfortable. They'd had to dig into the loose topsoil near the cliff face to carve out a shallow foxhole, which meant lying prone and wriggling forward under a low camouflage net to peer over the edge of the cliff face. It was vertiginous, cramped and windy with nowhere to move to get comfortable. Moving out from under the camouflage to stretch your legs wasn't a good idea and if they had raised the net any further, it would have changed the profile of the butte. An observant Deathless trooper interested in landscapes might notice, even from the plains, that the top of the enormous and distinctive rock had changed its skyline.

Milton squeezed herself into the foxhole alongside Marine Watson and peered out over the camp.

Camp North was all about shooting ranges. The whole thing. Come to sunny Camp North and spend all day, every day, shooting an exciting variety of weapons until you can actually hit the targets. The brochure would have made it sound exciting, but for most people, static range shooting was only fun for the first hour or two. The people who continued to find range shooting engaging after half a day tended to become snipers, since patience and an inability to suffer from the boredom of repetitive action were key traits in sharp-shooting. Detailed knowledge of wind and gravity could be trained into someone but if they didn't have the natural ability and the right personality, they probably weren't going to be great snipers. It was the truly dedicated, detail-oriented obsessives that you wanted on your team.

"Anything interesting?" asked Milton.

"They're burning through a lot of ammo," replied Watson. "The shooting is continuous and they're cycling their people."

As Milton watched, it became clear that the Deathless had no qualms about giving their troops as much ammunition as they needed to learn to shoot straight. There were at least a dozen gun ranges of various designs, as well as grenade emplacements and buildings that looked like they might be killing rooms simulating urban environments.

"Just make sure you're recording everything," said Milton, "and see if you can learn anything about their accuracy." She paused, watching a squad practising with railguns on a range that the HUD measured at five hundred and twenty metres. "Especially those fuckers," she said, tagging the snipers in the HUD for Watson to see, "they're a bit of a worry."

But it was Camp East that most worried Milton. Something about the camp had seemed wrong, even at first sight, but she hadn't been able to figure out exactly what.

In the observation post, she found Lance Corporal Bailey and her spotter, Parker, sitting in a scoop-like depression on the edge of the cliff. There were shrubs along the front edge of the coop and room for four or five people to sit and move around. The Marines had strung a camouflage net between the tops of the shrubs at the front and the wall at the back so that it wouldn't be visible from the ground as a disruption in the profile of the cliff.

There was even room to stand, just about, and the Marines had improvised seats from some of the flatter rocks to make this by far the most comfortable of the three observation posts.

"Morning," said Milton, stepping carefully into the scoop and crouching down. Bailey and Parker barely moved, testament to their ability to ignore distractions. "What's new and exciting?"

Parker shifted and glanced over his shoulder.

"Morning, Colour," he said, and it was clear from the tone of his voice that he, too, was worried by Camp East. "We've been watching them put their recruits through their paces. Look." Parker dropped a couple of flags into the HUD and Milton looked down on the camp.

"What am I look..." she began. Then she froze, seeing it for the first time, and shivering with recognition.

Parker had flagged a section of the camp that had been laid out as an extensive assault course. There were dozens of platoons on the course, hundreds of troops in total, all being put through their paces first thing in the morning.

"It gets worse," muttered Bailey, flagging an entirely separate course where a large squad practised in power armour. Even from here, they could see the telltale signs of live fire being used to acclimatise the troops to the sound of bullets flying over their heads.

"Well, bugger," said Milton quietly, because now it was obvious what had worried her about Camp East; it looked exactly like the first training camp she had ever attended, all those years before, when she had first signed up. She shivered.

"And look there," said Parker, flagging a group that stood along the edge of the assault course, watching, "we think they're the instructors and that they're taking notes on recruits' performance, evaluating them."

Milton nodded and brought her HUD to bear. The instructors had data slates and were clearly assigning ratings to the individual troops. Exactly as happened on the Commando course.

"Keep an eye on that for me," she said unnecessarily, trying to cover her mounting feelings of disquiet, "we need to know what they're doing."

She watched the power armoured recruits as they completed their assault course. When they reached the end, they climbed a high wall then ran down a steep hill on the other side. Rifles at the ready, they advanced to a firing position and emptied their clips into the targets at the end of the range. As each recruit cleared their magazine, they raised their rifle. Within a few seconds, every rifle was held high and, even from here, Milton could see triumph in the way they stood.

Then a team of instructors, also in power armour, popped up on either side of the jubilant troops. They advanced and fired immediately, rounds clattering from the armour of the shocked recruits, who quickly began to panic. Some curled up into balls, some sought cover or dove to the ground, others ran.

Milton gave a sickly grin. It was certainly an intense introduction to live fire and obviously a complete surprise for the recruits. It was over in moments and whatever ammunition had been used didn't seem to have penetrated the recruits' armour.

The instructors strutted around, calming their recruits. Then they lined them up and gave what looked a stern lecture, probably explaining in small words why using all your ammunition when you didn't know what was coming next was a bad idea.

"Brutal," she murmured, although it was undeniably a dramatic exercise. "Did you get that?"

"Yup, safe and sound," replied Bailey.

Milton wondered if something similar would be added to the training programme for the bootnecks after the Puzzle Palace saw the video. The exercise was harsh and tough, but the intention was clearly to teach the recruits a lesson in ammunition conservation and force them to focus on the limits of their armour's protective abilities.

They had not yet seen any surveillance drones, but Milton still checked the skies before heading back to the main campsite to review the information they had collected. Then she issued new orders to the team and set a countdown timer to get them cycling between the observation posts.

"And now we wait," she murmured to herself, replaying the video of the assault course and trying not to worry too much about the possible implications.

10

The jungle proved to be as thick and unaccommodating as Mueller had warned. Their yomp from the drop point to the first target looked like a beach-side promenade compared to the virgin jungle through which they now trekked. Beneath the canopy, it was gloomy even at midday, and a continuous spatter of falling water meant that Marine X was soaked within minutes of re-entering the jungle.

"Fifteen kilometres through this could take a while," muttered Ten as they hacked their way through the vegetation and around the trunks of the vast plants whose leaves formed the light-blocking top canopy. Goodwin grunted, pushing past saplings and diving through bushes, her power armour making light work of the plant life as she led the way.

And then Goodwin stumbled out onto a wide track that ran dead straight and due west, heading in almost exactly the direction they wanted to travel. The three Marines stood in the middle of the track and peered suspiciously first one way and then the other, looking along a wide green tunnel of trampled undergrowth that stretched as far as they could see before disappearing under the green gloom.

"What the hell did this?" muttered Warden, kicking at the bushy plants that had been crushed and flattened against the jungle floor. "Look at the way this is all churned up; it looks like a herd stampeded through here."

"Well, if it was a stampede, they won't be back, will they?" asked Ten, stretching his wings and giving a gentle flap. Even fully extended, he couldn't reach the edges of the tunnel. "It's going the right way and it'll be a hell of a lot easier to follow this path than to keep pushing our way through the jungle."

Warden hesitated, suspicious. "I don't like it," he said eventually. "What if the things that caused the stampede in the first place are still on the trail?"

"Don't worry, sir," said Ten in a reassuring tone. "I won't let the nasty monsters get you."

Warden gave him a flat look but the penal Marine had already turned back to the tunnel and was staring at the marks on the ground.

"What kind of thing do you think made these prints, eh?" he asked, focussing on something towards the edge of the tunnel. "I mean, they don't look like hooves, more like toeless feet of some kind. Really big feet from lots of beasties, but footprints nonetheless."

"Let's just keep our minds on the job, Marine X, and see where this damned tunnel takes us."

An hour later, Warden's team were still following the tunnel that cut through the dense vegetation and rich loam; it looked for all the world like an underground rail tunnel and was easily wide enough for two trains.

Even after they had travelled six kilometres, it still headed west as if following a line set down by some ancient cartographer. The tunnel showed no sign of coming to an end, and Warden had begun to wonder if it would carry them all the way to their second target. That was a worry, though, because, for all its convenience, it suggested that the Deathless had made the tunnel. They had assumed a herd of animals made it, but now he was considering other possibilities.

A little further on, the tunnel changed direction slightly to curve around a huge trunk. A series of scrapes and gouges ran around the side of the tree as if a massive vehicle had been driven too close and had rubbed against the bark, scraping loose the weird blue-flowered moss-like stuff that clung to every vertical surface.

"A tank of some sort?" suggested Ten, frowning. Then he shrugged, not really all that interested in solving the problem. Warden stared at the marks a little longer then shook his head. This wasn't a puzzle they were going to solve anytime soon.

Ten was first to feel it, a slight rumbling in the ground. He lifted his head and stared back down the tunnel, looking east. Around them, the jungle had grown quieter, as if all the nearby beasties had fallen still. For a long moment, Ten stood and stared as Warden and Goodwin loped off down the tunnel, heading west.

Then, his sense of unease growing, he turned and charged after them.

"I think we need to get off the road," he said when he caught up a few moments later, "and I think we need to get off right now." Warden looked at him, searching for evidence of a joke, but then he too felt the rumbling.

"You feel that?" he asked.

Ten nodded. His lighter clone was more sensitive to vibration and whatever was making the drumming was getting rapidly closer. Even Goodwin, in her heavier lizardman clone and wearing power armour, could feel the earth rumbling.

"Umm. Yup. Yup, yup, yup," Warden said as the ground began to vibrate beneath them and an ominous sound that was reminiscent of a high-pitched cement mixer overlaid with the pounding thunder of stampeding creatures. "Move. Now. Move, move, move!"

They sprinted along the tunnel, looking for an easy way into the undergrowth.

"There!" shouted Goodwin, pointing at a warped tree at the side of the tunnel. She jumped as she reached it, grabbing vines that hung

from the upper branches and beginning to climb as quickly as possible. Warden and Ten followed her, and they moved swiftly into the
lower branches.

"Fuck me, would you look at that," Ten said. The forest floor was
visibly shaking, rippling the water pooled on the flattened ground of
the tunnel. A few hundred metres down the tunnel, the trees at either
side were shaking as something brushed and trampled past them.

They had been perched in the tree for only a moment before the
rainforest divulged its secret. An enormous armoured beast thun-
dered along the tunnel. Its segmented body undulated as hundreds
of thick legs pounded the jungle floor. It was as tall as a house and it
moved with frightening speed. As it ran, the spines on its flanks cut
through the vegetation as if they were salad leaves and scraped
chunks from the trunks of the larger trees. The thing's head, easily
the size of a medium tank, was a nightmare of mandibles, antennae
and jet black eyes.

It slowed as it drew nearer, the antennae twitching back and forth
as if it searched for something. What the hell did this thing eat?
Warden glanced at Ten, whose winged form prohibited power
armour and meant he alone was not completely sealed inside an
airtight suit. Could this behemoth smell Ten's sweet, tender, Deathless clone-flesh, maybe?

"Stay very, very quiet," Ten hissed, stating the bleeding obvious.
Warden had to remind himself not to hold his breath as they waited
to see what the hellish creature would do.

"Hey, Ten, I think I've won the bet," Milton said cheerfully over
the comms.

"Really?" Ten whispered.

"You won't believe this thing; it's the biggest insect you've ever
seen. Well, arthropod, I think, strictly speaking. Horrible beasty, long
and wriggly, the mouth on this thing is straight out of some cheesy
horror holo-vid."

"You don't say," hissed Ten as the giant monster lowered its head
to the ground, snuffling back and forth across the tunnel. "Long and
wriggly?"

Warden glared at Ten, chopping his hand across his throat in the universal gesture of 'shut the fuck up'.

"Oh yeah, this thing was huge, two metres long, easily. Had to shoot it to get rid of it. No way you're going to beat it."

<I'll buy a barrel of gin for the company if I can't beat it, but right now we're a little bit busy. Take a picture for me, eh?>

<Roger that. Pictures to follow. Looking forward to the cocktails, Ten>

<Yeah, me too, if we make it out of this>

Warden chewed his lip as they waited. He had imagined all sorts of ways the mission could fail – capture by the Deathless, *Ascendant* blown out of orbit, Goodwin unable to hack the information, shuttle shot down on their way back to *Ascendant* – but he hadn't considered the possibility of being eaten by a hundred-ton nasty.

And then suddenly its head reared up and it screamed, a great cry that went on and on, like a meth-crazed foghorn. Then it began to move again, gathering speed until it was charging along the tunnel, passing by the three Marines fast enough that they could feel the wind rush past them. The stench of the thing surpassed even the ever-present scents of the rotting vegetation on the forest floor. A hundred metres long or more, it went on until, abruptly, it had passed.

They waited in the trees until they could no longer hear it screaming as it barreled down the tunnel, nor feel the vibrations from its passage. As the rest of the jungle began to come back to life, they climbed gingerly down from their platform in the canopy and stepped back into the tunnel, peering both ways. Then Marine X sniffed, gagged for a moment from the stink it left and spat on the on the floor.

"That was unexpected," he said, a masterful piece of understatement. "How do they turn around?"

Warden looked at him then grunted, utterly disinterested in the question, and set off along the tunnel, yomping away in the long, loping strides of the power armour.

Goodwin quickly followed but Marine X stood for a moment longer, looking at the tracks and thinking about how a train-sized monster might use a network of tunnels in the undergrowth. Then he sighed and began running. The sooner they were out of this jungle, the better.

W arden called a halt only a little way further along the track. The tunnel had opened out into a wide clearing where a second tunnel crossed the first. Two hundred metres across and heavily trampled, it was clear that the monsters were doing more than turning around in the clearing.

"What do you think they eat?" said Goodwin as the Marines stood in the crossroads. Warden and Ten looked at him, and Goodwin shrugged. "Just wondered. I mean, it's not like we've seen much in the way of game, is it, and something with huge jaws that moves at that sort of speed isn't likely to be a herbivore."

Warden shuffled uneasily. "I think I would have preferred you not to verbalise that thought," he said, scanning the tunnels and jungle uneasily.

"At least we're only four kilometres from the target," said Marine X, checking his HUD, "another hour and we'll be there, and then we'll see what's going on." He took a swallow from his water flask then unwrapped another energy bar. "Maybe there's some sort of monster buffet at the end of the tunnel."

Warden shook his head, finished his own snack and stretched his neck. "Let's keep moving. I want to get set up well before dusk."

T hey pushed on until they reached the end of the tunnel and the edge of the jungle. The valley had been clear-cut; massive tree stumps could be seen across the expanse between the jungle and the base. The buildings stood right in the middle of the valley, surrounded by nothing but low shrubs and crawling vines.

The colossal plants of the jungle marched no closer than the edge of the valley, reaching over a hundred metres above the low ridge and heavily hung with great leaves and trailing vines. The animal calls and sounds that had been a near constant accompaniment so far had died down and, for the first time, the jungle seemed subdued, quiet and ominous.

A maglev line emerged from the forest a kilometre away, dropping to a station near the base before rising again to head back out of the valley. Beyond the pylons that supported the line as it approached the base, the valley fell steeply away so that the base seemed to perch at the end of the world.

"There must be another base to the north," said Warden, checking the plans that Mueller had provided, "but there wasn't anything on the map."

"More gasbags," said Goodwin, peering out across the clearing towards the base. The walls were over two hundred metres away, ten metres tall and topped with the familiar curved spikes. Above the canopy, at the head of the valley where a small river dropped from the hills, a flock of the floating creatures hung in the air, seemingly tethered to the plants.

"Like jellyfish back home," said Marine X, "but with electrically charged tentacles instead of venomous barbs," he went on, remembering the scorch marks on the outside of the shuttle. "Nasty."

"I don't recall ever seeing a zeppelin-sized jellyfish floating above the treetops back home but yeah, just like that," Goodwin replied.

As they watched, the vines on one of the nearer gasbags jerked and shook then began to retract slowly. The Marines watched, open-mouthed, as a large animal was dragged up towards the underside of the floating body. Then it disappeared, stuffed into a huge maw that opened to receive its gift. The empty vines fell back to the forest canopy, and the gasbag hung there, giving no sign that it had just consumed a creature the size of a cow.

Ten cleared his throat, breaking the silence. "The locals are a bit unfriendly," he observed.

"Maybe that's why the Deathless didn't settle here," said Goodwin. Then she paused and frowned as another thought struck. "I wonder what those cow things eat?"

Marine X glared at the tech and shifted uncomfortably.

"We need a higher vantage point for the surveillance kit," said Warden eventually, "to give us a view down across the base. This ridge isn't high enough, not with those bloody walls in the way." Marine X looked at his commander then glanced at the nearest plants before finally looking at the Gasbags.

Then he sighed and rummaged in his bag for a remote camera kit. He stuck it to his webbing and looked up at the tree.

"Maybe there's a convenient branch with a clear view," he said unenthusiastically. "I guess I'd better have a look, right?"

"Probably for the best," agreed Warden. "You're the lightest, there's less chance of you falling, and if you do, it won't matter."

"Yeah, I do have wings, I suppose."

"Wings, right, I'd forgotten about those," Warden replied with a smirk.

Ten's eyes narrowed and he pursed his lips, then he cocked his head and looked hopefully at Goodwin, just in case the tech was keen to place the camera.

"Don't look at me," Goodwin said quickly, raising her arms, "this armour isn't really suited for climbing trees."

Marine X narrowed his eyes to slits but said nothing more. He checked his blades then shuffled back from their viewing spot and circled around to the far side of the nearest tree. Then he crouched and sprang, leaping several metres straight up and landing on the trunk, fists gripping the fibrous growths on the surface. He paused to look once more at Warden and Goodwin, but they just waved cheerfully and went back to watching the base.

"Fuckers," muttered Ten as he began to climb, checking for gasbag vines with every reach and hold.

Seventy metres up, with the greenery showing little sign of thinning, he found a thick branch that poked into the valley, overhanging the edge of the ridge. He stepped out onto the metre-wide branch and gave an experimental jump. It barely moved, so he walked gingerly out, towards the open air of the valley, working his way around the numerous branches that speared out in all directions.

"That'll bloody do," he said quietly. The branch had narrowed quickly and was now getting distinctly bouncy, even with Ten's light-weight body. He unpacked the camera, a tiny remote unit with a zoom lens and wide-spectrum sensitivity. A proper Gucci bit of gear, far better than the stuff they were usually issued.

The kit included a telescopic carbon-fibre mounting pole. Ten fitted the camera then began unshipping the pole, raising the camera cautiously towards the top of the canopy. As it reached the top, he switched to his HUD and stared out through the camera's lens.

"Slowly, slowly," he muttered, focusing on his task. The feed showed the undersides of huge leaves and the thin, spiny lengths of the topmost branches. Then the last spiny leaf was brushed away, and the camera burst out into the open space above the trees. Ten had a moment of vertigo as the camera's focus shifted rapidly and adjusted to the changing light. Then it settled to show a clear view across the jungle to the base. He switched away from the camera feed, rammed the end of the monopole into the trunk and checked it was secure.

<You seeing this?> he sent to Warden and Goodwin.

<Yes>

<On my way back> sent Ten, edging back along the branch.

On the ground, Warden and Goodwin both keyed into the feed. The camera had a long view across the valley and into the base. They couldn't see everything that was going on in the base, but by zooming and panning around, they could build a pretty good picture of the Deathless activity.

The problem was that Warden didn't like the picture he was seeing.

"Any good?" said Marine X, when he re-joined them a few minutes later.

"The feed is good," said Warden, "but I don't think we'll get in and out quietly." He paused to flick some captured stills to his slate then showed them to Goodwin and Marine X.

"Apart from the walls, the killing ground all around the outside of the base, the maglev station for rapid reinforcement and the wall-mounted cannons, this looks very straightforward."

"The cannons might be for the gasbags, sir," said Goodwin, "you know, to keep them from hunting inside the compound."

Warden switched his HUD to zoom out to the gasbag and then back to the walls, inspecting the cannons.

"Maybe," he conceded, "but the bits I really don't like are the towers," he said, flicking back to the remote camera feed and focusing on one of the four tall towers that held high watch positions above the base. "We might sneak in under their gaze, but they're going to make exfiltration really bloody difficult if things get noisy."

They spent a few minutes scanning the base and reviewing the feed from the camera, but nobody could see a way to avoid the towers.

"How many Deathless are in there, do you think?" asked Warden.

"If those two long buildings are barracks or apartments of some sort, maybe thirty bunks, then another fifty or so in the guard houses over there," said Marine X, panning around with the camera and flagging the buildings in his HUD. "That looks like some sort of conference facility and there's a big open area that might be a parade or exercise ground, and maybe a rec room?"

"Maybe eighty to a hundred then, in total," said Warden, grimacing. "I don't like our odds."

"There's a shitload of Ruperts down there," observed Marine X, "far more than any normal base, I'd say. And I can't see any specialists. No ogres or harpies, just lizardmen and Ruperts."

Warden frowned. "So this is what, exactly? A training campus?"

Marine X shrugged. "Could be they've erected an officers' stately pleasure dome," he said, grinning, "you know, somewhere they go for a bit of a jolly." Warden raised an eyebrow. "Or a retreat, maybe, where the brass meet to set strategy." Warden looked at him strangely, and Marine X frowned. "What?" he asked. "We have them at home, why not here?"

That was news to Warden, but he nodded, remembering that the well-preserved Penal Marine had acquired a wealth of training and obscure knowledge over his decades of service. How he knew about the habits of the most senior officers was a question for another day.

"An officer's retreat, then," said Warden quietly, "set far enough from the other bases to ensure privacy but still connected to the maglev network for convenience. Sounds ideal for what we need, I just wish it wasn't so bloody large. I would have preferred a nice, modest hunting lodge, to be honest. And at least there's no sign of a runway or a landing pad."

"Wouldn't want to fly too near the surface, sir," pointed out Goodwin, "not if you thought there might be gasbags floating around. Rail makes sense."

"And the maglev lines are on stilts because those giant millipede things might disrupt the trains," mused Warden.

"Nah," said Marine X, "I reckon it's just easier to sink piles to hold up the rail than it is to clear the ground and build on it. But there might be other megafauna, herds of giant herbivores maybe, that we haven't seen yet. Wouldn't want them sitting on the track as you were speeding along at three hundred kilometres per hour."

"Millipede shish kebab," murmured Goodwin in a rare moment of humour.

"Anyway," said Warden, dragging the conversation back to the matter at hand, "the point is that there are lots of them down there, they've probably got guards in the towers, and we've got to sneak right in there to grab one of their top brass. That's not something we can do quietly."

Goodwin nodded and Marine X, absorbed in the feed from the remote camera, merely grunted. Warden sat and thought for a few minutes, trying to see a way to do it.

"Nope, sooner or later it'll get hot," he said eventually. "It only needs one of those guards to sound an alarm or to get off a decent shot as we're retreating across the killing ground, and this whole thing will have been for naught."

He looked at Marine X and Goodwin. "I'm going to call in Milton and her team. Goodwin, you and I will infiltrate as planned. You'll run overwatch, Ten, and we'll have Milton to back us up when things go pear-shaped. Then we'll all head to the secondary extraction point."

Marine X flicked up his HUD. "Risky, very risky," he said, grinning, "but I like it."

11

"Come on, look lively," said Milton. Warden's orders had made it clear that time was of the essence, so now the camp was a hotbed of activity as the team packed away their gear and tidied the site.

"Leave no traces behind, people," said Milton as she folded down her own gear and stowed it in her pack. Bailey and Parker, lacking power armour and its advanced processing facilities, were bagging their solid waste for exfiltration along with the rest of the gear they'd brought for the two-day reconnaissance. Watson had drawn the short straw and was now packing bags of solid waste into his pack, carefully checking that each was properly sealed and surrounded by soft, non-piercing objects.

Had they been in the jungle, Milton might have risked burying the solid waste and trusting to the vegetation to hide both the evidence of digging and any lingering smells. Up here, with only dusty rock and thin soil, there was no option but to bag the crap and take it with them. Nobody's favourite job, but Warden had been clear: the enemy was to learn nothing from the site.

And so it was being scoured. Once they had finished, all the enemy would learn – if they ever came to look – was that someone had been up here for a while.

The observation posts were dismantled as well, all traces carefully removed, every stone and plant checked to make sure it looked natural, untouched. As each post was dismantled, Milton checked for any signs they might have left behind, but her team were professionals and she found nothing that would indicate they had once been there.

In fact, the only thing they left behind was the body of the millipede thing that Milton had shot. She looked at it as it baked in the sun then decided that as there was no practical way to hide it or take it with them. Their only option was to leave it where it lay. Besides, it had been shot with a Deathless pistol so even if the body was found and examined, the enemy would learn nothing about the Marines.

"That's looking good, people," said Milton as she completed her last round of inspections and the Marines shouldered their packs, "but we've got a long way to go and a short time to get there, so let's get moving."

It was still light when they left the site, which meant travelling less quickly than Milton would have liked and taking extra care with the route to ensure they stayed out of sight. Progress was slow, but they couldn't afford to be silhouetted against a skyline or spotted by a passing aircraft, not that the Deathless seemed to find much use for aircraft.

Bailey and Parker took the lead, scouting ahead to find the best route and checking for Deathless troopers and vehicles. The harpy clones made excellent scouts and even though they flew only a few metres off the ground, they were able to make much faster progress than the rest of the team.

Every five hundred metres, Bailey would halt and take up overwatch, scanning the sky for signs of enemy movement while Milton and the rest of the reconnaissance team yomped on. When they had almost caught up, Bailey and Parker would push on to their next overwatch point, searching continuously for signs of the enemy.

Slow and steady wins the race, thought Milton. With bases on every side of the butte, they would be easily surrounded if the Deathless discovered them.

The sun had just finished setting when Bailey sounded the alarm.

<Freeze> Bailey broadcast to the team, the command flashing an urgent red across their HUDs.

There was no cover, just the rocks and contours of the ridge, so the team crouched motionless on the ground, trusting their dust-coloured armour to hide them from hostile eyes.

<Problem?> sent Milton.

<Movement in Camp East>

<Do you have eyes on?>

<Just about – feed open now> confirmed Bailey.

Milton switched her HUD to show the world from Bailey's perspective. Down in the camp, vehicles were moving out, their head-lights shining in the dim light. Bailey tagged them in her HUD, which showed the vehicles moving at fifty kilometres per hour. Considering the terrain and the complete lack of roads, that was dangerously fast.

<Where are they going?> Milton asked.

<Not sure, Colour. They're heading roughly east but can't tell why or what they doing>

<Roger that> Milton replied, wondering what the hell was going on. Had they been discovered or was this merely a night exercise?

She flipped to an overhead map display and extrapolated the current path of the small convoy. They planned to board the maglev train just past the point where the ridge curved a little to the north-east. There was a long tunnel passing through the hills, the Deathless having simply dug straight through to maintain a fast line rather than go around or over the hills, and the station that seemed to serve the camps was on the northern side of the tunnel.

That was where Milton and her team needed to be; then it was a clear shot to the rendezvous with Captain Warden. They were still almost ten kilometres out, though. The Deathless convoy could be coming up into the hills between them and the station. If they'd detected them, it would be logical to get ahead of them and either set up an ambush or force them back up towards the butte and the other camps.

"There's nothing on the map," muttered Milton, tracking the convoy's likely path, "so they must be heading to the station." The more she thought about it, the more likely it seemed. If they had planned an ambush, they would have been driving with night vision rather than headlights, which surely even the Deathless knew would be a giveaway. The troops she'd been watching in Camp East seemed to be disturbingly competent and she couldn't imagine them making such an easily avoided error.

<We have to assume they're going for the station. We need to pick up the pace and see what happens. Bailey, Parker, get to an overwatch point for the station as quickly and quietly as you can. The rest of us will follow as quickly as possible. Notify us of any major changes> Milton ordered.

<Roger that, Colour> Bailey confirmed. Milton could just make them out in the distance as they unfurled their wings and ran forward, gliding along the line of the ridge, as low to the ground as possible. They should reach the station in about ten minutes, depending on the wind and altitude.

At daylight pace, Milton and her team could expect to take an hour to complete their yomp to the station, but the power armour did have some advantages.

"Switch to full night-vision mode," she ordered as her HUD scanned and mapped the terrain ahead, laying down an amber route for her to follow. "Stay close and look sharp. And if this takes us more than thirty minutes, I'll have you all doing drills until you spew pavement pizza, understood?" Milton looked around at her small team then nodded and broke into a loping run, following the route her HUD overlaid onto the ground in front of her. They might not reach the station before the Deathless, but she was damned if she would give them time to prepare an ambush.

～

<B ad news, Colour Milton> Bailey sent.
<Busy hoofing it, Bailey, we don't all have wings. What's up?>

<We've reached overwatch position and you have less than twelve minutes to make it to the train>

<We'll get the next one>

<Negative, Colour. There's an illuminated sign on the platform and maintenance on the line after this train; the next one isn't for another twelve hours>

<Buggery bollocks! Get a fucking shift on! If we don't make that train, we'll miss the RV with the captain and that means we won't get picked up by *Ascendant*. We are not getting stuck on this shithole>

<Permission to use stims, Colour?> requested Harrington.

Milton thought quickly as she huffed into the rebreather of her helmet, which sucked away her moist breath and condensed the water out of the air before returning it to her reservoir.

<Confirmed> she sent, issuing the order to the team and authorising their suits to dispense stimulants, increase the oxygen supply and deliver a cocktail of mild painkillers and anti-inflammatories.

<Dial up the servos> she sent, tweaking her own suit's settings so that she could run faster. It would cut the operational time of the suits' batteries in half, but they needed to reach their train more than they needed the power reserves.

The Marines accelerated, hurtling through the night, pushing their clones to the very edge of their design envelope. Even in the suits, there were risks, especially over terrain as rocky and broken as this. More than once Milton stumbled or missed her footing or found that the ground was sloping up rather than down. Their night vision gear was excellent, but it was easy to misinterpret, especially at speed, and there were limits to what the power armour could do to protect them.

Worse, they had no clear idea what the extra oxygen might do to the Deathless clones they wore. Their standard RMSC clones were better at handling oxygen than their biological bodies, but it could still do funny things to their minds. And while the painkillers were great for hiding the ache of sore limbs, they also cut the feedback loops that prevented small injuries from getting more serious.

Own it, thought Milton as she ran, teeth gritted, *fucking own it and push through it.*

Run or fail. Catch the train or get left behind on an alien planet and commit a very thorough form of suicide in order to protect the mission.

The Marines ran for all they were worth.

<Bailey. We need a solid plan to get straight on that train> sent Milton.

<Working on it. Those soldiers from Camp East are standing ready to board the train. Looks like they're going in our direction>

<Then we still need that plan, Bailey, and it better be a bloody good one>

A minute later, Bailey came back on.

<Sending a new route. Faster>

<That's fucking close to the edge>

<Only way you'll get here in time, Colour>

<Roger that> sent Milton, <changing course>

The new course took them far closer to the edge of the ridge. If there was anyone down there, all they needed to do was look up and they'd see the four Marines pounding along for all they were worth, illuminated by the stars that shone brightly through the clean air. And who knew how much noise they might be making as they steamed across the rocky slope? Sound did funny things in the desert at night.

No point panicking though, thought Milton. *Just put one foot in front of the other until you're finished.*

Jenkins stumbled when a small boulder slipped as his foot landed on it, and he almost went down, face first. Rebecca Watson was just close enough to grab his webbing and haul him up short before he could break his head open. Milton was bringing up the rear, and she reached down and grabbed him under the left shoulder, helping him to stand and get moving again.

<Four minutes, Colour>

<I bet these bastards have the only trains anywhere that bloody run on time> sent Milton, cursing to herself as she ran.

<Yeah, looks that way, Colour Sergeant. We clocked it as it approached the other side of the ridge. It's below the ridgeline now, but the HUD estimates its speed will put it in the station at the time shown on the platform sign. You have no slack> Bailey responded.

<So what's the boarding plan?>

"Say that again, Parker?" Milton hissed incredulously. They had made it to the rendezvous point about sixty seconds before the train was due to depart.

"There are Deathless in all the carriages that aren't still in the tunnel," said Parker apologetically, speaking quickly, "so we have to wait until the train moves off then get on an empty carriage. It's okay, I checked; there are four more carriages."

"No," Milton seethed, "it is most definitely not okay, Parker. Have you ever seen a maglev accelerate out of a station? They do not hang about. You want us to jump onto a moving maglev train and get ourselves attached to it before the wind shear yanks us off?"

"Well, I don't want to do it either, Colour Sergeant," Parker protested, "but there's not much choice. Oh, and you're going to have to hold on to me and Bailey because without power armour we probably won't be able to keep a grip." He grinned weakly and raised his thing, graceful hand.

"Oh spiffing, this just gets better and better."

"Sorry, Colour," Parker glanced at the train, "but there isn't time for us to get into the carriages at the back and the tunnel is too tight for us to crawl down it and get ready. Even if we did, we'd be clomping our boots all over the roof of one of the carriages with Deathless in it. On the plus side, the station isn't manned, so we can get right up to the lip of the tunnel ready to jump onto the second carriage. All at once of course, or it'll be too late."

"Fuck, fuck, fuckity fuck, fuck," Milton spat, "bollocks to it, we don't have a choice, do we?" She paused, chewing at her lip but there was no other way and she knew it. "Let's give it a go. This night can't get much worse, anyway."

"That's the spirit, Colour Sergeant," Bailey said with a broad grin. Easy for her to say, of course; she and Parker had wings to get them out of trouble if it all went wrong.

The team shuffled to the lip of the tunnel. Parker was right – it was less than a metre above the roof of the maglev carriages, and there was no way they could get in without giving themselves away.

"I think we just need to drop onto the second carriage. Better to have an empty carriage between the Deathless and us, yes?"

"Agreed. At least this thing is wide enough that we don't have to do it one by one. Three abreast, folks," said Milton, more confident now that the decision had been made, "and get your carabiners ready so that we can rig ourselves together. This is going to be a punishing ride. Once we're aboard, we'll be on this thing for a few hours before we get to the rendezvous with Captain Warden."

Below them, a whining noise indicated the maglev train was about to depart the station and that the time for talking was over. Milton checked her gear was securely strapped and that the rest of the team were in place.

Then they leapt.

The train was moving under them as Milton landed on the carriage roof. She heard the rest of the team land a few metres behind her and it sounded like they were down safely. Now, if she could just hold on to the edge of the carriage for a few hours, everything would be rosy.

"Sergeant!" Bailey shouted into the comms channel. "You seem to be hanging off the side of the train!"

"Thank you, Bailey, I hadn't noticed," she said sarcastically through gritted teeth as she gripped the rail at the edge of the carriage roof, "and it's 'Colour Milton'."

"I'm on my way, hang on," Bailey said, "you know, in case you weren't doing that already."

"Hadn't planned on letting go," hissed Milton as the train accelerated.

Bailey swooped in low and grabbed a rail at the side of the carriage to bring herself to a sharp stop. With her wings for lift, it was easy for her to get back up on the roof of the train. Milton, on the other hand, was clinging for dear life to the edge of the carriage with one hand while she tried very hard not to loosen her grip.

Then the train began to bank to the left, which would have been helpful if Milton had been on the right side, but a fifteen-degree tilt left her dangling in thin air, over at least a thirty-metre drop. With the train now travelling at over a hundred kilometres an hour and still accelerating rapidly, this was not helpful. Even the power armour wouldn't save her if she fell off at this speed but the bigger risk was someone in a leading carriage looking back and spotting her.

"I'm here, Sergeant!" Bailey said.

"If you tell me to hang on or take your hand, I will end you, Bailey."

"No, that would be stupid. If I have to tell you to hang on, why would I want you in charge? You'd be too stupid to live and if you could get your spare hand to me, you'd pull yourself up," Bailey replied as she busied herself with something.

"Good to know. Do you have anything useful to say?"

"Yes, I plan to say, 'Attach this carabiner to your webbing so we can haul you up'. Just prepping the line."

Thirty seconds later, the aforementioned article dropped over the side of the carriage, and Milton was able to grab it on the third try with her dangling left hand. She clipped it on to her shoulder straps and checked they were still tight.

"You've got a live one here," she shouted, left hand clutching at the line above the carabiner, just in case, "reel me in."

The line went taut as the Marines pulled her up the side of the carriage. She scrambled onto the roof and took a few seconds for a breather. Then, as the train pushed past a hundred and fifty kilometres an hour, she checked that the team was roped together and clamped to the roof.

A few minutes later, the train returned to an even keel and began to accelerate to maximum speed. Bailey and Parker were squeezed between Jenkins and Harrington in their power armour, with Milton at the front to take the brunt of the wind and Watson at the rear. They had used their climbing claws to give them extra grip, and each Marine was clipped to two others by a short length of cord and a carabiner.

The battering from the wind was severe and they squirmed and adjusted their positions until each had found the lowest possible profile to minimise the drag. Now, all they could do was cling on for dear life. This was going to be a gruelling couple of hours.

Milton cast her mind back to the Commando course, the final milestone of the Royal Marine Space Commandos training programme. Centuries before, the course had been only a week long but now, with all the extra combat roles the Marines faced, it took a full month with only a few precious 'rest' days between the various tests of endurance and confidence. The location had shifted as well, with the second half of the course now taking place on the harsh terrain of Mars rather than the relatively friendly Devonshire countryside.

Now, tied to the roof of an enemy train as it rattled across an alien planet at over four hundred kilometres an hour, Milton compared it to the last gruelling training week on Mars and decided it merited only 'challenging'. Then she chuckled as she remembered the weeks of paperwork and administration that had followed the earning of her Green Beret, and she downgraded her evaluation of the wind rushing past her to 'bracing'.

12

For Warden's small team, dusk took a very long time to fall. They lay at the edge of the jungle, one sleeping, one on guard, one watching the Deathless base, all waiting for the sun to sink below the horizon.

Marine X assembled and checked his railgun while the light was still good, tweaking the sights and making sure that they were set to take account of the light breeze. Then he propped it against the trunk of the tree and settled down to wait.

At dusk, a train rocketed across the valley and drew to a halt at the station on the edge of the compound.

"Sixty-five seconds," said Warden as the train pulled away again, "a few on, a few off, maybe." He shrugged. They hadn't found a timetable in their stolen data cache, so it was impossible to say when the next train might arrive, where it might come from or what it might be carrying.

All they knew for certain was that Milton and her crew were riding a train at that moment, inbound at something like four hundred kilometres an hour, all clinging to the outside of the carriages.

"Rather her than me," Ten had said when Warden described what

Milton's team were having to do. "What if there are tunnels or carriage scrapers or something? What if the train runs through a station and someone sees them?"

But nobody had been able to come up with a better idea and it seemed to be working, so far. Milton's last report had said they were making good progress and that she had a newfound respect for tumbleweeds.

Across the valley, the train finally slipped from view and a flock of something that looked like large, leathery birds flapped its way across the compound before disappearing over the trees.

"That's our entry point," said Warden after watching the video of the train arriving and pulling away several times, "we'll wait for full night, creep down, infiltrate the station and then go in from there."

Around the Marines, the nightlife was starting to emerge from the jungle, and the calls and noises were growing louder, more insistent.

"Why through the station, sir?" asked Goodwin, watching the video again in her HUD.

"Whatever the walls guard against, it's not people," said Warden, "so they probably don't have guards in the station, and they might not even lock the doors. It would fit with their previous performance."

Goodwin nodded but looked doubtful.

"And this is our target," said Warden, sharing an image from the files they had liberated earlier in the day, "he's got the right rank and job title and, with any luck, he'll get us into the secure spaces."

Goodwin nodded again but still looked sceptical. Sneaking around was something they were all happy to do, but kidnapping enemy officers was just a little too much like spying, and it didn't sit within the tech's comfort zone.

"It'll be alright, Goodwin," said Marine X cheerfully. "What could possibly go wrong?"

~

"That's late enough," said Warden eventually, one eye on the clock and the other paying attention to the base. Activity had died down an hour before, and now the compound was silent and still. They had plotted a route to the base that took them around the side of the valley to the maglev lines. "And then we just follow the pylons. Easy, and no chance of being spotted."

"It'll take a while," said Marine X doubtfully. "Hacking through the jungle in the dark won't be a lot of fun."

"Two hours," said Warden, "possibly a little more, but no chance of getting lost."

Marine X nodded, almost invisible under the thin starlight that penetrated the canopy.

"Milton's hours away, but by the time we get out, she should be pretty much here," Warden went on. He paused to check his kit again then he looked at Goodwin.

"Ready, sir," said the tech.

"I'm going to edge around the top of the valley, find somewhere with better visibility of the rail," said Marine X as he loaded his rail gun and re-checked the mechanism, hands moving quickly and confidently despite the dark.

Warden nodded to him, checked his rifle and webbing one last time, then he set out along the edge of the valley, following the route they had mapped out earlier in the day and that now pulsed dully in his HUD. The jungle was thick and progress, as Marine X had predicted, was slow. It took more than an hour to reach the first of the tall foamcrete stilts that supported the maglev line.

"That's our marker," said Warden. Goodwin nodded and followed him down the slope at the edge of the valley. Tracking the maglev rail took them across the valley, where the jungle's greenery was already trying to reclaim the open ground. They reached a small river, not much more than a stream, that flowed under the maglev line before diving into the deeper valley beyond.

An hour later, they had crept across the river and over the mangled remains of the local foliage so that they were only a hundred metres from the maglev station. The rail, ten metres above their heads, flew on towards the station as Warden and Goodwin advanced in its shadow, all the way to the train station.

The fifty-metre long train platform stood on more foamcrete stilts, an elegant structure that Warden might have considered architecturally interesting in other circumstances. At the back of the station, a short walkway led to the wall and then into the compound. From the ground, they couldn't see enough to spot movement, but there were no sounds from above, only the distant animal calls of the jungle.

Then there was some sort of animal alarm call from the jungle, far off down the valley, a high-pitched screaming cacophony that split the night air. Warden and Goodwin looked around, trying to spot the source of the problem, but even the HUDs couldn't resolve the details of the jungle where Marine X was hiding.

<Problem?> sent Warden, crouched behind a foamcrete stilt.

<Space monkeys> came the reply, <dealing>

"What the fuck?" breathed Goodwin.

Warden shrugged, the gesture almost invisible without the vision-enhancing capabilities of the HUDs.

<We're at the station> sent Warden. <Are we clear to ascend?>

<Hold, still dealing> came the reply. Warden frowned. Marine X was rarely unreliable.

Warden squatted down, resting his back against a foamcrete stilt. Goodwin scanned the area then she too settled down to wait.

"What the hell is going on?" muttered Warden after they had been waiting for a few minutes.

<Update, Marine X> he sent, marking the message urgent.

There was no reply, and Warden was beginning to fear that something untoward might have happened to the Penal Marine.

"This is taking too long," he said after giving Ten another ten minutes. "We have to get going." He gestured at the stilt, preparing to climb. Goodwin nodded, shifting so that she could see the platform and cover the captain.

Warden took a deep breath and began to heave himself up the

foamcrete support. The clone was well-suited to this sort of activity and the power armour made it all seem easy. In seconds, he was at the top and sliding silently over the parapet and into the station.

He scanned left and right, rifle at the ready, checking for Deathless sentries or other staff. Satisfied, he signalled Goodwin.

<We're in the station, all clear> sent Warden. <Are you ready?>

<Still dealing> sent Marine X, <give me a minute>

<No time for jokes, Marine X. Are you ready?>

There was no reply. For twenty long minutes, Warden and Goodwin crouched in the shelter of the station. Warden switched from the remote camera video feed to the HUD's night vision, alternately scanning the compound and the local area then staring out towards the jungle where Marine X was supposed to be providing overwatch.

Warden was in the process of composing a forceful note and a formal reprimand when Marine X finally responded.

<Sorry, space monkeys. All sorted now>

Warden and Goodwin shared a look.

<Save the excuses, Marine X, we'll talk about this later> sent Warden, <just get to your position>

<Almost there> came the response. Then a few minutes later, <In position. Good visibility, I see you. No movement in the compound, guard towers quiet and dark>

<Copy that> sent Warden. He stood slowly, stretching his cramped muscles, then he and Goodwin began moving, heading to the back of the station and the raised walkway that would take them into the compound.

<Station clear, no signs of security> sent Warden as he and Goodwin moved quietly along the walkway. At the far end, a steel door barred their way. Goodwin searched in vain for a control pad that would allow them access before they noticed the handle recessed into the face of the door. Warden stood back, rifle raised, as Goodwin pulled gently on the handle and the door slid on silent runners into the wall.

<Door unlocked> sent Warden as he stepped over the threshold,

Goodwin following. The room beyond was empty, dark and window-
less but large enough to hold a company as they waited for a train to
arrive. Ahead, a door led out towards the compound; to the right, a
second door led somewhere else.

Warden shook his head, marvelling at the total lack of security.
Had he ever been on a base that lacked even basic mechanical locks
and guards? But then why lock doors on a planet where your nearest
neighbours were over a thousand kilometres away? Bloody amateurs,
they weren't much better than space pirates, only with a lot more
ships and people.

Goodwin slid the door closed, and they stood for a moment,
checking their surroundings and waiting to see if they had triggered
silent alarms.

<No sign of activity> sent Marine X. <Looks like they're all asleep>

Warden nodded and signalled towards the door that led out into
the compound. Goodwin sidled over and touched the control. The
door slid back, and a gust of warm air flowed into the room, carrying
with it the smells of the base and the jungle. Outside, a wide stairway
led down to the ground where foamcrete paths were laid between the
buildings.

"We're allowed to be here, remember?" said Warden quietly,
shouldering his weapon and standing up straight. Goodwin looked at
him for a moment then nodded and shouldered her own rifle. "But
keep your pistol ready." Warden held up his hand to show a
suppressed pistol, then he strolled casually down the stairs and into
the compound, not quite whistling but definitely walking with a
jaunty air.

Goodwin waited a few seconds then followed, her own pistol
hanging at her side. They had mapped a route to the most likely resi-
dential block, and now all Warden had to do was follow the trail
displayed in his HUD. A few minutes of stealthy walking took them
around the edge of the compound and to a long, low building that
seemed to be a series of apartments overlooking the parade ground.

"Looks like a holiday camp," muttered Goodwin, frowning.

But a holiday camp designed by military minds rather than fun-loving architects or anyone who had ever been on an actual holiday. The paths were all straight and neat, and the buildings were plain and utilitarian, unadorned squares and oblongs of bare, unpainted foamcrete.

Even the imported plants – bushes and small trees that were clearly descended from Earth originals – were arranged neatly but without imagination, as if the whole compound had been laid out with function as the only principle worth following. Warden felt that it gave the whole scene a strange, unfriendly feel, like old bases back home where the joy had been sucked out of everything by bureaucrats and pen-pushers.

"Pretty shitty holiday," he whispered, making for the long low building that they'd pegged as the officers' quarters.

The path took them straight there, lit by bright, overhead lights on simple galvanised steel supports.

"Look for nameplates," hissed Warden, checking the apartment doors. They hadn't found a layout plan that showed room allocations and their target could be behind any one of these doors.

"Nothing," whispered Goodwin, "just a number."

"Shit, nothing on these ones either," murmured Warden. "Well, that's a bugger." Neither of them said anything for a few seconds, then Warden shrugged. "I guess we just take whoever's in the biggest room, then." Goodwin nodded and pointed at a large apartment set slightly away from the others at the end of the row.

Warden nodded and switched from his pistol to the suppressed rifle. Then they padded down the row of apartments towards the one at the end.

"Keep an eye on that tower," muttered Warden as they moved beyond the shelter of the apartments and back into the open space between buildings. He stopped by the door, checking that Goodwin was in place, then reached for the opening control.

<Movement on the tower> sent Marine X as Warden's hand brushed the control, <changing guard, maybe>

"Bugger," muttered Warden as the door slid open. The lights were off inside but the HUD gave them excellent night vision, and nothing seemed to be moving. He slipped into the room, and Goodwin followed, tapping the door control so that it slid shut behind them.

The room was large but sparsely furnished. A pair of sofas were arranged in front of a large display that hung on the wall. A desk and chair sat against another wall.

"Grab that," hissed Warden, pointing at a small computer of some sort that sat on the desk. Goodwin sidled over and picked it up, slipping it into her pack. She slung the pack over her back and turned back, collecting her rifle as she went. Then there was a bang and a crash as she caught a desk lamp with his arm and knocked it flying.

Goodwin stared in horror for a moment then both Marines swung round to look at the other door, the one they assumed opened into some sort of bedroom. From beyond the door, there came the sounds of stealthy movement.

Warden flicked his finger, gesturing to Goodwin to get out of sight. Then he moved the other way, trying to get close to the bedroom door. He was about halfway there, with Goodwin still moving the other way, when the door opened, and a Rupert clad only in light trousers stepped out into the room.

There was a moment of quiet surprise as they all stared at each other, then the Rupert said something, head turning to look at Warden, whose clone was essentially identical. The HUDs translated but the mangled text didn't help much.

<Who the sexual act is you? I will call the guards who are covered in blood!>

Then Goodwin smacked the Rupert in the head with the butt of her rifle and knocked him unconscious.

<Target acquired> sent Warden. <Beginning exfiltration>

<Hold> sent Marine X, <movement, two lizardmen heading your way>

"Shit," muttered Warden. He looked around then moved so that he was standing in front of the door. "Grab him," he said quietly to Goodwin, "and get ready to move."

<Two coming your way, no shot, under cover>

Warden readied his rifle as Goodwin picked up the unconscious

Deathless officer. The power armour made light work of the job as Goodwin slung the clone over her shoulder and drew her pistol. She nodded at Warden.

Then there was a knock at the door, and a question was asked in the Deathless language. Warden and Goodwin froze, still and silent, then the question came again, louder and with more insistent knocking.

There was a pause then came the gentle chime of the lock and the door slid open. A surprised lizardman stood on the threshold wearing only a light uniform. Then Warden shot him, his suppressed rifle spitting three times to punch neat holes in the clone's chest.

<Contact> sent Goodwin as the captain moved, looking for the second lizardman before the first had really processed the fact that he had been shot. Warden leapt forward, grabbed the stunned Deathless by his shirt and dragged him into the room. The clone collapsed across the floor and his partner, only now realising that something was wrong, yelled and made a grab for his pistol as he dived away.

Warden let loose a short burst but wasn't sure he hit anything. He stepped quickly over the threshold of the apartment then ducked back as the Deathless clone fired three quick rounds from his pistol.

<The guard towers are awake> sent Marine X, <eyes down for a full house. Firing>

"Move," shouted Warden, their chances for a quiet escape had been comprehensively blown by the lizardman, who had shuffled around the edge of the building away from the Marines and was yelling for all it was worth, "fast as you can, please."

Goodwin needed no further encouragement. She moved quickly across the apartment, sleeping Rupert on his shoulder, and followed the captain out onto the veranda.

Warden's rifle spat again but the lizardman had gone, ducking away into the gloom beyond the apartments as around them the compound began to show signs of life.

"Time to go," said Warden, leading the way. They retraced their steps, heading back to the station. A door opened ahead of them, and another Rupert stepped out, pistol in hand. Warden shot him several times from near point-blank range then pushed the corpse off the doorframe and back into the apartment.

<Stop> sent Marine X and Warden skidded to a halt just before the end of the apartment block. There was a whistle of a passing railgun round then the unpleasant fleshy sound of muscle and bone being torn apart and the familiar crack of equipment falling onto foamcrete.

<Check right> sent Marine X.

Warden poked his head around the corner to see two lizardman corpses, both with rifles but neither wearing power armour, laid out on the path.

"Come on," he said, waving Goodwin forward and hurrying for the steps.

<Firing> sent Marine X again. <Targeting guard towers>

Warden jogged towards the steps, rifle swinging every way as he tried to cover all approaches. A pair of lizardmen came around a corner, and the captain fired a quick burst in their direction, sending them scurrying for cover but not doing any real damage. They were almost at the steps when a guard on one of the towers started shooting.

They ducked back into cover, unable to see exactly where the shooting was coming from, and Warden switched out his magazines. He raised his head cautiously above the steps and then whipped it back down as rounds pinged off the foamcrete, altogether too close for comfort.

<We're pinned> he sent. <Can you help?>

<He's firing from the western guard tower but he's out of sight> sent Marine X. <I'll put one close and see if I can keep him down>

<Roger, ready to move>

Warden edged away, rifle ready, Goodwin behind him.

<Go now> sent Marine X. Warden came up firing, aiming in the rough direction of the tower and hoping they'd done enough to keep the Deathless guard down.

They hadn't. Two rounds went past Warden's head then a third pinged off his shoulder, knocking him around. Goodwin charged past, the Rupert still slumped over her shoulder, as more rounds rained down. Warden fired again, no better aimed than his last burst, and surged up the steps pushing Goodwin before him.

They dived in through the open door and sprawled across the floor of the large waiting room.

<More coming> sent Marine X, <move now>

Goodwin swore under her breath as she forced herself back to her feet and picked up the unconscious Rupert. Warden grabbed his rifle, punched in a new magazine and pushed himself upright.

"Gah!" he said, staggering sideways. He caught himself on a seat and managed to stay upright by holding the back of it. "I've been shot," he said quietly, faintly outraged by the very idea, "in the leg."

Goodwin spun around and peered at Warden's leg, eyes slightly wild behind her HUD.

"Walk it off, sir," she hissed, "we have to go!"

Warden nodded and hobbled after Goodwin, putting as little weight on his injured leg as he could.

<Captain Warden's hit> sent Goodwin. <Flesh wound only but it's going to slow us down>

<Keep bloody moving> came the reply, <straight across the walkway then drop down on the far side>

<Acknowledged> sent Goodwin, shaking his shoulders to resettle the Rupert. "Come on, sir," she said, gesturing urgently to Warden. The captain hopped and staggered across the waiting room as Goodwin fired her pistol at the unseen shapes lurking on the station steps.

Warden yanked the door handle, but this time the door didn't budge. He pulled it again as Goodwin emptied her pistol at their pursuers.

"The door won't open," he hissed through gritted teeth. Goodwin looked at him as he heaved again, putting his whole weight on the handle. Nothing happened. Then he noticed the keypad beside the door and cursed; it looked like the Deathless did sometimes lock their doors, even if there was nobody else on the planet.

"Shit," said Goodwin, "let me take a look." She dropped the

Rupert to the floor and peered at the control as Warden stepped away. "Base is locked-down," she muttered, "no way to open this from here." Warden boggled at her. "Sorry, sir, we're trapped."

Warden looked around wildly, desperately searching for a way out.

"That way, through that door," he said, edging along the room, his back against the wall as his leg dripped a trail of blood.

"Seriously?" said Goodwin, slamming a new magazine into her pistol before heaving the Rupert back onto her shoulder. "What's that way?"

"No fucking clue," said Warden through gritted teeth, "but we can't stay here."

He heaved the door open just as a pair of black objects sailed over the threshold from the stairs and clattered over the floor.

"Grenades," warned Goodwin, stumbling to the door. There was an almighty bang and a huge flash of bright light and both Marines were punched through the door and onto the narrow balcony that overlooked the compound.

<Can't see you> sent Marine X, <can't see much of anything moving>

Warden heaved himself back to his feet, shaking his head to clear the fuzz in his brain.

"Get up," he yelled at Goodwin, who was on her knees. The tech shook her head and pushed herself to her feet, settling her rifle across her shoulder. "Pick him up, get onto the roof," said Warden, louder than he needed.

Goodwin shook her head again but grabbed the Rupert, armoured hands slipping on the clone's now blood-slicked skin.

"Just get up there," said Warden, aiming his rifle across the waiting room then firing two quick bursts as a squad of lizardmen tried to storm the door. Behind him, Goodwin managed to get the injured Rupert onto her back and struggled up onto the rail that ran around the veranda. The top of the wall was only a few feet above the roof of the waiting room, but Goodwin was never going to reach it with the Rupert on her back.

"You'll have to pass him up to me, sir," said Goodwin. Warden swore and glanced up. Goodwin was right; there was no way either of them could climb to the wall with the Rupert on their back. He nodded, fired another quick burst at the doorway, then slung his rifle.

Goodwin dropped the Rupert into his arms and Warden staggered slightly, his wounded leg protesting mightily.

Unburdened, Goodwin simply reached up to the wall and heaved herself up. Then she lay flat and reached back down for the Rupert. Warden stood up and lifted the clone as high as he could, holding out its arm so that Goodwin could grab it and heave it up alongside her on the wall.

"Shit," murmured Goodwin as shots rang out and bullets pinged off the foamcrete wall, "we're a bit exposed here, sir."

Warden nodded and fired a last burst at the lizardmen clustering around the door.

"Get down there," he said, pointing over the wall. "I'll drop him down to you."

Goodwin looked surprised for a moment then nodded and slid over the wall, lowering herself as far as she could go before dropping and trusting that the armour would protect her.

Warden slung his rifle and heaved himself up onto the wall. He peered over the edge but couldn't see Goodwin in the gloom. More rounds bounced from the foamcrete on the wall as the guard in the tower opened up again, letting rip in a long, sustained burst.

"Fuck this for a game of soldiers," muttered Warden. He pushed the Deathless officer off the wall in the hope that Goodwin would catch him, slid a little further along then rolled himself over, intending to hang and drop in a controlled way, just as Goodwin had done.

A round struck the foamcrete sending shards rattling across Warden's faceplate. He flinched as he rolled and another round hit him in the shoulder, knocking him back. One hand scrabbled desperately for the edge of the wall and then he was over, bouncing off the wall as he fell to the ground.

13

<Ascendant, this is Marine X>

The message flashed up on the main monitor in the bridge and Cohen frowned in annoyance.

"How is he doing that?" he asked the room in general. Before anyone could answer, there were more messages.

<Be warned that Captain Warden and Marine Goodwin are in the Deathless compound. The enemy is aware of their presence>

"Oh," muttered Cohen, "that might make things a bit more interesting."

He turned to check his other monitors. Nothing moving nearby, nothing showing on the long-range passive scanners.

"Launch the dropship," he said, settling into his chair and checking the mission timer on the principal monitor, "get it clear and lined up for the extraction." He paused to check the status of the near-space sensors again then nodded to himself. Warden might have made a mess of the extraction on NewPet but, up here, everything seemed to be going very well indeed.

"Message from Soyuz," said Midshipman Wood, the communications officer, "translating and putting it on the forward monitor."

·   ·   ·

<<V*arpulis*. Dock at gate six immediately.>>

"W ell, that's not good," muttered Cohen. "I guess that means they're on to us as well." He stared at the message for a moment, pondering his response. "Send this please, Mr Wood: 'Docking gear being serviced. Full function in six hours. Will dock once repairs are complete.'"

"Translating," said Wood, "and sending."

Cohen focused on his breathing as he watched the monitor. He just needed to win a few more hours for Warden's team to complete their mission. Once they were safely back on *Ascendant*, he could relax.

<<V*arpulis*. Remain in current orbit. Prepare to be boarded by warship *Posvist*.>>

T hey all stared at the message for a few seconds. Then Cohen cleared his throat.

"Time to go to work, ladies and gentlemen," he announced. "Give me an update on the dropship."

There was a pause then Midshipman Jackson said, "Dropship is on the rails, launching in twenty seconds, clear for us to manoeuvre in fifty seconds."

"Good, thank you, Jackson. Mr Wood, another message if you please. 'Acknowledged, *Varpulis* standing ready.'" He paused while Wood sent the message.

"Dropship has launched, clear in thirty seconds," reported Jackson.

"Helm, get ready to move. Navigation, how far to the closest body of any size?"

"Helm ready, sir," said Martin.

"The second planet's orbit is about twenty million kilometres in towards the sun, sir," said Midshipman Martin, "but it's sixty degrees ahead."

"Too far to be useful, then," said Cohen, "so plot a course that will take us directly away from Soyuz and prep for high-G manoeuvres as soon as the dropship is clear."

"Aye, sir, preparing," said Midshipman Martin, her hands flicking over the controls.

"And let's find that warship, please. I'd like to know where she is before we break cover."

"Scanning, sir, nothing showing up at the moment," said Wood, peering at the scanners. Then, "I think I've found her, sir. Drone scans are showing a large ship near Soyuz, manoeuvring away from the station." The drones had been left behind when *Ascendant* had left Soyuz, a dozen tiny machines watching the station and relaying back images and information.

"If she's by the station, we've got, what, maybe five minutes before she has line of sight?" said Lieutenant White, Cohen's XO. "Do we fight?" he added quietly.

Cohen closed his eyes for a moment, considering the question. Then he took a deep breath and blew it out slowly, remembering how Admiral Staines had behaved and acted during the battle over New Bristol. This was his first combat command, and out here, far from home, there was nobody to hear him scream. He grinned briefly, then forced himself to focus on the monitor.

"One on one? Let's see what she does before we make any decisions," said Cohen in a low voice.

"Dropship clear in fifteen seconds," said Jackson, as calm and disinterested as if he were announcing the late running of a train.

"A blip on the scans, sir," said Wood, popping images onto one of the main monitors, "looks like a second warship, similar size to *Posvist*, coming around the planet in the other direction."

"Sneaky," muttered Cohen as he inspected the images, "very sneaky." He turned to White. "Discretion today, I think." White nodded his agreement. "We'll jink out a little, get some distance, then head off at a tangent and try to lose them." White nodded again; a solid, if risky, plan.

"Take us to action stations, Mr MacCaibe," said Cohen.

"Sir," acknowledged Midshipman MacCaibe, punching the command. A klaxon rang out and the bridge crew's seats reconfigured automatically for high-G combat manoeuvres.

"Dropship is clear," said Jackson.

"Spin us around, Ms Martin," said White, "and sound the warning for high-G manoeuvres."

"Acknowledged," said Martin, punching the ten-second warning and triggering the attitudinal thrusters. The ship rotated smoothly, like a swan gliding across a pond, until her engines faced the planet. "Manoeuvre complete."

Cohen watched the monitors as crew stations reported their readiness. He drummed his fingers on the arm of his chair for a tense thirty seconds as the crew raced to secure their areas and themselves. After what seemed like hours, the counter hit one hundred per cent and Cohen nodded.

"And away we go, please, Ms Martin."

"Acknowledged," she said, sounding the high-G klaxon again, "sixty-five-second maximum power firing of the main engines in three, two, one." She punched the control, and the ship shot forward, pressing the command crew into their flight chairs and making every simple movement ten times as difficult.

All eyes turned to the display to watch the timer tick slowly down to zero.

"Main burn complete," said Martin eventually. The release of pressure as the engines switched off was like being gifted with a super-power that allowed easy use of arms and hands.

"Let's launch a few drones, Mr White," said Cohen, "just in case they try to follow us."

White made the arrangements, dispersing a dozen of the tiny machines in a random pattern, some to float in the wake of *Ascendant*, others to move outward in an ever-growing sphere.

"Spin us around to ninety degrees from the orbital plane, Ms

Martin, and sound the warning for high-G burn in ninety seconds," said Cohen, watching the monitors on which the positions of the *Posvist* and the second warship were plotted.

"Low-G manoeuvres in three, two, one," said Martin before triggering the controls. The attitudinal thrusters fired and the ship span, no more than a gentle push compared to the massive compression of the main engines. "Manoeuvre complete."

"It's going to be close," said White, watching the monitors and reviewing the course that Cohen was planning, "we'll have to trim the burn to stay out of view."

Cohen nodded.

"Twenty-five seconds on the main engines please, Ms Martin, full power."

"Acknowledged," said Martin, sounding the high-G klaxon again, "firing in three, two, one." The acceleration pressed them into their couches as the main engines pushed them at right-angles to their trajectory. There was a pause before Martin said, "End of burn in three, two, one."

"Enemy vessels still out of sight around NewPet," said White.

"Everything off," said Cohen, "we'll run dark for a few minutes then see where things stand."

"Active sensors offline," reported MacCaibe, "passive sensors only, weapons powered-down."

"Running lights and transponder off," said Martin.

"Better hope there isn't a friendly-fire beacon," said White, "or this is going to be the shortest escape attempt in history."

"How long till the enemy comes out from behind the planet?" asked Cohen, peering at the monitors.

"*Posvist* will be out in just over thirty seconds, sir," said Wood, "the other ship in maybe fifteen minutes."

"A quick flare of the starboard and aft attitudinal thrusters please, Ms Martin," said Cohen, "just enough to give us a gentle tumbling roll."

"Firing thrusters," said Martin, "thrusters fired for a half-second burn, our roll is stable at one revolution every ninety minutes."

"Just like an asteroid," murmured White, eyebrows raised.

"Exactly so," said Cohen, "it won't fool everyone but they've got a lot of bodies to scan and maybe it'll stop them looking too closely."

"And now?" asked White.

"And now, we wait," said Cohen, "until Warden completes his mission and Smith signals that they're ready for the pick-up."

14

<Nice move> sent Marine X as Captain Warden heaved himself upright, leaning against the wall, <elegantly executed>

Warden ignored him and focused on his leg, which hurt a lot and wasn't moving quite properly. His neck and shoulders ached, as did his back and his other leg, but nothing seemed to be broken.

"You okay, sir?" asked Goodwin, hurrying over.

Warden nodded, although in truth he could have done with a week off, a massage and a decent meal.

"The Rupert?" he asked, looking around as boots banged across the foamcrete paths and gravel on the other side of the wall and shouts floated through the night.

"I mostly caught him," said Goodwin apologetically, "but he's not dead yet."

<Ware above> warned Marine X. Then there was the familiar thrumming of a railgun round and a new bout of frenzied shouting from the walkway that led to the station.

"We need to move," said Warden, shaking his head to clear the last of the daze.

<Situation update> he sent as he picked up his rifle and checked it was in good order.

<Activity on the walkway, lots> came the reply. There was a long pause then another rail gun round thrummed over the wall. <Move now>

Goodwin snatched at the Rupert and slung him over her shoulder. Warden backed away from the wall, rifle raised, searching for anything to shoot at.

<Clear, move fast> sent Marine X.

Warden gritted his teeth as Goodwin, one hand wrapped around the Rupert to stop him sliding off her shoulder, began to jog awkwardly across the open ground.

<Slow works as well> sent Marine X but neither Warden nor Goodwin had the time to respond.

As Warden and Goodwin slogged their way across the open ground, Marine X fired again and again. They had made it nearly halfway before one of the Deathless returned fire. The sound of the rifle was strangely loud against the backdrop of the jungle.

"Keep going," said Warden, staggering on as fast as he could go, "just go!"

Goodwin pounded on. The armour took most of the weight but it was still heavy going; carrying bodies across the ruined undergrowth of an alien jungle probably wasn't in the design brief.

<Keep moving, Captain> sent Marine X as Warden crashed down into a stream.

He lay there for a moment then heaved himself around to look back at the base. The station was only a hundred metres away, which was absurd given the amount of effort Warden had put in. The Deathless were firing from the wall, and Warden ducked into the stream, unable to overcome the fear of being shot despite the incoming rounds all going well over his head.

<Get up, Captain> sent Marine X, <can't stay there, this jungle is most unhealthy>

"Fuck," said Warden quietly with gritted teeth. Marine X was right but that didn't make it any easier. Ahead, over the low bank of the stream, his HUD picked out the shape of Marine Goodwin, still plugging away across the open ground with the Rupert on her back.

<Two vehicles coming your way> sent Marine X, <thirty seconds max>

Warden swore again and pushed himself to his feet, clambering out of the stream and staggering after Goodwin. He could hear something, some sort of engine, and suddenly there were lights blazing out across the mashed vegetation. Ahead of him, Goodwin was nearing the edge of the open ground where the valley began to slope up towards the jungle where Marine X was hidden.

<Ware monsters> sent Marine X but Warden wasn't sure he'd read that right. The vehicles were turning towards him; he could see the headlights reaching for him through the misty night.

"Shit," he said, unslinging his rifle and standing on his good leg.

<Get clear> he sent as he aimed at the first vehicle.

<Negative; ware monsters>

Warden ignored the message and squeezed the trigger, firing short bursts at the lead vehicle as it closed rapidly on his position. Was he hitting anything? He couldn't tell, he just kept shooting.

And then there was a sudden noise of stampeding cattle and the lead vehicle flipped into the air. It flew end-over-end before crashing down in a spray of mud and water in the middle of the stream, engines screaming.

In front of Warden, a huge millipede beast reared up, standing on its back legs to claw at the night sky. The second Deathless vehicle swerved wildly as the driver veered away from the enormous creature. It bounced across the wrecked ground and over the stream then turned on a hairpin to flee back towards the compound.

<Captain? You still alive?> sent Goodwin.

Warden looked around but all he could see was the side of the millipede-thing as it charged after the second vehicle. The ground rumbled as it rocketed past, then the Deathless troopers on the wall opened fire and the monster screamed. It changed direction again, thrashing around as it searched for the flies that bit and stung its armoured hide.

<Captain?>

<Here> managed Warden. He almost dropped his rifle as he

turned to continue his stumbling escape towards the safety of the jungle. Now that the millipede-thing had moved on, he could see the dim shape of Goodwin as she slogged up the slope ahead.

His HUD showed the route to the rendezvous point. Only two hundred metres away. He gritted his teeth, slung his rifle and put his head down, grinding his way down the path in half-metre steps.

Behind him, it sounded like the Deathless troopers were letting rip with every weapon in their arsenal. The monster roared and screamed and then a great boom sounded across the valley.

Warden turned to see the great animal rearing up again, this time against the walls of the compound. It towered over the walls as the Deathless fired at it again and again. Then there was a sudden flash of light as the millipede fell against one of the curved spikes that jutted out from the top of the wall.

The huge beast screamed in pain and flopped back down to the ground, stunned and staggering.

<Move> sent Marine X and Warden resumed his trudge, glancing over his shoulder every few steps to see what was going on behind him.

<Survivors from crashed vehicle> sent Marine X, <dealing>

There was a thrumming noise as a railgun round flew overhead. Another followed a few seconds later, then a third.

Then Goodwin arrived out of nowhere, grabbed Warden's arm and hoisted him up off his bad leg.

"Got to move now, Captain, only a hundred metres or so, but those buggers are getting ready to come after us, I'm sure of it."

Together they half-climbed, half-crawled up the slope of the valley towards the jungle.

"Almost there," encouraged Goodwin, "just a little further, then tea and biscuits."

Warden grunted at the quip, focussing on the hill in front of him and staying upright as Goodwin dragged him steadily to safety.

"Where's the Rupert?" he managed through gritted teeth.

"Ten has him," said Goodwin, "jammed him full of meds and he's out for the count. Got some waiting for you as well when we've covered the last twenty metres."

A shape appeared on the edge of the jungle in front of them.

"Get a fucking move on," said Marine X, waving an exasperated arm at them. "They're heading out and we've got places to be." Then he swore and dropped to his knee, raising his ridiculously long gun. "They're getting bolder, need to teach them another lesson," he muttered, squeezing the trigger.

Then he dropped the rail gun and jumped down the slope, grabbing Warden's other arm to drag him the last few metres.

As he moved, there was a loud crack and the tree he had been standing beside sprouted a ten-centimetre hole.

"Sniper," shouted Goodwin in alarm as they all bundled over the edge of the rise and thrashed their way back into the jungle. They jinked left, back towards their temporary camp, and another rail gun round smashed through the foliage behind them in a cloud of splinters and flying leaves.

"Too close," said Marine X as they dropped down behind one of the huge tree-like plants, "far too fucking close." He fished in his bag for a painkiller and rammed the needle into Warden's leg.

"Ah, that's done it," said Warden as the drugs took effect. He shook his head and looked around, able to really focus on his surroundings for the first time in what seemed like ages. He paused as more railgun rounds crashed through the trees a metre or so above their heads.

"Firing blind," muttered Marine X as they all crouched, "any word from Milton?"

Warden checked his HUD then shook his head.

<Milton, sit-rep> he sent, hoping she was within range.

<Still on the train, disembarking in the next few minutes> came the reply.

"Right, we need to get to the extraction point," said Warden, checking his HUD for directions, "that way, about four kilometres." They had set a pick-up point away from the compound to avoid enemy fire, but now that felt like an extravagance.

Warden grabbed his kit and slung the bag over his shoulder.

Marine X looked around for his rifle before remembering he'd dropped it at the edge of the jungle. "Shit," he said, slinging his pack over his wings, "guess we'll manage without a railgun."

Goodwin collected her own bag then looked at Marine X.

"You need a gun," she said, again demonstrating her supreme ability for stating the obvious.

"I need a weapon," countered Marine X, glancing at Captain Warden, "but I guess I'll make do with a pistol."

15

"Three minutes, Colour," Bailey said, counting down as the train approached the station.

"Noted. Get ready to move, everyone. Looks to me like we need to go off the south side," said Milton, "and make sure you stay out of sight." The reconnaissance shots showed the station buildings to be on the north side of the track, which made sense as the camps Captain Warden had been investigating were also in that direction and they hadn't seen anything to the south from orbit.

The station itself was at the top of a steep, almost cliff-like, slope covered in the dense jungle foliage that blanketed the area. The pylons supporting the maglev track were much taller at this point on the line, particularly on the south side, which was going to present some issues. They'd had a good view as they approached the hillside and the total drop was about a couple of hundred metres.

Power armour had all sorts of advantages and could climb tough slopes with relative ease, but jungle terrain added its own dangers and even the best suit wouldn't save you from a two hundred metre fall. Rolling down a steep slope in power armour would be almost as bad as a straight fall. Milton had wanted a nice, safe platform but there was no such luck.

On the plus side, they'd had nothing to do for a couple of hours except cling to the train for dear life so the whole team had been able to review the reconnaissance shots and talk about their next steps. They now had a plan that should see them disembarking without being spotted, injured or left too far from Captain Warden's position to make the rendezvous. Probably.

"Everyone ready?"

"Sniper team, standing ready," confirmed Bailey. She and Parker would be disembarking as the train approached the station, making use of their clones' wings to glide away to the west before circling back to find a perch in the jungle where they could take up overwatch positions.

"Ready, Colour," said Cooke.

"Ready," said Harrington.

"Ready as I'll ever be, boss," Watson said, her voice breaking a little.

"You okay, Watson?" Milton asked.

"Just a bit nervous about dangling off the side of a train, Colour."

Which seemed reasonable, in Milton's opinion. Unlike the snipers, the rest of the team couldn't launch from the train and flap away.

"We could jump off right before the train reaches the station and let the armour take the pounding," Harrington had suggested, but staying out of sight would mean disembarking while the train was doing more than seventy kilometres an hour. Nobody fancied hitting a tree at that speed if the jump went a little wrong, so they had swiftly binned the idea.

Instead, they were going to have to disembark stealthily at the station in such a way that they weren't spotted by the Deathless in the station, in the base or on the train. There wasn't another station on the next thousand kilometres of line, which suggested that the Deathless troops on the train would be disembarking here as well. Either that, or they were going halfway across the continent, and Milton didn't think her luck would be that good.

The best they'd come up with was to attach climbing cords and rappel off the side of the train, then reattach under the tracks, preferably to one of the support columns. That seemed achievable, not fancy, not noisy and, hopefully, survivable.

"It's no big deal," said Milton cheerfully, hoping to persuade Watson and the rest of the team that high-speed train-surfing was a normal part of a deployment, "Ten does this sort of thing all the time and he always gets away with it."

"Can't be trusted with a piano, though," quipped Harrington to a round of laughter, although Watson didn't seem too amused.

"Yes, Colour. I'll try to do what Ten would do," Watson said.

"Er, well, maybe not everything, eh? Don't want to end up calling you Eleven. Right, Bailey, Parker, the train is slowing down, you think you can make it at this speed?"

"Soon find out, Colour," said Parker as he raised himself up into a crouch and unfurled his wings. They snapped wide like a parachute and he was immediately lifted clear of the train. He banked away to the south and was quickly lost in the night.

"It's fine up here, no bother at all," said Parker a moment later. "I'm off to find a perch." At that, Bailey took to the air as well.

"Watch out for those gasbag creatures, I don't want you two getting electrocuted and eaten," said Milton as she adjusted her own position on the train.

"Colour, there's a firefight going on by the base. Looks like the captain has made his presence felt," Bailey said.

"Roger that. Continue as planned, find a perch and get us covering fire," ordered Milton.

The train was slowing to a stop. Captain Warden had said that the earlier train had been stationary for about a minute but surely this one, laden with troops, would need longer? They couldn't wait for the Deathless to clear the station. As soon as the train came to a stop, Milton gave the word.

"Go, go, go!" she ordered, dropping off the side of the carriage and into the night, her team following close behind.

Milton pulled up short as the rest of the team dropped below her. She turned to face the tracks and fired her grapnel then reeled herself in towards the track.

"Colour? Where are you?" Harrington asked.

"Making plans for Nigel. Get yourselves over to that pillar, I'll catch up." Milton hauled herself up, under the train. It took her only seconds to turn her plan into reality and then she detached her grapnel and wound the cable in before forward rappelling off the track into the air again.

She was glad it was so dark; the drop really didn't matter so much when she couldn't see the ground. If she didn't hurry, though, she'd still be attached to the train when it departed and that would be a thrill for all of about two minutes before it became seriously unpleasant and likely quite grisly.

The rest of the team had made it to the pillar and their lines had disappeared, so they must have detached their magnetic clamps and reeled them in. Milton brought herself right way up and began to swing her legs to generate a pendulum effect so she could get closer to the pillar.

"Colour, you don't have time, just use your grapnel," said Watson.

"Negative, I could hit one of you at this range," Milton replied.

"Good point, aim for the sound of Harrington's voice," said Watson.

"Hey!" said Harrington. "Sorry, Colour, we're all fine but you know these lines, they're great but too light to be able to throw them to you."

"Yeah, I know, Harrington. I'll be fine this way," Milton said, doing her best to keep the scepticism from her voice. She'd only thought of this plan at the last minute and hadn't had time to discuss it or warn the team. It might be helpful if it worked, but this bit was harder than she had imagined.

She felt the pendulum motion begin to change and it took a moment to realise it wasn't the wind blowing her about or her suddenly working out the best way to rock her body back and forth to generate a swing. It was the train moving away from the station.

"Fuck," she muttered, as the train began to accelerate. "Get climbing! I'm coming in fast!" she yelled.

"Roger that," said Harrington, calm as anything.

Milton prepped her grapnel and turned her night vision to max as the train reeled her in, slowly at first, but getting steadily faster.

With only seconds to go before she was mangled against the pillar, there wasn't time for more thought. She picked her target, aimed the grapnel and fired. As soon as the bolt bit home, she hit the quick release on her line and fell away, thumb jabbing desperately at the launcher control until the motor began to spin.

It whined loudly against the strain of her downward motion, reeling in the line as she swung toward the pillar that her team were climbing. For a moment she feared it would be heard by the Deathless over the noise of the train.

She reached the end of the arch with only a metre to spare between her and the foamcrete pillar. The launcher's motor screamed its objection but it held, another admirable demonstration of the quality of the Deathless kit. The sudden stop almost wrenched her arm from its socket, only the power armour saving her from a nasty injury.

Then she began to swing back the way she'd come, dropping away from the tower. She let the grapnel pay out some line.

"I'll be back!" she yelled, as the team receded from her view.

"We'll throw you a line, boss, see if you can grab it," said Harrington.

"Yeah, should be a doddle," Milton replied as she started the return trip.

She could see Harrington hanging on to a line with his left hand and spinning something around in his right. Was that a gun attached to the line? Oh, bloody hell.

He released his improvised weight just as she approached the pillar. It was a pretty good throw, the weapon arcing through the night sky to only just miss her. But Harrington was attached to the pillar on her left side and he'd thrown the weapon so it passed in front of her to the right. She couldn't grab the gun but she collided neatly with the line and managed to loop it around her left arm.

She swung back again, the line paying out behind her.

"Have you got it tight, Colour?" asked Watson.

"Yup, I've got it."

"We'll haul you in as quick as you can when you come back then. Is your arm okay?"

"Hurts like you wouldn't believe but nothing the med-suite can't handle."

"Now!" said Watson and Milton felt the line go taut in her hand. She dangled there for a moment as the Marines fought against the gravity that tried to drag her backwards, then they had her. She thumbed the switch on the grapnel and payed out more line as they dragged her slowly towards the pillar. She ended up a few metres below them, clutching the pillar for all she was worth and breathing heavily while the suit pumped painkillers and anti-inflammatories into her shoulder.

"That was exciting, Colour Sergeant. What was that little diversion in aid of, if you don't mind me asking?" Bailey enquired.

"I realised that we'd been a bit rude to our hosts, so I left them a little present to remember us by."

Bailey nodded and Harrington said, "Ooh, that's nice. When will they be opening it?"

"I'm sure they'll pick the right time," Milton replied, "but we need to get cracking. There's a firefight going on up there."

They began to clamber around the supporting pillars, heading to the north side of the line. The climbing gear built into the power armour suits simplified the exercise but the need for stealth slowed everything to a crawl. As they climbed, Milton checked in with the sniper team.

"Give me an update please, Bailey."

"We have a good solid perch, Colour. We have LOS to the train station and the base."

"What's going on at the base?"

"Looks like there are Deathless on the walls firing at something and troops in vehicles heading west from the base towards the jungle. Someone has been returning fire from the jungle and the Deathless have a sniper on their walls."

"If you can take him out, do so, but first tell me about the station."

"A full company of Deathless getting ready to move out, piling into vehicles like those large APCs we captured on New Bristol. I don't see them being able to actually get into the jungle with those, though, not unless they've got a road they can follow."

"Anything else I should know about?"

"I'm pretty sure you lost your bet with Ten," Bailey replied, "because there's another megafauna out here, thrashing about between the base and the edge of the valley."

"One of the gasbags?"

"Er, no. Looks more like a giant millipede, if you can believe it."

"Yeah, I already saw one of those, a couple of metres long."

"Yes, Colour, if at your school 'a couple' meant about a hundred and fifty."

Milton was silent for a moment as she focused on her climbing.

"So, we have a base full of Deathless troopers firing into the jungle, a sniper, some kind of special forces company-in-training between us and the captain and, to top it off, a millipede the size of a train."

"Oh no, Colour, it's much bigger than a train."

Milton took a moment to order more painkillers from her med-suite to dull the pain of a headache she could feel building behind her eyes.

"Right, sort out that sniper and anyone else who thinks he looks clever. Keep an eye out for this company of special forces recruits as well. If they're the best they've got and full of vim and vigour, I really don't want to tangle with them tonight. Oh yeah, and watch out for space monkeys, according to Ten."

"Roger, will do," said Bailey, ignoring the weird comments about 'space monkeys'.

<Captain> sent Milton in a private message as her team moved out, walking west under the canopy provided by the train platform and station, <we are at the train station, flanking west. A company of Deathless arrived on the same train from what looked like a special forces training camp. Otherwise, we're having a good day>

<Roger that. We have the prisoner. I have a light injury, Goodwin and Ten are fine. Get to us as quickly as you can. What's the status of that Deathless company?>

<Looks like they're moving out to chase you. Will you be able to stay ahead?>

<Possibly. Don't put yourselves at risk to hold them up, though. There's no way you can cope with a full company>

<Acknowledged. Will avoid engaging if possible>

<We have eyes on the enemy sniper on the wall. Permission to engage> sent Parker.

<Update first. We've made it to the rainforest. What's happening with the Deathless company from the train?>

<They're lining up to get into lightly armoured trucks, six in all> sent Parker. <They'll probably head out in maybe three minutes. It's a target rich environment>

<Sniper first, then officers and NCOs. Don't hang about too long before you change your roost. Understood?>

<Roger that, Colour. We can probably hit the truck engines as well; they look like normal vehicles. Should we engage them as well?>

<Only after the officers. And I repeat, don't hang about too long. They're bound to have snipers in that company. Over>

<Acknowledged, we'll check in when we're moving. Out>

Milton glanced at her team. They were making good progress through the rainforest, having found a tunnel that must have been punched through the foliage by a seriously large machine, probably a resource gathering vehicle of some sort. It didn't go in precisely the direction they wanted to travel but it was only off by a few degrees and it allowed them to maintain a good speed-marching pace.

Without the power armour, that would have been impossible. Even with the flattened plant life, their gear would have cut their speed. They would have to enter the pristine rainforest further ahead but, for now, the HUD showed they were gaining on Captain Warden.

"Colour, once Bailey starts taking out their officers, they're going to start moving much quicker. Do we need to stand and fight them off?"

"No, but we'll stop here and leave some deterrents for anyone who comes after us. Harrington, get it done for me, I have to check Bailey's progress."

She wondered if it was time for her present to be opened yet. Opening up the feed from Bailey and Parker, she surveyed the situation as she slowly walked away from the traps that Harrington was laying for the Deathless.

Milton watched as Parker flagged targets for Bailey, scanning back and forth with the range-finding scope on his rifle, picking out Deathless officers. Each figure was flagged with a yellow box and a number with the target count showing in the HUD for Bailey to work through.

Then he was done and the view flashed back to show the Deathless sniper on the wall. Milton switched to Bailey's feed, watching as the enemy's railgun swept gently across the jungle. The sniper was clearly completely oblivious to Milton's team, still focused on finding Warden and the kidnapped Deathless officer.

Parker gave the go instruction and Bailey squeezed the trigger. The helmet of the Deathless sniper snapped back as the round punched through it, but Bailey's viewpoint was moving before the Deathless had finished collapsing, swinging towards a target labelled '2' in the right of her scope.

A yellow box appeared around an officer on the wall, who was looking away from the sniper. Whoever they were, they hadn't yet registered what had happened further up the wall. Bailey squeezed again and the officer's head was removed from his shoulders.

Then they were on to the Deathless from the training camp. Milton had to fight the urge to puke as Bailey's rifle panned across the open area in front of base, inducing momentary motion sickness.

Bailey's gun spat again, delivering a round through the armoured windshield of one of the transport trucks. It passed through the neck of the officer in the passenger seat and out into the back of the vehicle.

As Milton watched the view from Bailey's scope, she could see that Parker had opened fire as well. The targets were at the extreme range of his rifle's capabilities but Parker was an excellent shot and his efforts were already being felt.

Parker fired burst after burst into groups of Deathless as they ran for cover, looked around for the enemy gunmen or just stood around in shock. Between bursts, he marked priority targets for Bailey, who had changed clips twice already.

"Hurry it up," muttered Milton, tense despite her team's obvious impact on the enemy.

They were targeting the vehicles now. They had no protection against railgun rounds and Bailey quickly shot through their engine blocks, freezing the light transports in place.

Around the station there was chaos. Milton watched, waiting for the moment when the Deathless would scatter and run; special forces they might be, but these troops had clearly not yet seen action and were unprepared for the murderous fire laid down by the sniper team.

"Time to open the present, I think," she muttered to herself. She glanced at a pair of icons blinking on her HUD and activated them in sequence. The explosives on the maglev train detonated in the distance, somewhere beyond the valley, and the night sky lit up. That drew looks from the Deathless, wondering, no doubt, what the hell had gone wrong over there. With any luck, the track had been destroyed and the train had crashed off the track into the ground at high speed.

Then the device under the station exploded and any coherence the Deathless might have had was blown away. They stared as a large part of the station structure and building above the track crumpled and fell down the slope into the jungle.

Milton grinned with satisfaction. The damage wouldn't really affect the Deathless war effort but it was a pretty good hit for the effort and, more importantly, it was causing consternation amongst the troopers, who couldn't tell what had happened, where the enemy was or how many they faced. The Deathless scattered and ran, their resistance broken even as Bailey's rounds continued to fall amongst them.

Milton wondered for a moment if the grenade launchers might be brought into play but her HUD showed they were too far from the enemy even if the rainforest canopy wasn't blocking their line of fire.

<Parker, time for you to leave. Join us as soon as possible. We're moving out as soon as Harrington has finished with his booby traps>

<Roger that, Colour Sergeant. We'll break the last two engine blocks then pull out>

<Acknowledged>

Milton switched off the feeds and looked over to Harrington and the team. They had set up several lines of simple traps, covering a hundred metre radius. It would be hard for the Deathless to come near to their trail and not set off at least one, and one was all it would take to slow them down. The moment they lost someone to one of Harrington's traps, the doubt and fear would grow. Where was the next one? What if they couldn't see them? What if I let the man next to me go first and I hang back a little? Is the woman next to me hanging back? Hey! She's using me to check the path. Will I be next? What was that beneath my foot, was it a twig or a tripwire?

"Don't use all your supplies, Harrington, let's leave something further up the trail."

Harrington laughed, "Did you get back from a psychological warfare training week just before we shipped out here, Colour?"

"No, I simply remember the last time I did a barracks locker inspection and the shock you get after finding a few clean ones and then you stumble upon the next horror show," Milton replied. "Let's move out!"

<Pursuit disrupted, Captain> sent Milton, <on our way to the rendezvous>

<Good work but don't hang around> replied Warden. <We're almost at the dropship and I'm looking forward to my kippers>

16

Smith punched the controls and the dropship began to lift even before the doors had finished closing. The Deathless troopers kept firing as the ship climbed past the canopy and into the relative safety of the early morning sky.

"*Ascendant*, this is dropship four, come in," said Smith as the main engines fired and the ship rocketed forward, pulling away from the enemy base and moving beyond the range of their small arms. "Come in, *Ascendant*, this is dropship four," Smith repeated.

"Problems, Smith?" said Milton, dropping into the vacant co-pilot's chair.

"There's something funky going on, Colour," said Smith, concentrating on the distant mountains as the dropship climbed past a flock of gasbags.

"Funky?" said Milton, not liking the sound of this. "I thought the flight paths and rendezvous points were agreed before we left?"

"They were," said Smith as he wrestled the controls and threw the dropship across the jungle canopy, keeping it deliberately low, "but when Captain Warden's little jaunt went hot, the Deathless got suspicious and sent two warships to intercept and board *Ascendant*. When I came down to land, she was heading out to avoid an uneven fight."

He slowed the dropship and pulled up a little to skim it over a ridge. "I'd hoped she would be back by now."

"Hoped?" said Milton, really not liking where this conversation was going. "And what do we do if she isn't back?"

Smith spared her a glance that said everything. Without *Ascendant*, they were in serious trouble.

And then a message showed on the comms monitor.

<<*Ascendant* incoming. Flightpath by secure link. Rendezvous in seventeen minutes. One pass only>>

Then a data dump arrived and Milton flicked it onto the main monitor, updating their rendezvous plan. Even to her eyes, it looked like an aggressive course.

"Shit," murmured Smith as he glanced at it, confirming Milton's fears about the flight plan, "that's going to be tricky." He glanced at Milton and then back at the monitor. "Can anyone in your team fly? It would be really useful to have another set of eyes on these problems."

Milton snorted. "We're Marines. 'By Sea, By Land', remember? You deliver us and we'll fix it but we don't drive the planes."

"Then you'd better bloody learn," snapped Smith, "because I can't do this all by myself." He pushed the controls and heaved the dropship around a looming mountain peak, then dropped it into a long, thin canyon on the other side. A lamp glowed suddenly red, and a klaxon sounded.

"What's that?" said Milton, alarmed.

"It's the fucking missile lock warning," snarled Smith, heaving the dropship sharply up and out of the canyon, "so buckle up and check the monitors and try to work out what's bloody shooting at us!"

"Shooting?" said a happy, carefree voice from the doorway. "Are we home already?"

"Shut up, Ten," said Milton, in no mood for the penal Marine's jokes, "unless you can help fly this thing."

"Nope, sorry Colour, it's been years since I flew anything and my qualifications have lapsed."

Milton stared at him, mouth open. Then she shook her head. Of course Ten could fly, why was she even surprised by these things anymore?

"Then take a fucking seat and help Smith with the flight plan," she said, thoroughly hacked-off with the entire situation.

"Right ho!" said Ten, dropping into the navigator's chair and peering at the monitor. "This is a joke, right?" he said, his sense of humour rapidly evaporating as he scrutinized the flight plan and compared it with the location data on the other monitor.

Smith yelled something and flicked the dropship across to starboard, dropping suddenly back into the canyon. A rocket screamed overhead and struck a cliff. "Aargh!" said Smith as he hauled back on the controls to avoid following the missile into the rock. "Which way?" he yelled.

Marine X concentrated on the flight path, suddenly focused. He blinked, scanning the numbers and shaking his head. The UI on this ship wasn't anything he was used to and it took a few moments to work out how to push the flight path into the nav-computer. Then he punched the warning klaxon, just in case anybody hadn't already noticed the sudden manoeuvres and was still sufficiently alive to take precautions.

"Sixty degrees to port, come up to forty-five degrees and punch it with everything we've got," said Marine X, his voice calm and cool.

"That'll put us above the mountains," pointed out Smith, "and they're already shooting at us."

"Gotta fly higher than the mountains to reach the stars," said Ten, "and if we don't move soon, our only option will be to wipe out against a mountain and redeploy, which means failing the mission." He leaned over to rest a hand on Smith's shoulder and whisper in his ear. "Don't make me fail a mission, lad."

Smith shook off Ten's hand and muttered something about 'psycho Marines' then glanced at Milton. "You okay with this?"

"Live fast or die trying, Smith," said Milton through gritted teeth.

Smith looked at her and shook his head. "You're both fucking mad," he opined. Milton grinned at him, wide-eyed, and Smith shook his head. "Fuck it," he said, hands flying across the controls. The dropship shuddered as Smith pushed it around a mountain and flipped it up to aim well above the horizon.

"How's that for you?" yelled Smith, as the engines screamed and the dropship blasted across the sky.

"Come to port by another five degrees on my command," said Marine X calmly as he concentrated on the screens before him, "rockets to the left of us, railguns to the right," he muttered. "And now!"

Smith swung left, and a rocket blazed past, so close that he could almost read the message scrawled on the casing.

"And up another ten degrees, please," said Marine X, watching the nav computer's interpretation of *Ascendant*'s flight path and plotting the intercept course. It was going to be tight, very tight.

"What's that?" said Milton, frowning as she pointed at a monitor showing an external view of the world behind the dropship.

Smith glanced at the monitor but couldn't make out what she was pointing at. Marine X flicked at his screens until they showed the same image. He zoomed in and grunted.

"That looks like a fighter craft of some sort," he said quietly. "Strange, wouldn't have expected to find those on a planet like this." He looked at the dropship's trajectory again, trying to work out what they could do about the fighter. It was closing fast, and the unarmed dropship wasn't ideally equipped for countering enemy attacks.

"Goodwin," said Marine X as he flicked at the screens and tried to make the intercept course work, "are you available for a little improvised weapons duty?"

"It's a bit bloody bumpy back here, Ten," said Goodwin, as if Marine X could possibly have failed to notice. "What do you need?"

"Could you be a dear and pop back to the loading bay? Need you to open the rear doors and throw out anything explosive that comes to hand."

"Are you fucking joking?" yelled Goodwin, apparently not entirely happy with Ten's request.

"Right now, if you would be so kind. We're about to be shot down by a Deathless fighter and we need another minute or so to clear the atmosphere."

Goodwin closed the comms link, and there was a moment of quiet during which Ten could almost hear the tech yelling at him from the far end of the dropship.

"Come up another five degrees, Smith," said Marine X, his hands now very heavy as he operated the controls that were dangling above him as the dropship powered through the atmosphere.

"Five degrees," acknowledged Smith. The dropship tilted a little further as Goodwin shouted obscenities across the comms link.

Then the alerts sounded to indicate that the rear doors were opening. Marine X zoomed out on the rear camera and saw that the fighter was now very close, only hundreds of metres behind the dropship.

"He's an enthusiastic little fucker," said Marine X with no small degree of admiration in his voice, "getting very close, bravely doing his duty, determined to bring us down." He checked the interior loading bay camera and saw that Goodwin was wedged onto a bulkhead, still wearing her power armour and with a crate of grenades by her side. He frowned as he watched, not quite able to work out what she was doing and why she wasn't moving.

Something flashed at the front of the fighter and Smith shouted a contact warning. In the loading bay, bullets pinged off surfaces as Goodwin worked, hidden behind her bulkhead.

"Come on, hurry up," Ten muttered to himself. Then he blinked as the fuse warnings on the grenades all went live at the same time, flashing up proximity warnings on the HUDs of every nearby Marine.

Goodwin grabbed the crate and tipped out its contents, emptying three dozen grenades out the back of the dropship. They bounced across the steeply inclined floor and fell through the open doorway, hurtling towards the fighter.

Half a second later, the first exploded. Then another, then a whole load of them as the fighter flew right through their midst.

"Nice move," muttered Ten as he watched the fighter break away.

Goodwin tossed a second crate of grenades out but by now the fighter had peeled away and the second batch exploded harmlessly. Then Goodwin slammed her hand over a button, and the rear doors began to close.

"That's it," said Smith, "we're pulling free." The dropship, which had bumped and rumbled its way through the thick atmosphere of NewPet, finally began to fly more smoothly as the last wisps of air fell behind. The shutters had closed over the forward windows and now the monitors showed only the vastness of space, huge and empty.

"Come around ten degrees to port," said Marine X, his focus back on the nav-monitors, "and up another five degrees, then give it everything we've got."

"Attitude thrusters firing," said Smith, somewhat more relaxed now that the missile lock warning alerts had stopped screaming for attention, "pushing to one hundred per cent on the main engines in three, two, one." The acceleration kicked them again as the dropship surged forward, heading for its rendezvous with *Ascendant*.

"Is that *Ascendant*?" asked Milton, peering at one of the forward monitors and pointing at a black shape that drifted across the suddenly bright and full starscape.

Smith and Marine X looked at it for a moment then shared a glance.

"No," said Marine X quietly, "that looks like a Deathless warship, a big one."

"And we're going to get pretty close to it," said Smith as he checked the monitors, "about three hundred kilometres, I think." Not good. At that range, the unarmed dropship would have no hope of avoiding whatever ordnance the Deathless choose to deploy.

"So where the fuck is *Ascendant*?" asked Milton, not unreasonably.

They spent a frantic few minutes checking the monitors, tweaking their trajectory to hit the flight path *Ascendant* had sent and trying to make sure the sensors were all working before Smith spotted a likely candidate.

"There," he said, pointing at something dark moving fast towards them along *Ascendant*'s planned flight path, "there she is." He sat back with relief and looked at Marine X. "How are we looking?"

Marine X flicked at the nav-monitors and nodded to himself. "Need some minor adjustments, but we're looking good."

They sat silently for a few minutes, nothing to be done but watch the monitors and wait to see what happened next.

"How's the captain?" asked Milton to fill the time.

"Fine," said Marine X, "flesh wound. He lost a fair amount of blood but these Deathless clones are pretty tough. He'll be okay." He stretched, just remembering not to flick out his wings. "And the Rupert's still alive, so we got what we came for. Goodwin's going over the files she pinched at the moment."

He sat up as if just remembering something important. "If she didn't fall out the back of the dropship or get shot to pieces by that fighter. I'm going to check on her." And he heaved himself out of the seat and headed off to the loading bay.

"Nothing from *Ascendant*," muttered Smith, "she must be coming in hot and quiet."

"How long?"

"According to the flight plan," said Smith, flicking through the nav computer's screens, more relaxed now that the hands-on flying was done, "about six hundred and forty seconds."

"And how long till we shoot past that warship?" Milton looked at the main monitors where the dark bulk of the Deathless ship was helpfully circled in yellow, its trajectory picked-out in a dotted line.

Smith looked at her then back at the flight path. "About same," he said in a strangled voice.

"And does *Ascendant* know about our little friend?"

Smith glanced at the monitors then looked at Milton, eyes darting around.

"*Ascendant*. Be advised. We have an enemy vessel in our vicinity. Coordinates attached," said Smith, triggering the secure comms system to convert his speech to text and send the enemy vessel's position and flight vector to *Ascendant*.

They waited for a response. Nothing.

"Then I guess all we can do is wait," said Milton, sitting back in her chair.

"Only five hundred and forty seconds," said Smith, setting a timer.

"Nine minutes and hope," murmured Milton, "story of my life."

17

"**W**here are they?" murmured Cohen, staring at the monitors as if he could uncover the enemy ships by willpower alone.

Space was big, and the two Deathless vessels had played their hand well. Combat between capital ships was a long, dull game of waiting followed by a short period of intense action and then, for one or more vessels, an eternity drifting through space as an expanding cloud of radioactive debris.

Now, Cohen assumed, the two Deathless warships waited, lurking near the planet, ready to charge in when *Ascendant* returned to collect the dropship. It was all getting a little bit dicey.

"Where are they?" Cohen murmured again, chewing his lip. Then a message flashed up on the comms screen.

<<**A**scendant, this is dropship four, come in>>

Another message came in a few seconds later.

. . .

<<C ome in, *Ascendant*, this is dropship four>>

"T hat's our cue," said White, "how do you want to do this, sir?"
Cohen paused, not absolutely convinced that he wanted to
do it at all. He looked at the monitor, which now showed the dropship's location on the planet.

"Fast and hot, please, XO," said Cohen eventually, "but keep us
quiet for as long as you can."

"Acknowledged," said White, settling into his chair. "Taking us to
action stations, prepare for high-G manoeuvres." He flicked a couple
of buttons, and a ship-wide broadcast went out in a computerised
voice, deliberately tweaked to make it stand out from orders given by
the bridge directly.

"Prepare for high-G manoeuvres. All personnel to assigned seating, immediately."

"And let's bring the weapons online, Mr MacCaibe," said White.

"Aye, sir," said MacCaibe as the action stations klaxon sounded
half a second later, "firing solution available in twelve seconds."

"Helm, put us on the straight and narrow, prep for main engine
burn as soon as Mr Jackson has a course."

"Acknowledged," said Midshipman Martin, "twenty-second low-
power burn on attitudinal thrusters in three, two, one." There was a
very small kick as the thrusters fired and the ship's spin slowed and
stopped. "Manoeuvre complete."

"Navigation solution plotted. Course laid in and on screen," said
Midshipman Jackson, flicking the series of points she had plotted to
fulfil Cohen's orders across to the main viewers.

The course was conservative and safe, putting them comfortably
into a neat orbit to rendezvous with the dropship. A simple, textbook
flight plan.

"Thank you, Mr Jackson, but that's no good at all. We need to go in much harder, much faster," said Lieutenant Commander Cohen. "We need to be on top of the dropship before anyone knows we're there, then we need to burn our way out again before the dropship has come to a rest."

Jackson frowned and looked at his numbers. "We can burn longer at the start, sir, but then we would be moving far too fast for the dropship to dock safely. There won't be time to match velocities before we'll be well past them."

Cohen nodded and grinned. Jackson was right, of course. He knew his stuff but like all of them, he lacked real combat experience despite the training and the vast number of hours logged in the simulators.

"Let me suggest another way," said Cohen, leaning forward to describe his plan.

"That might work, sir," said the navigator his uncertainty obvious in his voice, "but the dropship would need to be carefully positioned. It's a precision job."

"Your concerns are noted, Midshipman. I have every confidence in Smith's abilities, so let's plot the course and send him the details."

"Are you sure about that, sir?" asked White with a frown, leaning in close so that only Cohen could hear. "What if the transmission is intercepted?"

"If we don't tell him where we're going, Mr White," replied Cohen, "they're really going to struggle to meet us at the rendezvous point."

White settled back in his seat, clearly still worried about the situation. That was fine by Cohen; he was more than a little worried himself.

"Course plotted, sir," said Jackson, flicking the new course onto the monitor. Cohen peered at it for a moment, nodding. It was aggressive, very aggressive, but it might just work, even if it did put great stress on the crew of *Ascendant*.

"Million to one shot," Cohen murmured. Then he stretched his neck and nodded again. "Send it to the dropship, Mr Jackson, and lay in the course."

"Acknowledged, sir, sending now," said Jackson, flicking controls. "Sent and laid in, ready to go."

"Then take us out, Ms Martin, quick as you can."

"Aye, sir," said Martin, hitting the high-G warning klaxon, "one hundred and sixty-second full-power burn in three, two, one."

"That never gets old," muttered White as the engines fired and they were all pressed firmly into their seats.

"At least these clones are engineered to take the Gs better than our Navy standard issue," said Cohen, frowning. "I wonder if that says something about the Deathless attitude to space combat?"

"Or maybe they're just over-engineered," pointed out White as they watched the numbers count slowly down to zero.

"Main burn complete," said Martin finally, "on target for rendezvous in eight hundred and fifty seconds." Her hands flashed across the console, and a timer appeared on the main monitor alongside the planned trajectory.

"Thank you, Ms Martin," said White, easing himself into a slightly more comfortable position. "What's the status of our weapons, Mr MacCaibe?"

"Ready to fire as soon as we have something to fire at, sir," said the weapons officer.

"Eyes open, people," said Cohen, "passive sensors only, but find me *Posvist* and any other Deathless vessel in the volume."

"Eight hundred seconds to rendezvous," said Martin. "No sign of the dropship."

"Incoming transmission from dropship four, sir," said Midshipman Wood. "There's a data package, pushing to monitors."

scendant. Be advised. We have an enemy vessel in our vicinity. Coordinates attached>>

. . .

W ood hummed to himself as he pushed the new information to the monitor so that it now showed the trajectory of drop-ship four and the presumed location of the enemy vessel alongside the charging flightpath of *Ascendant*.

There was a moment's quiet while the bridge crew reviewed the new information.

"Target that vessel," said Cohen eventually. "I want a full broad-side of railgun and missile fire available on my command, Mr MacCaibe."

"Aye, sir, preparing now."

"We'll send them a 'vessel in distress' signal as soon as they give any sign of having seen us, Mr Wood."

"Ready and waiting, sir."

"Let's warn the docking bay crew that dropship four might come in a little warm," said White, "and have fire suppression systems and damage control teams standing ready, just in case."

"Six hundred seconds to rendezvous and closest approach to the enemy vessel," said Martin.

"We're rendezvousing at the closest approach point?" muttered White, shaking his head at such staggeringly bad luck.

"Ready countermeasures, Mr MacCaibe," said Cohen, "and give them everything we have at the first sign of enemy fire."

"Already queued up and ready to go, sir," said MacCaibe.

"Dropship four is moving at a fair clip, sir, but we'll need to brake aggressively to pick her up safely," said Martin as the main monitor showed the updated trajectories.

"No movement yet from the Deathless vessel," reported MacCaibe, who was peering at his screen with a frighteningly intense look on his face, "assuming it is a vessel."

"Mr Wood, send dropship four a message, give them our ETA and let them know this will be a hot and untidy pick-up."

"Aye, sir, sending now."

"Ms Martin, get ready to spin us around for the braking manoeu-vre," said Cohen.

"Program laid in and ready, sir. Three hundred and seventy seconds to main engine burn for deceleration."

"Then let's do it, Midshipman."

"Aye, sir," said Martin, sounding the low-G manoeuvre klaxon, "minimal burn, attitudinal thrusters only, firing in three, two, one." There was a gentle nudge as the ship slowly spun until it faced back the way it came, following its engines. "Manoeuvre successful, ready for deceleration burn."

"Thank you, Ms Martin. Anything from that vessel or Soyuz?"

"Soyuz is behind NewPet, sir. Deathless vessel is just sitting there, no obvious signs of life."

"Sixty seconds to main engine burn," said Martin.

"Incoming message, sir," said Wood, "can't tell where it's coming from." He flicked it up onto the main monitor.

<< V*arpulis*. Enter orbit around New Petropavlovsk-Kamchatsky. Surrender immediately>>

"P redictable," muttered White, "but at least they're still talking."

"Send this reply, Mr Wood," said Cohen, clearing his throat. "'Acknowledged. Entering orbit in two hundred seconds.' Let's see what they make of that."

"You think they'll fall for it?" asked White quietly. Cohen shrugged because it didn't really matter. Their trajectory was locked in, they had to collect the dropship four and they were out of options.

"Thirty seconds to main engine burn." Martin waited a little longer then sounded the high-G manoeuvre klaxon. "Main engines firing on full power for one hundred and thirty seconds in three, two, one."

"Anything from that Deathless vessel, Mr MacCaibe?" asked Cohen through gritted teeth as the deceleration rammed them into their chairs and pressed heavily on their lungs.

"Nothing, sir, and no sign of the other warship."

Cohen pondered that, looking for meaning as the counter ticked steadily down.

"Dropship is slightly off course," said Martin, frowning even as the deceleration tried to flatten her features, "I think we can adjust but it's going to be bumpy."

"Do it, Midshipman," said Cohen, "and let's warn dropship four."

"Sending now, sir," said Wood.

"Attitudinal thrusters firing now," said Martin. There was an indiscernible change in pressure for the briefest time as the huge ship twisted slightly.

"Manoeuvre successful," reported Martin, her voice a little tense. "Ten seconds left on the main burn."

"Sound the combat alarm, everyone remain calm," said Cohen, so hyped that he could barely follow his own advice. "Grab us a dropship, Midshipman."

"Bay doors opening," said White, "and for what we are about to receive, may the Admiralty be forever grateful."

"Firing attitudinal thrusters," said Martin as her hands flew over the controls. The ship shook and twisted as it bore down on dropship four. All eyes were on the monitors as the dropship suddenly appeared on the monitor and rushed towards them.

"That's a bit bloody quick," said White, then the dropship's engines fired and the rate of approach fell as she accelerated.

There was a brief moment when the dropship was so close to *Ascendant* that every scratch on her hull was visible to the bridge crew. Then it was gone, and there was the most awful screeching of metal scraping against metal followed by a long, drawn-out rumbling crash.

"Bay doors closing," said White quietly.

"Attitudinal thrusters firing, four-second rotation manoeuvre, main engine burn in six seconds," said Martin.

<<*Varpulis*. Heave-to and prepare to be boarded>> came the translated orders from the Deathless ship.

"Fire everything, Mr MacCaibe," said Cohen.

"Aye, sir," said MacCaibe grimly, punching controls on his

console, "rail guns firing, random spread, four-second burst. Missiles away, counter-measures deployed."

"Main engines firing now," said Martin, "one hundred and fifty seconds, full power."

"Keep firing the rail guns, Mr MacCaibe, we don't need to hold onto the ammunition."

"Firing again, sustained burst," said MacCaibe. "No incoming fire yet, three seconds till delta-v renders weapons ineffective."

"Active sensors, find *Posvist*, please," said Cohen.

"Sensors online," said Jackson, "scanning."

"Firing paused, out of effective range," said MacCaibe, "railgun ammunition depleted by forty-two per cent, six hours to replenishment, auto-manufacture beginning now."

There was a pause, just a few seconds long when nothing happened.

"That went about as well as could have been hoped," said Cohen, "thank you, ladies and gentlemen." There was a murmur of quiet celebration, muted slightly by the continuing acceleration.

"Ten seconds left on the main engine burn," said Martin before she counted them down to zero.

"Excellent," said Cohen, standing up from his chair. "Let's see what we caught, shall we?"

Then Jackson gave a strangled cry.

"*Posvist*," he said, horror in his voice. There was a flash on the forward-facing monitors as something huge and dark flashed across them. Kinetic rounds ripped into *Ascendant*. The ship shuddered and shook.

Then the hull-breach alarms sounded.

18

"Hull breaches across all decks," said Midshipman MacCaibe, "primary weapons bank inoperative, ammo-fabs offline."

"Forward sensor array offline," said Jackson, voice shaking, "starboard sensor array damaged and only fifty per cent operational, all other sensors functioning correctly."

"Focus on the hull breaches," said Cohen, more loudly than he had meant, "what's our status?"

"Interior doors are closed, atmospheric pressure is stable," said White as he reviewed the monitors, "multiple punctures to the hull but no explosive concussion detected." He paused to change the view on his screens. "No radiation leaks, no obvious damage to the power plant or distribution system."

"Get the repair teams out," said Cohen. "I want a full assessment inside an hour and details of everything that's been damaged. And get me a list of casualties."

～

"All hail the conquering heroes," muttered Goodwin to herself as she peered out through one of the holes in the hull. The stars stared back at her from the cold vacuum of space. Then she sighed and removed the inner panel, flicking away insulation and shattered components to clear the area.

Whatever had hit them – and Goodwin hadn't yet found a projectile – had punched a seventy-millimetre hole in the hull and decompressed the room beyond. This one had been empty but she had already fixed holes in two rooms with frozen corpses.

She shook her head. The hole in the outer hull was ringed with torn metal where the projectile had struck. The angle was awkward but the plasma cutter attached to the arm of her engineer power armour suit made short work of the metal and it fell quickly away.

Goodwin fitted a slab of armour plating over the hole and welded it in place. Then she sprayed insulating foam across the whole area, filling the gap between the outer and inner hulls before replacing the inner plate with a new panel.

"Almost as good as new," she muttered. On the other side of the room, a matching hole showed where the projectile had travelled further into the ship. Goodwin inspected the ruined panels but couldn't see any damage to critical systems. She slapped a lightweight internal patch across the wall, welded it in place then packed up her kit.

<Room four fixed and ready for re-pressurisation> she sent.

<Acknowledged. Area clear, re-pressurising now> came the response from engineering control as the HUD display listing breaches that to be sealed and damage to be repaired was updated again.

There was a hiss as air bled back into the room and in moments it was back to normal.

<Pressure holding, looks good> sent Goodwin. Then she checked her slate and moved on to the next room on the list.

"That's the last of the hull breaches sealed," said White as he reviewed the updates on his slate. It had been two hours since the attack and *Ascendant* was a hive of frantic activity as repairs were made and casualties triaged and patched up.

"What news on the primary weapons bank?" asked Cohen as he reviewed the casualty list again. It was bad – thirty Marines and seventeen crew – and with the deployment bay offline after the attack, there was no way to redeploy them.

"It's shredded," said White, looking at the pictures of the damage. "Looks like it took several strikes, at least one of which went through the primary fire controller. They're trying to rebuild it from spares but it's not looking good at the moment."

Cohen and White were in the meeting room behind the bridge. Monitors all around the room showed status reports and damage assessments. The encounter with *Posvist* had been short but brutal, and *Ascendant* was going to need some serious work to fix everything properly. Right now, all they could do was patch the holes and get as many systems as possible back online.

"The good news is that the personality backup systems are fully operational, as are the engines, life support and navigation systems. The secondary weapons banks and the counter-measure launchers escaped damage, but the ammo-fabs are going to be offline for a few hours while the manufactories churn out the necessary components. Given all the damage, they're running non-stop."

Cohen grunted, staring at his slate.

"How did we miss *Posvist*?" he asked quietly, replaying the video and sensor readings captured by the forward arrays. "Why didn't we see her coming up on us?"

White said nothing for a moment then sighed. "It was a bluff. All that 'prepare to be boarded' and 'heave-to for inspection by *Posvist*' stuff. They were playing us. They knew all along, ever since Warden's fuck-up at the base, that we weren't what we claimed."

"So why go easy on us? They must have fired their engines for that attack run well before we got there, did they see us coming?"

"Or did they intercept our comms? Yeah, I worried about that. We're using their kit, after all. Have we been hacked or do they just have the encryption keys? Maybe they simply snagged our comms and plucked the trajectory from dropship four."

Cohen looked up from his slate and swore. Then he cleared his throat, his decision made. "Right. Get the techs to run over the entire ship, check it for bugs, backdoors and anything that might be a listening device or an intercept. Then have the fabs make new comms kit, new nav-computers, new AI processors, new helm. Everything, internal and external. Every single piece of Deathless comms or processing tech is to be systematically stripped out and replaced, got it?"

"That'll take forever," said White, frowning. "Is it really necessary?"

"Hah! You said it yourself." Cohen grimly replied. "They knew we were coming. They've known everything since we left Soyuz. Every bit of intelligence we've shared over their kit, they've known. We have to assume we're utterly compromised, so our only option is to rebuild our systems from the ground up. Start with navigation, helm, life support and engine management, then move on to comms, weapons control, atmosphere management, fabs. Everything."

White nodded, realising that Lieutenant Commander Cohen's assessment was correct and that he was quite serious about the changes.

"Aye, sir," he said, "at least these are our slates."

"No! Dump the slates as well, and no mention of this across the wires or in a slate until we've cleaned the ship and we're certain we're secure, got it?"

"Got it," said White, slightly shaken by Cohen's vehemence.

"Only the paranoid survive," muttered Cohen, shaking his head.

19

The Rupert was tied to a medical gurney in one of the meeting rooms. Captain Warden, Marine X and Colour Milton watched the monitors as the med-techs finished checking his wounds and his restraints. He was hooked up to a drip that would keep him incapacitated but cogent; docile, but awake enough to answer questions.

"How do you want to play this, sir?" asked Milton as the med-techs left the room.

"Believe it or not, this will be my first interrogation of an alien prisoner, Colour Sergeant, so I think we'll play it by ear." Warden paused to look around at his team. "Anything else?"

Milton and Marine X both shook their heads. Warden found it surprisingly disconcerting that Marine X hadn't done something like this before. His unusual career history might be a patchwork of secrets classified way beyond Warden's pay grade, but this was the first time he could remember the Penal Marine failing to offer an opinion based on previous experience.

"Right," said Warden, squaring his shoulders, "let's get to it."

Limping slightly from the wound in his leg, Warden led Milton into the meeting room leaving Marine X to watch from next door. The head of the gurney had been raised so that the Deathless Rupert now faced into the room rather than staring at the ceiling. His eyes tracked Warden and Milton as they came in.

"Let's see how well this works," muttered Warden, flicking at his slate to activate the translation features. The techs had been furiously training the app in every spare moment but there were still gaps in its vocabulary and the output had already been shown to be less convincing than they had hoped when they had dealt with Soyuz.

"I am Captain Warden and this is Colour Sergeant Milton. Who are you?"

There was a pause as the machine worked then it spat out a sentence in what sounded to Warden like fluent Deathless.

The Rupert blinked in surprise then answered slowly.

"Corporal Uladimov Vyacheslav Savelievich, second class. Where am we?"

"This is the British Commonwealth Royal Navy vessel, *Ascendant*, in orbit around New Petropavlovsk-Kamchatsky. You are a prisoner of war."

The Rupert coughed, obviously surprised to learn that he was anything of the sort.

"What war? No war here."

"We don't think you are a corporal, second class," said Warden, ignoring the question, "you wear an officer's clone, and the attendee list for your retreat shows you as 'General Guryev Zakharovich'. We want to know why your troops invaded the peaceful colony of New Bristol."

"Never heard of it," said the Rupert. "Is above clearance level of humble corporal."

Warden turned off the translation device and glanced at Milton. "You think he's a corporal?" asked Warden in a low voice. Milton glanced at the Rupert then shook her head. "No, neither do I. Bring over the palm-reader." He flicked the translation device back on.

"We want to understand, General, but if you won't help us, we'll just get the information another way." The Rupert stiffened at the perceived threat and drew away from Milton as she stalked forward with the palm-reader. She grabbed his wrist, but the Rupert made a fist and refused to let it go.

"I could break his fingers, sir," offered Milton, only half-joking. The Rupert tensed as Warden's slate translated Milton's words.

"No need, Colour, I'll just increase his meds," said Warden, poking at his slate, "and we'll wait till he passes out to get a reading." The slate translated that, and the Rupert snarled. For a moment it looked like he might resist, then his fingers uncurled, and Milton was able to press his palm against the reader.

"Well, well," said Warden, peering at the results, "welcome aboard, General. I should apologise for the rough treatment at the base and your subsequent condition. We've done what we can and your wounds will heal, but I'm afraid your colleagues on the planet were rather more capable than we had expected."

"What do you want, Captain?" asked the Deathless general. "And what is this 'war' you talk about?"

"You really don't know? Your people attacked one of our planets, New Bristol, and began killing our civilians. My troops stopped the invasion then we captured one of your warships, destroyed two others and came here looking for answers. You're going to help us get those answers."

The Rupert snorted derisively. "You know nothing. I am soldier, not politician or leader. I have never heard of this planet you speak of or your people. I cannot answer your questions even if I wanted to. Kill me or send me back. I cannot help you."

"Why do your people make war, General? What is it you need from us, from our planet, that you cannot get elsewhere? What are your plans? Why are you training so many troops on New Petropavlovsk-Kamchatsky? Where are they all being sent?"

Warden rattled through the questions but Zakharovich remained silent, staring at Warden, unblinking, as the interview rolled on. After ten minutes of veiled threats, enticements and questions were all met with stoic silence from the prisoner, Warden switched off the translator and turned away.

"This isn't going anywhere," he said. "Any ideas?" Milton glanced at the Rupert then shook her head. "Right, well, we've got better things to do with our time talk to an uncommunicative prisoner. Get him locked away somewhere safe and make sure he's comfortable and secure." Milton nodded and flicked at her slate to summon the med-techs.

Warden watched, somewhat depressed about the vast effort they had expended to acquire a general whose knowledge was either too limited to be of use, or whose discipline was too great for him to be chatty. Then his slate pinged and a message from Goodwin appeared.

<Hand print and DNA accepted. File decrypted. You need to see this>

W arden and Milton slipped into the crowded briefing room to join Cohen, White and a host of other officers all eager to learn what Goodwin and Cornwell had found when the general's palm print and DNA had given them access to the encrypted file.

"The prisoner is General Guryev Zakharovich, not quite the most senior soldier in the system but pretty important," began Cornwell after Cohen had cleared his throat to silence the room. "He hasn't answered any of our questions but his palm print and DNA have unlocked the encrypted files that Captain Warden and Colour Milton took from Soyuz." There was a buzz of excited anticipation in the room.

"The contents aren't as explosively interesting as we had hoped," said Goodwin. She flicked at her slate to pull images onto the room's main monitor. "They don't give us any of the reasons behind the Deathless' actions, so we still don't know why they're here, why they attacked us or where they're shipping their troops."

"What we do know," said Cornwell, "is that although NewPet is an important part of their ground-troop training programme, it isn't the only such centre. Mention is made of 'Training Base 7', which we think is their name for the NewPet system's features as a whole, and that obviously suggests that there are at least another six training bases somewhere."

"Training Base 7 also isn't the only facility in the system," went on Goodwin, pulling up a manifest and punching it across to the monitor, "but it is the only collection of ground-based troop-training centres. The files don't tell us how many troops are being trained or how the programmes are organized but they have suggested somewhere we can go to look for more answers."

A picture of a large moon flashed onto the screen. Like NewPet, it was heavily wooded and studded with large mountain ranges that marched across medium-sized continents set in large blue seas.

"This base," said Cornwell as the view zoomed down from moon-sized to focus on an area only a few kilometres across, "seems to be some sort of command centre. It's heavily defended, as you can see from these shots, and appears to be the system's principle communication depot. If they have a wormhole link to their home planet, that's where it'll be."

Cohen cleared his throat again. "How do you know all this, Midshipman? Was there a file listing top-secret bases?"

"No, sir, but the moon's name and the station's designation appear in the meta-data for many of the files. The Deathless seem to have a file format that allows their top-secret documents to be tracked, so we can see how the transmission was routed and from which base or space station they came. That allows us to infer the existence of other places beyond the system but the names are meaningless without more contextual information.

"Importantly, though, it also shows that every single file in the data package that originated outside the system entered through the comms point on this moon, which strongly suggests it is their one and only wormhole endpoint," Cornwell concluded.

Cohen nodded thoughtfully. "Good work, Midshipman. What else do we know?"

"Unlike the officer's retreat on NewPet, this base is properly defended. Walls, guards, towers, all the normal things, plus some sort of ground-to-air defences."

"Do we have any recon shots of our own, or are we relying on Deathless files again?" asked Cohen, wary of being fooled into trusting the Deathless data or systems again.

"I'm afraid it's all Deathless data, sir," said Goodwin apologetically, "and the moon is too far away for our sensors to do more than confirm its existence."

"Well, Captain," said Lieutenant Commander Cohen as he looked at Warden, "it sounds like we have another job for you. Fancy taking a closer look?"

Warden caught Milton's eye briefly before looking at Cohen. "I think we might be able to help with that, if you can get us into position."

"Excellent," said Cohen, rubbing his hands together and sitting forward on his chair to look at White. "Have we switched out the nav-computer yet?"

"Let me check," said White, flicking through the checklist on his slate. "No, there's probably another couple of hours to go before we're ready to do that."

"Good. In that case, there's one last thing the nav-computer needs to do for us before it goes the way of all flesh."

"Okay," said White, frowning at Cohen's vagueness, "I'll send a note to the techs."

"Thank you, Mr White. I suggest we reconvene in, say, eight hours, by which time we should have some idea of the amount of work left to do to secure *Ascendant* and return her to full combat readiness." He paused to look around the room. "That'll be all for now, folks."

20

"I can't believe you've found us another base on another jungle-planet to assault," said Warden once the meeting room had emptied and the team had dispersed to carry out their assigned tasks. He pored over the limited collection of images they had retrieved from the encrypted files, looking for anything that might constitute good news. "Does it at least have a pool-side bar?"

Cohen snorted and shook his head. He and White were reviewing the trajectory that would take *Ascendant* halfway across the system and into orbit around the moon of the second planet.

"How hard do you want to hit this place?" asked XO White, pushing a list of ordnance and weapon systems to the main monitor. "I mean, we could take out their satellites and any probes they might have in the upper atmosphere. Maybe make them think we had a much larger force?"

Warden looked up from his slate and glanced over the weapons list. The forward weapons bank was still offline, not that it would have done them much good against a planet-side base, and the other options were somewhat limited.

"How do you feel about an orbital bombardment?" he asked

Cohen, not entirely sure that it was something he himself was comfortable with.

The lieutenant commander shook his head. "Tricky, very tricky. Apart from the fact that we don't have any appropriate ordinance," he wagged a finger at the list on the screen, "it pushes right up against our rules of engagement. It would need to be very finely directed, and we'd need to be dead certain it was a purely military target. If there's any possibility of civilian casualties..."

"But you're okay with missiles?" asked Warden, raising an eyebrow.

"Strangely yes, although they would probably burn up in the atmosphere before they did any harm to anything on the surface."

Warden nodded, somehow relieved that orbital bombardment wasn't really an option. He had seen what such weapons could do to a city; he had no wish to visit that on anyone else, even an enemy.

"The goal is to get to the ground before they blow us out of the sky," said Warden, restating the problem in an attempt to elicit new ideas, "and without giving them so much notice of our arrival that they're fully prepared with reinforcements on the way by the time we knock on their front door."

"And we need to make sure you have enough time to get back to *Ascendant* before *Posvist* and her evil twin turn up to put the boot in," said White, voicing the fear that cast its noxious shadow across the whole enterprise.

"That at least, I think, we can deal with," said Cohen, flicking away at his slate until he could push something up onto a monitor. "We load this trajectory into our hacked Deathless nav-computer, wait for it to bounce the information off to our friends on Soyuz, then we rip out the machine, replace it with our own and load the real course."

"Nice," said White, nodding appreciatively. "We send them on a wild-goose chase by feeding them false information. Do you think they'll fall for it, Sir?"

"Who knows?" shrugged Cohen. "But it's got to be worth a try. If we've found all their bugs – and that's a big 'if' – then the worst-case scenario is that we find the planet held against us, but we'll still surprise them."

"And if not? If they still have a bug on-board?" asked Warden.

"Then they'll probably be waiting for us," said Cohen darkly, "and things might get a bit sticky."

A*scendant* powered on. Patching the systems damaged by *Posvist*'s attack took hours; ripping out the comms infrastructure and sweeping the ship for bugs took much longer and nearly three days had passed before Cohen pronounced himself happy.

"I'd prefer to spend another week checking things over and re-working the tier two service hardware to make sure there aren't any bugs or backups hanging around in the system," said Cohen, "but time is pressing, and we've already waited long enough that they could have brought new forces into the system or moved things around."

The Marines were certainly bored with waiting. As soon as the cloning bay had come back online, they had redeployed the casualties from the *Posvist*'s attack, and now, back at full strength, they were ready for the next action and eager to head to the moon's surface.

"We're going in hard and fast," Warden said when he briefed his officers. "Brown, you'll take the majority of A Troop in drop pods, into the southwest quadrant of the base. Hayes, your pods will drop B Troop outside the wall, again in the southwest. Lewis and C Troop will arrive in the dropships. A Troop will secure the southwest quadrant, and B Troop will breach the wall to join them, creating our exfiltration path. A and B troops will then storm the base, take down any opposition with maximum aggression, grab everything they can find that looks like intelligence before exfiltrating through the breach. C Troop will secure the dropship landing zone, provide overwatch and cover the retreat."

He paused to look around at his team.

"This has to be done quickly. We'll be using every pod in *Ascendant*'s inventory and we get only one shot at this. We don't know what sort of opposition we face or how long it will take them to organise a meaningful defence. We go in, we grab anything that isn't nailed down, the techs take anything they can find that looks interesting, then we're out. Fifteen minutes tops, if it goes well. If not, we'll give it another ten to find the intel we need, then pull out. Lieutenant Commander Cohen can't give us longer than that."

He paused again. "Questions?"

"What's the priority, sir? Intelligence or destroying the base and eliminating personnel?" asked Lieutenant Linda Hayes, who would be leading B Troop.

"I'll be leading the team to gather intelligence," said Warden, "with Bailey and Parker on overwatch to identify likely targets for us to investigate. The priority for the rest of A Troop is to sweep the southern quadrant and eliminate the opposition. B Troop needs to get breaching charges in place on the wall and then assist A Troop. The breach can be made as soon as the Deathless rumble us. After that, both A and B Troops should focus on taking out any Deathless between my team and the wall to secure our retreat but make sure everyone knows that they should take any opportunity to grab intel. Make sure your techs have drones up, keep the HUD updates coming. Standard operating procedures, basically."

There was a little shuffling; then Lieutenant Hayes cleared her throat.

"Will Marine X be on this mission, sir?"

Warden rolled his eyes and ignored the question. "If there's nothing else, get your squads ready. We're eight hours out."

<F our hundred seconds to drop>
    The message flashed across the HUDs of the Marines as they sat in their drop pods. *Ascendant* hurtled in at a huge speed,

bearing down on the Deathless moon base like a badly thrown Roman candle.

Warden sat in a four-body pod with Milton, Goodwin and Harrington, who would be supporting Goodwin's data exfiltration work.

<Main engine deceleration burn, full-power, in one hundred and fifty seconds>

Ascendant's command messages were being relayed from the bridge to Warden's officers. The Marines were only getting timing updates, although Warden suspected that Goodwin and Harrington were both listening to the command channel.

<Full-power burn for one hundred and sixty seconds in three, two, one>

There was a brutal kick from the main engines as *Ascendant* began her final approach to the moon base.

<No sign of *Posvist* or any other Deathless vessel>

A rare piece of good news.

<End of main engine burn in three, two, one. Thrusters firing for attitude correction>

Getting the pointy end to face forward, as Warden always thought of it. The main weapons bank, at the front of the ship, had been one of the last systems to come back online but it was now, Cohen assured him, one hundred per cent operational.

<Reorientation complete>

<Forty-five seconds to pod deployment>

<Orbital weapons platforms identified. Targeting>

<Incoming messages, translating>

<Thirty seconds to pod deployment>

<Firing railguns, firing missiles>

The flow of messages was both reassuring and alarming. It was good to see Cohen's team working so smoothly, but a quiet, easy entry would have been even better.

<Incoming fire, deploying counter-measures>

<Attitudinal thrusters firing in preparation for pod deployment>

<Five seconds to pod deployment. Good luck>

Then there was a bang, and suddenly the pod was free of *Ascendant* and on its one-way journey to the Deathless base.

21

The pod shuddered as it slammed through the soupy atmosphere of the moon the Marines had designated 'Puzzlewood', after the weird trees in the forest they were now hurtling toward. The drop pods were little more than guided bullets with brutally simple deceleration systems intended merely to bring the craft to an abrupt stop right before they impacted the target site. The ride was not comfortable.

Warden watched the feed from the hardened cameras on the outside of the pod as they fell towards the Deathless base. A neat 'X' glowed to show the target landing point, well within the perimeter. The pods had little in the way of guidance features and nothing that was accessible to the Marines, relying instead on the accuracy of the initial launch.

They should miss buildings and other obstructions, but they were still dropping directly into a hot zone, a bold and risky tactic that would expose them to immediate fire if the enemy were on the ball.

"Fifteen seconds to impact," intoned the pod's onboard computer.

Warden was sharing the pod with Milton, Goodwin and Harrington, the first three members of the team he would be operating with on the mission. Marine X, Parker and Bailey were in a separate pod aiming to land outside the base so they could find a suitable sniping perch. Chief Science Office Mueller had reported that the megaflora on the moon were even taller than those on NewPet, so they hoped to find a good, high spot to work from.

There was a great roar as the pod's engines fired, pressing the occupants firmly into their seats.

"Brace for impact in five seconds. Inertial dampeners do not exist," intoned the strangely philosophical onboard computer.

Great, thought Warden, *even the drop pod has a sense of humour.*

Then the engines stopped, and the parachutes deployed, snapping out to take away the last of the speed before the pod slammed into the ground with bone-crunching force. As drop pod deployments went, it was pretty smooth, thought Warden, since he hadn't bitten off his tongue or heard the alarming sound of metal twisting and shearing.

Warden was first out of his seat. He slammed his fist against a large red button, under which some joker had written, 'Inflight Entertainment', and the side panel of the pod blew open, falling to the ground with a thump to form an exit ramp.

Warden shouldered his rifle and leapt through the doorway into the compound as the last swathes of parachute rustled back into the pod's nose, clearing the way for the disembarking troops.

He scanned the compound, checking for immediate threats, then looked for falling pods; they should all have hit the ground at about the same time. Lieutenant Colonel Atticus had once been killed by a late-arriving pod, and Warden had no intention of going the same way.

"Come on," he said, waving an arm, "get moving, people." Milton, Goodwin and Harrington emerged from the pod, weapons raised, and began to move out. Warden shuddered, glad to be clear of the pod, which was a potential death trap if it came under fire.

The base compound was eerily quiet. There were a few final thumps of landing drop pods from outside the base walls, and then only the sound of the Marines deploying. The temperature and humidity were oppressive, and the thick atmosphere made every-thing sound strange.

"Nobody around," muttered Warden, frowning as he scanned the open ground.

The Deathless must have noticed their arrival. The pods had parachutes but, since the purpose was a speedy arrival, they screamed through the atmosphere until the rockets fired to slow their descent so that the parachutes could usefully deploy. At night, they looked like a meteor shower but they sounded like a jet with a damaged engine, and they often made a booming noise like a dropped shipping container when they landed.

Warden headed across the compound and Milton, Goodwin and Harrington were quick to follow, all seeking cover against a sturdy-looking building to the north. Not knowing where to look, they planned simply to crash the most likely building then go from there. Goodwin worked on the lock while Warden checked-in with the rest of the team.

<Command team is down> he sent, <at the first building. Troop leaders check in>

<A Troop down, sir, all on target. Securing the southwest quad-rant now> sent Lieutenant Luke Brown. He'd been brought in by General Bonneville to take over Warden's troop when he was promoted.

<B Troop landing was clean. Approaching the south-west wall and preparing to breach> confirmed Lieutenant Hayes.

<C Troop present and correct, securing exfiltration route. We have good LOS to the base and are setting up overwatch for B Troop assault> sent Lieutenant Felicity Lewis.

<Roger that, troop leaders. Let's try and keep it quiet as long as we can. Wait until the Deathless sound the alarm before letting rip>

Behind him, the door to the building opened, and Harrington slipped inside, suppressed pistol ready.

<Bailey, Parker, Ten, we're going into the flagged building. Let me know when you're in position>

<Roger that, Captain> acknowledged Parker,

Warden slung his rifle, drew his own pistol and followed the team into the building.

~

Ten scanned the treeline, picked a likely target and sprinted towards it. He pulled his grapnel launcher and sighted on the trunk, as high up as he could see. The grapnel bolt bit home and the indicator on the barrel went green. After giving the line a good tug to check it was secure, he thumbed the motor's switch and began to ascend.

Bailey and Parker followed suit. The trees didn't offer much cover, having an unusual pattern of leaf growth where thin, vine-like shoots wrapped around thick branches that sprouted from the trunk-like needles. As they were about to go into a full-on attack, though, these details really didn't matter to Ten.

He climbed further through the branches until he had a good perch and a clear view of the compound. Their pod had been one of the first launched, along with C Troop's dropship, to ensure they had time to get into position before Captain Warden and his small team arrived in the compound, and A Troop landed to clear the exfiltration route.

Ten sighted down his railgun at the tower closest to the captain. It was manned by four Deathless troopers. The tower itself was fifty metres high, about the height of Nelson's column. He chuckled to himself, imagining what old Horatio would have thought of all this; he'd probably have been thrilled at the prospect of taking *Ascendant* into battle against overwhelming odds.

The guard tower was topped by a square room, each wall with thick, and no doubt bulletproof, windows. The roof was a shallow pyramid, with a communications antenna protruding from the peak. A narrow balcony wrapped around the tower above the windows, creating a firing point that the guards could use in the event of an attack.

Inside the tower, the guards all looked very agitated, pointing towards something within the compound. It was odds on that they had seen or heard the drop pods of A Troop landing.

Ten twisted to face Bailey and Parker and said, "England expects," before he unfurled his wings and dove towards the base. He shot across the open ground, flapping his wings for height before gliding the rest of the way to the guard tower.

"Bailey, Parker, Ten, we're going inside the flagged building. Let me know when you're in position," Captain Warden announced. Ten let Parker deal with it so he could concentrate on the task at hand.

"Roger that, Captain," Parker acknowledged, "we have our first perch, and Ten is approaching the tower now. I'll update once we have overwatch. Over."

Marine X alighted on the roof, angling his wings to form billowing air brakes as he approached, slowing him to walking speed so he could drop neatly onto the tower. He took a few paces forward, grabbed the antenna and he was in control again.

Ten worked quickly, attaching a line from his waist to the base of the antenna. Then he ran off the roof, jumping face first over the balcony and swinging back to the wall as he dropped. His feet hit the wall under the balcony, and his knees protested about the impact, though he wasn't sure why since they were brand new, unlike his real knees, which were safely in storage back home. Or at least somewhere, closer to home. He had a sudden horrible thought that he couldn't actually remember where he'd left his body. Was it in one of the bases or in a storage unit at his home?

With the ease born of regular practice, he flipped himself over and payed out more rope, dropping to just above the window. He crouched, upside-down, and reached out to slap something sticky onto the glass in two places. Quickly, he pushed himself left along the wall, then pushed out as hard as he could, swinging away from the tower.

As he swung away, he activated an icon on his HUD and the charges on the window detonated. That definitely got the attention of the guards inside, who had apparently been so distressed by the arrival of the drop pods that they had completely failed to notice him landing on the roof or running down the side of their guard tower.

Ten let go of the belaying device, and it clamped down on the line, leaving both his hands free as he came around the tower towards the gaping hole in the window, feet first. He drew two pistols, and they coughed simultaneously as he burst into the room through the remains of the window.

He landed unceremoniously on his arse and slid across the floor. His guns spat, once at the face of the guard on the far left, once at the neck on the far right, then he followed up with two more head-shots on the middle pair of guards as he rose to a crouch before giving them all another double-tap, just for good measure.

"Bailey, Parker, all clear for you to join me," he said as he moved to the window the guards had been looking out of.

"Roger that, incoming," Parker acknowledged.

Ten casually reloaded his pistols as he looked out of the window, working out which building the captain had entered. It didn't look like much but going in was the right thing to do, even if it wasn't the building they needed. Then he unslung his railgun and leaned it up against the wall before placing more charges around the windows.

Bailey and Parker arrived on the roof just as he was finishing.

"Hold there for a mo'," he said, hunkering down in the corner of the room. Then he detonated the rest of the charges in a series of pops that neatly destroyed the remaining windows. "Clear."

The two Marines dropped down to the balcony and climbed down the ladders into the guard room.

"Bailey, take the north tower," said Ten as the sniper unslung her rifle. "I'll deal with the one near B Troop if they haven't done so already. Can't let them get involved."

"Roger," said Bailey, moving to the north wall as Ten began rifling through the armoured cabinets on the west and east walls of the tower. Each contained a variety of heavy weapons, rifles, grenades and worst of all, railguns. If any of the guards were trained snipers, they could cause some serious damage.

Bailey aimed through the blown-out window as Parker began targeting for her.

"Lieutenant Lewis, the guard towers are equipped with heavy weapons, including grenade launchers and railguns. Repeat, the guard towers contain railguns. Recommend immediate counter-sniper measures. We have taken this tower and are eliminating the guards in the adjacent towers, flagged on the HUD."

"Understood, Ten. I appreciate the heads up. We'll get them dealt with immediately," Lieutenant Lewis responded.

Ten was already shooting, taking down two guards with one round before the others could react. His felt his eyebrow, or rather the brow ridge of the harpy clone, which didn't really have eyebrows as such, rise in surprise. That almost never worked; the odds of two of your enemies being so neatly lined up and the round going so straight that it would pass through two armoured heads was slim at best. It was so rare he hadn't achieved it more than a dozen times in his entire career.

The third guard turned to look for where the enemy fire was coming from. He had left himself exposed, and that did him no favours, he went down a mere second after the other two.

The fourth guard thought he was smarter and had dived for cover, grabbing a rifle on the way.

Good for you, son, thought Ten as he aimed. *Maybe next time you'll remember what railguns can do.*

He squeezed the trigger, his chosen target a spot fifty centimetres below the window, just in line with the barrel of the rifle that poked up from below it. He followed with second and third shots at close but different locations. The rifle disappeared from view and a second of scanning back and forth with his scope brought him a glimpse of a bloodied corpse through the massive holes the railgun rounds had made in the wall.

Ten scanned across the visible buildings, checking for snipers, his HUD letting him see through the night as if it were noon on a bright day. Then, satisfied there were none, he moved to the nearest gun cabinet. Bingo. It was like a toy chest in here. He grabbed a couple more magazines for the railgun, reloaded his gun then distributed some of the contents around the room, passing spare magazines to Bailey and Parker. The downside of a flying clone was the weight restriction, which limited their use of ammunition and prohibited heavier options like grenade launchers.

Here, though, they could use ammunition like it was going out of fashion, dramatically increasing their combat effectiveness.

"Right, let's see if we can't work out which building the captain should be looking at," said Ten as he looked out of the eastern window holes again, "because I'm pretty sure it's not the one labelled 'Virtual Reality Training Facility', is it?"

22

"What the fuck?" Warden breathed as he followed the team down the corridor and into the first room in the building. It was a sizeable warehouse-style space, with heavily insulated walls and a foamcrete floor. In itself, that wasn't too surprising, but the Deathless wandering around in it were another matter.

<Looks like they're in a virtual reality training session, Captain> Harrington broadcast to the team. <Might be a sound-proof room>

That made sense. The Deathless were spread out all over the otherwise empty space, some crouching, some jogging, all holding brightly coloured weapons of some kind. Presumably, the offensive colour scheme indicated that they were training replicas rather than live firearms.

<Yes. It doesn't look like we'll find anything useful here> Warden said as he watched the troops going through the motions, aiming and firing as their weapons made loud bangs and recoiled realistically. It was hard to tell quite how well they were doing, as he couldn't see the simulated enemy they were firing at. He wondered what models they were using for their enemy – Deathless in a different uniform or perhaps they were now training against Royal Marine avatars?

<So...> Harrington sent, waving his pistol meaningfully.

Warden glanced at Milton. She returned an exaggerated shrug.

<Okay, let's take them, quick and clean> Warden responded.

Harrington nodded and quietly padded up to his first target, clamping a hand over his mouth and swiftly pushing his F-S dagger up through the neck into the brain.

Milton was on the move too, also using her dagger – silence and stab then gently ease the victim to the ground. Goodwin was using her pistol, applied to the back of the skull and catching the corpses as they fell. Warden waded in, opting for his dagger. It was grim work but over in less than a minute.

They were almost rumbled when one of the Deathless tripped over a fallen comrade – it looked like the VR simulation wasn't programmed to account for obstructions in what was supposed to be a near-empty room, aside from the other players.

"Find an officer or NCO, we want their ID cards to open doors," Warden ordered as he cleaned his knife.

<Captain, I don't think you'll find much in that building> sent Marine X. <The HUD is translating the signage, and it says it's a VR training area>

<The translation is working then. We just found a section in here going through a training exercise. They're down. Any better idea where we should head next?>

<There's a covered walkway on the first floor of your building. I think that will take you into a good target but get in position and we'll update, sir> Ten replied.

<Roger that, moving to the first floor>

Harrington and Milton had both found cards by the time he'd finished his conversation with Marine X, so they moved immediately up the metal staircase in the corridor outside.

They gave the first floor a cursory check, but it was quiet, only empty observation and control rooms for the simulation space downstairs and some toilet facilities.

The covered walkway was a fully enclosed tunnel that ran the twenty metres to the next building, presumably a way to avoid the local weather. The analysis done by the science team on *Ascendant* suggested the conditions here on the jungle moon could get rough, so it made sense the Deathless would want to keep inside whenever possible.

The walkway was dark, but there were lights on the ceiling. Warden waved a hand experimentally into the passage, and the first light came on. He ducked back out of sight.

<Any joy, Ten?>

"Goodwin, can you hack those lights and keep them off? I don't want to be exposed out there if we can avoid it," Warden whispered as an aside.

<I had to move along the wall a bit to get a line of sight on one of the signs. It reads 'Command Operations Centre', so I think you're golden and that's the one you want to head for>

<Excellent news> Warden replied.

"Got the lights off, sir, we're clear," Goodwin said. "Permission to deploy micro-drones, sir?"

Warden nodded at her, motioning down the corridor.

<The lights are down in the corridor and we're heading in> he sent to Marine X. In the background, the whisper-quiet whirring of tiny rotor blades faded into the distance.

<Understood, sir. It's all very quiet here. Do you want me to have a shufty around some of the other buildings?>

<Yes. Feel free to leave some surprises for our semi-immortal friends but focus on intelligence gathering> Warden confirmed.

<Yes, sir. I'll be as quiet as a mouse until you tell me otherwise. Over> Ten confirmed.

Warden turned back to the team. "Ready?" he asked, and they all gave affirmative hand signals. It was a redundant question, of course. They were ready but you needed to maintain the habit, in case you had someone fresh out of training in your squad, or someone had been injured and wasn't responsive.

He tapped Harrington on the shoulder lightly, and the commando specialist moved off down the corridor, suppressed pistol at the ready. Goodwin's drones had mapped the open space beyond already, sending the floorplan to their HUD maps.

They came out of the walkway onto a balcony overlooking an atrium. On the ground floor, there was a reception desk, thankfully unmanned at this time. There were seating areas, and an archway led off to a cafeteria which was mercifully as dark inside as the sky was outside.

<Where to, sir?> asked Harrington.

Warden pondered for a second and then turned around. He grinned as he found exactly what he was looking for and he motioned for Milton to look too. It was a large building, and its size stood out even on such a large base. The architecture reminded him of a hotel or conference centre. As with many such buildings, someone had put a nice big floorplan on the wall to direct visitors to the correct room.

They scanned it with their HUDs and waited while the information was absorbed and the legend was translated. Then their HUDs generated a neat, augmented reality overlay with floorplans and room labels.

<Second floor, Colour Milton, that big room> sent Warden.

Milton nodded. The label said 'War Room', which sounded ominously interesting. Warden turned left and led the team towards the staircase. He opened a double door and began to move up the stairs, much to the surprise of the Deathless Rupert who was coming up from below.

Colour Milton acted first. Moving swiftly forward, she clamped her power armoured fingers over the throat of the unfortunate officer, barrelling him backwards and to the left. Her dagger came up once, twice, three times and he gurgled his last. She lowered the body quietly to the floor, wiped her dagger on his uniform and sheathed it. Then she picked up the body by the waistband and collar and jogged down the stairs to the ground floor, where she stowed the corpse under the first flight in the unused shadowed area beneath the stairs.

Warden continued up to the second floor, cursing his carelessness. They weren't going to remain unnoticed forever but longer was definitely better. He moved up the steps as quickly as he could without making too much of a racket. Even though the boots of his power armour suit had advanced composite soles that gave superb shock absorption, there was still a world of difference between a light step and stomping around as if your shoes were made of lead.

On the second floor, they found an empty corridor and another map. Warden scanned it while the team covered him and watched the corridors, then they followed the directions in their HUDs to the war room. It occupied a substantial portion of the second floor, somewhat more than half of the area on this level was devoted to it. The other end appeared to be offices and administrative areas.

<Captain. We've gone hot out here. You might want to get a move on> Parker sent.

<A bit more detail, Parker?>

<The southwest quadrant is a war zone, looks like a couple of mess halls emptied out. There's a railgun or two on the other side of the base. They're probably in the guard towers we can't see because they're on the other side of the buildings. They're causing problems. B Troop have breached the wall, but they were already over it before the real shooting started>

<Hayes. Parker sees railguns on the guard towers on the eastern side> Warden sent as they crept towards a large pair of wooden double doors that bore a brass plaque with the legend 'War Room'. It was a rather old-fashioned style, and he guessed senior staff liked their creature comforts in the Deathless forces as well.

<Yes, sir. They're hampering us>

<Marine X, if you can assist with those, do so. Lieutenants Hayes and Brown, I suggest getting some serious fire directed at those guard towers in case Ten is engaged. If you can get a targeting laser on them, get C Troop to send them a bunker buster> Warden ordered.

<Roger that, sir> Brown confirmed.

<Negative, sir, I'm too far away> sent Marine X. <Advise immediate action to be taken by A and B Troop>

That sealed it; if Ten couldn't make it in time, Hayes and Brown would have to deal with the towers another way.

Warden left them to it. Callous though it might seem, looking after his junior officers was not the mission priority. They were here to get the data to help the fight the Deathless across a battlefront potentially much larger than New Bristol. All their lives were somewhat less important than the hundreds of millions of citizens that might be at risk.

From the map alone, he knew the war room was huge, far too big for a four-person team to control properly, but they didn't have time to pull anyone else in. The situation outside could deteriorate at any moment, and *Ascendant* couldn't afford for them to hang about. Warden motioned the team to make their move. Milton and Goodwin pulled the doors open gently and he and moved in with Harrington.

An enormous circular table took up the entire centre of the room, and a holographic 3D representation of a dozen or so local star systems seemed to float above it. Various lines and symbols hung in the air between the systems, indicating strategic movement of fleets and troops, Warden imagined. Each wall was festooned with view screens, and they too displayed lists, some of which might have been the destinations they'd seen on the space station's departure gates.

A dozen Deathless Ruperts in sharp-looking uniforms peered at the displays, pounded at keyboards or shouted into communicators. Warden knew he needed to get a handle on the Deathless rank insignia, but it was a safe bet that some of these dignitaries were admirals and generals. There was space around the table for plenty more, but it looked like their planning session had petered out.

There were only a handful of other Deathless in the room, presumably junior officers and NCOs not involved in the planning but hanging around to make a good impression.

Don't go home before the boss, Warden thought wryly.

A frowning Rupert clone in a what was presumably a junior officer's uniform crossed the room to intercept them asking something in their Russian-based language. Warden tapped the side of his head with the barrel of his pistol as if there was something wrong with his audio feed. He didn't much like the tone this person was using.

And then, finally, a klaxon sounded as someone on the base raised the alarm.

The effect was predictably electric. The hapless officer's eyes went wide as he finally noticed the pistol, apparently having been unfazed by the Marines' power armour. The Rupert spat out another angry line at Warden and gesticulated to the door. He had no idea what the man was saying and couldn't be bothered to get the HUD to try the live translation the Puzzle Palace had concocted.

He recognised the tone, though. A green officer, unused to command and incapable of giving orders properly. Instead, the man was immediately throwing his toys out of the pram and issuing demands like a toddler given too much sugar. Warden cocked his head and wondered if this young idiot was actually trying to order him to go and find out what the klaxon was all about.

What an absolute arse he must be. Finally, something seemed to click in the Rupert's mind. Possibly it was the splatters of blood on his armour from their work in the VR training room, maybe just that he hadn't taken off his helmet or saluted or possibly even the fact he was wandering around an officers' area with a drawn weapon. Either way, he reached for his pistol in a way that suggested he hadn't done the drill necessary to draw a weapon quickly and smoothly.

"*Prosti, tovarisch*, not today," Warden said as he punched him hard in the face with his left gauntlet. The officer's head snapped back in a spray of blood, and he staggered backwards, falling over a trestle table covered with glasses and coffee cups and sending everything flying. That was one for the video album, thought Warden.

And then one of the senior officers at the conference table took notice of the commotion. He stood up and shouted.

"*Gospoda, vy ne mozhete srazhat'sya zdes'! Eto voyennaya komnata.*"

All eyes turned to the intruders, and more of the officers stood up.

"Prisoners, sir?" Harrington asked.

"Fuck no, slates and data only. I'm not carrying one of these moody bastards again. Goodwin, do we need any of them alive to access their slates?"

"No, sir, we should be able to crack it now that we've had more access to their systems," said Goodwin, "that said, it wouldn't hurt to have a couple of open slates; I have a way to keep them unlocked," she said, holding up a small device.

Warden nodded and walked up to the general, or whatever he was (he really did need an *I Spy* book of Deathless uniforms). He picked up the data slate by the man's plate and said, "I just need your signature on this, if you don't mind, sir," as he slapped the man's hand on the screen. It unlocked, and he passed the slate to Goodwin.

"Will that do?"

"All done, sir," said Goodwin, pocketing her hacking device and slipping the slate into her bag.

"Good," said Warden, and he shot the general in the head, "that's for New Bristol, and for wherever else you arseholes are."

The room exploded as the officers burst into action, reaching for weapons, yelling for guards or just diving for cover.

"Move," shouted Warden, firing his pistol until he emptied the magazine then unslinging his rifle. The Marines opened fire, their weapons shattering the peace of the war room as they worked their way through the officers.

In moments, it was all over. The air stank and the floor was littered with shell casings and corpses. Warden slammed a new magazine into his rifle as he stalked across the room, checking behind obstructions for targets they might have missed.

Goodwin grabbed a couple more slates and slapped their owner's hands on them before they finally expired and the device's security would no longer accept their authorisation.

Nothing moved as the Marines efficiently padded quietly around the great room.

"Clear," said Harrington from the far side of the room.

"Clear," echoed Milton.

"Harrington, watch the door. Milton, help Goodwin grab the slates," Warden ordered as he began rifling through the pockets of the officers, taking ID cards, data chips, personal slates and a small amount of actual paperwork.

It was all fodder for the intelligence section back at the Puzzle Palace. After a quick trip to a cloning bay, these officers would be back, and they would come back angry. The more they could learn about the enemy, the better. It also didn't hurt to take personal knick-knacks to vex them further. That thought sparked another one, and Warden checked the mission clock; time was tight, but they still had spare.

He cast his eyes around the room until he found what he was looking for. He jogged over to a rack of flags on poles near the door, pulled out his Deathless knife and thumbed the vibro control. A few quick cuts and his prizes came free.

There was a glass display case next to the flag poles, and he stuck the knife in that experimentally as well. It didn't so much punch through as shatter the glass into tiny fragments from the vibration. That might be useful in an entry situation.

He grabbed a few more mementoes from the case and hurried back to Harrington.

"Got some pressies for you, hang on," said Warden, opening the small pack on the Marine's back and dropping the loot into it.

Goodwin and Milton had grabbed every data slate they could find and installed several of Sierra's hacking boxes. The tech specialist pulled out her own slate, setting it to grab every file it could find.

"How much longer do you need, Goodwin?" he asked a little testily.

"There's a lot of data, Captain. We'll need about, er," she paused, calculating, "about twenty minutes to grab everything, but if we leave now we'll still get more while we're in range of the boxes." She looked at him across her slate.

Warden glanced at the timer in his HUD. From outside the conference room, the sounds of the firefight were now clearly audible. Warden shook his head. Twenty minutes was too long.

"No, that'll do, we've already burned more time than we had allowed. Let's move, ladies and gentlemen," he ordered, setting a route on his HUD to guide them back to the extraction point. Harrington and Milton began circling back to Warden's position as Goodwin flicked at her slate.

"Move, Goodwin, we're leaving," Warden shouted. The tech

nodded and finally slipped her slate into her bag. She shrugged her rifle from her shoulder as she jogged around the room.

And then, as she passed one of the Deathless, he raised himself onto his elbow and emptied his pistol into Goodwin's back. The tech cried out and stumbled, knocked forward by the impact of the bullets.

Harrington turned on his heel and loosed a burst of fire into the face of the Deathless officer, turning his head to bloody mush.

"Grab her," shouted Warden as Milton and Harrington moved towards Goodwin. The tech was on her knees, one hand on the floor, the other on her arse.

"Get up, Marine," shouted Milton, heaving Goodwin up with no regard for her injuries. "Where are you hit?"

Goodwin grumbled something through gritted teeth in reply as she was pulled her to her feet and bodily dragged through the door by Milton and Harrington. Warden grabbed her rifle and slung it across his back, determined to leave behind nothing that might give the Deathless information.

They stumbled together down the corridor towards the lifts, carrying a cursing Goodwin between them.

23

"Permission for Marine X to use performance-enhancing stimulants in the performance of his duties, sir?" Ten muttered to himself as he used his HUD to order his med-suite furnish him with a shot of combat drugs. "Why yes, you may absolutely do that, Marine X, and while you're at it, maybe you'd like to take an energy booster drink with a healthy dose of caffeine? Why thank you, sir, I'd just love to suck down a violently green concoction that makes my eyes water and my mouth feel like a sweaty retro-hipster has been living in it. Nothing like sipping from a tube on my webbing rather than a good old-fashioned cup." He could probably get by, but if the relatively green Lieutenants Hayes and Brown didn't get it right, a lot of Marines could take a railgun round to the head before they got the situation under control.

Resisting the urge to preemptively puke, he sought out the water tube that protruded from his webbing and ordered the HUD to inject the water supply with an energy cocktail, courtesy of Mueller.

Was this version still a virulent green that looked like a cross between a pressed juice from a trendy tearoom and an energy drink strong enough to keep a university student dancing until seven in the morning? Ten didn't know, and he had long since stopped looking when he'd realised the stuff resembled pond water. It was better not to know. The combination of sugar, caffeine and what tasted like heavily salted grass clippings, was more than enough to make the experience unpleasantly memorable.

It was undeniably effective, though. In a winged clone, you could either drink the stuff or stick to gliding. It was better to drink than try to get off the ground with your wings and wake up the following morning unable to move from the strain it had placed on your muscles.

<Parker, I'm moving to the wall, per the Captain's orders to help out the kiddies with their sniper problem. Are you two copacetic?>

<Copa-what-the-fuck?>

Fucking kids, thought Ten, shaking his head.

<Are you okay on your own while Daddy takes care of some bad guys?> he sent as he shot his grapnel up to the highest roof he could hit.

<Oh yes, Daddy, we'll be fine. Will you bring us back a present?>

<Only if you do your homework. I want to see ten kills before I get back from work. Over> replied Ten as the grapnel motor reeled in the line and he more or less ran up the side of a building. He clambered over the edge of the roof, releasing his grapnel as he did so and ended up on the highest nearby roof, which just so happened to be above the captain's team.

A present, eh? What do you bring the sniper team that has everything it needs? A double-barrelled railgun? No, that would be silly. Under what circumstances would you need two shots at once? he thought to himself as he worked.

He found a ventilation duct and ripped off the grill. He lowered a small package inside, tied it to the remains of the grill and attached a detonator.

Then he sprinted towards the east side of the building, lobbing a couple of other packages over the side to his left and right as he approached the edge. It wasn't effective, but he didn't need any extra weight for this next bit.

He leapt forward off the roof and immediately extended his

wings, allowing the air to catch them before he flapped to gain altitude. Below his feet, the base pulled away as he rose through the air. It was easier than he remembered, but despite the assistance of his med-suite, it was still a huge effort to get sufficient lift to achieve a rapid gain in altitude.

Observing the battlefield below him, he picked out the towers that were causing a problem for A and B Troops. He flagged them in his HUD and sent a broadcast, <Enemy railgun positions visualised. Flagged in tactical map. Moving to take out first target, Lieutenant Brown>

<Roger that, Marine X. Much appreciated. We have two Marines down trying to get a laser to bear on the towers> Brown responded.

<Recommend flanking the south tower with a drone while they concentrate on you, sir. Heading for north tower now> Ten responded, thankful that it was a HUD message and the lieutenant couldn't later whine about his exasperated tone.

<Acknowledged> came the terse reply. Ten imagined the young officer was cursing, angry that he needed a Penal Marine to suggest solutions to his problems.

He dropped into a steeply banked dive, coming around to glide north to south along the east wall of the base. As he dropped he pulled his railgun around and put three rounds through the windows of the north tower. Then he hit the walkway atop the wall hard and at speed, skipped a couple of paces and fell forward into a diving roll to absorb the impact.

He came up into a kneel and he found he had misjudged the landing, ending two metres short of the door. Cursing he shouldered the railgun and squeezed the trigger, sending two rounds in quick succession through the lock. He rose and dashed forward, dropping the railgun and drawing his pistols.

He wrenched the door open and dived forward into a roll that finished in the centre of the room. There were three Deathless left standing, one sprawled against a wall opposite the door, bleeding out. The guards were raising guns towards him, and he executed a neat three-sixty spin as he unfurled his wings, sweeping them from their feet. Ten felt and heard something snap with an unpleasant sound, but the enemy all lost their footing.

He was rising to his feet as his rotation ended, the barrels of his weapons extended in front of him. He was pretty sure he looked like an avenging angel, though if his wing was broken, it probably didn't look that impressive. He was still turning as the weapons in his hands dispatched the uninjured guards with neat precision.

When he stopped, he felt a little sick. Shit. All that rolling combined with the revolting energy drink cocktail was not agreeing with him. He ordered his med-suite to dispense an anti-emetic then turned to the Deathless guard, whom he must have hit when he breached the door. They were still coughing up blood, so he put it out of its misery with a double tap to the head.

Ten furled his wings, which confirmed that one was broken. He added a painkiller to his bloodstream and resolved to stick to walking for a while. Perhaps he'd need a new clone and could finally get one of the ogres to play with. That was well worth the discomfort in his estimation.

There was no way he could get airborne again with his wing as fucked as it was, so he went out and grabbed his railgun, reloading as he returned to the room. The next tower was directly along the wall to the south and seemed to still be intact. *What the bloody hell are the kiddies playing at?*

He sighed. Daddy would have to fix this one as well, it seemed. Sometimes they really tired him out. He looked down at the weapon in his hands. Yes, sometimes the new commandos were a bit like having a bunch of kids running around screaming their heads off, and that was wearisome. But then, sometimes, there were railguns. Railguns and improvisation were a heady combination for Ten.

Walking over to a gun cabinet he grabbed a roll of all-purpose tape and a second railgun. Double-barrelled railgun indeed. *What purpose could it possibly have?* he wondered as he calmly but swiftly taped the two weapons together. As he worked, he kept an eye on the tower to the south, tagging the guards in this HUD. Whistling softly to himself, he tore off the last strip of tape and checked his newly modified weapon.

He rested the barrels on the frame of the shattered window. The wonderful thing about railguns, other than the insane speed the rounds travelled at and the consequently colossal amount of damage they inflicted, was the comparatively spare frames they required, which meant the two triggers were very close to each other.

Extending both the stocks as far as he could, he grabbed a cushion that the sniper had been resting his arms on and shoved it between his shoulder and the railgun's butts. This might sting a little, but it should just about work.

Ten braced himself and took a grip in each hand, then began firing, two rounds at a time. The recoil was insane. The rounds were small, but their velocity was huge. A small mass, moving at a very high velocity had significant advantages, but if there was more energy going out the front of the weapon, there was more coming out the back as well. *Bring on the wormhole guns*, he chuckled to himself.

He was shooting as fast as he could bear. The twin rounds weren't nearly as accurate, but they utterly demolished the cover behind which the targets were hiding. At least a couple of Deathless troopers took direct hits as the south tower was torn apart by the railgun rounds that smashed through the walls and windows, turning chunks of foamcrete into deadly shrapnel.

After he'd emptied both magazines, he fell to the floor and roared in pain. Fucking hell that hurt. His shoulder felt like it had been hit with a wrecking ball. He dispensed more painkillers from his med-suite and rolled over, crawling towards the gun cabinet to grab a new weapon.

His experiment over, he loaded and shouldered the weapon, yelling again as he realised instinct had overridden his intention. Bollocks. He swapped to his left shoulder, struggled to his feet and pointed the weapon out of the window towards the shattered tower. Two guards were staring at him over the broken windows and bringing rifles to bear. The rounds they sent his way began to shatter against the wall below him, and in response, his weapon bucked in his hands as he fired it cack-handed.

He fired three times then ducked before their rounds could find their mark in his head. Ten had barely slumped to the floor before the explosions detonated. He patted the grenade launcher with his left hand. "Good girl."

A few seconds later, he gritted his teeth and risked sticking his head up to take a look. The south tower was gone, or more accurately, the roof had collapsed, the walls supporting them reduced to a small pile of rubble.

<Targets destroyed, Lieutenants Brown and Hayes. Anything else I can do for you?>

The captain cut in at that point. <Brown, Goodwin is wounded, we have the intel we need, but we need cover while we exfiltrate>

<On our way, Captain> Lieutenant Brown broadcast.

Ten checked his HUD and saw the icons for A Troop and B Troop start moving as one. The rate of fire increased dramatically as the Marines moved more quickly, freed from the threat of the railguns. Their aggression was restrained, but there were almost two troops of commandos in power armour down there with C Troop defending their rear. They moved by teams, smashing enemy positions with grenades or simply leaping over their cover and engaging them in close quarters.

Ten checked the location of the captain and his team. Still on the top floor of the operations building.

<Need a hand, sir?> he sent privately.

<We're a bit stuck, the lobby is full of Deathless, and we need a way out. The stairwell is blocked>

<Roger that, en route. Get to the south side if you can> Ten responded.

He moved to the gun cabinet and made his preparation, keeping an eye on his HUD as he did so, waiting until Captain Warden had got to the south side of the building. As soon as the captain's team had reached the south side of the building, he detonated the mines he had left all over the base.

The one in the vent blew out the windows on the north end of the operations building. A series of explosions detonated around the base at various points. *That ought to cause a few of them to need a change of trousers.*

<A little warning next time, Ten>

<Sorry, Captain. On my way to your location>

He moved to the west side of the guard tower and picked up the first weapon he'd set out there, emptying the magazine of the launcher as he sprayed grenades widely across the northern end of the compound. He followed up with a second grenade launcher and then emptied a few magazines of railgun ammunition in the general direction as well. If there was anyone over there, they'd have their heads down for a while. Assuming they still had them, of course.

Now all he needed to do was get to the captain. He slit the tape binding the two railguns and took his own back, then added the other to the pile he'd made in the corner, before taking a few extra grenades and some spare magazines. Then he looked out the window again and checked the mission timer on his HUD.

He sighed. This was not going to be fun. He climbed the ladder in the corner and walked out onto the wrap-around balcony at the top of the tower, then clambered up onto the thin wall that protected it, balancing precariously for a few seconds before he unfurled his wings. Pain shot down his broken left wing, but he gritted his teeth and ignored it, diving off the tower towards the captain's position.

It wasn't graceful, and he almost passed out from the agonising pain. The left wing tip wouldn't properly extend so he had to compensate by leaning his body, but the rush of air against the broken limb wrenched it uncontrollably. It might be a limb added to a basic human frame, but it still had a blood supply and nervous system, and it registered pain just as any other limb would.

His barely-controlled fall carried him towards the south side of the operations building, and he thought he was dealing with the lopsided nature of his wing remarkably well, right up until some bastard began shooting at him. A squad of Deathless troops were pinned down by the advancing Marines, hiding behind a squat enclosure of foamcrete that served as storage for several large, wheeled, rubbish bins. One of them was facing him directly and had fired at him with a combat shotgun.

Pellets shredded the membranes of his right wing, and he plummetted toward the ground, desperately trying to stabilise his fall with one broken wing and one shot to pieces as he scrabbled for something in his webbing. With just metres to spare, he pulled the trigger, holding the launcher with both hands and thumbing the motor switch as the grapnel bit home in a rooftop ahead of him.

It tugged him back skyward, directly towards the Deathless squad, and he snatched a random grenade from his webbing, hurling it towards them. His feet touched the ground at the bottom of his arc, even as the grapnel was pulling in the line and he ran a few faltering steps until it wrenched him up again. The flashbang he'd thrown detonated, and he detached the grapnel bolt, launching himself at the squad of Deathless troops.

Landing with an agonising crunch that brought him to one knee, he forced himself up and forward, straight at the trooper with the shotgun. He threw out his right hand to grab the top of the barrel and push it flat against his enemy's chest, even as his left hand closed over the Deathless trooper's trigger hand. He thrust his thumb into the trigger guard, pushing the trooper's finger down with the trigger.

The shot rang out and took the head off the soldier to Ten's right. He wrenched at the shotgun, ramming the butt into its owner's face, once, twice until he let it go. Ten flung it away and drew his vibro-knife, jamming it into the soldier's chin with a snarl then snapping a kick to his left as one of the troopers turned to face him. He lobbed the knife at the trooper behind him, and it plunged into his shoulder. Despite the safety having turned off the vibro function, it was still a heavy combat knife, and it wasn't the first time Ten had thrown one.

He pulled his pistols, and turned to his right, as the last trooper came at him with his own knife. Ten's suppressed weapons discharged in the soldier's face and he dropped to the floor. Five down or injured. Done. Good job that flashbang had disoriented them or they might have given him trouble.

Wait a minute, weren't there six?

He swayed to his right, even as a huge blade slammed down into the ground to his side. Ten screamed as he lost half a metre of his broken left wing entirely, sliced away by the glowing blade. It was just like the sword he'd looted, only working reliably and wielded by an ogre class clone.

Ten turned to face the uninjured final opponent, dancing a few steps back to stay out of reach of the sword. The troopers he had he had kicked in the face and thrown the knife at were recovering and going for their rifles. Ten dropped a pistol and scrambled over a foamcrete planter that protected the walkway from the passing vehicles, desperately seeking cover from the gargantuan fencer.

In any other circumstances, he'd have felt quite secure behind a three-metre long foamcrete planter with a few tonnes of soil and some massive bushes in it. But the ogre's vibro-sword was at least two metres long, and the hugely muscular Deathless clone swung it down in a vicious arc.

The blade sliced through shrubs, soil and the foamcrete planter as if they were nothing more than cheap bio-plastic. Ten scrabbled backwards, and the tip of the sword slammed into the road surface between his feet. The ogre pulled it out, and only the impact of bullets from Ten's pistol held him back.

The Deathless swordsman dropped to a crouch behind the remains of the planter, which was great cover from bullets but bloody useless against a vibro-sword. His magazine empty, Ten decided to try something else.

He dropped the pistol and pulled out his second vibro-knife, thumbing it on as he rose to his feet, screaming a challenge.

"Fucking come on then! Let's be having you, you big beautiful bastard! I'll be wearing one of you sooner or later! Come on!" he yelled at the top of his lungs.

The ogre rose up from behind the planter, with a huge and menacing grin on its face. Whether or not the Deathless had a working translation system, it understood the challenge, and it stomped one heavy foot onto the planter, then the other.

"Yeah, that's right, you climb up on that and roar impressively. You want to fight? You want to fight me?" Ten screamed at it, nodding encouragingly and waving his knife. The ogre roared back at him, presumably an acceptance of the challenge.

"Well, I fucking don't, you gullible twat," Ten giggled happily, pressing the detonator in his left hand as he hurled himself back to the road. The grenade he'd pressed into the soil as he went over the planter exploded beneath the ogre. Ten expected him to disappear in a shower of blood and guts.

Instead, there was a dull bang, and a streak of fire shot up the ogre's legs. Soil exploded upward, and the distinctive thunderclap of the flashbang echoed across the plaza. The ogre staggered back, falling on his arse on the remains of the planter. Ten swore and struggled to his feet, rushing forward, as the ogre snarled and rose up to meet him, swinging the huge blade one-handed from Ten's left, ignoring the flames on his legs.

Ten saw the blade coming in a fearsome arc, but instead of trying to leap back, he barrelled into the surprised ogre, grappling it around the chest. The small, winged, clone tackled the giant ogre, causing it to stagger back. The Deathless trooper dropped its useless sword, but it was too late.

Ten wrapped his legs around the Deathless warrior's chest and squeezed, hanging on tight, then he slammed his head forward to bring his scaly forehead straight into the bridge of the ogre's nose. It shattered in a gout of blood, and the ogre roared, horribly loud in Ten's ears.

But now the vibro-knife hummed and sizzled as Ten plunged it into the chest of the ogre, again and again, stabbing in a frenzied attack until the Deathless trooper finally toppled backwards.

The Penal Marine staggered upright and hopped painfully back from the corpse. Then he reached down and grabbed the sword, heaving the ridiculous blade awkwardly onto his shoulder. He stalked over to the terrified soldier he had kicked in the face and the one he'd thrown his knife at. They cowered in fear as he stood over them, sword still resting on his shoulder.

Ten leaned down and grinned at them, covered in blood and muck, eyes wild. He reached out his hand and the soldiers whimpered.

"That's mine, sonny," hissed Ten through bloody teeth, "and I need it back, so you'll want this morphine." He jammed a tube against the soldier's chest, and it hissed as it delivered its load of drugs through the skin. Then he gripped the knife buried in the trooper's shoulder and pulled it free. The soldier fainted.

Ten looked at the other soldier and saw him glance at a discarded rifle.

"Don't," warned Ten, shaking his head expressively. The Deathless trooper seemed to understand, drawing his hands together and sitting as still as he could.

Ten walked back to the ogre, dragging his new sword behind him, and picked up his guns. He slammed home another round of painkillers and looked around, trying to remember why he was here.

<Ten. We're in a bit of a jam here. How are you doing?>

24

Warden stared out of the window as Ten rounded the corner of a building. Behind him, Harrington and Milton were laying down covering fire and throwing flashbangs down the corridor towards the staircase. The lobby was full of Deathless troops, both trying to reach the top floor and get up out of the stairs.

What they didn't realise was that some of Goodwin's micro-drones were still active, so each time they tried to rush out of the staircase, Milton and Harrington could see them coming. It was like shooting fish in a barrel but it wouldn't last, not least because their ammunition was running low.

The courtyard below wasn't much better. Warden couldn't get too close to the windows because every once in a while the Deathless below would take a shot at them. They were struggling to hold back the advance of A and B Troops, who Warden could see pushing forward to capture the space around the operations building. It was not going fast enough.

"Too long," he muttered to himself, shaking his head as he watched another Deathless trooper make an attempt on the stairs, "it's all taking far too long."

Then Ten appeared, looking a total mess, coming around the

corner behind some of B Troop. His wings were bleeding ruins, his face and chest were covered in blood and dust and he didn't look at all happy. Warden was sure that wouldn't last; Ten might not be looking his best, but he was in his element.

Marine X propped the largest sword Warden had ever seen against the wall the Marines were hiding behind, and snatched a grenade launcher from a protesting colleague. Warden sniggered.

"What's so funny?" Milton asked over her shoulder.

"Ten just arrived," Warden said as he smashed the windows out completely with a few rounds from his pistol. Then he pointed it into the courtyard without aiming and emptied the rest of the magazine. He wasn't going to hit anything, but he didn't need the weight and it might distract the Deathless troopers.

"Goodwin, get your drone out there, I want to see what's happening without getting my head blown off," he ordered.

"Yes, sir," Goodwin responded, throwing the large combat drone out of the window and wincing as she did. They'd given her a plethora of antibiotics and painkillers, but she had indeed been shot and wasn't moving well, even if she had mostly stopped whining.

"Where are you hit? Where are you hit, Goodwin?" Milton had demanded as they half-dragged, half-carried the staggering tech along the corridor. The colour sergeant performed a basic first-aid check as they went, a simple enough exercise with a conscious patient.

"They shot me!" Goodwin had mumbled in surprise as Warden's quickly-rigged booby trap went off at the top of the stairwell.

"Yes, I know that. Where did they shoot you, Goodwin?" Milton asked insistently.

"In the arse! They shot me in my arse!" Goodwin said, apparently incredulous at the thought of it.

"The cheeky bastards," Harrington said.

"Oh for fuck's sake," said Milton and motioned Harrington to stop for a moment while she used her HUD to call up an override on Goodwin's med-suite via and dispense more painkillers and stimulants. She took a quick look and determined it was most likely a flesh wound, a very fleshy wound actually, that had penetrated a joint on the power armour, slipping between some of the armour plates and into Goodwin's left buttock.

"Well, you've been injured now, Goodwin, so you'll have to bring up the rear while we get out of here," Harrington said.

Goodwin wasn't so out of it that she didn't notice the dreadful pun. "Hey! Stop that, I've been shot, it's not funny."

"First time?" Milton had asked sympathetically.

"Yeah."

"Well, it won't be your last if you don't stop pissing about. It's only a flesh wound, Marine," the Colour Sergeant had responded, with substantially less sympathy than the tech had expected.

"Yeah, if you whine about it too much, you'll be the butt of loads of jokes in the company, Goodwin," quipped Harrington.

"Stop it!" Goodwin complained.

"Find us a way out of here, and I'll not only stop, I'll buy you a beer."

"That's a bloody miraculous offer right there, Goodwin. If you can get Harrington to stand his round, nobody is going to have time to make jokes about you getting shot in the buttocks," said Milton.

Ten's commandeered grenade launcher popped repeatedly as he emptied the magazine as fast as he could. There was a pause for a magazine change, then it began to pop again, just as the first barrage of grenades detonated. Warden could tell it was Ten because he'd never known any other Marine to fire a hand-held grenade launcher on full-auto with such aplomb.

He brought up the overhead view from Goodwin's combat drone and saw the Deathless cowering, heads down behind whatever cover they could find. Ten was saying something to Brown and pointing towards the building. Brown was apparently arguing with him. Ten turned towards the troops around him and shouted at them, pointing at the building and they began to let rip. Brown seemed to be protesting.

The Deathless, meanwhile, were keeping their heads down after the incredible barrage of grenade fire. Quite a few were mangled beyond repair.

Ten cracked his neck and Warden could almost hear the noise, almost as if he were stood right beside him. Then he grabbed the sword and shouted again at the commandos near him. He leapt over the low wall in front of him with a painful-looking pump of his mangled wings, and charged.

The Penal Marine ran directly at the Deathless, his ridiculous over-sized sword held high above his head as he screamed like a banshee. The sword began to glow as he reached the first group of Deathless troops and he pumped his shredded wings again to leap over their cover. He let rip another blood-curdling scream – whether of rage or agony from his wounds, Warden couldn't tell.

He twisted in mid-air and kept turning as he landed, swinging the sword in a wide arc and slicing through three Deathless in one blow. Warden winced at that then switched back to his main feed.

"Let's get out there and help, shall we?" he said to Milton, turning toward the shattered window. He kicked the ruined frame its setting, sending it tumbling to the courtyard below. Then he unslung the combat shotgun he'd been carrying as a backup and blasted the suspended ceiling, bringing it down in a cloud of dust.

He clipped his grapnel launcher to his waist then fired it through the hole in the ceiling so that the grapnel buried itself in the foam-crete floor above.

Warden grinned briefly at Milton, grabbed his shotgun and walked out of the hole where the window had been. The line payed out behind him as he rappelled head first down the side of the building, shotgun held before him.

Ten rushed another group of Deathless lizardmen as they began to rise from cover. Warden pulled the trigger repeatedly, and one of them went down. The rest tried to bring their weapons to bear, torn between the sword-wielding maniac on one side and the gun-toting horror running down the wall on the other. They weren't fast enough. Ten disembowelled or dismembered all four of them before Warden even hit the ground.

<Milton, get Goodwin and the intelligence package out the moment we're inside> sent Warden.

<Roger that, Captain> she replied.

He turned back to the building and charged. The Deathless troopers on the ground floor laid down a barrage of fire and Warden ground his teeth, blasting away as he ran. He knew Ten was close behind, using his power armoured captain as cover.

And then a roar erupted behind him. A Troop were following the lead set by their captain and Ten, charging the enemy position and yelling for all they were worth.

<Goodwin, have you got all the data you need?> Ten broadcast.

<At 98% of available data> she replied.

<Tell me when you hit 100%>

<Roger>

Warden didn't have time to think about that as low-calibre rounds pinged off his armour. He vaulted through a shattered window and slammed his foot into the face of a Deathless trooper.

Despite the onslaught of small arms fire, Warden strode into the room firing his shotgun in rapid bursts, not bothering to deal with anyone he missed. He simply pressed forward; the mission data was all that mattered, and Goodwin needed time to complete the exfiltration.

Ten came in behind him and went right, dancing amongst the enemy troopers and lashing out with his sword. The Penal Marine moved continuously, even as bullets sprayed everywhere. The tattered remnants of his wings were spread out by his sides and twirled around in a manner that Milton would later describe as 'like an extremely angry fairy ballerina who's had way too much coffee' although not to Ten's face.

In moments, it was all over. The rest of A Troop were in the building, mopping up what little resistance the Deathless still had to offer after Captain Warden and Ten's onslaught.

<Done, that's all the data, Ten> Goodwin broadcast.

<We should leave now, Captain, while they're confused> Ten sent privately.

Warden really wanted to know what the Penal Marine had up his sleeve, but he knew better than to waste time asking questions. Cohen wouldn't thank them if they fell further behind schedule.

<Fall back to the RV> he ordered on a broadcast channel, triggering the display of the exfiltration route to appear on the HUDs of the Marines.

Ten was ahead of him, having stuck to the edges of the massacre in the lobby of the operations building. He was sprinting away, following A Troop and still carrying that ludicrous sword despite his injuries.

Warden was the last to leave the building, chasing out Milton and Goodwin as the tech stumbled down the steps and into the open compound. The moment he was clear, Ten popped up from behind a wall almost a hundred metres away. The harpy clones had a fair turn of speed, but Marine X must be on combat drugs to keep going with the wounds he was carrying.

Ten grinned and tapped his wrist suggestively. Warden sprinted as hard as he could, and a second later there was a devastating explosion on the north side of the base. The shockwave blew him from his feet and sent him tumbling end-over-end. Half the troop was blown over, but by the time Warden had cleared his head enough to notice, all he could see was Ten, and grinning like a Cheshire cat, as if all his birthdays had come at once.

Warden looked around as he stood up. There was hardly anything left in the north end of the base. Half the operations building had collapsed and the night sky was now lit by the flames that rose from the shattered ruins. Whatever Ten had used, it packed a punch.

The Deathless seemed similarly stunned, their resistance shattered. Those that could were backing away or nursing their wounds, no longer at all interested in fighting.

Warden checked his HUD for casualties and saw that Bailey and Parker were still in position and apparently, still shooting things.

He ordered them to get out immediately and they dove off the wall, gliding back towards C Troop. Behind them, the guard tower blew itself apart in a series of explosions, mere seconds after the snipers were clear.

Warden made notes in his HUD as he watched his troops retreat. He would need to discuss Lieutenant Brown's performance with Lieutenant Colonel Atticus. Whatever his problem with Ten, it should not have needed a heavily injured Marine to lead the charge, secure the success of their mission, and help Goodwin to safety, which had been the only important objective by that point. It was their first time working together, but that was no excuse.

He surveyed the Deathless base one last time and then turned to the assembled Marines. "Let's get going. I'm gasping for a cup of tea."

EPILOGUE

The conference room of HMS *Iron Duke* was crowded and Captain Warden, the last person to arrive, had to shuffle around the table to find space next to Lieutenant Colonel Atticus and Governor Denmead. When he finally squeezed past the throng and took his seat, he was only mildly surprised when a familiar voice whispered in his ear.

"Morning, Captain," said Marine X quietly, "are you ready for the bad news?"

Warden sighed and half-turned in his chair.

"Should you really be in here, Marine? This briefing is supposed to be restricted."

Then Vice Admiral Staines cleared his throat, and Marine X's opportunity to explain was snuffed out.

"Good morning, thank you for coming," he said, looking around the room at the attendees, his face unexpectedly grim and serious. "Thank you to our colleagues joining us by wormhole transmission," he finished, gesturing to the view screens lining the walls from which General Bonneville and a number of other military dignitaries looked on.

"I know you've all been looking forward to a little downtime after *Ascendant*'s mission to NewPet, but I'm afraid, given the information retrieved by Captain Warden, that you'll have to put your plans on hold for a little while longer," said Staines.

A ripple of disquiet passed through the offices until Staines held up his hand for silence.

"Settle down," he said, in a largely reassuring tone. "We've all seen a lot of action over the last few weeks, some more than others, admittedly, but we can't go back to our day jobs just yet." He paused to poke at his data slate until new images were pushed to the holographic display that hovered over the conference table.

"The purpose of this briefing is to bring everyone up to speed on the developments since *Ascendant* left to reconnoitre the Deathless facilities in the NewPet system. A great deal of data was recovered at various stages of the mission, and it is now being analysed by the combined brainpower of the Commonwealth's military intelligence agencies," he paused to allow the wave of tittering to calm down.

"If you have all quite finished with your amusement at a joke that has to be at least a millennium old," Staines admonished sternly, "we'll move on.

"You've all seen these images from *Ascendant*, of course," he said, zooming in to show an image of a large structure in orbit. "This is the Deathless space station Soyuz, in orbit around the planet NewPet. Captain Warden visited the station and confirmed that it is a staging point through which the extensive troop training facilities on NewPet itself are funnelling tens of thousands of well-trained and well-equipped troops to destinations unknown.

"Having established that the Deathless are shipping troops to more than one location – which of course means they aren't just attacking New Bristol – it was clear that the mission of *Ascendant* should be extended in the hopes that we might identify the targets. Further excursions, conducted on the planet itself, established details of the Deathless training facilities and methods, as well as supplying the majority of the information gathered over the mission as a whole. However, those details are best discussed in further briefings and are not what I wish to focus on today," said Staines, clearing his throat.

"We have now received the decrypted intelligence in full, and the first results of the analysis are troubling, to say the least. This star chart," he said as the projection changed to a view of the Milky Way with a large three-dimensional section broken into volumes distinguished by colour, "shows the extent of space currently claimed by the Commonwealth and other Sol governments."

Another blob appeared, further out from most of the Sol space but almost as large as the Commonwealth itself. The edge of the area touched the volume of space in which the solar system of New Bristol could be found. Warden had to resist an urge to whistle. Behind him, Ten whispered, "Wow."

"As I'm sure you can guess, this region is the area that the gathered intelligence shows as being claimed by the Deathless government already." Staines flicked at his data slate again, and a new volume was marked, with shipping routes all leading from NewPet. "These are the systems to which NewPet has been sending ships."

A murmur of horror went around the room. If the data was correct, the Deathless were not just attacking Commonwealth space, but planets and systems claimed by other Sol governments as well. Simultaneously.

"Those aren't just colony planets, are they?" Lieutenant Commander Cohen asked.

"No, they are not. As well as invading the indicated first stage colony worlds, the Deathless are also occupying systems that Sol governments have, to date at least, deemed unsuitable for colonisation," Staines confirmed.

"Does anyone have a theory as to why?" Governor Denmead asked.

"The prevailing opinion is that they require vast resources for economic growth and are strip-mining asteroid belts and uninhabitable planets to gather the materials they need," Staines said.

"But, if they aren't building colonies, why would they need to mine systems on an interstellar scale? Surely they're not building a Dyson sphere?" Denmead joked, the very idea being universally considered a laughable waste of time.

"Actually, that's exactly the scenario that our intelligence analysts say is our best case, Governor. If that is what they're doing, their expansion would have a theoretical limit, and they would be concentrating on building up one system to an unprecedented level. Other data have suggested this is, unfortunately, not the case," Staines continued.

He flagged another system, well outside the boundaries of Sol space and a significant distance from the known volume of Deathless control. "Now we come to this system, as yet unnamed but designated U-235 for the time being, due to the likelihood of it exploding into something unforgettably nasty. This is the information that has caused the most alarm."

"More alarming than a multi-system interstellar invasion plan?" asked Lieutenant Colonel Atticus.

"Yes, very much so. U-235 contains a shipyard and only a shipyard. It has no colony, as far as we can tell, no troop training facilities and its planets are likely uninhabitable. What we do know is that it contains vast wealth in metallic elements, far beyond what is found in the average solar system. This may explain why they've gone so far out of their existing space to build these facilities. The boffins estimate that the production capabilities at U-235 equal or exceed those of the Commonwealth," Staines concluded, allowing time for that information to sink in.

Warden stared at the highlighted system in a mixture of awe and horror. Ten leaned forward and whispered in his ear, "Told you it was bad news."

Warden frowned. It didn't sound like Ten was being his usual cynical self, it sounded like he had known already. Oh dear. He should probably mention it to Lieutenant Colonel Atticus and get Goodwin to sweep their systems for signs that Ten had breached them for some reason. He wouldn't put it past the Penal Marine to nose around the Commonwealth's classified databases out of idle curiosity.

"On the off chance that any of you missed your courses on the importance of economic power to the conduct of long-term or large-scale military endeavours, let me put it in simple terms. If correct, our analysis of this system, which has been entirely dedicated to the production of ships that we assume are military in nature, can out-produce the combined capabilities of the Commonwealth shipyards across all our systems," Staines said to further horrified mutterings.

"In short, ladies and gentlemen, it appears they have not only the means and the population to start a war against us, the Death-less have the capability to launch attacks against all the other Sol governments at the same time. They've also been preparing for decades and we are already hopelessly outmatched. Have a think about that, and let me know your questions," he finished.

There was another pause while everyone absorbed this.

"Given all this, Vice Admiral, what is the Admiralty planning to do next?" asked Governor Denmead, one of the few civilians in the conference room. "I mean, if the Deathless are almost as numerous and widespread as the entire Commonwealth and they have been on a military footing for some time, we are in a rather worrying position."

"You are quite correct, Governor, both in your estimate of the scale of the problem and your assessment of the concern being displayed by the Commonwealth government on Earth. They are, to put it bluntly, panicked, and I think you'll agree they have good reason. A number of measures are being put in place. New fleets are being commissioned as we speak, recruitment is being stepped up, the colonies are being informed of the existence of a new threat, and intelligence is being passed through channels to other Sol govern-ments," Staines said.

"What about the other systems they've already attacked?" Governor Denmead asked.

"The Admiralty currently plans to launch missions to each of our colony worlds that may have been attacked, and strike back. They will use New Bristol as a staging post for those fleets, which will mean that we will regularly have more ships here to defend the system."

"Does the Admiralty even have enough ships to defend the frontier, Vice Admiral Staines? I mean, without wishing to be rude, we haven't come close to anything on this scale for a very long time," said Atticus.

There was a pause, and it was clear Staines was uncomfortable with the question.

"No, we don't have enough ships," he admitted. "We're bringing everything we can out of mothballs and placing new production orders. Old capital ships are the priority, but anything that can be pressed into service will be seized and made available. Former personnel are being re-activated to provide crews, and they'll be used for lower priority patrols. We're also reactivating retired Royal Marine Space Commandos and other military personnel across the Commonwealth," Staines said.

"That's all reassuring, sir and I'm glad to hear they're taking the situation seriously. Do we have new orders yet?" Warden asked.

"Yes, Captain. We're being sent all the ships the Admiralty can spare to defend New Bristol, as well as ships to form a strike and reconnaissance fleet under the command of Admiral Morgan." There was an audible groan from Ten behind him, causing the Vice Admiral to honour him with a frown. There was an awkward silence and Warden wondered why Ten had reacted poorly to news of Admiral Morgan's imminent arrival. He coughed politely and posed his next question.

"So I'm guessing we'll be going back out to investigate the shipyard?"

"General Bonneville and I are still discussing the details, but yes, you and Lieutenant Commander Cohen will be part of the fleet we select to investigate U-235. Your company of commandos will join *Ascendant* for boarding actions and ground missions, though we anticipate this will be a largely Naval affair," Staines said.

"Thank you, sir," said Warden. Then he turned to Cohen with a malicious grin. "Looks like it's over to you for the next one, Lieutenant Commander Cohen."

GUNBOAT

RMSC OMNIBUS - BOOK 4

PROLOGUE

Captain Yegorovich felt the subtle shift in the decking beneath his feet that signalled an engine power change. He pressed the comm button by his vid-mirror. "Borisovich, how long to the target?"

"Fifteen minutes until the colony is within range of our primary weapon systems, Captain," replied the pilot.

"Asteroid, Lieutenant, not a colony. It is an unlicensed mining operation, held by outlaws. GK Industries frigates do not open fire on legitimate colonies," Yegorovich admonished the pilot of GKI *Jacobo*. "We are not savages. We are merely securing GKI's legitimate interests in this system, for which they have mining rights."

A flush rose up from the collar of Borisovich's uniform to the close-cropped hair around his ears.

"Yes, Captain. My apologies."

Yegorovich nodded and released the comm button as he jutted his jaw towards the mirror, checking for any remaining soap. He grunted, satisfied. This was an important call, and he had spent an hour ensuring that he looked the part. His valet had pressed immaculate creases into his uniform and polished every surface in his ready room.

One last pat down with a warm towel and he was ready to make the most important call of his career, to a man with a reputation for placing a premium on the comportment of his staff.

If this mission went smoothly, Yegorovich would be perfectly placed for promotion to command of one of the company's new battleships, maybe even a capital ship. Yegorovich was young for such a position, but GKI executives groomed the subordinates who impressed them for high positions, and none were better placed to further his career than the man he was about to call.

He sat at his desk, straightened his shoulders and tapped a button. The viewscreen popped up from the back of his desk, and he opened a connection to the bridge.

"Junior Lieutenant Germanovich, open a wormhole to headquarters and put me through to Chairman Giacomo Khan," he said in his best commander's voice.

This is it, he thought, *this is your chance to impress Giacomo Khan himself, founder and principal shareholder of Giacomo Khan Industries.*

"Yes, Captain. Right away, Captain," Germanovich replied, initiating a wormhole transmission to establish interstellar communications with the regional company headquarters of GKI. Moments later, the transmission connected and was routed through to the captain's ready room.

"Good morning, Captain."

"Good morning, Chairman," he replied, trying to keep the excitement from his voice.

"Hold for the Chairman, please," said Ms Afanasievna with a sniff that somehow conveyed utter contempt. The screen changed to show a holding vid.

His personal assistant. Not the chairman. Yegorovich shut his mouth with a snap and waited as a monotonous hold video played on the screen.

His collar felt tight. That idiot, Orlov, had over starched his shirt again. He stuck his finger in and tried to loosen it a little. Was he perspiring? His forehead felt damp, and his throat was dry.

Yegorovich swallowed, eyeing the glass of water, then the waiting video. He swallowed again, then reached for the glass to take a sip, his hand trembling nervously.

"Captain Yegorovich, what is your status?" snapped Giacomo Khan, his words clipped and impatient as he glared from the viewscreen. Well, he was a trillionaire. His time was no doubt valuable.

"We're almost ready, I mean, uh," Yegorovich stammered, spilling the water over his hand as he set the glass down, "we are almost in position to attack, Chairman Khan. We are ten minutes from primary weapons range."

"Good. Any problems?"

"No, sir. These thieves have only minimal defences on their improvised mining station. We will eliminate their pathetic anti-ship cannons and missile defence lasers with one barrage of surgically targeted strikes. After that, they have nothing to prevent our corporate security forces from storming the station, eliminating any armed opposition, and securing their other personnel," replied Yegorovich, feeling a little more confident now that he was speaking about the military matters that he had already discussed at length with his team.

"Remind me. Who will lead the assault?"

"Captain Katerina Petrovna of the 6th Company, GKI Counter Insurgency Troopers, sir. She will conduct the assault and secure the station for GKI. She is confident that her troopers can complete the assault with a minimal number of CIT casualties and secure the enemy personnel before they can regroup to offer effective resistance. If you are happy to authorise us to proceed with the seizure of these criminally obtained assets, Chairman Khan," Yegorovich said.

There was no hesitation, no delay for further thought. Giacomo Khan had not created the largest conglomerate in Koschite history by being indecisive. "You have your authorisation, Yegorovich. You are to proceed with the operation and take justice to this band of criminals. Happy hunting, Captain."

"Borisovich, what's our time to intercept the target?" Yegorovich asked as he lowered himself into his command chair and began drumming his fingers on the arm. He crossed his legs, straightened his jacket, cracked his neck and then uncrossed his legs.

"Four minutes, Captain," Junior Lieutenant Borisovich confirmed. "Optimum launch window for the boarding pods opens in three minutes and fifteen seconds."

"Captain Petrovna, what is your status?"

"Boarding team ready to launch," Captain Petrovna replied. "Weapons are locked and loaded, all systems fully operational."

"Excellent. Standby for launch." He turned to his XO. "Germanovich, do you have a firing solution?"

"Yes, Captain. Targets locked in, the first window opens in two minutes. Optimal engagement results are expected at two minutes, thirty seconds," said Germanovich.

"Very well, engage targets at the optimal range. I would like one clean volley, if possible. Identify failed strikes and re-engage immediately if any first strikes miss their mark. Launch boarding pods once the window opens," Yegorovich ordered. The relevant personnel confirmed his orders as he gave them.

He leaned back and steepled his fingers under his chin, waiting impatiently, eager for the plan to proceed.

"Volley fired. Nine point eight seconds to impact. Six. Three. Impact. Assessing damage," Germanovich stated in flat, calm tones. "Impact data returned. All targets successfully struck and no longer operational. One hundred per cent success rate, Captain."

"Excellent work," Yegorovich said.

Presently, a rumble could be felt through the deck plating and Borisovich reported, "Boarding pods away, Captain."

"Good hunting, Captain Petrovna."

"Thank you, Captain Yegorovich. Impact in fifteen minutes. Switching to stealth mode," replied the mercenary commander.

And that was it. Now all they could do was wait and monitor the surrounding regions for trouble. There was some manoeuvring for Borisovich to do, of course, to keep them in the best position to defend themselves and fire on the mining facility, should they need to, but that was it. Unless another ship arrived, it was now up to the GKI infantry to secure the station.

~

"Captain, the pod will land in four minutes. We have three safe impact zones. Which is your preference?" asked Specialist Popov, looking up from his data slate as he guided the pod to its target.

Petrovna looked at the slate as he presented it to her.

"What is this?" she asked, pointing at a fourth area.

Popov was taken aback. The captain was pointing at a part of the colony that wasn't a valid target for a boarding pod to create a hull breach. Surely she knew this? Captain Petrovna wasn't keen on waiting, though, so he answered as quickly as possible.

"Captain, it is a bio-dome, a recreational area filled with plants and trees to provide a pleasant environment for the miners to relax in. It has no strategic importance, and if it is opened to vacuum the flora will be destroyed."

"It is surplus to company requirements," said Petrovna calmly, "and gives immediate access to internal doors and multiple areas and levels. It is only windows and some thin supports, so we can breach it, yes? A perfect landing site."

"Yes, Captain, but it will depressurise, and we won't be able to seal the breach behind us. We'll crash right through the window panels and be left in hard vacuum," he protested, for all the good it would do.

"Are you questioning my decision, Specialist?" she asked.

He gulped and shook his head. "No, Captain."

"Then set the course. But there is no need to be dramatic; after all, who likes a bumpy landing?" she said with a cruel laugh.

The destruction would be wanton, but Popov knew the captain

didn't care about such things as leisure and mental health facilities for the miners. The company's needs were all that mattered.

He issued the final course to the pod, firing the thrusters to align it with the target then the retro-engines to slow the pod so that it would be well below the normal impact speed by the time it struck the beautiful domed garden. Then he reached above him and pulled down the helmet of his power armour.

Popov took the opportunity to shudder in disgust at the demands placed on him by his employers. If he could, he would have transferred away from Captain Petrovna's command, but she wouldn't take that well and she had a reputation for spiteful reprisals. No, if he wanted to be surrounded by people who didn't terrify him, he had to find some way to get promoted to a senior role elsewhere in GKI. He wished he had joined the army instead.

Petrovna broadcast to all pods. The sycophants around her signalled their amusement and gave her the thumbs up. It was the same joke every time, but she always got an enthusiastic laugh. Popov grinned broadly through his faceplate and gave her two thumbs up as well, and she laughed, punching his shoulder. At least he wore power armour. Out of the suits, her idea of a playful punch was unpleasantly sadistic.

Popov was pretty sure Petrovna's psych report would confirm psychopathic tendencies, if it weren't for the fact that her last shrink had died in a horrible accident shortly after suffering a failure in her backup hardware. For a Progenitor to suffer the final death was almost unheard of, and Popov did not believe in coincidences.

He checked his straps one more time, then tried to relax into his seat, insofar as that was possible while he was surrounded by this bunch of quasi-criminals and borderline psychopaths. He hadn't known, before joining up, that the GKI mercenaries were every bit as, well, mercenary as the Libertarian-aligned news shows always portrayed them to be. The vid shows told stories of corrupt corporate mercenaries being pursued by honest cops, but they had always seemed like exaggerated melodramas.

Now, from the inside, the shows disturbingly accurate. Tame, even.

The countdown began, and Petrovna's main team whooped and hollered over the wide band. He slapped a volume limit on them via his HUD. He didn't need to hear it, but he knew he had to listen to every comment they broadcast in the next hour and that Petrovna wouldn't discipline anyone for anything they said, or did. Not unless they shot a friendly or damaged company property.

The pod struck the network of carbon-nanofibre filigree with far less force than in a normal boarding pod procedure. The diamond-glass glazing, whose panels made the dome sparkle like a bejewelled egg, shattered as the supports gave way.

Popov watched through the hardened cameras embedded in the nose as the seemingly delicate shell first crumpled, and then tore, when the boarding pod punched through it. The atmosphere rushed out, and Popov's worst nightmare was fulfilled.

First one body, then another, then a third, was pulled from the dome by the escaping gas, dragged into space to die in a horrible fashion. They had been hiding in there, he was sure of it, safe in the least valuable, and most welcoming, part of the facility. When the station was attacked, the garden dome had probably seemed like a safe place to send their most vulnerable residents. How wrong they were.

Popov could see the last of them, a woman, struggling to hold on to a tree branch with one hand and a small figure with the other. He could see her screaming in agony and terror, then the last breath left her body and her strength failed. Her child was ripped from her grasp and the woman lost her purchase on the tree. Both bodies tumbled past the boarding pod, sucked out into the frozen void beyond.

Popov closed his eyes and wondered if he could ever forgive himself for the crimes he had committed today. He felt a little piece of his mind snap, and his eyes misted with tears that he couldn't wipe away unless he, too, wanted to feel the icy touch of space on his skin.

Blinking furiously to clear the tears from his eyes, he followed

Captain Petrovna through the door of the pod and into the ruined garden. The mercenaries were waiting at the first door, which he hacked and forced to open, venting more atmosphere from the facility.

Each door from the destroyed bio-dome fell before his hacking skills, and he followed his captain and two of her best soldiers into the station, resealing the door and repressurising the chamber.

<My team will head to the command centre. All other teams secure assigned targets, round up squatters, and bring them to the central square for processing. If any of these criminals resist our assertion of GKI's legitimate mining rights, put them out of my misery> Petrovna ordered on a wide band to all her troops.

Any of these criminals? thought Popov bitterly. *We're the criminals here.*

⁓

This time, Captain Yegorovich waited until an image appeared on the screen in his office before he spoke, which turned out to be wise as the secretary did not pick up. Instead, the view was of a large office with a commensurately enormous leather topped wooden desk.

Behind the desk, a high-backed office chair faced a panoramic view over the city of Bratsk, with its beachfront villas, bars and restaurants, and the sparkling blue bay of water which lapped against the white sandy beaches.

Yegorovich hoped to be invited to a company event in the luxurious city one day, but he couldn't afford it on his salary. Bratsk was the vacation destination of choice for many Koschites, regardless of their political leanings.

The view from GKI's regional headquarters was spectacular, thanks to the vigorous efforts of GKI's in-house terraforming gurus. Bratsk Bay had once been a provincial backwater full of river silt and bounded by shingle beaches, but the terraforming team had transformed it, changing every aspect of the bay.

The work had been extensive. The terraforming team had obliterated the native ecosystem, swapping the flora and fauna for non-native species. They had dredged the bay, scraped away the shingle, and constructed sweeping beaches of pristine artificial sand. A kilometre upstream, an artificial lake had been constructed, partly to host water sports but mostly to filter contaminants from the water, such as silt and native fish, before it flowed into the bay.

Downstream of the lake, the river was a beautiful, sparkling ribbon of unnaturally clear water. Even the river bed had been dredged, the original muck being replaced with thousands of tons of picture-perfect pebbles and semi-precious gemstones. The plant life in the river and along its banks and been razed or plucked out and exchanged for more visually appealing species.

Yegorovich had heard that each regional headquarters had a penthouse office space reserved for the use of the chairman and his staff, but he had never seen one. Bratsk might have been only a minor regional office, but it must surely have the most spectacular vista offered by any of them.

According to company gossip, the chairman wouldn't visit any company site that didn't yet include an office equivalent to the one on his home planet. Chairman Khan would surely never set foot in this system, nor have personal involvement in the day to day operations. He was, however, in the habit of checking in on the direct actions of GKI's military, and many of Yegorovich's colleagues had told him that they, too, had been honoured by direct communication with Khan during a critical mission.

Then the occupant of the huge and opulent chair turned slowly to face him, and the audience began. The screen in Yegorovich's office was large and had such excellent image quality that it felt almost as if he was in the same room as his superior.

"Ah, Captain Yegorovich. Do you have good news for me?" Khan said. As he spoke, his fingers gently scratched between the ears of a large albino mandrill. The monkey was perched on a platform built into the right-hand side of the chairman's chair. The creature looked content, tilting its head to encourage scratching in a different area.

Most of the mandrills wore engineering power suits which aided them with tasks such as forest clearance or shipboard maintenance and repair. This one wore a suit that was clearly military, and to Yegorovich's eyes it seemed to be dramatically more expensive than the equipment issued to Petrovna and her CIT team.

Rumour had it that the monkey had received comprehensive combat training and was, in fact, a bodyguard. Wild stories were told of the capabilities of Khan's mandrill and its famous suit of power armour. Some said it had cybernetic limbs, or that its gauntlets fired vibro-bladed shuriken, or there was a railgun mounted in the forearm.

Then Yegorovich realised he'd taken too long to reply, distracted by the infamous albino monkey, and he spoke suddenly. "Yes, Chairman Khan. The assault on the mining station went to plan. Captain Petrovna controls the facility."

"It would be more accurate to refer to this as the recovery of a GKI mining claim, Captain Yegorovich, and I expect your official reports to reflect that. Casualties?"

"I understand, sir, my report will use the correct wording. The miners – I mean, the pirates who were illegally mining the asteroid belt – did sustain some casualties."

Khan cut him off irritably. "Not the criminals, Yegorovich. Where there GKI casualties?"

"Oh, no, sir. Captain Petrovna said the pirates crumpled before her troopers like the cowardly scum we took them to be. One or two of her team took minor scrapes during the boarding pod impact, but she assures me that her troops incurred no serious injuries and that getting banged about a bit is expected in an action like this."

"That is excellent news. Since this is your first such action, I will remind you to keep your report brief and to the facts. We don't need colourful descriptions of this minor operation leaking to the press. Gather Petrovna's report, write your sections and submit a draft to Ms Afanasievna. My team will check for inappropriate language, potential factual errors or missing information. Understood?" Chairman Khan asked, his demeanour unexpectedly that of an employer who cared about the future of a junior employee enough to help them improve their reporting skills.

Yegorovich went with it. "Yes, sir. Thank you for your help, sir. I'll send my draft shortly."

"First things first, if you haven't already, get the installation of cloning bays under way. It is critical that the deployment of GKI mining personnel and the permanent security team take place as soon as possible. I want that facility turning a profit as soon as possible."

Yegorovich only had time to acknowledge the order before the chairman cut the call. He waited a moment then let out a sigh of relief. Reaching for a tissue, he wiped the sweat from his face and neck.

He wondered if he would ever get used to dealing with the founder of the company. Then he winced as he played back the conversation in his mind.

Of course the chairman of GKI wouldn't need to know about the casualties amongst the pirates who had set up a rogue operation in the asteroid belt. They'd even had the gall to have families here, probably kidnapped from some unprotected merchant ship or another small outpost. Worse still, they had put children in harm's way, according to Petrovna, and their criminal actions had gotten them killed. Petrovna had said the bodies were irretrievable and there likely weren't any records they could use to deploy the pirates' victims to new clones.

What an appalling life these people must lead, he thought, as he loosened his collar and poured himself a stiff drink. One day, perhaps, he would be able to put an end to all such pirates, and then he wouldn't have to see the frozen remains of a child tumbling out into space. Yes. That was a fine goal for his career. Commodore Yegorovich, the man who ended space piracy and organised crime throughout Koschite space.

He sat back with his drink, lost in his daydream.

1

―――――

"Good morning, ma'am," said Admiral Morgan, sitting upright before the video link. In front of him, at the other end of a wormhole that stretched untold hundreds of lightyears across the galaxy, sat the always serious Admiral of the Fleet, Norma Crown.

When they had last spoken, she had been calm, serene even. Now she was agitated, and she seemed to have aged over the last few weeks. This crisis, the arrival of the Deathless at the colony world of New Bristol, had aged them all.

"Morgan," nodded Crown, her tones clipped and precise. "Your mission briefing is downloading at the moment," she said, flicking at a tablet Morgan couldn't quite see, "but it's really quite simple. You are to take your fleet and proceed to the location identified by Lieutenant Commander Cohen and his team. In a number of systems en route, you will deploy intelligence drones to forewarn us of any future visitors."

Morgan's eyes narrowed at the mention of Cohen, but he kept the rest of his face carefully neutral. Everyone else seemed to think Cohen could do no wrong, especially his mentor, Vice Admiral Staines. But Morgan had seen Cohen come up through the training academy and he knew better. Whatever Staines thought, Morgan wasn't going to let an over-promoted puppy like Cohen derail his mission. Crown went on.

"This shipyard, U-235, and the other facilities we suspect accompany it," she said as the lower right quarter of the screen broke out to show a star chart and a route, "are key."

Morgan nodded, grinding his teeth at the ridiculous identifier Cohen's team had given the shipyard. U-235. A stupid, child-like joke, as if this was something exciting and interesting, and now it was the official designation and they were stuck with it. He hid his annoyance and nodded.

"Yes, ma'am." He had seen the files, but he couldn't quite bring himself to believe them. The details were sparse, but they showed that U-235 was immense. The boffins had estimated that a structure the size of U-235 could host a dozen fleets and churn out new ships at a rate that far exceeded the production capacity of the Royal Navy's combined ports. That was an unsettling thought, and the Admiralty was collectively in a state of mild panic.

"The rest of the fleet, all that could be gathered in the available time, is either waiting for you at New Bristol already or will be there in the next eighteen hours. How long till you arrive?"

Morgan checked the countdown timer on his data slate. "A little over three hours."

"Good," said Crown, nodding, "and how long will you need to resupply?"

"I don't think we'll need to. *Duke of Norfolk* is fully provisioned, so our in-system time should be short. A few hours, maybe, but no more."

"Very well. Go to U-235," repeated Crown, "find out what's going on, and then take whatever action is necessary to end or critically degrade the station's ability to threaten our systems. Is that clear?"

Morgan nodded, face hard and expression grim. "Yes, ma'am."

"Vice Admiral Staines commands the in-system forces. He will remain at New Bristol to coordinate the ongoing defence and oversee the construction of a London-class starbase."

Morgan nodded, carefully keeping the surprise from his face. The

London-class had only recently entered service and there were, so far, only two. That Staines had been given the task of constructing a third was, to say the least, unexpected.

"A starbase?" he said, forcing out the words. "That should keep him busy."

"Indeed," agreed Crown, "and it will eventually give you a base of operations, should it be necessary."

"I had rather expected this to be a short-lived deployment," said Morgan, frowning slightly. "Get in, do the job, and then come home," he summarised.

Crown gave him a flat, mirthless smile. "That rather depends on what you find at U-235. I wish you the best of luck, Admiral. Happy hunting."

Then she was gone, and the display showed only the Royal Navy's bland screen saver and a countdown timer to the next Trafalgar Day.

Morgan sat back in his chair and shook his head. Investigating enemy starbases was one thing, but having to deal with idiots like Staines was quite another. If there was one person that Morgan truly couldn't stand, it was Staines, who had an annoying knack for landing in the right place at the right time to scoop up the credit for someone else's work.

And now he had been charged with building a London-class starbase. The ability of the man to fall on his feet and collect tasks beyond his limited capacity was truly astonishing.

Morgan shook his head again at the ridiculous situation and stood up, smoothing down his uniform and flicking away a non-existent particle of dust.

U-235 might be the mission, but Morgan was also going to get to the bottom of whatever it was that was going on at New Bristol. He was going to find out what Staines was up to.

∾

"That is a big ship," said Captain Tom Warden, watching in awe from a viewing port on *Ascendant*. He was in the small observation room above the bridge with Lieutenant Commander Alistair Cohen and his XO, Lieutenant Tim White. All three men wore captured Deathless clones, a relic from their mission to infiltrate an enemy base on the planet of NewPet.

"That's HMS *Duke of Norfolk*," said Cohen as the huge ship drifted across their view. Almost half as long again as *Ascendant*, it was one of the biggest and most modern ships in the Royal Navy's fleet. "Admiral Morgan's flagship. Makes *Ascendant* look like a pleasure cruiser."

Warden grinned. "You're too hard on yourself, sir. I've always thought of *Ascendant* as more of a passenger ferry than a pleasure cruiser."

Cohen sniffed but didn't respond.

"A ferry might be more comfortable," said White morosely. "A pleasure cruiser would definitely be more comfortable. Probably have a better supply of booze as well."

"They let people disembark from ferries," observed Warden with a hint of bitterness, "even if only for a few days." The ongoing emergency meant they had to be ready for action at short notice, so shore leave had been cancelled.

"Even the rum on this ship is grim. I'm sure the machines are watering it," complained White. "And the port is frankly awful. I wouldn't use it to clean a table back home."

"Okay, knock it off," said Cohen wearily. The good-natured complaints had been amusing at first, and Cohen had endured with little more than a tired frown. Now, after days in transit and longer in orbit around New Bristol awaiting orders, the novelty had worn off.

"Have you met the admiral?" asked Warden to change the subject.

"No," said Cohen, "but I know a few people who served under him. He seems to be well respected, although he's got a bit of a temper."

"He doesn't like Staines," said White. The other two looked at the XO. "That's the chatter anyway. Some sort of falling out, years ago.

They haven't seen eye to eye since, and that's the main reason Staines is stuck out in the backwaters with only two ships to his name."

Cohen looked back out at *Duke of Norfolk*, frowning. If there was one thing he liked less than inappropriate humour, it was rumour-mongering and gossip.

"Let's focus on the job at hand," he said. "Is everything ready for our departure?"

"Yes, sir, pretty much," said White, pulling out his data slate. "The damage we took at NewPet has been repaired, and the external hull inspections were completed a few hours ago. We've taken on fuel, raw materials for the fabricators and our supplies of organics for the cloning bays have been restocked. The dropship has also been patched up, but the admiral has asked that we leave it here, so it's preparing to leave."

"Good," nodded Cohen, although he had kept tabs on the progress reports as they had come in and already knew most of this. "And the drop pods?"

"Ah," said White, "yes. The news there is less good. The techs think that the pods are loaded from outside. There's certainly no way to load them from inside *Ascendant*. The theory is that they were installed when the ship was built and that, once used, the ship has to return to base for a refit."

"Use once then refit?" said Cohen, frowning hard at White. Then he shrugged. "I suppose they're not a core part of the ship's day-to-day operations."

"No, and if you've used them, your troops have been deployed, so you don't need any more. The good news is that the fabricators can make the parts," said White, "and the automated assembly suite can put most of them together. The bad news is that the final assembly has to be done by hand, and then they have to be walked around the outside of the ship. It's fiddly work, and installation will be dangerous without a properly equipped shipyard."

Cohen didn't like the sound of that. Spacewalks, even in high-quality modern suits, were inherently risky. Manoeuvring large pieces of equipment at the same time would cause a serious set of problems.

"Then let's leave the drop pods to one side for the moment. See if *Albion* can come up with a way to fabricate and install them. I don't want to go to the effort of building our own only to find they get stuck in the tubes when we try to launch them."

Warden nodded his agreement. Getting stuck in a drop pod, half-deployed from the ship and unable to move in either direction, did not sound like a lot of fun.

"Will do," said White. "That ought to mean we're about done."

"And the crew?"

"Last of the redeployments should be finished later today, sir. Growing the clones took a little longer than expected, and the cloning bays are still only able to produce Deathless models."

"Really?" said Cohen, frowning. "I thought we were going to redeploy to standard RN models now that the need for secrecy is over." Warden's face held an expression that suggested he was no happier with this state of affairs.

"The techs are looking into it, sir," said White, "but there's some fundamental incompatibility or a technical restriction in the bays themselves. They'll turn out all the Deathless models we might want, but uploading new patterns doesn't seem to be possible, so RN and RMSC deployments are all being done on *Albion*."

Cohen held up his hand and looked at the long, slender fingers of the Rupert clone. These models had their advantages. They were fast, well-suited to high-G manoeuvres and tough. But they were also unfamiliar, and some of the crew were finding it difficult to adjust. The sooner they could get back to the RN's standard clone, the better.

"Keep working on the problem. I want the option to produce RN or RMSC clones as soon as possible."

"Will do." White made a note on his slate. "Apart from that, everything is shipshape and in New Bristol fashion." He grinned at his wit, but the room remained quiet.

"How are the Marines holding up, Warden?" said Cohen, neatly passing the steaming corpse of White's joke.

"All redeployed, equipped and ready to go, sir. They seem to have settled into their Deathless clones," said Warden. In fact, he was a bit worried that some of his team might be getting rather attached to their new flesh.

"Anything else you need?" asked White, although as he reviewed the list of items the Marines had requisitioned from stores or had custom fabricated by the ship's manufactories, he couldn't imagine what more they could possibly want.

But Warden only grinned. "Actually, we were wondering about making a few tweaks to the armour."

"Fine," said White before Warden could begin giving him the details. "Talk to the techs and keep it reasonable. No gold-plated pauldrons or gem-encrusted shin guards." Warden raised his eyebrows, but White just shook his head and sighed. "A story for another day."

"Understood, sir, thank you," said Warden, heading for the door. "I'll let Milton know. No gold-plated Marines."

2

Admiral Morgan's flagship, HMS *Duke of Norfolk* led the fleet into hyperspace, closely followed by Rear Admiral Harper's flagship, HMS *Caernarfon*. The rest of the fleet followed in strict order and within minutes, eight ships of the line and a dozen smaller vessels had left New Bristol with their support ships. Twenty-seven ships in total, making this one of the most formidable fleets ever assembled by the Admiralty.

Ascendant was to remain in reserve with the support ships unless called on to deploy their complement of marines. Rear Admiral Harper had informed Cohen in no uncertain terms that Admiral Morgan had no intention of performing boarding actions and therefore, didn't need a 'glorified troop ship' at the front of the battle formation.

Now Cohen sat in the command chair, face cupped in his hand as he frowned at the monitors. Not that there was anything to see while they flew through hyperspace. All he was really doing was keeping the seat warm. He sighed and picked up his data slate checking the ship's current state for the umpteenth time, before heading to the command suite to brief his executive officer, Lieutenant White and Captain Warden of the Royal Marines.

"You've read the background information?" asked Cohen, taking his seat.

"Yes," said White, "but I had an espresso, if you can call it that, and I'm awake again, sir." Warden seemed too intent on glowering to notice the quip.

"*Ascendant* is to hold back? That doesn't make any sense, does it? Shouldn't we be in the fight?"

Cohen shook his head. "Not our call. The admiral wants us as the back, so that's where we'll be."

"And you're okay with that?" persisted Warden.

"Not my decision to make, Captain," said Cohen, emphasising Warden's rank, "or yours."

"Is there to be a ground assault on U-235," asked Warden, "or will everything be done by bombardment?"

"There's nothing in our orders instructing us to stand by for a drop," said Cohen, "and as yours is the only company in the fleet, I guess that means no assault."

Warden sat very still for a moment, face schooled to immobility.

"Right," he finally said. "Ours is the only company. Is that normal?"

"For Staines, no," answered White. "He likes to have Marines on his ships."

"Admiral Morgan is a different beast," said Cohen, "with different ideas about how to get things done."

Warden shrugged, his face an open book.

"I guess we'll sit this one out."

The command suite on HMS *Duke of Norfolk*'s was the polar opposite of *Ascendant*'s. It sat behind a bright, spacious bridge and unlike the command suite on the former Deathless ship, lived up to its name by consisting of more than one room.

The main room was dominated by a large conference table; a galley and lounge area were on the other side of the corridor that led from the bridge. Then there were several rooms for junior intelligence personnel and smaller meetings.

Admiral Morgan sipped at his coffee as he stood before the bank of monitors that covered one wall of the command suite. He wore a Royal Navy clone with custom command implants, and was clothed in a white shirt and dark trousers, as was standard for officers on general duty.

A hologram of Rear Admiral Harper sat bolt upright at the table. Of course, Harper wasn't necessarily sitting in the command suite onboard *Caernarfon*, it was just easier if virtual avatars sat still in a designated spot. Similarly dressed and wearing the same clone type, Harper was flicking at a data slate.

The main monitors showed the state of each ship in the fleet, their locations relative to *Duke of Norfolk* and their readiness. In the top right, a countdown timer showed *Norfolk* would exit hyperspace in a little over six minutes.

"For the record, do you have any last-minute questions about the plan?" Morgan asked in a bored voice.

"No. Just the same as the last time. Get in, drop the drones, get out."

"Keep an eye out for the Deathless. You can never be too careful," Morgan replied.

"Vigilance never hurts, I suppose," Harper agreed before signing off the conference call.

Morgan didn't take his eyes from the screens. He rubbed at his short-cropped beard and took a turn around the conference table, pausing at the coffee machine for a refill.

Then the counter hit zero, and *Duke of Norfolk* dropped back into normal space. Morgan stood before the monitors, mug half-raised, as he waited for the rest of his fleet to emerge from hyperspace.

For ten seconds, nothing happened. Then HMS *Molesworth* and HMS *Virtue* appeared, followed by HMS *Caernarfon* a moment later. They were exactly on time and each exactly a kilometre away from Morgan's flagship. More ships followed, dropping into position behind *Duke of Norfolk* to form a loose cone a few kilometres wide and deep.

As each ship emerged into real space, the indicator on the board flashed, confirming the reconnection of real-time communications. Morgan counted them all off, then scowled as the last, *Ascendant*, took its place at the very rear of the cone.

A new counter appeared on the top right of the display bank. Ten thousand seconds till the next jump began. Long enough to complete the in-system work and prepare.

On the displays, the ships' statuses began to flash with updates as they prepped for the next hyperspace jump. *Virtue* and *Apollo* began their drone deployment tasks, each sending a dozen autonomous vehicles into the system to scout, monitor and search for anything that might be of interest.

Apollo's drone deployment reports flashed across Morgan's screen. The last deployment was a small fusion-powered wormhole generator to provide a communication link back to Sol once the fleet had departed. The drones began to spread out, their small but efficient solar sails unfurling to recharge their power supplies.

So far, so good.

Then the proximity warning flashed red, and everything went to hell.

Aboard *Ascendant*, Marine X and Colour Sergeant Milton were sitting in the mess watching the forward displays and working through a jug of coffee.

"Not the worst I've ever had," said Ten.

"High praise. What was the worst?"

"Tricky," said Ten, leaning back in his chair. He was quiet for a moment. "Ever been to Epsilon City? Did a job there, way back. A provincial commander went rogue, tried to declare his own kingdom. Started attacking nearby towns."

Ten took another sip as Milton leaned forward, eager to hear the story. He seldom spoke about his past, but his tales were always entertaining.

"The job took longer than expected. We were stuck there for months, cleaning up and chasing the buggers down. The locals had this idea that coffee needed improving. Something about the soil, I think they said. They did all sorts of shitty things to the plant to make it grow in their crappy climate. They couldn't stop tweaking the plant strains."

He snorted and shook his head.

"Never did understand why they didn't grow the bloody plants in greenhouses. Long story short, their beans were evil and their roasters incompetent. The locals loved it but, to me, it tasted like shit. Even this muck is better."

"Morgan has beans from Earth," said Milton, "or so I hear."

Marine X's face went unusually blank at the mention of Morgan.

"You know the admiral?" asked Milton, frowning.

Marine X ignored the question as *Ascendant* dropped out of hyperspace and the status displays switched to show the relative locations of the ships in the fleet. He frowned hard at the screens, coffee forgotten.

"Something wrong?" asked Milton as Marine X moved to stand in front of the displays to get a closer look. She followed his gaze but couldn't see anything unusual on the screens.

"Not sure," he muttered, glancing around the room before his eyes settled back on Milton. He seemed worried, as if some nagging doubt was troubling him, but he couldn't quite work out what it was.

"Why is the fleet so close together?" he asked quietly, staring again at the displays.

"Is that important?" asked Milton.

Ten was silent for a moment then he shrugged and shook his head.

"Nah, probably not, just a feeling, you know? Like when the wind changes or you see something out of the corner of your eye, know what I mean?"

Milton frowned. A disturbed Ten was a strangely worrying thing to see, given his normal carefree disposition. Then the displays updated to show drone deployment had begun. All perfectly normal. Ten shook his head again and sat back down.

"Sorry, a twinge of déjà vu. Nothing to worry about." He picked up his coffee mug and grinned.

Then the proximity warning klaxon sounded.

3

"Talk to me, Captain," barked Morgan as he strode onto *Duke of Norfolk*'s bridge. "What's going on?"

Captain Stevens, commander of *Duke of Norfolk* since it had launched a few months before, glanced up from his command chair as Morgan came onto the bridge.

"A small craft, forty metres long and likely a scout ship, dropped out of hyperspace about thirty seconds ago, sir," said Stevens. The enemy ship hung against the stars, sleek and heavily armed, with a disproportionately large hyperspace engine wrapped around its hull.

Morgan glanced at the floor to ceiling viewscreens that dominated the curved wall of the bridge. The intruder's position was highlighted by a blinking red circle.

"Is that it?"

"Yes, sir," said Stevens.

"A scout? Where did it come from?"

Then the proximity warning again.

"Two corvettes emerging from hyperspace in spread formation," reported Midshipman Todd. "Two hundred kilometres ahead, one fifteen degrees above and the other fifteen degrees below."

"Identification, Ms Todd?" asked Stevens as Morgan, peered over the shoulders of the crew as they worked.

"Deathless, sir," said Todd, putting a close-up of one of the ships onto a large viewscreen. "They aren't using Sol transponders and don't match designs of any friendly governments." The corvette, like the scout ship, was heavily armed, with railgun clusters and missile launch systems along its flank. A bruiser of a ship, ready and looking for trouble.

"Confirmed, unknown vessels are of Deathless origin," said Stevens.

Morgan heard this and rolled his eyes. What else would they be out here? Stevens was already getting on his nerves. He would like nothing more than to replace the man. If it weren't for Royal Navy protocol, he would already have done so.

"Take us to action stations, Ms Todd," Stevens ordered.

"Belay that order," said Morgan, head whipping around. "Send my orders to the fleet to stand our ground. We will remain stationary as if nothing had happened, as per my plan for an unexpected encounter. We will not provoke an incident."

Stevens frowned at him. "Sir? I understood we were to seek out the enemy and we have some right here. Shouldn't we engage them immediately?"

"Don't forget the bigger picture, Captain, you have your orders," said Morgan, as he took the chair next to Stevens. "Let's just see what they do before we respond rashly."

"Order relayed to the fleet, sir," said Todd.

"I'm not sure I follow, sir," said Stevens, lowering his voice so that only Admiral Morgan could hear. "What bigger picture?"

Morgan ignored him as his data slate pinged with alerts. It seemed that Stevens wasn't the only captain who couldn't visualise the theatre of operations. If he'd been able to pick his own people, this would all be so much easier. Instead, he had to make do with the ships the admiralty had sent. Annoyed, he sent a templated reply to each message to reiterate the order to hold fire.

"More hyperspace points opening," said Todd as part of the main viewscreen switched to show first one huge ship dropping into normal space, then more. "Three more coming – no five, no nine!"

"Sir, please!" hissed Stevens, leaning over to speak to Morgan. "We must go to action stations and order the fleet to attack. We're sitting ducks!"

"A little patience, if you please, Mr Stevens," said Morgan with an air of infinite wisdom and calm. "I know what I'm doing."

On the display, the Deathless ships accelerated rapidly towards *Duke of Norfolk,* racing to close the gap and bring the fleet into weapons range.

"They're coming in from all angles," warned Midshipman Rees.

"Sir, we need to manoeuvre," pressed Stevens. "We have to break out before it's too late."

"Incoming signal from *Virtue,*" reported Todd. Stevens frowned in frustration as Admiral Morgan's attention whipped across the bridge.

"To my screen only, Ms Todd," said Morgan. He turned to his screen as the message was decrypted and displayed.

<*Virtue* stands ready to attack. Request permission to engage the enemy> sent Captain Gladys Ainwright, commander of HMS *Virtue*.

<Await my signal>

<We have hostile ships within fifteen kilometres> sent Ainwright. <Request permission to engage>

<Permission denied. Await orders> replied Morgan, frowning as he typed out the message. Maybe Ainwright wasn't the stalwart and reliable commander he had thought.

"Three scout ships will pass within four thousand metres in thirty seconds on their current course," reported Rees.

Morgan ignored the stares from around the bridge, waiting for the perfect moment to launch his plan. He raised one hand, a finger pointed into the air.

"Action stations," he said solemnly, "take us forward." He dropped his arm and pointed at the enemy fleet, "Engage!"

～

Warden sat beside Captain Cohen on the bridge of *Ascendant*, waiting. His HUD told him it had been only a few minutes, but he'd never sat so long under the gaze of an enemy. It was distinctly uncomfortable. The viewscreen showed the Deathless vessels approaching quickly, their trajectories lit in red on the tactical display, probable targets picked out in blue.

He leaned toward Cohen. "Why we aren't attacking, sir? They're getting a lot closer, and I thought you'd want us suited up by now."

Cohen gave him a puzzled frown, seemingly surprised that anyone would even ask. "Our orders are to remain here until Admiral Morgan tells us to engage. The forward portions of the fleet will engage the enemy while we remain in reserve."

"Are you pulling my leg? *Ascendant* just waits? That's it?"

"No, Captain, I am not pulling your leg. Now if you don't mind, I have a ship to command."

This is nuts, thought Warden.

<Heads up, Milton. The admiral has put *Ascendant* in reserve. Nothing moves without a direct order. Get the company suited and booted, just in case the Jacks need help>

<Help with what, sir?>

<No idea. Breaches. Boarding actions. Torpedoes, maybe. Just be ready>

<Do the Navy know it's harder to hit a moving target?>

<I'm not sure they do, Colour. I'm not sure they do>

Ten strutted confidently into the battery, a stream of bullshit ready to roll over the occupants if they challenged him. He was almost disappointed to find the loading bay and secondary fire control room were empty.

He checked the toilet for good measure. No sign of the weapons crew at all. In theory, the railgun battery didn't need to be manned, but it still that seemed strange.

Never one to look a gift horse in the mouth, he pulled a cold can of cider from the fridge, grabbed a chocolate bar and sat down at the fire console.

These Navy boys really do have the good life, he thought, as he swigged the booze and took a bite of the Uranus bar, which fortunately didn't taste as bad as it sounded.

"Now then, what do we have here?" he muttered to himself as he surveyed the battle displayed on the viewscreen above the console. He chewed his bottom lip as he looked at potential targets.

"Where do you think you're going?" he mused as he tapped a couple of icons. "Three scout ships, eh?"

<Standing by to prevent hull breaches, sir. Do we have permission to prevent breaches from becoming a problem on our own cognisance, or do we need authorisation from Captain Cohen?> he sent to Warden.

<Yes, Marine X, you may act as expected of you. No need to ask>

<Roger that, sir, just making sure I dot and cross. Out>

"Permission granted," he muttered with a slight smile.

"I am the very model of a modern Major-General," he mumbled as he picked his targets, worked out a firing solution, and fired.

"I understand equations, both the simple and quadratical, you Deathless bastards," he intoned with satisfaction as the leading edge of the barrage struck the first of the scout ships.

"What the hell just happened?" demanded Cohen as the tactical display updated.

"Er. The forward railgun batteries fired, sir," said MacCaibe. "two scout ships destroyed, one crippled, before they could fire on the fleet."

"I didn't order that. We have strict instructions not to engage the enemy. Which of you fired?"

"It didn't come from the bridge, sir. The command came from the secondary fire console in the forward battery itself."

"Show me the feed for the battery," Cohen snapped. When he saw the Marine in power armour sitting at the console and swigging from a can, he heard Warden sigh audibly.

"What's the meaning of this, Captain?"

"It would appear Marine X has engaged the enemy," Warden replied, stony-faced.

"Get him up here, on the double, Captain."

~

"Why did you open fire, Marine X? Our orders were to stand by!"

"When a squadron of enemy vessels dive through the fleet at high speed with weapons primed and targets locked to target a support ship, I figure they aren't out collecting donations for the Natural History Museum," Marine X growled back at him.

Cohen's eyes bulged as he bellowed, "Captain Warden, confine this man to await court martial!"

Marine X cocked his head, expression grim. "The most recent Articles of War grant a Royal Marine the authority to take command of an unmanned Royal Navy gun battery with no assigned target if they identify an enemy vessel and deem it a threat to the fleet. I identified three vessels and I deemed."

Cohen could feel his face flushing red, "And another thing, you were drinking on duty!"

"Ah, well, sir, there you've got me. I did indeed have two units of apple-based alcohol. You can keelhaul me at your convenience. But I was obligated to defend the fleet, Captain Cohen. You can charge me for it, but the court martial will support my actions." Without waiting to be dismissed, he snapped a salute and left the bridge.

Cohen rounded on Warden. "We'll discuss this later, Captain."

~

arden's unease was growing, and he squirmed in his seat.

"Control yourself, Captain," said Cohen, not looking away from the main viewscreen. "This is how these things are done."

"But we're sitting ducks!" he snapped.

"Despite the cavalier actions of your Penal Marine, *Ascendant* will await orders before moving from our assigned position."

"Still?" said Warden incredulously. As a Marine used to a degree of freedom to act, the Navy's rigid adherence to orders was alien to him, especially when Morgan's orders made no sense.

"New orders," said Cohen, glancing at his slate. "Open fire, Mr MacCaibe."

"Yes, sir," said MacCaibe, calmly professional. "Railguns firing now, all batteries. Missiles away, drone weapon platforms deployed." The relief on the bridge was almost palpable.

Then *Apollo*'s status indicator went grey.

"What the hell was that?" snapped Cohen, staring at the display. One moment *Apollo* had been part of the fleet, firing on the enemy as expected. And then it was gone. Part of the viewscreen zoomed in to focus on the ailing ship as it tumbled, dark and drifting, across space.

"It's an ambush," Warden said at a volume perilously close to shouting, "and we're right where they want us to be."

"Patience, Captain," said Cohen, although his own nerves were starting to fray a little. "I'm sure the admiral knows what he's doing."

Warden was pretty sure that the admiral didn't have a fucking clue, and he damned sure as mustard didn't have any experience. No-one did. But there were limits to what he could say, even now, so he bit his lip and kept his own counsel.

Cohen tapped his fingers on the arm of his chair, leaning forward despite himself, as if he would somehow see the viewscreens more clearly. His slate pinged with new orders from the admiral. *Finally*, he thought.

"We have orders," Cohen announced, "take us forward. Ten-second burn on the main engines, full power please, Miss Martin."

"Aye, sir, laying in. Five seconds." A warning klaxon sounded.

"Keep firing, Mr MacCaibe," said White, "target anything we have a clear shot at."

"Aye, sir. There's nae shortage of the wee buggers."

Warden looked around, wondering if he was the only sane person on the bridge. The fleet was moving, but slowly, far too slowly and far too late.

Then the engines fired, driving *Ascendant* forward and keeping pace with the support ships in the centre of the fleet.

Warden watched, a sick feeling in his stomach. Morgan was taking the entire fleet forward in a completely predictable manoeuvre.

"Turn around," Warden suggested. "Break formation, get us out of here before–"

There was a flash on the forward viewscreens and HMS *Virtue*'s status indicator went from green to grey.

"What the hell was that?" asked Warden, confused.

"Looks like *Virtue* exploded," muttered Cohen, staring at the status updates and trying to make sense of the barrage of data.

"Get us out of here," implored Warden, "back off, circle around, come at them again from a different angle. This is an ambush," he repeated, "we're in the kill zone, right where they want us, and the longer we stay here, the worse it's going to get."

Cohen threw an angry glance at him, and it was clear he wasn't happy with either Warden or the admiral's orders.

"Be quiet, Captain. That's an order."

Warden seethed and reached for his data slate. The Navy might like blundering around in the space the enemy had chosen for their ambush, but he was damned if he was doing nothing. He tapped out a quick message to Milton.

<Ambushed. Prep for incoming>

He snorted to himself. Milton didn't need orders in a situation like this, and what the hell did he expect her to do anyway? He shook his head.

<Acknowledged> came the terse response. Warden put the slate away. He'd done what he could for his team, however little that

might be, and now he could only watch as events unfolded before him.

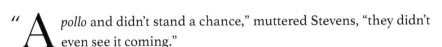

"*A* pollo and didn't stand a chance," muttered Stevens, "they didn't even see it coming."

"Press the attack, Captain," said Morgan calmly, sending more orders to the fleet. "Take us forward; let's see what else they have." The admiral looked as if the loss of his second ship was nothing more than a minor inconvenience.

Stevens nodded and took a deep breath, impressed by Morgan's self-control. "Get us moving, Mr Church, full power to the engines, thirty-second burst."

"Aye, sir," said Church initiating the manoeuvre as the high-G warning sounded.

"*Molesworth* has been hit," said Lieutenant Sturgis. "She's falling behind, engines damaged."

"More incoming ships," said Barnes as warnings flashed across the screens.

Morgan's slate pinged with a direct message from Captain Soberton, commander of *Molesworth*.

<We're drifting. Main engines dead, but we have thrusters and hyperspace ability. Request permission to withdraw and return to New Bristol>

<Request denied> replied Morgan, tapping furiously at his slate. <Victory is close. Stand and fight>

<Weapons offline, unable to comply. *Molesworth* returning to New Bristol>

<NEGATIVE> sent Morgan. <Remain on station, close with the enemy and engage>

<Impossible> came the reply from *Molesworth*. Morgan thumped his fist against the arm of his chair. <Hyperspace course laid in, departing in twenty seconds>

<I'll see you court-martialled for this> threatened Morgan.

<Gladly, Admiral. *Molesworth* out>

"Where's *Molesworth*?" Morgan shouted. "Show me what damage she's taken."

"Aye, sir," said Todd. "On screen now." The main display switched to show a close-up of *Molesworth*, which was clearly badly damaged and leaking atmosphere from a dozen or more holes in its flank.

Morgan ignored the barrage of incoming messages on his data slate, "Comms, fleet-wide broadcast. Admiral Morgan expects every ship to do their duty. The Royal Navy does not retreat and does not surrender!" He stuck his chin out proudly but Steven's sloppy crew of layabouts gave his rousing speech no recognition.

Then there was a great flash of light from *Molesworth* and all eyes turned to the zoomed-in view on the main screen.

"What was that?" snapped Morgan.

"Liquid oxygen release on *Molesworth*, sir," said Todd as she reviewed the video. A much larger flash followed and for a moment the image went flat white. When they could see again, *Molesworth* was exactly where she had been, still venting plumes of burning gas, still tumbling through space.

<Mayday, mayday> came the plea from *Molesworth*. <Main power lost. Require immediate assistance>

<Confirm your status, *Molesworth*> sent Morgan, his eyebrow twitching as he watched the fleet being torn to shreds.

<Abandoning ship. *Molesworth* is lost>

Molesworth's life pods launched, barely a dozen of them as her decimated crew fled their stricken ship.

4

The alarms sounded continuously now, too frequent and too close to separate, as more enemy vessels appeared.

Morgan watched as the crew of HMS *Duke of Norfolk* struggled to cope with the rate of enemy fire and the overwhelming numbers of craft that were appearing on all sides. Then he began tapping out new orders.

The engines kicked in and *Norfolk* shot forward, pressing the crew back into their seats. Then there was a series of bangs and the engines failed.

"Impacts detected," said Barnes, voice rising as she watched the reports. "Multiple impacts across the starboard flank. Hull breaches," she paused, searching for a way to explain the magnitude of the damage, "everywhere."

"Engines offline," said Todd unnecessarily, "some sort of leak in the fuel system."

"Engineering," yelled Stevens over the impact and hull breach alarms, "what's going on?"

A bright flash of light from the main displays rolled quickly across the bridge and was gone.

"What was that?" shouted Lieutenant Sturgis, scrabbling around for news.

"HMS *Virtue*," muttered Morgan, his frown deepening as his fleet disintegrated around him. A quarter of his ships now showed amber or grey on the status monitor and all were engaged. He flicked at his slate, ordering the fleet to press forward and shoot their way free from the trap.

"*Stingray* and *Colossus* are gone," said Church numbly. There was another flash of light, smaller this time but still bright.

"What was that?"

"Where is *Molesworth*?"

"Wormhole comms system inactive."

"Are we still firing?"

"Fire suppression systems activated."

"Atmosphere venting on lower decks, casualties unknown."

"Starboard sensor arrays damaged. Multiple incoming contacts. Brace for impact."

"Engines damaged, unrecoverable."

"Aft weapons bank offline. Forward weapons bank inoperable. Starboard railguns overheating."

"Hyperspace engine shielding punctured, status critical."

The ship creaked as another wave of projectiles washed over the hull.

"Multiple hull breaches, internal doors closed and sealed."

"Hyperspace engine offline," murmured a horrified Church. He looked round at Morgan, fear obvious on his face. Without the hyperspace engine, there was no way to escape the ambush.

Then there was a rumbling explosion from somewhere beneath the bridge. The floor bucked as shockwaves blasted through the ship.

"Artificial gravity failing," said Sturgis redundantly as the bridge crew felt themselves suddenly become weightless.

Morgan still sat serenely in his chair as the disaster unfolded. Ship after ship reported incoming fire, then hull breaches and failures. Status indicators went orange, then red or grey as ships were crippled, abandoned or destroyed. Morgan sent orders to each of his captains, designating targets amongst the swarm of enemy vessels that flashed across his view.

"*Hawk* has been abandoned."

The display shifted to show a view of the support ship, HMS *Hawk*. Along its length, escape pod doors had opened, and *Norfolk's* bridge crew watched helplessly as launch rockets flared. Only a handful of pods left their tubes.

"Get the engines back online," shouted Morgan over the din, abruptly engaged in the drama, "and get those bloody alarms switched off."

The alarms suddenly stopped as Todd punched at the controls. The silence was unsettling.

"Negative on the engines," came a voice across the comms. "Engineering is down, the whole area is offline. Looks like a hull breach. Everyone behind the blast door is dead."

More groans swept across the bridge.

"Target those vessels," shouted Morgan, pointing at the main display where a small squadron of new Deathless scout ships had appeared only four thousand metres from *Norfolk*. "Hit them with everything we have."

"Targeting," said Barnes, running on automatic, hands moving swiftly over the controls, but her mind elsewhere. "Firing."

There was a pause.

"Weapons inoperable. The railguns are all offline, missile systems unresponsive." Barnes turned in her seat to look at Stevens. "What do we do, sir?"

"Switch Shard Storm to fully autonomous operation," said Stevens, "and let's hope it's as good as everyone says."

"Shard Storm operating at ten per cent capacity," reported Ellis. "Not likely to be very effective now," he went on, voice bitter.

There was another rumbling explosion, deep in the heart of the ship, and the lights flickered. Some of the monitors failed. Then the main lights went off and the bridge was suddenly cast into total darkness. Someone yelled. Stevens shouted for light, then the emergency power kicked in, bathing the bridge in a dim red glow.

Stevens looked around, appalled at the scale of the disaster. Then he unstrapped himself from his seat and gave the only order left to him.

"All hands on deck," he whispered, triggering the final klaxon, "abandon ship."

The situation was deteriorating. The fleet moved forward as ordered by Admiral Morgan and the Deathless pressed their attack. Again and again, the Deathless vessels dove through the fleet, firing at close range and escaping unharmed. Outnumbered, outgunned and clearly outmanoeuvred, the Navy fought hard but the odds, even to Warden's inexperienced eyes, looked hopeless.

Warden watched in dismay as Cohen and White strove to follow the admiral's orders and play their part in his plan. He was struggling to work out exactly what that plan might be, but Cohen seemed ready to follow orders and issue his own in line with the admiral's, regardless of the tactical realities. He shook his head. From the Marines' perspective, none of this made any sense.

"Railgun ammunition down to twenty-two per cent. Exhaustion in," MacCaibe peered at his monitors with disbelieving eyes, "forty-five seconds."

"Keep firing, Mr MacCaibe," ordered Cohen, although the midshipman had been targeting every enemy ship he could find and firing continuously, for all the good it was doing.

"Aye aye, sir," said a strained MacCaibe, hands flashing across the controls. The railguns were running hot, close to their operational maximum. Any hotter and their performance would be seriously degraded.

"Let's get the automated manufacturing plants running, Mr White," said Cohen.

"Yes, sir, although they can't do much with everything locked down to action stations."

Ahead, a support ship split in half as if a giant sword had cleaved it down the middle. Warden couldn't see what had done the damage, but it looked like the ship had just come unstitched.

The two halves tumbled apart, each spewing supplies and bodies into the vacuum. One part was burning as liquid oxygen splashed across the hot steel. An explosion tore at the dismembered vessel, punching new holes in her hull and blasting debris across the fleet.

Then the status indicators for *Duke of Norfolk* flashed orange. Cohen saw it and shivered.

"Just keep shooting," he said, "and let's get the missiles underway as well. No point keeping them in stores, they won't do us any good there."

"Aye, sir," said MacCaibe. He triggered a broadside of missiles towards the Deathless capital ship, not that he expected it to do any good. "Spread burst against the scout ships," he muttered under his breath, "another against those buggers down there, and let's paint these little chappies as well."

MacCaibe worked fast, marking targets for the computer to launch against as soon as their trajectories brought them within range. *Ascendant* ground forward, weapons firing on all sides as around them space filled with the detritus of battle.

The strategic overview now showed the fleet finally beginning to break up, but from where Warden sat, it looked like the Deathless were simply mopping up. More enemy ships had appeared, and they dove through the Royal Navy's fleet, firing at will and almost unopposed.

Warden couldn't take his eyes from *Norfolk*, now shown in one corner of the display, as internal explosions made the hull shudder and buckle. The ship was clearly stricken, no threat to anyone, and yet still the Deathless pounded it.

Norfolk's indicator went from orange to grey. For a few seconds, nothing happened. Then an escape pod launched from *Norfolk*, and another, then a handful more until the pods were streaming away.

Cohen poked at his slate as he tried to make contact with Admiral Morgan or Rear Admiral Harper. He tried the other ships, but still received no answer.

"Morgan's dead," said Warden. "He's dead, and we're dead as well if we stay here much longer. We have to leave before –" said Warden.

"Shut up!" snapped Cohen, his temper finally breaking. He rounded on Warden, finger raised.

"Incoming," shouted MacCaibe, voice raised in panic. "Brace for –"

They felt the impacts before MacCaibe could finish. His words were drowned out by the titanic noise of multiple projectiles, both solid rounds and explosive, tearing into *Ascendant*.

And, just like that, the world shifted.

The emergency power came on almost immediately, casting a grim red light across the bridge. The klaxons were mercifully silent, although whether through action or damage was unclear. The familiar background whine of the life support system, usually ever-present, was gone.

Warden could hear his own breathing, and he could hear the bridge crew working to re-establish control. The rest of the ship was silent.

"Like a tomb," he muttered.

"Which it will quickly become," said Cohen harshly, "if we don't get this under control."

"Status report, Mr MacCaibe," said White, calm despite everything.

"Nothing, sir," said MacCaibe, his voice near hysterical. "Nothing at all. Everything's off. We're blind!"

"Get a grip, Mr MacCaibe," said Cohen, "and start solving the problems."

MacCaibe nodded and took a few deep breaths. Then he started working through the troubleshooting and emergency procedures that had been drilled into them during countless simulations at the academy.

"That goes for the rest of you too," said Cohen, raising his voice.

"Focus on the job in front of you, get me information, bring your systems back online." The bridge was silent. Cohen clapped his hands together. "Move, people."

The crew snapped out of their shock and began to work. Slowly, carefully, they investigated their areas.

Cohen turned to Warden, who was still sitting in his chair, hands locked to the arms.

"Not a word," he hissed. Warden nodded. In the dim red light, Cohen looked stressed, almost manic.

"Passive sensors are online, sir," reported Midshipman Wood at the communications desk, "but all the active sensors are down, and the processors are still rebooting. We'll know more in," he checked the countdown timer, "about fifteen seconds."

"Weapons control systems offline," said MacCaibe as he poked the reboot buttons, hoping for any sort of response. He shook his head. It was hopeless. "About as much use as a chocolate teaspoon, sir. We need to get to Engineering."

"Internal comms are down," said Wood, "and so are the sensors. Can't tell if there's anything still working outside the bridge."

Or alive, thought Warden, keeping it to himself.

"Processors coming up, configured for minimal power use," said Wood finally.

"Engines are dead," said Midshipman Martin, her voice quieter than normal. "No diagnostics."

"Hyperspace drive remains operable, sir," reported Midshipman Jackson. A rare piece of good news. "But the guidance system is offline."

A monitor flickered awake in the main display as power trickled back from somewhere. It showed a cut-down strategic overview with the limited information available from the remaining sensors.

"Get the rest of it back, Wood," snapped Cohen. "We need more than just flashes and snippets."

Warden peered at the monitor, but it was too far away for him to see the details. He pulled out his data slate and hoped the comms were working. "Come on," he muttered as he poked at the screen. Then he had it, the overview.

"Oh shit," he said, louder than he'd intended. Cohen's head snapped round, and Warden wordlessly passed over the slate.

"Where's the fleet gone?" murmured Cohen, not quite understanding what he was seeing.

"It hasn't," muttered Warden, "it's right where it was."

And then Cohen saw it. The ship status reports were blank, lost when the external comms system had failed, but the passive sensors told the story. The fleet had ceased to exist.

"External comms coming back online," said Wood.

"–advised." A sudden noise blared over the bridge speakers.

"That's external, sir," clarified Wood.

"Message repeats. This is HMS *Palmerston*. If you receive this message, please respond. We are in urgent need of assistance, and our immediate vicinity remains hostile. Discretion is advised."

"Get the channel open, Wood," said Cohen. The midshipman flicked at his controls then turned to Cohen and nodded.

"This is *Ascendant*. What is your situation, *Palmerston*?"

"*Ascendant*? Thank fuck for that. We have casualties, but we're mostly airtight. Life support is pretty much working, and we have manoeuvring thrusters. Everything else is offline. You?"

Cohen ground his teeth.

"Comms," he said, stating the completely obvious, "probably hyperspace capability."

"That's it?" said whoever was crewing *Palmerston*. "Okay, it's better than nothing. Hang on; we're coming to you. Can you get your hanger doors open?"

"Hanger doors?"

"The doors to your hanger," said *Palmerston* with admirable self-control, "can you open them to allow us to dock?"

"What?"

"Because we have hyperspace capability, sir," said White, leaning over. "We can get them out of here."

"Never mind, *Ascendant*. We're on our way. Course is laid in, and the thrusters are firing. Get your doors open in about thirty seconds, or we'll be knocking them down."

"Wait, what?" shouted Cohen, looking around.

"*Palmerston* out."

"Shit," muttered Cohen.

"Internal comms are still offline," said Wood, "but the processors are bringing some of the sensors back online."

"Can we open the hanger doors?"

The strategic overview flashed as *Palmerston* was highlighted and its new course flashed onto the display.

"There's no atmosphere in the hanger, sir," reported Wood.

"Twenty seconds to impact," said Martin.

"Fuck," muttered Cohen. Then he pulled himself together. "Get the hangar doors open, Mr Wood. And let's make sure they are at least facing toward *Palmerston*, Miss Martin."

"Aye, sir, calculating now." Martin's hands flashed across the controls. "Thrusters firing, manoeuvring only, short bursts."

"*Palmerston*'s coming in faster than a greased whippet," said MacCaibe, tracking the gunboat as it crossed the last few kilometres.

"Hangar doors are open," said Wood, hardly daring to believe the monitors. Then he squinted. "Or they might be."

"What? Are they open or aren't they, Mr Wood?" said, White.

Wood shrugged hopelessly. "Don't know, sir. Might be open. Might be damaged sensors. Can't even be sure that part of the ship is still attached."

"Holding steady," said Martin, "manoeuvring successful." She switched monitors and yelped, "They're almost on us."

"Close the doors as soon as they're in, Mr Wood," said White, still pushing at the dead controls of his own monitors, trying to find something that would tell him what was going on.

"Incoming," said MacCaibe. "Looks like the Deathless have noticed we're still moving."

There was a long rumbling bang that reverberated around the ship, as if a rake had been dragged across a huge steel container.

"That was *Palmerston*," reported Wood. "They've, er, landed."

"Then get the doors closed, Mr Wood," said White.

"Lay in a course to New Bristol, Mr Jackson," said Cohen. "Take us home."

"Negative, sir, guidance computers are still offline. They don't seem to be restarting. We can engage the hyperspace engine, but until the navigation computers can be repaired, we won't know which system we're heading to. I'll be able to give you an estimate in about thirty minutes if I put some data into my slate."

Cohen cursed in frustration. An unguided hyperspace trip could leave them travelling for far longer than usual before they reached the next system. You couldn't simply make a U-turn in hyperspace, after all. The ship would travel in the general direction of 'forward', but they wouldn't know if that was taking them directly at a nearby system or fifty degrees away from anything closer than ten light years. They wouldn't be worrying about that if they didn't go somewhere, though.

"Fifteen seconds to impact," said MacCaibe. "Brace yourselves."

"Hanger door probably closed," said Wood. "*Palmerston* probably sort of secure."

"That's very vague, Mr Wood," snapped White.

"Best I can do, sir. Most of the sensors are shot, and even the internal video in the hold is out," Wood said apologetically.

"Brace for multiple impacts," said MacCaibe, hands locked to the arms of his chair.

"Punch it, Ms Martin," ordered Cohen.

Martin, her hand already over the control, activated the hyperspace engine.

Ascendant vanished.

5

scendant flitted through hyperspace, carrying the crew away from the ambush. Klaxons screamed, demanding attention as the ship shook and creaked.

"Everyone okay?" asked a shaken Cohen. There was a murmured chorus of confirmations from around the bridge. "Then let's work on the damage reports."

The primary displays were still off but one small part, which had shown the strategic overview, now flashed a 'hyperspace travel' notice. Ordinarily the bridge was bright and well lit, but now it was dark and ominously shadowed. The only light at all came from the sparse low-power emergency system, accompanied by the angry red glows of the warnings that flashed across the remaining screens.

"Hyperspace drive working correctly," said Martin.

But that much was obvious. *Ascendant* had left real space behind and with it the immediate threat from the Deathless vessels. There was a pause, a long moment of silence while Cohen waited for more reports.

"Well?" he snapped, looking around the bridge. "Anything else?"

"Multiple hull breaches I think, sir," reported MacCaibe. "Er, but sensors are as stable as a newborn lamb, so I can't tell how many or where."

"But we're losing atmosphere? Mr MacCaibe," said White when he didn't receive an answer, "are we losing atmosphere?"

MacCaibe turned to look at White and shook his head. "I don't know, sir. The sensors aren't reporting," he said in a small voice.

"So what do we know? Come on, people, start working the problem," said White, stealing a worried glance at Cohen. The commander was sitting back in his chair, face pale as he poked at his data slate. "Gravity is off, power is limited, sensors aren't working," he summarised, "but what else?"

"Wormhole communicator has gone, sir," said Wood at the communications desk.

"Gone?" queried White. "What do you mean 'gone'?"

"No response to diagnostic requests, sir, although the hardened systems that connect the bridge and the wormhole communicator appear to be functioning. It looks like the WC itself has been destroyed."

"Shit," muttered White, entirely without irony.

"Internal comms are down, sir. There's no way to know what's happening in the rest of the ship," reported Midshipman Wood. "Looks like life support is offline, but that might affect only the bridge."

Then there was a metallic banging on the door as if someone were requesting entry, the sound ringing loudly across the bridge.

"All the power's being routed to the hyperspace engine, sir," said Wood. "There's nothing left to open the doors."

"Great," muttered White, shaking his head.

"Pity we didn't leave sooner," murmured Warden. White shot him a look but didn't say anything.

Then the knocking came again, longer this time and in a recognisable rhythm.

"Morse code," muttered Wood. "A - N - Y - O - N - E - A - L - I - V - E. Anyone alive." She looked at White. "They don't know if we're alive, sir."

"I get that," snapped White, releasing his straps and pushing himself out of his chair. He floated over to the door, his zero-G training coming back to him in a rush. He pulled out a multi-tool from his belt and steadied himself against the door, waving for quiet. He couldn't hear anything at all through the thick door, but that wasn't surprising. He began tapping out code.

"A - L - L - A - L - I - V - E - W - I - L - L - O - P - E - N - D - O -" he began, positioning himself so that he could reach the door's manual controls.

A rapid and insistent banging from the other side interrupted his careful tapping.

"B - R - E - A - C - H - A - W - A - I - T - O - R - D - E - R - S."

White stared at the door for a moment then carefully removed his hand from the lever. He glanced at the pressure indicator by the handle and saw that it was showing a big red cross, indicating an absence of atmosphere on the other side of the door. He stared at it for a moment, appalled that he had forgotten to check it – a schoolboy error. He tapped an acknowledgement, slipped his multi-tool back into its pocket, and pushed himself away from the door.

"I guess we stay here for now," he muttered. He looked at Cohen, still strapped in his command chair and staring blankly at the main display. "Are you okay, sir?" he asked quietly, floating over so that the two men could speak privately.

Cohen's head snapped up and, he looked round at White. For a moment, he said nothing, then he took a deep breath.

"I am fine, XO, thank you," he surveyed the bridge, taking in the crew's inactivity as they all watched from their seats. "Hull breaches, dead sensors, life support offline, power shortages, failed internal comms," he said, summarising the situation. "Anything else?"

"Isn't that enough?" asked White. But Cohen was back on top of things now, and he just raised an eyebrow. "Yes, sir, that's everything we know of so far," said White.

"Good," said Cohen, releasing his seatbelt, "then we're still afloat. All hands to the pumps, people. We might not be able to leave the bridge, but let's at least do what we can to quantify the damage."

Goodwin had begun fighting her way into a suit as soon as Colour Sergeant Milton had relayed Warden's warning. She, Milton and a dozen others who had been close to the stores had moved quickly to climb into the bulky outfits.

Suited and booted, they had spent an anxious few minutes waiting to see what would happen. Then the first projectiles had ripped into *Ascendant,* and it was suddenly apparent what was going on.

"Helmets," Milton had shouted, even as she reached for her own. As the ship shuddered and groaned around then, the Marines struggled into their helmets and checked each other's suits for fit and function.

"Comms check," ordered Milton, and the Marines counted off. Their names appeared in the HUD of Milton's suit.

Then the lights went off and the gravity failed.

"Whoa," said Goodwin, grabbing a strap to halt her motion. "What's going on?"

"Nothing good," snapped Milton. "Strap in, stay quiet." The emergency lights flicked on, dim and red.

"Internal comms are offline," said Goodwin, although that was obvious to everyone since their suit HUDs were warning of connection failures. The suits themselves had a mesh network feature allowing their wearers to communicate without needing to route connections through the ship's systems.

The Marines looked at each other in the glow of the emergency lamps. With nothing to do but wait, they sat and waited as the ship shook and grumbled around them.

Finally, after what seemed like hours but was actually only a couple of minutes, there was a long-drawn-out rumbling bang followed quickly by the familiar tug that signalled the shift to hyperspace.

Milton waited a moment longer to see if anything else was going to change, then she unstrapped.

"Time to work for a living, people," she said, pushing away from her seat and making for the door. She pulled the lever and braced a foot against the door to open the door. Then she tugged herself forward to float through the doorway, kicking off against the frame to give herself just a little momentum. The passageway beyond the door was dark, and the head torches on her helmet came on automatically to compensate.

"Work in pairs, stay in touch, find out what's going on, and make a note of any problems you find. And remember, you may be the only ones in suits, so take care opening doors, especially if the pressure indicators show there's no atmosphere in the area beyond." She held her position as the Marines floated out into the corridor and dispersed into the ship. "Goodwin, you're with me. We're going to find the captain."

"That's it, Colour, all good," said Goodwin, pushing back from the corridor wall. It seemed that much of the ship was still airtight, but the corridor that led to the bridge had been punctured several times, and the surrounding chambers were a mess.

Between them, Goodwin and Milton had found and patched seven holes, two of which led directly to the vacuum of space.

They had re-pressurised several rooms already, and now Milton hit the button to flood the corridor with air. A plume of gas shot soundlessly into the room, and the atmosphere quickly thickened until the pressure indicators showed a good level.

"That's it, three-quarters atmosphere," said Goodwin, checking the suit's readout. "Enough to be going on with."

"Right, let's get this door open," said Milton, pushing gently off the wall to float down the corridor. She stopped outside the bridge, checked the pressure indicator in the door, then pulled the lever to force the door to open. It slid smoothly open in a hiss of air as the pressures equalised.

Milton floated into the bridge and looked around, checking that everyone was in good shape. Then she removed her helmet.

"Milton," said a relieved Warden, floating upside down and grinning at her. "It's good to see you. Was that you tapping Morse code on the door?"

"Yes, sir. It was a bit fresh out there, didn't think you'd want to try it. We've patched a few holes, but the ship's riddled, and we didn't do much more than come straight here."

"Casualties?" asked Warden, dreading the answer.

"We don't know, sir, sorry. There were a dozen of us close enough to the stores to suit up after your message. Goodwin and I have found a score of bodies or more, all killed by sudden atmosphere failure, but the rest of the team are still searching." She glanced up at Lieutenant Commander Cohen and the XO who were floating in to listen. "It's bad, sir. Very bad."

A*scendant's* main bay was a mess. From where Cohen and White floated in the observation room above the bay, the damage done by *Palmerston's* arrival was clear.

"We're not going to get back our deposit," muttered White as he looked down at the huge scars of torn metal where the gunboat had scraped and bounced its way into the bay. The main doors seemed to have closed correctly, despite what the sensors had shown on the bridge. "Do you think it's airtight?"

Cohen shrugged. There was no way to know without flooding the chamber with air, and they didn't have enough left that they could take the risk. They wouldn't be able to test it until full life-support systems were back online and they could generate new atmosphere.

"Suits, I think," said Cohen, heading for the airlock. They grunted their way into the environmental suits and cycled through the airlock into the main bay. *Palmerston* sat against the far wall, covering half the bay but twisted over and stacked against the bulkhead. Even from across the bay, they could see the puncture wounds in the side of the vessel, the ones that had incapacitated *Palmerston*'s main engines and weapon systems.

"She's seen as much action as *Ascendant*," said Cohen as they pushed off from the airlock door and floated across the bay. "And looks like she's taken about as much damage. Can you imagine going to war in something as small as this? It's not even as big as the fabricator ship the Deathless had in here."

Palmerston's external airlock door appeared to be intact, so Cohen triggered the opening mechanism. The door slid smoothly open to expose the small chamber of the airlock.

"Snug," said White as they pushed their way in. The door closed behind them, and the airlock was flooded with air. Cohen removed his helmet as the inner door opened.

"Are you Cohen?" asked a suspicious voice from the corridor beyond the inner door. Cohen turned to see a pistol being pointed at him. He froze, hands in front of him, still holding his suit's helmet.

"I am. Lieutenant Commander Alistair Cohen," he said, suddenly aware that he was still wearing a Deathless clone. "This is my XO, Lieutenant Tim White."

"Those aren't standard clones," said the voice. "How do I know you're human?"

"It's a long story," said White, removing his own helmet. "How about you let us in and we talk about it over a cup of tea?"

The figure in the corridor stared at them for a long moment, then the gun disappeared, and it waved them through.

"Okay, can't imagine an alien asking for tea. Come on in. I think we lost the last of our tea in the cross-fire," the voice said apologetically, "but we might find you a shot of rum, if that'll do instead?"

"Maybe later," said Cohen. "Who's in command here?"

"Sub Lieutenant Corn, sir, at your service." Corn held out her hand and Cohen tried to shake it – an awkward manoeuvre since they were inverted. "Let me help out, sir," said Corn, flipping herself around so that she was the right way up from Cohen's perspective. "Welcome aboard *Palmerston*, sir."

"Is this your ship, Corn?" asked White.

"No, sir, but Lieutenant Ruskin was killed during the opening exchange. Bit of bad luck. Some sort of projectile – a railgun round probably – came through the wall of the bridge and near sliced him in half. Decompression almost killed the entire bridge crew before anyone could get an emergency patch panel in place."

"So you're the surviving senior officer?" asked Cohen. "Was it you we were talking to on the comms channel?"

"Yes, sir. We were waiting for Admiral Morgan's orders when something went past us at high speed and raked *Palmerston* with railgun fire."

"Then you're in command now, Captain Corn," Cohen pointed out.

"Yes, sir. I suppose I am."

"Take us to the bridge, Captain. Let's see what's left of your ship."

"Aye, sir," said Corn, leading the way.

They floated down the corridor to a bulkhead door that slid smoothly open as they approached.

"You have internal power?" asked Cohen as he looked around the bridge.

"Yes, sir," said Corn, "although only enough to run the vital systems. Life support was mostly functional when we arrived, but the landing must have shaken something loose and the air scrubbers are offline. We're trying to restore them, but without fabricators, we're probably screwed."

"*Ascendant* has functioning maintenance fabricators," said Cohen, peering at the status displays. They showed, as Corn had said, that *Palmerston*'s systems were largely inoperable. "But we only have minimal power at the moment and it's all going to the hyperspace engine at the moment."

Corn nodded sympathetically. "Do you have cloning bays? We have casualties we'd like to redeploy."

"Yes," said White, "but we don't know what state they're in or whether the clone stock has survived, and in any case, we don't have enough power to run them."

"What the hell is this?" said Cohen, plucking a small white ceramic ball from the air as it floated across the cabin.

"Sample projectile, sir. We make them to test the mass fabricators when proving the system, although the real missiles are about a three hundred times the diameter of that thing. You can keep it, sir, it's no use to us," said Corn.

"Who else is left from your command crew?" asked Cohen, pocketing the ceramic sphere.

"Lieutenant Ross was the only fatality on the bridge," Corn said, gesturing around the room, "the other five bridge crew survived, thanks to Midshipman Meeks's quick reactions. He saved the ship when it was hit – fitted the emergency patch over there, and piloted us safely into your hangar. Well, mostly safely. I was amidships, or I wouldn't have been able to contact you."

"Which one is Meeks?" Cohen asked.

A man on the other side of the small bridge who was fiddling with his console, stood up and saluted.

"Well done, Mr Meeks. Carry on." Meeks nodded and went straight back to what he had been doing.

"You mentioned casualties other than Lieutenant Ruskin?" Cohen asked.

"Yes, sir. We lost most of the weapons and engineering team, another six crew in total. I only have Stent and Yards left. Small ship, small crew."

"And your role, Corn?" asked Cohen, pulling his attention from the status monitors.

"I'm the XO on paper, but in practice, my main role is running engineering and weapons, sir. Stent and Yards work for me – we feed the weapons, manufacture projectiles and make sure everything's working. Of course, my team is well understrength right now."

"You're the XO and the chief engineering officer?"

"Yes, sir. As I say, *Palmerston* is as small a ship as it is possible to make. Everything's wrapped around the rail cannon and geared to supplying it, so the crew complement is restricted to the bare minimum. Everyone has to be cross-trained to fulfil more than one role."

Cohen nodded. "What's your assessment of the damage? Can you get *Palmerston* operational?"

"Yes, sir," said Corn confidently. "If we can get some time on your fabricators, we'll have her up and running again in a week or so, although not back to top form and, of course, without a full crew..."

"Very good," said Cohen, nodding. "Give Lieutenant White your list of requirements and he will find you time in our fabrication roster as soon as our power issues have been resolved. But you have only three days, then I want *Palmerston* ready for action."

"Understood, sir, we'll do our best."

6

"Right," said Cohen, strapping himself into his chair on the bridge and looking around at his team, "let's do this. Ms Martin, drop us out of hyperspace and let's see where we are."

The journey through hyperspace had allowed them to escape the Deathless ambush and given time for some basic repairs, but it had pushed the ship to its limits and shaken loose every worn fitting and damaged panel.

Ascendant limped along on emergency power and every hour brought new reports of damaged or failing systems as the remaining crew worked their way across the huge vessel. Unable to repair the core systems, the crew had concentrated on getting far enough away from the enemy that they could recover in peace before attempting the return journey.

"Aye, sir," she said, hands on her control deck, "disengaging hyperspace engine now."

Cohen's stomach fell as the ship dropped back into normal space. Then the main display, still only partly functional, changed to show the view ahead.

"Get our location, Mr Jackson," ordered Cohen.

"Aye, sir," said Jackson doubtfully, "might take a while." They had rigged a personal data slate to stand in for the navigation computers, and although it worked, the incomplete sensor array and reduced processing power meant nothing was happening quickly.

"Anything nearby, Mr MacCaibe?"

"Checking, sir. Looks quiet so far, but without the starboard sensor arrays, it's difficult to be certain."

"Get me what you can, then," said Cohen, containing his frustration. Almost everything they tried to do, anywhere on the ship, was disrupted by the vast amount of damage done by the Deathless.

The fact that the maintenance team's primary spare parts store had been breached by at least one explosive projectile had not made life any easier. Much of the fabricator suite had survived the attack, but with the hyperspace engine taking all the available power, they weren't able to spare enough energy to manufacture replacements.

At least they had managed to cobble together enough spares to repair the power systems that supplied the main engines. Cohen hoped that was the case. They had certainly spent a lot of time relaying cables and swapping out shorted or destroyed power circuit components. Whether anything would work, however, was still unknown.

"What's the status of our engines, Sub Lieutenant Mantle?" said Cohen, triggering the link to the engineering department.

"They're still broken, sir," said Mantle, somewhat testily. "We're working on them. News to follow." She cut the connection before Cohen had a chance to ask another question. He ground his teeth, but there was really no point in pressing the matter. Mantle was hard-working and reliable; if she wasn't telling him what he wanted to hear, it would be because the news wasn't yet good enough.

"Still broken," muttered White, shaking his head. Mantle's attitude to non-engineers was dismissive and abrasive, but she knew her stuff.

There was a whir of fans from the vents near the ceiling, and fresh, warm air started to flow into the bridge.

"That's a good sign," murmured Cohen as he looked at his slate. The life support systems had been restored to minimal function soon after *Ascendant* had entered hyperspace, but they had run only intermittently to minimise power drain. Supplies were low, and if they ran short of power for the hyperspace engine, it would execute an uncontrolled stop and give them something new and horrible worry about.

A report from Mantle flashed up on Cohen's data slate.

<Main generator now operating at twenty per cent capacity>

Cohen snorted and showed the slate to White. A week ago, that would have been extraordinarily bad news. Today, it was more than he had hoped for or thought possible, given the state of the ship.

It wasn't going to be enough to run the exotic matter conversion systems within the advanced fabricators, but the basic matter assemblers would be able to function, which meant they could begin building the sub-systems they needed to repair the rest of the ship.

"A rare piece of good news," said White quietly, echoing Cohen's own feelings.

<And the engines?> Cohen queried.

<News to follow. You can reinitiate the bridge systems now> was Mantle's terse reply. Cohen sighed. He shouldn't have expected anything else.

"Right, people. The air-con is back on, and Sub Lieutenant Mantle says we have enough power to do something useful. Let's see if we can boot the bridge systems and start taking control of our ship."

There was a general work-like muttering from the bridge crew as they began to fiddle with their computers, restarting and reactivating where necessary.

"And let's get the forward view up on the main screen," said White. "I want to see what's going on out there."

"Don't know which system we're in yet, sir," said Jackson, "but we seem to have emerged on the edge of an asteroid belt."

"Very good, Mr Jackson. Gather everything we can, people, I want to know what's going on. Mr White, you have command." And Cohen left the bridge in the capable hands of his XO.

<E ngines working> came the message from Mantle.

"Finally," muttered Cohen, slipping his slate into his pocket and pushing away from his hammock to head for the door. The artificial gravity still wasn't working, so the crew were floating everywhere using the handholds conveniently built into the ship's walls and ceiling.

He worked his way back down the ship towards the bridge. The lights were still on and the air was fresh, both of which he took to be good signs. After days of work, the ship was at least reasonably airtight and warm, two critical factors in space travel.

"Good morning," he said to the skeleton crew manning the bridge as the door slid shut behind him. He took his chair and strapped himself in. It was comforting to see everything the right way up, even if the whole concept was essentially meaningless.

<Good news> he sent to Mantle once he had arranged his slate in its holder on the arm of his chair. <How soon till we can get underway?>

There was no immediate response, which Cohen took to be ominous.

<I'm coming to the bridge> came the reply, which Cohen thought was even more ominous. Mantle seldom visited the bridge, preferring to remain in the engineering section whenever possible.

Most of the command team were away from their consoles, either sleeping, eating or working on repair duties, but there was little enough going on and no need to call them back. Only Jackson was at his station, diligently monitoring the systems that had so far been restored to working order. The monitors and sensors showed nothing of interest – they were floating a long way from the local star, far from the dozen or so planets that made up the system.

The door slid open and Mantle floated in. She had redeployed to a standard RMSC clone as soon as they had reached New Bristol, claiming she hadn't felt truly at home in the lizardman she had worn at NewPet. Cohen hadn't ordered or authorised the redeployment, but the head of the engineering team had both the personal sway and the access necessary to make her own decisions.

"Lieutenant, good morning," he said.

"Is it?" she grunted, hooking her foot around a nearby console to anchor herself in place. "I'm not sure you'll think that when we've been through this shit," she said, pulling out her slate.

"I was hoping with the air and lights still working and the news about the engine..." he trailed off as her expression darkened. "Go on. What else do I need to know?"

She flicked at her slate to call up a list, but Cohen was sure she could recite it from memory.

"The main engines are working," she began, "but at no more than five or six per cent of normal output. And they might fail at any moment or suffer fluctuations. That means no sudden manoeuvres, very limited control and absolutely no combat."

Cohen nodded, his face a mask. That was worse than he had hoped, but still better than he had feared.

"What about the wormhole comms system?" asked Cohen. "Is that back online yet?"

"Negative. We've lost most of the system's exotic matter, so we can't activate the mechanism to form a wormhole."

"Lost?" said Cohen incredulously. "How?"

Mantle shrugged, as if it were a minor matter. "Some sort of armour-penetrating explosive round by the amount of damage. It destroyed the core wormhole generator and spread the exotic matter across vacuum."

Cohen frowned. "But we have spare parts? Backups?"

Mantle shook her head. "We had spare parts, but they were largely destroyed during the attack." She put her head on one side. "I don't think you've quite grasped the sheer quantity of damage done to the ship, the engineering team and our backup systems, sir."

Cohen took a deep breath and blew it out in a long sigh. "Maybe I haven't, Lieutenant, maybe I haven't." He stretched his neck to try to relieve the tension. "I don't suppose the fabricators–" he began, but he stopped when he saw her face. "No, I guess they're damaged and we don't have the power to run the matter fabs in an case." Mantle gave him a curt nod. "Fine. I had hoped to make repairs in-field, but without a wormhole communicator, we'll have to head straight home and deliver the news in person."

Mantle raised an eyebrow and Cohen groaned, just a little. Then she gave him rest of the bad news. "The hyperspace engine needs work, sir. We've taken it offline for repairs."

"What?" snapped Cohen, frowning hard. He had assumed the hyperspace engine was going to be his emergency escape route, if something else went wrong. Once the navigation computers were restored and operational, getting home by hyperspace was the obvious next step. "Is this really the time to take the drive down for a bit of maintenance?" he asked, the stress obvious in his voice.

Mantle sniffed. "We do maintenance to a schedule," she said. "We plan it, make sure it's flagged well in advance, get all the parts ready and make sure our teams all know what they're doing, and then we do it somewhere safe and quiet where it won't cause any problems." She flicked at her slate and passed it to Cohen. "This isn't maintenance – these are repairs. We do them when forced and because there's no other choice. They're necessary now because the engine has been damaged by being over driven for too long with inadequate, fluctuating power supplies. It's a miracle it lasted as long as it did, given the abuse it's taken."

She waited while Cohen skimmed the slate, reviewing the list of necessary work that her team had identified and planned.

"But this suggests you need weeks to complete the repairs," he protested, letting go of the slate so that it hung in the air between them, spinning slowly. "We don't really have weeks, Lieutenant. What are the other options?"

She sniffed again, obviously unimpressed. "These are just the things we know about now. We could cut back on testing, skimp on the repairs, stretch the operational lifetime of the strained components and generally half-ass the job, sir, but I wouldn't recommend it."

"But how long would it take?" said Cohen. A six-week repair

schedule made a lot of sense from one perspective, but he couldn't get the image of the HMS *Apollo* rolling through space and spewing bodies from the gaping hole in its side out of his mind.

"If we cut corners – and I really wouldn't advise it, sir – then maybe we can get a minimally functional engine together in seven to ten days. That might be enough to get us home, but it might also blow us to pieces as soon as we switch it on."

"Do what you must, Ms Mantle, but get us moving. You know the state of the ship, and you've seen how the fleet was ripped apart. We don't have weeks to spare. We need to get back to New Bristol and get word to the Admiralty."

"Then find me somewhere quiet and safe to work, somewhere with a ready supply of elements to feed into the fabricators."

"Like an asteroid," murmured Jackson from his seat. Then he realised that both officers were staring at him and that he had spoken more loudly than he had meant to. "Sorry, sir, ma'am, but I couldn't help overhearing. We're a long way from the nearest planets, but we're practically on top of the asteroid belt."

Cohen looked at Jackson then turned to Mantle, who nodded. "A large asteroid would do nicely," she said. "I'll return to engineering and make the arrangements." She plucked her slate from the air where it floated and stuffed it into a pocket. Then she pushed off the console towards the door and disappeared.

"Right. Mr Jackson, find us a nice large asteroid, the bigger the better, and set a course. And sound the call to action. I want the bridge fully crewed and ready to run."

"Aye, sir," said Jackson, punching the control that would summon the rest of the bridge crew.

Cohen tapped his fingers against the arm of his chair as various crew members floated onto the bridge and took their positions. Ms Martin arrived last, apologising for the delay.

"Let's just get things moving, shall we?" said Cohen. "Mr Jackson, what have you found for us?"

"Difficult to say for sure, sir. Most of the sensors are still out, and even the ones that are working aren't backed by fully operational processor arrays, so resolution is low."

"Yes, understood, but given the data we have, what do we know?"

The bridge door slid open one more time and White floated in, pulling himself quickly into his chair. Cohen nodded at him, then turned back to Jackson.

"I think there's a large asteroid, more of a dwarf planet, really. Our drift has actually taken us very close, and it's actually heading our way, no more than a hundred thousand kilometres ahead, sir," said Jackson. He flicked at his controls and pushed a low-res image to the main display. Then the image pulled back to show the route that would take *Ascendant* to the asteroid.

"Thank you, Mr Jackson. Ms Martin, if you're quite ready, let's start things gently with one per cent engine."

"Aye, sir," said Martin. "Manoeuvring thrusters, short bursts, then an initial sixty-second burn at one per cent."

Manoeuvres complete, Ms Martin triggered the main engine. For a few brief seconds there was a gentle push of acceleration, then it stopped. Martin frowned at the controls and tried to send the command again. Then an angry message flashed up on the main monitor.

<Engine troubles, fixing>

Mantle, working on the issues, Cohen supposed. The bridge crew could do nothing but watch the asteroid approach and wait for Mantle to work her magic. A few minutes later she sent another message.

<Try again – BE GENTLE>

Martin triggered the engine again and this time it fired correctly, delivering a continuous gentle acceleration. She recalculated the thrust operations required to take *Ascendant* to the asteroid and laid in a new course.

"Two per cent burn for twenty seconds," she announced as punched the engine control again.

Again the engine fired, but again it failed. No message from Mantle this time, just an expectant pause. Eventually, an 'Engine

Ready' status message flashed onto the main screens. Martin tried again and was rewarded with another gentle burn. She shook her head. This was going to take a while.

But it took less time than anyone thought. The engine lost thrust a few more times, but they were able to reach a steady three per cent, which took them sedately towards their target. And the asteroid, which Jackson titled *Ceres II* in honour of its counterpart in the Sol system, was moving towards them at a good rate, bearing down on *Ascendant* as the ship pushed through the belt. Martin and Jackson worked to move *Ascendant* into position, manoeuvring to match the asteroid's velocity and bring them safely to a halt.

"It's the rotation that's tricky, sir," said Martin after another round of manoeuvres. "The sensor degradation means we can't be sure exactly where the asteroid is or how quickly it's spinning, which makes landing risky."

But it couldn't be avoided, and Cohen ordered the final approach. Jackson and Martin worked in near silence, battling the vast mass of *Ascendant* and forcing it to obey their commands and align with *Ceres II*.

"Corn is asking if she should put *Palmerston* alongside, just in case something goes wrong," said White. Cohen looked at his XO in annoyance. He didn't much like the implications of Corn's request, but he couldn't fault her logic.

And I should have considered it sooner, he thought, annoyed that Corn had had to suggest it. He nodded agreement to White and the XO made the arrangements with Corn.

"*Palmerston* will be out in about three minutes," reported White. "Flight status is unproven, and she'll be back for further repairs once we're safely down." Cohen grunted and went back to watching the main display.

At some point, the door to the bridge opened and Warden floated in. Cohen glanced his way, annoyed at the distraction, then snapped back to stare at the Marine when he realised he was wearing full power armour.

"That's not a big vote of confidence, Captain," said Cohen as

Warden flipped himself around to sit in one of the empty seats. "Do you really have so little faith in our abilities?"

"Not at all, sir," said Warden, setting his helmet on his legs while he strapped himself into the chair. "But this isn't the easiest of manoeuvres, even with everything in good working order, and *Ascendant* isn't really in the best of shape." He grinned as Cohen glared at him. "Just being cautious, sir."

"Four minutes," said Martin, her voice taught but calm. "Firing thrusters again. Main engine burn in thirty seconds to match *Ceres II*'s velocity."

The engine fired again, this time with the main engines facing towards *Ceres II* as the ship fought to change direction and catch the asteroid before it passed them by completely.

Warden watched the screens with no small amount of interest, but the low-resolution sensors and degraded processors meant that the crew were flying almost blind. He shifted uneasily in his seat and quietly fitted his helmet, just in case.

"Forty seconds to landing," said Martin, hands flying across the controls as Jackson adjusted the trajectory and fed new information to the helm. "It's going to be tight," she warned. "Firing main engine and manoeuvring thrusters for last adjustment, hopefully."

The engines fired, and the crew watched as *Ceres II* span slowly towards *Ascendant*.

Cohen leant forward, barely daring to breathe as he watched the final approach. They were going to come down close to the forward edge of the enormous rock, where it looked like it might be fairly flat.

Then the main engines failed.

"Oh, shit," said Martin quietly as she flicked at the unresponsive controls. She turned to look at Cohen, her fear obvious. "Sorry, sir."

Then *Ceres II* struck *Ascendant* from below, and there was a terrible grinding of metal as the ship crashed and bounced across the face of the asteroid.

Everything went dark.

7

"Mantle," Cohen practically screamed into the comms channel. "Damage report!"

There was a crackle from the speaker then a whoosh of gas.

"Lots of damage," yelled Mantle. More gas – fire extinguishers – then a lot of swearing and shouting.

There was a whining alarm from engineering, then Mantle shouted something in the background. A moment later there was a crunch, then a bang, and the alarm abruptly stopped.

Cohen waited impatiently while the bridge crew, who seemed remarkably intact, reviewed *Ascendant*'s status. Sensors had registered damage across the ship but most of the decks were still pressurised.

"It's bad, sir," coughed Mantle, "almost as bad as the damage we took during the battle. We're back to square one in some areas. Three weeks of repairs, if things go well? Four if they don't. The damage on the port side will be worse, and it's hard to be sure until we complete a proper inspection. There could be breaches that are sealed against the surface."

Her estimate seemed like guesswork to Cohen, but he couldn't expect more right now. Given enough time, crew and fabricators, there was a chance of getting operational again.

What they couldn't deal with was loss of atmosphere and a long-term reduction in hull integrity. Each time the hull was compromised, the ship became a little less safe and a bit more complicated to repair. Unless you were about to face a meltdown, patching hull breaches was always the priority, and for that to be done efficiently you needed operational hull and room pressure sensors. Ensuring they had comprehensive service from these sensors had been one of Mantle's top priorities.

"Atmospheric pressure looks good, sir. Is the bridge secure?"

"Yes, no obvious leaks."

"Good. We need to get everyone into suits and start patching the breaches."

"Roger that. We have pressure suits here, so I can spare you a few people to come and help. It's not as if the ship is going anywhere for a while."

"Tell them to take care, sir. This rock has gravity, but only just. My rough calculation is you could jump over thirty-five times higher than normal on this dwarf planet, so if people go storming about the ship, we'll have a lot of concussions. They should treat it more like zero-G. Slow but steady."

"Noted, Mantle," said Cohen. "Captain Warden, it would be greatly appreciated if you and your Marines could assist with sealing our breeches." It had been mildly irritating when the Marine had opted to stand out the landing procedure in his power armour, but now that precaution was going to prove useful.

"Absolutely, sir, we'll be more than happy to assist you with your breeches. We'll make a start immediately," came the reply, with just a hint of amusement. "My team are all standing by in their suits. Just in case." The Marine officer floated over to the door and left.

"Right, Mr Wood. Let's see if we can contact *Palmerston*," said Cohen.

"Already tried, sir, so I could tell them we're still alive."

"So external comms are down?"

"Afraid so, sir. I've begun diagnostics," said Wood. "They're running now, but the results might be unreliable, given all the damage."

"What can I do?" Cohen asked.

"Maybe start the diagnostics on the internal communications systems?"

"We've just used that system," pointed out Cohen.

"Yes, sir, but there were still problems even before we crashed – er, had that rough landing, sir. If we can find the problems, we'll be able to identify new damage, which might help us direct engineering."

Cohen nodded. "You've got details of the working areas and problems from before the," he chewed his lip for a moment before continuing, "the crash. It was a crash, plain and simple, so we should just call it that. All right?"

Wood nodded.

"Good. So you've got the data on which systems were working before *Ceres II* tried to mate with our hull?"

"Yes, sir."

"Then let's get to it, Midshipman. We have a lot of work to do."

∽

"Give me data, people! I need to know what's happening," Captain Corn barked.

"*Ascendant* is down, Captain," Midshipman Parks said.

"Brilliant deduction, Parks. I meant something we don't all know already," Corn said with what she sincerely hoped was withering sarcasm. "Anyone else got any helpful insights? What's their status? Casualties? Any massive holes in the ship? Are they alive down there? Come on, people, we need to create solutions to problems here, and for that we need to know what's going on!"

"Captain, *Ascendant* is beached on her port side, she's got multiple hull breaches," Midshipman Robinson said.

"I'm not getting any responses, Captain. Not from the bridge, or the engineering section," Midshipman Shepherd said, pulling his headphone back from his ear as he spoke.

"Noted, comms," Corn acknowledged.

"They're going to need to patch those breaches soon, Captain," Midshipman Meeks said. "I've analysed the data on the atmospheric loss they're experiencing based on the flow rate of escaping gas. Their breaches are severely compromising hull integrity. The impact has probably affected a lot of systems, and without the breaches being sealed, their work rate to identify and repair damaged components will be compromised. If there are any badly damaged systems that are unstable, they could become critical by the time they've finished fixing breaches."

"Well, okay then, let's find some solutions people," said Corn. "What can we do to help?"

There was a long pause and some uncomfortable shuffling in chairs. Someone coughed.

Corn looked around, but no one seemed to want to catch her eye.

"Right. We need to do something to help them. What can we do to help them with those breaches?" she asked.

"We have engineering suits, Captain. Could we run a skeleton crew on the bridge and get everyone else out there to help them?" Robinson suggested.

"Captain, we can't know what the situation is with them until we establish comms. If I go down to *Ascendant*, I could patch in a short-range transmitter so we can establish ship to ship comms," Shepherd suggested.

"How do we get down to *Ascendant* safely? Even if we can spare bridge crew."

"Can we use the grabbers? Stent and Yards could take anyone we can spare down to the asteroid, and then it's just a short trip to *Ascendant*," Robinson said, drawing a circle around a spot near the stricken ship's hull on the viewscreen, and another around an airlock that would be accessible. "They can get access through that hatch. Shepherd could get access to the ship to set up her transmitter, and anyone else can either patch external breaches or get in to help inside the ship."

Acting Captain Sub Lieutenant Corn pushed an internal comms

button on the armrest of her chair. "Stent and Yards, we need you on the bridge."

She turned back to the bridge crew. "Shepherd, go get your transmitter and suit up. Elson, if we need weapons now. We're stuffed anyway, so get prepped for engineering duty. Parks, you too, we aren't going to need a navigator for the time being. Meeks, I want to get your analysis of any breaches ready in a summarised format for the engineering team on *Ascendant*. Robinson, you and I will work out how close we can get to *Ceres II* without joining *Ascendant*. I want the grabbers to have a short journey."

Before she'd even finished, they were unbuckling their harnesses and getting on with their new assignments. Corn moved forward to sit at Parks' navigation console next to Robinson's helm console so they could plot a flight path that would strike the optimum balance between proximity to *Ascendant* and not getting hit by an enormous asteroid.

Mr Stent and Mr Yards arrived on the bridge a few minutes later.

"Captain. How can we help?" asked Stent, always matter-of-fact.

Corn turned to face him. "Gentlemen, how do you fancy taking a field trip in the grabbers to *Ceres II*?" She pointed at the floor to ceiling viewscreen, where *Ascendant* looked to be in terrible shape, like an ancient shipwreck languishing at the bottom of a deep ocean. At least they didn't have to worry about space sharks or drowning.

"The weather looks good, Captain, and I have my travel sickness tablets. I'm up for it," Able Rate Yards said.

"Actually, I have a note from my mum, Captain. I'm to be excused highly dangerous space walks in power armour that's several generations behind current standard," Able Rate Stent added.

"Well, unless you neglected to mention that your dear old mum is also an admiral, I think I'll take my chances and tell you to get suited up, get in the grabbers and get Shepherd, Elson and Parks over to *Ascendant*. Shepherd needs to get inside and set up a transmitter so we have ship to ship comms. The rest of you are to assist with patching any breaches you can find. Understood?"

"Aye, Captain," they echoed, snapping smart salutes.

"And, gentlemen, this is not the day for jokes. *Ascendant* is in trouble and we have no idea what state she or her crew are in. I want total decorum and professionalism today. And don't crash my grabbers. *Ceres II* isn't the type of small rock we pull in to launch in our rail cannon. It's a dwarf planet, so make sure you adjust for gravity. If any of you crash because you didn't, I promise you will never hear the end of it or see a head you won't have to clean by hand."

Suitably chastened, they chorused another round of acknowledgement and exited the bridge with all possible haste.

8

"Right, so the plan is to right *Ascendant* using *Palmerston*'s asteroid grabbers, then patch the remaining hull breaches on the port side," said Lieutenant Commander Cohen, looking at the officers assembled around his conference table. "This is something that hasn't been done before, as far as we can tell from the records. Because this will be a first, it might put too much strain on the structural integrity of *Ascendant*, which we're still not entirely confident of. Does that about sum it up?"

"Yes, sir, it does," Mantle confirmed.

"And yet, you don't seem all that bothered, Sub Lieutenant Mantle. Why is that?"

"She's a good ship, sir. Well built. I'll only be bothered if you're expecting to get her on an even keel in less than six weeks."

There was a stunned and awkward silence to which Mantle seemed oblivious, interested only in her ship. Cohen noted that everyone else's gaze had slid casually across the table, onto the floor and found a new home near the ceiling or checking the number of visible rivets on a wall panel. Not a man jack of them was looking at him.

He took several deep breaths but still didn't feel entirely calm.

"What about *Palmerston?*" he asked. "Do we have any good news about that at least?"

"Umm. Not really, sir. *Palmerston* is essentially spaceworthy, but we don't have hyperspace capability at the moment," Sub Lieutenant Corn said. "I'm sure it'll be a lot easier once Captain Ruskin is redeployed to a new clone, sir."

Cohen shook his head. "I don't need Ruskin, or anyone else who isn't vital to maintaining and repairing HMS *Ascendant* and HMS *Palmerston*. Even if we had operational cloning bays, we can't afford the food, water, atmosphere, cloning materials or energy expenditure for redeploying crew. An engineering expert might be one thing, but an officer whose skillset is leadership is a hindrance, not an asset, at the moment. You're the acting captain of *Palmerston*, Corn, and you're an engineer. That's what I need. How long until your hyperdrive is operational?"

Corn gulped. "I'm afraid I don't have a timescale yet, sir. It depends on what components *Ascendant* can make available. Sub Lieutenant Mantle and I have assessed the damage with our teams, and *Palmerston* will be much easier to bring online because the damage isn't so severe, at least to the complex systems which are more time-consuming to repair. Our hyperspace capability could be restored in a week."

"I'm sensing a 'but' in that sentence, Corn. Spit it out. What aren't you telling me?"

Corn shifted uncomfortably in her chair. "We can only achieve that timescale if we make *Palmerston*'s repairs a priority, which means limiting the work on *Ascendant*. Our manufactories are limited, and we've looked at repurposing the ones we have, which has helped, but ultimately the more complex spare parts can only be made by complex manufactories. There's a lot of manual assembly of the components, some of which can only be carried out by highly trained personnel, of which we have none."

"Fine. XO, have you established some timelines on getting the crew evacuated using *Palmerston*? If we abandon *Ascendant*, can we get everyone back to New Bristol?"

Lieutenant White shook his head firmly. "No, sir. We have too many survivors to fit in *Palmerston*, even if we gut some combat systems from her and just turn her into a transport. The nature of the ship's design means she doesn't carry enough storage space to transport large numbers. She has a shuttle bay that isn't large enough for a dropship, just a local run-around to transport crew. There's a bay for the asteroid grabbers and the rock they retrieve to manufacture sabots for the rail cannon. That opens directly onto the rail cannon bay to facilitate loading the weapon."

"I'm looking at the schematics of *Palmerston*. Isn't that bay large enough to hold a lot of people? Can we refit it if we strip *Ascendant*?" Cohen asked.

"The problem is that life support in there is minimal, sir," said Corn, "and it's designed as a purely functional space. There's little in the way of systems already in place that we can use to patch in life support. We would have to complete a retrofit of *Palmerston*'s hull and internal conduits, and essentially strip out and replace most of the systems throughout the ship. Even then, we'd have a jury-rigged system with no guarantee that we could launch into hyperspace without it failing. It would also take several weeks to complete, at best speed."

There was a pregnant pause.

"I see one option," White said.

"As long as it's not that we euthanise people and redeploy them when we get to New Bristol, I'm listening."

"It's not quite so drastic," White continued, "but it doesn't really fit with the standard policy of not leaving people behind. We would shore up *Ascendant* so that it's essentially a working space station – stable, pressurised, with everything it needs to last for the time being. Then we focus on *Palmerston*, get the hyperspace working, get back to New Bristol and bring help which would, of course, take weeks of travel."

"You don't seem enthusiastic about that plan," said Cohen, and his face made it clear that he wasn't too keen on it either.

"No, sir. Firstly, there's no guarantee the Admiralty will want to retrieve those left behind on *Ceres II* or have the ships to spare. We just suffered a massive defeat and we're somewhere in what we believe is Deathless territory. Our scans can't confirm any activity here and it's certainly not a well-populated system, if they have a presence at all due to the lack of class M planets. But I believe the Admiralty will only come to retrieve crew once they're confident of success, and the build-up of a new fleet might take months," White said.

"Agreed, as soon as we're back at New Bristol, we'll be working on the new plan to defend the Commonwealth and preparing for counter-attacks. What are your other points?" Cohen asked.

"My second concern is that if we leave personnel behind, they'll be unprotected and susceptible to capture and subsequent interrogation by the Deathless. We have to assume they aren't going to follow the rules of war and treat prisoners well or refrain from torture. If the Deathless find *Ascendant*, we would have given up valuable intelligence as well as condemning those left behind to a horrible fate. My third and final major concern is that we can't afford to lose *Ascendant* after losing the fleet. I think we're better off taking time here, returning with both *Ascendant* and *Palmerston,* and bolstering the fleet. It's a lot quicker to repair both ships than it is to build two new ones to replace them."

"Does anyone wish to offer an argument against Lieutenant White's assessment of our options? No? Good then, we'll proceed on the basis that repairing both ships is in the long-term interests of both ourselves, the Royal Navy and the Royal Marines. Sub Lieutenant Mantle, tell us about our options for wormhole communications."

"*Ascendant* lost her wormhole capability during the Battle of Akbar. The generator is little more than scrap, and these are highly complex systems. The internal systems are in better shape but also require repairs. We will not be able to establish a stable wormhole for burst transmissions until the later stages of our plan," said Mantle.

"Can we move it up the schedule?" Cohen asked. "Communicating our intelligence about the battle could be crucial."

"The nature of the generators means they're the most complex systems we have aboard ship. With so many personnel deceased, we can either aim to get hyperspace capability back or wormholes. We can't do both at the same time," said Mantle with her usual lack of visible distress, "and even then, we need to find a new source of exotic materials."

"Hyperspace it is then," said Cohen. "We have to get back into the fight, and we can't do that sitting on our arses on a spinning rock. Our lack of communication will be sufficient for the Admiralty to conclude that the mission went badly wrong, but unless they come looking, they won't know exactly how or why, and they may not feel they can spare resources for a search."

He looked around the table, considering his options before giving the orders that he hoped would put them on the right course.

"Our first goal is to get *Palmerston* spaceworthy again. I want her hyperspace capability back first. We need a ship that can function properly. Then we'll switch our focus to *Ascendant*. The cloning bays are compromised and the reports I'm seeing here don't suggest we'll get more speed even if we put in the effort to repair them and use them to deploy more personnel."

Captain Cohen nodded and looked again around the table. "Does everyone understand our priorities?"

"Yes, sir," came the response, followed by the assembled officers saluting him. Cohen returned the salute and exited the room, heading for the bridge, where he would continue to pore over work schedules and damage assessments, looking for any way that he could improve their situation.

Images of the Battle of Akbar replayed in his mind as he moved through the ship. The terrible destruction wrought by the Deathless and the questionable decisions of Admiral Morgan constantly pushed themselves to the front of his thoughts. Stopping for a moment, he tapped a few icons on a nearby viewscreen and brought up a feed of space around the ship. There was nothing in this system but the asteroid belt. It was a bleak, hostile place to be stranded.

Breathing deeply and closing his eyes, he fought to tamp down the vision of exploding ships and frozen bodies tumbling through space as the Deathless fleet pummelled them. The frightened edge to the voices on the bridge as his crew struggled to remain calm in the face of withering fire. The horror he'd felt at having to order them to flee and abandon their colleagues.

When he opened his eyes, he saw space, empty but for the tumbling asteroids of the belt. Somewhere out there, the Deathless fleet waited for him. He was going to find a way to repay them for the Battle of Akbar if it was the last thing he did.

9

C ohen was in the command suite behind the bridge when the message arrived. The internal comms were still flaky, even from the bridge to the command suite, and so the crew had adapted by moving from one location to another to deliver messages in person. It was horribly inefficient.

"Sir, there's a message," said Martin as she floated in the doorway between bridge and command suite.

Cohen frowned and looked up from his data slate.

"A message? But the wormhole communicator is offline," he said. Then he paused and peered suspiciously past Martin towards the bridge. He twisted around, reorienting himself so that he floated the same way up as Martin.

"Yes, sir," said Martin, "the WC is still offline. The message came in by radio."

Cohen glared at her then nodded to the bridge. "I'll come now," he said, pushing off the wall to float towards the door. Martin spun easily and led the way back to the bridge, heading for the communications console.

"Right, let's have it on the main display," said Cohen as he flipped himself around so that he could float in a sitting position above his command chair. "And find Lieutenant White and CSO Mueller," he added. "I have a feeling we'll need them."

"Aye, sir," said Jackson, attempting to use the internal comms system before giving up in disgust. He despatched a rating to find Lieutenant White and CSO Mueller, then went back to monitoring his systems.

"Here's the message, sir," said Martin. "This is the original, and that's the translation."

"It's in Koschite? It's from the Deathless?" asked Cohen, alarmed. He looked up at the message, skipping the Koschite original to focus on the English translation.

< T his is the belt mining vessel *Child of Starlight*. Your presence contravenes the agreement. Identify yourselves>

C ohen stared at the display for a moment.
    "Take us to action stations, Mr MacCaibe," he said, painfully aware that *Ascendant* couldn't support any action more aggressive than a dignified death.

"Aye, sir," said MacCaibe. He triggered the command and the lamps on the bridge flickered and dimmed, changing subtly. He frowned at the controls and flipped them back and forth, but nothing else happened. "Sorry, sir, the old girl's given us all she has."

Cohen sighed. "What do we have to do to get a red alert around here? Change the lightbulbs? Just add it to the list of things to fix." It would probably be a trivial repair, but the never-ending stream of problems was sapping both resources and morale.

Then the bridge door opened and White floated in, followed by Mueller and, Cohen was less pleased to see, Captain Warden. The Marines had suffered many casualties in the Deathless attack, and their sentiment was that the Navy was responsible. They remained completely professional, and had worked immensely hard to help keep the ship running, but a certain frostiness currently tainted all dealings between the Marines and *Ascendant*'s command team.

Cohen nodded at the new arrivals.

"We seem to have been noticed," he said drily, gesturing at the screen.

"The Deathless?" asked White, leaping to the obvious conclusion. "Should we not be at action stations?"

Cohen glared at him. "We are. Can't you tell?"

White looked around as Warden and Mueller took vacant chairs and strapped themselves in.

"Ah, right. Another broken system, I guess?"

"And to answer your other question, the message was in Koschite, so I think we can assume it's from the Deathless."

"If it's the Deathless," said Warden, "why aren't they shooting at us? It's not as if they feared us when *Ascendant* was fully operational. Like this..." He gestured at the gaping panels, the trailing cables and the mess of half-repaired systems, his point made eloquently by the ship's obvious state of disrepair.

"Thank you, Captain," said Cohen acidly, "but I think we are all well aware of the situation." He turned back to the display.

"If it were the Deathless," began CSO Mueller, "what agreement might our presence contravene?"

Cohen stared at the science officer for a moment. "Are you suggesting the message didn't come from the Deathless?"

Mueller shrugged.

"Mr MacCaibe," said Cohen, turning back to the bridge crew, "find out where that message came from."

"Aye, sir," said MacCaibe, although his tone suggested deep scepticism about his chances of success.

"Another message, sir," said Wood, taking over at the communications desk.

· · ·

< This is the belt mining vessel *Child of Starlight*. You must identify yourselves or your presence here will be treated as a hostile act under the terms of the agreement>

"Okay, that sounds more like the Deathless," muttered White. "At least we know where we are with threats."

"Send this, Mr Wood: This is HMS *Ascendant* of the Royal Navy. We have suffered extensive damage and require time to make repairs. Are you able to offer assistance, *Child of Starlight*?"

"Translating," said Wood, "and sending."

< Your details match archive entry for the Koschite warship, *Varpulis*. Confirm>

"Tricky," muttered White, as Cohen flexed his fingers and considered his response.

"Mr MacCaibe, any news?"

"Nothing, sir. We're short of sensors, but there's nothing obvious within range. No idea how big *Child of Starlight* is. She could be hiding amongst the asteroids."

"Very well, keep searching. Mr Wood, send this: Confirmed, *Ascendant* formerly known as *Varpulis*, now in the service of the Commonwealth Royal Navy. Peaceful intent only. Damaged in recent encounter and crash-landing. Require time to make repairs."

The bridge was quiet as the team awaited a response. It was some time before the next message arrived.

< *Ascendant*, hold position. Do not power your weapons or engine. Failure to obey all instructions will bring immediate and dire consequences. Estimated time for repairs?>

. . .

Cohen opened a channel to the engineering department. "Sub Lieutenant Mantle, can you give me an estimate on the remaining repairs to get us spaceworthy?"

"About a week," she snapped, "if you stop crashing us into asteroids." She cut the channel and Cohen sat back. Then a thought occurred to him.

"How do we translate a week into a period they'll understand?" he asked the room in general.

"From what we've read in their literature, the Deathless use a time system based on decimal numbers of seconds. One hundred thousand, or ten to the power of five seconds, equates to one of their days," said CSO Mueller, "so a week is a little over six hundred thousand seconds."

"Right. Forget that, let's keep things simple," said Cohen. "Send this: *Ascendant* requires two weeks to make vital repairs. Some elements will be taken from the asteroid on which we have landed."

"Sent, sir," said Wood. All eyes turned to the display as they waited for the response.

Negative, *Ascendant*. Mining prohibited. *Child of Starlight* will provide processed resources to facilitate rapid repair. Await further orders>

"What's all that about?" muttered White, echoing Cohen's own thoughts.

"Doesn't matter," said Cohen, shaking his head. "Whatever their intention, we're not going anywhere." His hand hovered over the control that would open a channel to engineering, then he thought better of it. "Mr White, get down to Engineering and update Mantle. She'll appreciate the personal touch, and make sure she's not already planning to strip-mine this asteroid."

"You think they'll deliver the resources we need?" asked White doubtfully.

"I have no idea," said Cohen wearily, "but until we know more, we can't afford to antagonise them."

"Aye, sir," said White nodding his agreement, unstrapping himself, "on my way."

"Anything for us, sir?" asked Warden.

"Not yet," said Cohen tiredly, "but I don't trust this situation. Get your team ready, just in case *Child of Starlight* turns out to be more than the mining vessel she claims to be."

"Aye, sir," said Warden, nodding grimly. "We'll be ready."

10

"I can repair all the damage," said Mantle, "but there's a limit to what can be done with our current resources. I need new supplies, and if I can't scrape them off this rock, where do you suggest I look?"

Mantle's voice grew colder even though her tone remained professional. White knew it wasn't the damage inflicted by the Deathless that had infuriated her – that was all part of the job – it was the crash-landing onto *Ceres II*. That little mishap had made her seriously angry, and she was not shy about sharing her feelings. She didn't tolerate incompetence in her own team and couldn't stand to see her work undone by the failures of other crew members.

"The Deathless vessel, *Child of Starlight*, has offered to give us what we need," said White, trying to stand on the wall in the low gravity of *Ceres II* while Mantle sat in her chair. It was most disorienting.

She stared at him for a moment, seemingly completely at ease despite the cockeyed gravity.

"Why would they do that? We're defenceless. Why not just finish us off?"

"I don't know," sighed White. "Maybe this ship hasn't got the message. Or maybe she really is a belt miner, and this is a ploy to keep us here till the warships arrive."

"So where is she? And when will we get the materials?"

"We don't know, not yet. She's not showing on the sensors, probably because she's small and our sensor array is severely degraded."

Mantle snorted. Repairs to the sensor suite were on the list of emergency fixes, but they weren't anywhere close to the top. Then she sighed and White thought he detected just a hint of give in her posture.

"I'll see what I can do to speed things along. If you can avoid doing any more damage for a few days, it'll help."

White nodded his thanks with a tight smile. "We'll do our best."

"Have you found that Deathless vessel yet, Mr MacCaibe?" Cohen asked.

"No, sir, sorry. I'm using what sensors we still have to sweep the belt, but the resolution is so low they could be breathing down our neck and we'd probably never know."

Cohen grunted at that image. "Keep searching. Maybe we'll get lucky."

"Aye, sir."

Cohen stared at the main display, which showed little more than a plethora of alerts, warnings and damage reports. It was a dispiriting body of information.

He flicked at his slate, but that showed nothing new. He let the slate go and then snatched it quickly from the air as it was tugged gently sideways, towards the wall. After days of free fall, it was taking time to adjust to the asteroid's low gravity, especially with *Ascendant* laying on her side.

"Incoming message, sir," said Jackson. Cohen dragged his attention to the screen as the message flashed into view.

.   .   .

<T>his is *Child of Starlight*. Open doors designated 'C2' to receive resource delivery>

"E r, what?" said Cohen frowning at the screen. "Where the hell is that ship, Mr MacCaibe?"

"No idea, sir," said MacCaibe, frantically checking his screens. "There's nothing on the scanners."

"Give me a view of the outside of the ship at door C2," snapped Cohen. While Jackson worked to bring the camera feed to the main screen, Cohen opened a channel to Warden. "*Child of Starlight* claims to be making a delivery. Get a team to door C2 immediately and find out what the hell is going on."

Warden barely had time to acknowledge the order before Cohen closed the channel.

"Oh," said Jackson in surprise. Then he shook his head. "Camera feed, sir."

All eyes turned to the main screen as it switched to show an image of the outside of the ship. Mostly, it showed *Ascendant*'s hull, and beyond that, only darkness and stars. But standing on the hull with what looked like a pair of large sleds were two tall figures in suits.

Cohen sat back, staring at the screen, utterly nonplussed.

"Where did they come from?" he muttered. Then he switched back to Warden's channel. "What's going on?" he demanded.

"Almost there, sir," said Warden. "C2 opens into a cargo bay and nothing's as easy as it should be when the floor is a wall."

"Well, hurry it up," snapped Cohen. "There are guests waiting for you outside."

"Deploying now."

Cohen glared at his slate, almost willing it to update.

"We're ready," reported Warden eventually.

"Evacuate the air," said Cohen, "and open the doors."

The air was sucked from the cargo bay and the Marines stood ready, weapons at hand but not yet pointing at the door.

"Aye, sir," said MacCaibe. "Opening the doors now."

The doors slide open and the two figures dropped neatly in, falling elegantly into the cargo bay and anchoring themselves to the near vertical floor. The sleds followed and parked themselves inside the bay, squeezing in through the doors and settling against the wall. The doors slid closed behind them.

And then there was an awkward pause.

<S hall we talk, *Ascendant*?>

C ohen stared at the new message for a few seconds.

"Jackson, send this: Delighted to talk. Welcome aboard HMS *Ascendant*."

He opened the channel to Warden. "Bring our guests to the briefing room, Captain, and have someone take a look at those sleds to make sure they are what they seem to be."

"Roger," replied Warden. "Bay is pressurising, we'll be with you in a few minutes." Cohen nodded and closed the channel. Then he pushed himself out of his chair and headed for the briefing room.

11

The briefing room was not a happy place. The large display at the end of the room had been shattered by a railgun round that had gone on to tear through a column of chairs before punching a hole in the opposite wall.

Secondary damage from depressurisation was apparent in the rest of the room's fittings, and the repair crews had done nothing more than seal the breaches and clear the bodies. It was a grim setting for a diplomatic meeting, even without the inconvenience of the ship's angle and the malfunctioning artificial gravity.

Cohen rose from his chair when the door opened and the guests floated in. Even through the distorted perspective of *Ascendant*'s crazy angle, it was clear that the two visitors were far more familiar with low gravity conditions than either the Marines or the crew. They climbed nimbly into the room, pushing along to come to a halt a few metres from Cohen.

"Welcome," he said, remembering the lectures he had received on diplomacy and first contact protocols. "I am Lieutenant Commander Alistair Cohen, captain of HMS *Ascendant*."

When the two figures removed their helmets, Cohen barely

contained his surprise. Young and attractive, the two visitors were obviously human rather than the Deathless clones they'd expected.

One was clearly female, with blue hair and tattoos that climbed up one side of her neck. The other was bald, with striking grey eyes. Each wore a transparent eyepiece mounted on a thin arm, like half a pair of lightweight spectacles, which Cohen assumed was some sort of interactive display.

"Er, hello." Cohen glanced from one to the other, unsure how to proceed.

The woman spoke in the language that Cohen, like everyone else, now thought of as Koschite. He looked automatically at his slate for the translation.

"I am Anne Trygstad of the mining vessel *Child of Starlight*. This is my colleague, Kaare Ramberg. You are wearing a Koschite clone, and–" she paused when she saw the slate translating her words. "You wear a Koschite clone, you command a Koschite vessel, *Varpulis*, but you do not speak the language. Why is this?"

Cohen hesitated, unsure quite how much to divulge. He glanced past the two visitors to see that White had now arrived and was hovering near the door with Warden.

"It's a long story," he replied. "There was an engagement. We captured *Varpulis* and her store of clones, and renamed her *Ascendant*. But you are right, we are not Koschite and we do not speak the language. We are from Sol, and we represent the Royal Navy of the Commonwealth."

That seemed to surprise both visitors.

"From Sol? The Origin?" asked Ramberg, and the translation engine marked their tone as 'highly sceptical'. "Do you have a way to prove this? It seems more likely that you simply pretend to be ignorant, and that you claim to be not of the Koschite for some other reason of your own."

Frowning, Cohen said, "I'm not sure why we would claim that."

Trygstad raised an eyebrow. "Maybe you are pirates who have captured this ship and seek now to take our home, *Child of Starlight*. Is that it?"

"Madam, please," said Cohen, aware that the conversation was taking a potentially unpleasant tone and keen to restore some degree of control. "I can assure you that we are not pirates, that our capture of this vessel came at high cost to ourselves and that it was motivated entirely by the desire to prevent suffering and body loss amongst our civilian population. And as for taking *Child of Starlight*, well," he shrugged, "I am afraid we do not even know where *Child of Starlight* is. Our sensors are barely functioning. Right now, all we'd achieve by fighting would be to demonstrate a courageous determination to die with honour."

Trygstad and Ramberg exchanged a sceptical glance.

"You have seen our vessel, both inside and out, and you have kindly brought materials to enable repairs. Would any self-respecting pirate venture forth in a vessel as damaged as this one?"

"Venture forth? No," said Trygstad, a hint of steel in her tone. "Only an idiot would fly this vessel in its current state. But pirates often suffer at the hands of the Koschites. This damage could have been inflicted in battle."

"And it was, I can assure you," said Cohen, flicking at his slate. "A most awful and one-sided battle that resulted in significant loss for our side. Please, take a seat, let me show you images of the encounter." The two visitors made no move to sit. "They will demonstrate that we were not alone and that we were most vigorously attacked by a Koschite fleet."

"Wait," said Trygstad, holding up her hand, "you were attacked by a Koschite fleet? Why?"

"We are at war," said Cohen simply. "The Koschites attacked one of our planets, and we travelled as part of a fleet to find out why." *And to destroy their ability to wage war*, he didn't add. There was a time and a place to reveal these sorts of things, and this most definitely was not the right time.

Trygstad shook her head dismissively. "Convincing images can be created by even a halfway competent artist, let alone an AI. Show me something real, something that cannot have been faked. Show me something that proves you originated outside Koschite space."

Cohen blinked, uncertain. Then he nodded. "Of course, Ms Trygstad. Lieutenant White, please ask Mantle to join us."

"Aye, sir," said White, opening a channel to relay the request.

"It may take a moment," said Cohen, "so please, sit." He gestured again at the seats and this time the visitors sat, although they obviously found the angle and the associated discomfort amusing.

"You wanted to see me, sir?" Mantle pushed her way into the room, clearly ready to be gone as she had more important things to be doing. She stopped when the two guests turned to look at her.

Cohen waited a moment then nodded. "Thank you, Mantle, that will be all for now."

Mantle looked at him as if she couldn't quite believe what she was hearing. Then she snapped a surly salute and disappeared, heading back to the engineering department.

"Sub Lieutenant Mantle has been wearing that body, a standard Royal Navy clone, for a few weeks. As you can see, it is most definitely not a Koschite artefact or one that could have originated within Koschite space," he said, fervently hoping that this would be sufficient.

Trygstad stared at him so long he thought she might have fallen into a daydream. Then she gave him a chilly smile.

"The fact you think such clones might support your argument is charmingly naive," she said, "and I cannot imagine any genuine Koschite would ever believe that such things might lend credence to the fantastical story you have spun for us today."

Cohen opened his mouth to speak but Trygstad held up a finger to silence him.

"And so, strangely, I find your story more convincing. There are other anomalies with this ship, whether *Varpulis* or *Ascendant*. Handwritten Latin text on walls and doors, computing devices that are obviously not Koschite designs, a mode of address that seems quaint to our ears. These deviations from Koschite norms are indicative of something that originated outside their sphere of control, and so I will, for now, accept your explanation and relay it to *Child of Starlight*."

"Thank you," said Cohen, offering a polite nod of his head to cover his disquiet. The fact that the Deathless had clones sufficiently similar to RN standard that a quick glance couldn't tell them apart was disturbing. Neither he nor the boffins back at HQ had picked that up from the information retrieved by Warden and his teams on NewPet.

"You said you would need two weeks to make your vessel space-worthy," said Trygstad. "We have delivered two sleds of processed elements to speed your repairs but, by the look of your ship on the way to this room, you will need far more time and rather more material to complete the work."

"We will arrange further deliveries," said Ramberg, his quiet voice carrying a measure of authority.

"You are very kind," said Cohen, aware of something nagging at the edge of his mind, something he couldn't quite grasp. "But that will not be necessary. We will construct an automated mining machine and extract what we need from this asteroid with no further need to trouble you." He gave them a friendly smile that was not reciprocated.

Then his mind latched onto the strangeness he had noticed.

"What did you mean by 'their sphere of control'? Are we not within the Koschite sphere of control at the moment?" he asked, frowning.

"The Koschite volume is large and expanding. They have little interest in systems that lack readily habitable planets, like this one," said Trygstad. "And in the gaps, around the edges or in systems where the Koschites find nothing that meets their criteria, other groups gather."

"Other groups like us," said Ramberg.

Cohen sat back as the pieces clicked into place. The clones, the suits, the names. Even the way the visitors spoke. None of it seemed typical of the Deathless they had encountered so far.

"You aren't with the Deathless," he said quietly, shaking his head slowly as he thought through the implications.

"Deathless?" asked Ramberg, raising their eyebrows.

"What we call the Koschites," explained Cohen. "Their Ark was the *Koschei*, named after a Slavic god who never died, hence Deathless."

"It is a fitting name," nodded Ramberg solemnly.

"Regardless of the name or the history," said Trygstad with a hint of annoyance, "you are within the volume claimed by our people, the Valkyr."

"That is not a name with which we are familiar," said Cohen, glancing past his visitors at White and Warden. "Are you allied with the Koschites? Or under their control?"

Trygstad shook her head and Ramberg snorted derisively.

"We are similar, but separate," said Trygstad. "The Koschites have their priorities, we have ours. We keep to our own volume, they to theirs."

"Mostly," muttered Ramberg.

"We are a peaceful people," said Trygstad, ignoring her colleague, "as you will see. But we prefer to avoid contact with outsiders, and so we will do what we can to assist you to leave our volume. We have already delivered resources to aid your repairs and more will be arranged."

"That is most generous, Ms Trygstad," said Cohen with a slight bow of his head.

"Just Trygstad," she replied. "We do not typically use honorifics or titles, merely names."

"I understand," said Cohen. "Please, forgive my presumption."

Trygstad shook her head. "You could not have known, so your ignorance is forgivable." She pushed herself out of her chair, and Ramberg and Cohen followed.

"Thank you, Commander Cohen, for your time," she said. "It has been most informative."

"We will be in touch," nodded her colleague. Then both moved towards the door.

"Wait," said Cohen, pushing away from the table so that he could float gently after them. "You haven't explained why you don't want us to mine here, or where *Child of Starlight* is. How did you reach us so quickly?"

Trygstad stared at him for a long moment. "Your sensors must be more degraded than we thought," she observed. "We didn't reach you quickly, you came to us."

Cohen bewilderment was obvious.

"This asteroid, as you call it," said Ramberg, "is *Child of Starlight*. Your vessel crashed at our front door."

Cohen's mouth fell open, then he shook his head in astonishment. "The asteroid is populated?"

"Yes, Commander," said Trygstad. "Welcome to our home, *Child of Starlight*, an asteroid colony of Folkvangr, the people of Valkyr."

"They live here? On this rock?" asked Mantle incredulously. The visitors had gone, escorted back to the door by Captain Warden's Marines with many thanks for their generous gifts.

"So it would appear," said Cohen, his mind elsewhere. Asteroid mining was common throughout Commonwealth space, but almost everybody preferred to live on a planet. He had never heard of anyone colonising an asteroid permanently, especially not one orbiting so far from the system's star. "So we were never going to find *Child of Starlight* because we were looking in completely the wrong direction."

"We're the first visitors ever to crash onto their home," said White, oddly proud of the achievement.

"Well, I suppose that's something," said Mantle acidly. "But more to the point, they brought us four cubic metres of various inert materials. Aluminium, silicon, phosphorus, titanium, cobalt, nickel, copper, tin and a few others. A good mix, all useful."

"Enough to get the wormhole communicator working?" asked Cohen.

"No," said Mantle. "No exotics, nothing radioactive, nothing lighter than aluminium or heavier than gold. Which means the WC still can't be fixed, but we'll be able to make a start repairing all our other systems, given time and power."

"That's disappointing," murmured White.

"Maybe, but not surprising," said Mantle.

"And they promised to deliver more," said Cohen, "so let's get the fabricators working to turn these elements into useful materials."

"Already underway, sir," said Mantle.

"Good. I want us capable of flight and safe to travel as soon as possible."

12

Cohen walked into *Ascendant*'s command suite, pausing briefly at the threshold to clutch at the doorway and heave in a deep, calming breath as the gravity shifted suddenly beneath him. The ship's artificial gravity system had been restored only hours before, and it was still suffering occasional glitches that could produce unpleasant shifts.

He dropped into a seat and opened a comms link to *Palmerston*.

"What's your status, Corn?" he said, once he'd got the nausea under control.

"We're looking good, sir," she said from *Palmerston*'s small bridge. "Your engineering team has been feeding us spare parts, and all our critical systems are now operational."

Cohen looked over Corn's shoulder at the patches on the wall and the missing workstations.

"It looks like you're still short of a few things," he said, nodding at an empty desk. Corn followed his glance then turned back to the comms unit.

"We can manage, sir," said Corn confidently. "As soon as you have a target, we'll be ready."

"Good. When will you be ready to conduct main engine tests?"

"We're ready now, sir. All our flight systems are working, and the diagnostic tests have gone well. We're airtight, fuelled, armed and ready to go."

"Excellent. Then please proceed. *Ascendant* is some way from being ready, so *Palmerston* is our lifeboat and I want her proven and ready, just in case."

Corn frowned. "Are you expecting trouble, sir?"

"Expecting? No, Sub Lieutenant," said Cohen, staring at one of the battle damage repairs. "But let's prepare, just in case."

~

C ohen killed the comms link and walked through *Ascendant* towards the bridge, brow furrowed as he thought through their situation. Again.

The fleet was gone, lost to Morgan's incompetence. *Ascendant* was safe, for now, but stranded a long way from home. Cohen was horribly aware how quickly things might change if the Deathless discovered their location.

A message pinged into his HUD. Visitors in the conference room. He frowned again. Visitors could mean only the Valkyr, and since that first visit, they had communicated only remotely. He flicked an acknowledgement and changed course to head for the conference room.

When he arrived, he was astonished to see three Valkyr waiting for him. Lieutenant White was with them, a pot of coffee on the table and a selection of untouched cups arranged before the visitors.

"Trygstad, Ramberg," he said, "welcome."

"Commander," said Trygstad. Ramberg just nodded. "This is Miriam Haukland, the prime minister of *Child of Starlight*."

"I am honoured to meet you," said Cohen. "How can we be of service?"

Haukland clasped his outstretched hand. "Commander Cohen," she began, "your repairs proceed satisfactorily, I trust?"

Cohen opened his mouth to reply then frowned as he realised he hadn't needed his slate for translation.

Haukland saw his confusion and tapped her throat, upon which a tiny mic was strapped. "Sub-vocalising with automatic translation, speaker in lapel. Not perfect, but good enough. In time, I may learn your language, but only if you stay longer."

"I'm sure you'll be glad to see us on our way," said Cohen with a faint smile. "The repairs are going well, and once they are complete, we will leave."

"And your other ship, the small one?"

Cohen paused, face frozen to immobility. The Valkyr had been nothing but friendly so far, but discussing the functional readiness of his ships with anyone outside the Navy made him distinctly uncomfortable. "Other ship?" he said finally.

"The smaller one, *Palmerston*. She arrived in system in your main bay but launched to space shortly before your landing attempt. Is it ready to fly?"

"She is," said Cohen slowly, struggling to keep his face immobile. It was clear that the Valkyr knew an awful lot more about the situation than they had previously suggested. "How did you know she was in our main bay?"

Haukland gave a little shrug. "Your sensors are degraded, but ours function perfectly. We see everything, both inside *Ascendant* and in the volume around *Child of Starlight*."

"You've scanned the interior of our ship?" asked Cohen, mildly outraged by the intrusion.

"Of course, Commander," replied Haukland. "Would you not have scanned a vessel that crashed into your home?"

Cohen opened his mouth to say that there was no way he would ever countenance such an action, but then he realised that that was exactly what the Navy would do. Regardless of hostile intent, an inspection would be needed to search for anyone needing assistance. Or to check for life-threatening damage to critical systems.

"You're right, of course," he said and inclined his head. "*Palmer-*

ston is functional and about to begin main engine flight trials." Then he narrowed his eyes. "Why do you ask?"

"You asked how you could serve," said Haukland. Then she took a deep breath and looked suddenly uncertain. "We need help, and we think you may be the people to provide it. Maybe the only people who can help."

She glanced at Trygstad and gave a tiny nod.

"This is research station *Ornament*," said Trygstad, flicking at a tiny data slate until the conference room's main display began to show images. She moved on before Cohen could ask how she had circumvented *Ascendant*'s security.

"*Ornament* is just one of many stations we operate, but it is the largest dedicated to research." A scale was added to the picture and Cohen whistled. "With a radius of a little over two hundred kilometres, *Ornament* is one of the larger bodies in the asteroid belt, and it hosts an experimental facility conducting important research."

Cohen nodded, transfixed by the image that spun gently on the screen. *Ornament* was clearly artificial, a space station in the shape of a giant wheel. At its centre, a small hub hung at the end of delicate-looking spokes.

"Fascinating. What sort of research? And how can we be of service?"

"Approximately three hours ago," said Trygstad, ignoring Cohen's first question and tapping at her slate to zoom the display, "a hostile vessel docked at *Ornament*'s main bay here, on the outer rim of the station. Communications were lost soon after, and contact attempts elicit no response."

Cohen nodded, finally seeing the shape of the problem and the type of help Haukland needed. "And so you want us to take a look and rescue your people?"

"We want you," said Haukland, leaning forwards to emphasise her words, "to secure the station and remove the pirates before they escape."

Cohen sat back, eyebrows raised in surprise. "The station? That's what you're worried about? What about the people?"

Haukland waved her hands at him in irritation. "The people, yes, we wish to rescue them of course, but the station and the research data are less easy to replace or recover. Can you help?"

Cohen glanced back at the screen, taking in the huge scale of the station. The Admiralty would scream bloody murder if he put his crew at risk, but how could he refuse to help the very people whose materials he needed if *Ascendant* was ever to get home.

"You've been very generous to us," he said, "and it seems only right that we should seek to repay that generosity." He shared a look with White, who gave an almost imperceptible nod of agreement. "What did you have in mind?"

13

"Coming out of hyperspace in three, two, one," said Sub-Lieutenant Corn, who had left engineering to pilot *Palmerston* for the mission. The view on the main display changed, and for a moment all they could see was a field of stars. Then Corn fired the attitude thrusters, and *Palmerston* twisted, bringing *Ornament* into view.

"Target ahead," whispered Corn, momentarily awed by the sheer scale of the research station.

"Good work, Corn," said Cohen, checking the sensor readings. They had emerged from hyperspace inside *Ornament*'s ring, mere kilometres from the station's dock and far closer than would be acceptable under normal circumstances. At home, this sort of manoeuvre might cause an immediate response of the "shoot first, ask questions if anyone survives" type.

But Haukland had assured them that the station was unarmed and that their unannounced arrival would not be seen as hostile. Indeed, the ability to maintain some element of surprise was key to the entire mission.

"Any sign they've noticed us, Mr MacCaibe?" asked Cohen, not entirely trusting Haukland's assurances regarding the station's crew, and rightly cautious with regards to the pirates.

MacCaibe, seconded from *Ascendant* to replace *Palmerston*'s usual weapons officer and the third member of the tiny flight crew, shook his head. "Nothing so far, sir. But we're awful close. If they start shooting now, we could be in a pickle."

"Take us in, Corn, and be ready to step sideways pretty sharpish if anything happens."

"Aye, sir," said Corn as she triggered the control sequence that would see *Palmerston* dock on the inside of *Ornament*'s ring, with the sweeping bulk of the station between them and the pirates' ship.

Assuming it was pirates that had attacked the station. Cohen had his doubts about that, but Haukland had been adamant.

"The Koschites would never attack a research station like *Ornament*," Haukland had insisted. "What would they gain? We share our results, mostly, and if they need resources, they have only to ask."

But something still didn't feel right to Cohen, and his fingers drummed on the arm of his chair as *Palmerston* closed on the docking port.

"Some damage to the station, sir," reported MacCaibe as he watched the feeds from *Palmerston*'s cameras. "Looks like the pirates put a few rounds through the poor dear."

He flicked at his controls and brought up images of damage to the station's exterior, "Looks like railgun rounds to me, sir."

Cohen grunted his agreement and relayed the information to Warden.

"Twenty seconds," said Corn as the attitudinal thrusters fired to align *Palmerston* and slow her approach.

Cohen checked the internal monitors, which showed area behind the airlock where Warden's small team of Marines stood ready.

"Are you sure six will be enough?" Cohen had asked when he had discussed the plan with Warden. But the Marine captain had just shrugged.

"Given what we know of the station and the enemy, either six will be plenty or our entire force, everyone we have on *Ascendant*, won't be enough."

And so the Marines waited, a motley mix of Deathless lizardmen and standard RMSC clones, all wearing powered armour and carrying a multitude of weapons and other kit.

"Ten seconds," said Corn. Cohen nodded, then blinked in surprise as a message flashed onto the main display.

<Greetings, *Palmerston*. Welcome to *Ornament*>

Captain Warden waited on the inside of *Palmerston's* port airlock with his small team, watching the docking timer count down towards zero.

The plan was simple: storm the station, rescue the scientists and evict the pirates with whatever degree of force was necessary. At least, it had sounded simple when they had thrashed it out on *Ascendant*.

Here, faced with the enormity of research station *Ornament*, Warden found himself doubting the wisdom of the plan.

"Ten seconds," said Corn over the intercom.

There was a gentle clang as *Palmerston* docked with *Ornament*, followed by a pause while pressures were equalised.

"Stay sharp," said Warden, the helmet's mic conveying his words to the team. "Let's keep this tight."

There was a hiss as the airlock doors slid open, then Marine X was through, leading the way into *Ornament* with Goodwin and Milton behind him. Warden went next, with Harrington and Drummond bringing up the rear.

"Dark in here," murmured Goodwin, exhibiting again her inordinate skill at stating the bleeding obvious, as Ten had once described it. The corridor wasn't quite pitch black, but the main lights were off and only a dim glow emanated from what looked like an emergency backup.

<Be advised> sent Cohen, <*Ornament's* AI is on overwatch and may be chatty>

"A chatty AI?" muttered Harrington, mildly disturbed by the concept.

"Don't upset it," replied Ten, "or it might not open the doors when we ask."

"What?" asked Goodwin, thoroughly confused.

"Quiet," snapped Milton. "Focus on the job."

Marine X nodded and padded off down the corridor, following the directions laid out in the helmet's HUD. He was carrying a suppressed rifle, the heavier version of the carbine they had used when first deployed on New Bristol.

At the end of the corridor, they came to a T-junction. Marine X checked it was clear then made to turn right. A message appeared in his HUD from a sender identified as *Agent O*.

<Go left>

Marine X paused, glaring suspiciously at the message that hovered before his eyes. Behind him, the rest of the team paused.

"What's the hold up?" asked Warden.

"You didn't get that message? *Agent O* is giving me directions."

"Who the hell is *Agent O*?"

"At a guess, I reckon it's *Ornament's* AI," said Marine X. "Let me ask."

<Is this *Ornament*?> replied Ten.

<Correct, Marine X. Welcome aboard my humble abode. 'Agent O' is my *nom de guerre*, as you might say>

Marine X rolled his eyes.

"Got that one," said Warden. "I guess we have inside help."

<Go left to circle behind the aggressors>

"You want to follow its advice?" asked Marine X, still hesitating at the junction.

It comes down to a question of how much I trust the Valkyr and their weird AI, Warden thought. A foreign AI as a guide wasn't the weirdest thing he had ever encountered, but he still wasn't comfortable with the idea.

"Go left," said Warden, "but keep your eyes open."

"Sir," acknowledged Marine X, swinging left and following his rifle down the corridor.

<You can move freely> sent Agent O. <The aggressors are elsewhere>

Warden filed that under 'deeply suspicious', and the team proceeded with their normal caution, checking each room they passed and locking doors as they went.

<You are approaching the central atrium> sent Agent O, although the maps supplied by Haukland showed exactly where they were. <Take the next door on the right and ascend two flights of stairs>

<Roger> sent Marine X before swearing under his breath. "I'm talking back to a bloody AI."

"This isn't the route we planned," said Milton, her unease palpable even over the radio.

Marine X reached the door, checking carefully, then Goodwin triggered the controls and they flowed smoothly through into the next room.

"Bugger me," muttered Marine X, momentarily stunned by the room that lay beyond. 'Atrium', it said on the plan, but that didn't do the room justice. The space was cavernous, with a vast glass roof that enclosed the area and gave an expansive view of the inside of the wheel, *Ornament's* hub, and the space beyond.

At least four stories tall, the atrium was bathed in starlight and lit from within by a multitude of cunningly hidden lamps. A forest grew beneath the glass, leaves rustling in the gentle breeze of the air conditioning. It was serenely beautiful.

The Marines had entered on a balcony level that ran around the vast space, and now they had an excellent view of the park that flourished in the centre of the station.

"That's not something you see every day," said Goodwin.

"Keep moving," hissed Milton, "or this'll be the last thing we see today."

<The aggressors are ransacking the stores on this level, two hundred metres ahead and fifty to the right. Follow the path lights>

A line of gently glowing panels appeared in the floor, marking a line along the balcony, disappearing from view as it followed the curves of the walls.

"I hope that doesn't lead all the way to the enemy," muttered Ten as he made his way cautiously along the balcony. The same thought had occurred to Warden, who sent a question back to Agent O. Marine X crept a little further along the balcony, sweeping his helmet cams across the scene to capture everything they were seeing.

<Of course not, Captain! The path is lit only as far as you need it to be, and will not be seen by the aggressors> sent Agent O. <I have read over a thousand texts on military tactics and strategy, and several thousand accounts of skirmishes, ambushes, battles and wars since the assault began. I will make no mistakes>

Ten turned to look at Warden, who shrugged.

<You are approaching the next turn. Twenty metres along the next corridor, the path will dim. Bear left at the first junction you reach after that, then advance through the doors>

Marine X stretched his neck and blew out a long, calming breath. Then he turned the corner and led the way into the next corridor.

As Agent O had said, the path lights dimmed to nothing after twenty metres, leaving only the low-level emergency lamps to light the corridor.

<Agent O, can you kill the lights completely when we enter the next room?> asked Warden.

<A night assault!> replied Agent O, managing to imbue a simple text message with an inappropriate degree of youthful excitement. <Of course, Captain, although I have no low-light sensors in the stores, so I will see little. The aggressors have torches>

<Are they armoured?> asked Warden.

<No, Captain. They wear simple environmental suits and carry small calibre personal weapons that should pose no threat to your armour> Warden discounted that immediately. It was bad enough that he was taking tactical advice from an unproven AI, he certainly wasn't relying on its military judgement. <My crew is not in the vicinity>

<Any chance you can give us the precise locations of the pirates?>

<By the time you reach the door> sent Agent O, <the information will be yours>

"Use it," said Warden as the team's HUDs decompressed Agent O's information dump, "but don't rely on it. Mark I eyeballs for preference, and let the HUDs log everything."

He paused to look around at the team, then he glanced at the plan of the storerooms in his HUD, which now showed the last known positions of the pirates.

"When the lights go off, we go in," said Warden, checking his weapons one last time.

<We're ready> he sent. <Kill the lights>

The lights went out almost immediately, and the corridor was plunged into near total darkness. The Marines' helmets switched to infrared and enhanced vision as the door to the storeroom opened quietly in front of them.

Marine X moved smoothly through the open doorway, weapon up as he searched for the enemy. They could hear people moving and see the flash of lamps as the pirates, apparently unfazed by the sudden blackout, went about their work.

The storeroom was huge, laid out for automated trucks and stacked floor to ten-metre-high ceiling with crates and racking.

Milton and Harrington went one way, edging along a line of crates towards a group of people clustered around a loading truck of some sort. Ten and Goodwin went the other way, making their way around the back of the stores.

At the end of the row, Marine X stopped and crouched, hidden from the four pirates who were working only a few metres away, searching crates and moving some to a cargo truck. The lamps on their helmets swung about wildly as they continued to load their stolen cargo.

<Ready> he sent on the team's channel, hoping that Agent O either couldn't hear or would have the sense to remain quiet.

<Go on zero> sent Warden as a five-second countdown appeared in the Marines' HUDs.

Ten watched the numbers drop. When they flicked over to zero, he moved around the edge of the racking, sighted on the nearest pirate and pulled the trigger. His gun cracked and spat, and the first figure went down with a neat pattern of holes in its chest.

The weapon was a suppressed version configured for discreet assaults, but it was still a rifle and thus noisy. If the pirates hadn't been wearing environmental suits and helmets, the sound would have alerted them half a second later to the intruders.

Beside Ten, Goodwin fired controlled bursts at the others in the group. The muzzle flashes flared in the dark of the station. Torches jumped and span as the pirates fell. It was over in seconds, and nothing moved but a shell casing rolling away under a rack.

Ten and Goodwin swapped in new magazines and advanced between the racks of shelving. From ahead came the quiet pops of suppressed rifles, interspersed with sharp snapping sounds that must be enemy fire. The pirates might have been caught by surprise but the survivors had mounted a determined defence.

Ten and Goodwin rounded a corner to see the pirates crouching ahead of them, sheltering behind a vehicle; they had discarded their torches and were firing at the Marines from behind a truck.

"Harrington's down," said Milton over the comms channel.

Ten growled and opened fire, cutting into the nearest pirates.

Goodwin joined him, and their murderous fire had an immediate impact.

"They're done," said Ten moments later, swapping in a new magazine without lowering his weapon. He swept the area, Goodwin behind him, checking for movement or heat signatures.

"Clear," he reported, scooping up one of the pirate's pistols.

"Harrington's dead," said Milton, although they could all see his status in their HUDs. Ten and Goodwin made their way to Milton's position, where she, Warden and Drummond were clustered around a body.

"Small calibre," said Milton as she peered at the hole in Harrington's chest, "but effective."

"They were spraying the area, shooting at every bit of cover.

Methodical," muttered Drummond as Milton rolled Harrington's body to show the much larger exit wound.

Ten looked around, and now he could see the holes in the crates and drums behind which the Marines had sheltered.

"Right through," he murmured, inspecting one of the crates. The contrast with the controlled fire patterns of the Marines was stark. "Dumb luck," pronounced Ten, "just dumb fucking luck."

<*Palmerston*, Harrington is dead. Confirm status?> sent Warden.

There was a pause, then, <Confirmed. Backup intact>

"Harrington's safe," said Warden. "But these pistols are clearly a lot more dangerous than they look."

"Built to punch through Deathless armour," said Marine X, crouching down to inspect the damage. Then he pulled out the pistol he'd collected and looked at it for a few seconds. "What sort of pirates carry weapons like this?"

"And where do they get them?" added Milton.

"Problems for another time," said Warden.

<How many more aggressors, *Agent O*?> he sent.

<There are at least eight more in the station, and several in their ship>

"Time to go," said Warden. "Let's get this done, and remember that neither armour nor shelter is proof against these nasty little pistols."

<Return the way you came> sent Agent O, <and I will guide you to your targets>

Back in the corridor, Agent O restored the low-level lighting and lit the path to guide them to their next destination.

<The aggressors are heading your way> sent Agent O. <They know their comrades are dead and are proceeding with caution>

Warden nodded grimly to himself as the team moved out, following Agent O's path and making rapid progress through the deserted station.

<They are coming down the corridor ahead> sent Agent O as the Marines reached a large, galleried space that looked like a communal

dining hall. <You have thirty seconds. The gallery will give you an excellent ambush position>

Warden surveyed the room. It wasn't as open as he would have liked, but it was as a good a spot for an ambush as they had seen.

"Up the stairs," he said, pointing at the stairs, "and onto the gallery. You know how this works."

The Marines nodded and moved quickly to the stairs, spreading out around the balcony.

<Five seconds to contact> sent Agent O. <Here's opportunity for your preparation>

Warden was just wondering why that seemed familiar when the door slid open beneath his spot on the gallery. A group of figures moved quickly into the room, obviously following some sort of arranged route, and headed towards the doors on the other side.

Then the lights went out.

14

"Fire," said Warden unnecessarily, pulling his trigger and sending rapid bursts into the suddenly confused pirates. With the twin advantages of military-grade night vision equipment and surprise, the Marines cut down the pirates before they even realised they had been ambushed. It was over in seconds.

"Everyone okay?" asked Warden, although he knew from his HUD that none of his people had been injured. For a few more seconds, everything was quiet and still.

Then the lights came back on and they were able to see the corpses and the damage.

"That was you," said Ten, nudging Goodwin and grinning as he pointed at a neat cluster of holes in a table. "Not even close, Gooders. Awful."

"I was aiming for that one," snapped Goodwin, swapping out her magazine and nodding at one of the corpses. "But some stupid fucker shot its head off before I got to it. If you'd worked in from the right like normal, it would have been fine."

"From the right?" said Ten in mock exasperation as he reloaded his own weapon. He walked off along the gallery towards the stairs, shaking his head. "I don't know what the youth of today are coming to, I really don't."

"Knock it off," said Milton. "We're not done here yet."

<A most impressive display> sent Agent O as the lights came back on. <My sensors here are multi-spectrum, so I have video of the whole ambush. With the exception of the one nicknamed 'Gooders', whose inaccuracy makes her an outlier, your Marines achieved over ninety-seven per cent accuracy of fire. Would you like to see?>

"Told you, Gooders," Ten chided.

"I said bloody well knock it off, you two!" snapped Milton.

<Maybe later> sent Warden to the verbose AI. <Where are the rest?>

<There are only two aggressors left in the station, and they are in the control suite two hundred metres from your current location. The path will guide you. They hold a hostage, scientist Frida Skar, the only Valkyr on Ornament>

<You have a crew of one?> asked Warden incredulously.

<It might be more accurate to say that I currently have only one resident, Captain. But from another perspective, yes, I have an absurdly valuable crew of one>

<But this station is vast!> protested Warden as the Marines resumed their walking tour of the station, following more quickly now that Agent O had twice proved its mastery of the situation.

<A more accurate statement would be that the station has great volume. The space reserved for fleshbags is, however, only a tiny portion of that volume>

Warden shook his head and looked around as the corridor opened out into a wider passage with arched entrances leading in all directions.

<The command suite is at the far end, through the middle arch. Scientist Skar is being held captive inside by the two remaining aggressors> sent Agent O.

There was the sound of hissing steam and a line of holes were suddenly punched in the wall above the Marines. They scattered, taking such cover as was afforded by the arches as another burst of fire clattered from the command suite to pound the station's already bruised structure.

<They are firing blind, Captain> sent Agent O. <They know that their comrades are dead, but they cannot see you from their position. If you creep carefully to the arch, you will be able to surprise them>

"Sounds like a good way to get killed," muttered Goodwin. Nobody disagreed.

"We need a better way in," said Warden as another burst of fire punched holes on either side of the arch that led into the command room.

"I've got this, sir," said Ten, pulling out his stolen pistol and peering at the buttons.

Then there was a series of loud bangs and blast doors began to close in the nearby corridors.

"What the hell was that?" said Warden.

<Hurry, Captain. The aggressors who remain on their vessel are shooting at me> sent Agent O. <Railguns, at close range into sensitive areas, and some sort of missile tipped with explosives>

Another burst of noise, quieter this time and further away.

<Multiple breaches. I'm losing atmosphere and taking damage. You should move quickly> warned Agent O. <I am unable to calculate with accuracy when they might hit something critical>

A third round of fire echoed through the station, longer and more sustained.

<*Palmerston*, can you see what's going on?> sent Warden. <The pirates seem to be firing on us>

<Negative, no line of sight> sent *Palmerston*. <The pirate ship is still anchored to the station and we can't see anything while we're docked>

<Understood. Don't go looking, okay?> sent Warden, suddenly worried that Cohen might decide to hunt the pirates before the Marines had escaped the station.

<Acknowledged, but do hurry up. You're taking an awfully long time>

"The Navy boys are getting jumpy," said Warden.

"Really?" muttered Ten as another burst of fire from the command suite cut through the walls. "I'm none too happy myself. Let's get this bloody done, shall we?"

"What's the plan, Ten?" asked Milton, her unease growing as another volley of railgun fire shuddered through the station.

"Distract them," said Ten, nodding towards the remaining pirates, "and I'll saunter over and slot 'em." He waved the pistol and grinned.

"A distraction?" murmured Milton, grinning evilly as Ten wormed his way forward.

<I'm going to shoot them through the walls> Ten sent to Agent O, <but you need to show me where they are>

<Hmm, tricky. Let me see> The comms channel went quiet for so long Ten began to wonder if the AI was rebooting. <There you go> sent Agent O eventually.

Ten's eyebrows went up as an access request popped into his HUD. He tapped through the confirmation and ignored the warning that granting access permissions to a third-party breached the EULA and might invalidate his warranty.

<I have access> sent Agent O. <The aggressors are shown in red>

Ten grunted as his HUD view was overlaid with a wireframe model of the interior of the command suite. When he looked at the wall, he could see the figures and furniture within.

"Nice," he muttered, raising his pistol. He sighted on the first red figure. "When you're ready, Colour."

Another burst of railgun fire tore into the station and a wind sprang up as atmosphere vented from a small hole on the far side of the room. Then something metallic bounced across the floor, tumbling in the wind, before exploding with a loud bang and a bright flash.

The response from the pirates was immediate as they fired in the direction of the flashbang, rounds smashing through walls.

Ten adjusted his aim and fired twice, once for each pirate, and suddenly the only noise was the wind.

"Two kills," said a voice in the air. "But this area is no longer safe."

There was a burst of shouting and a figure stumbled out of the command suite looking distinctly uncomfortable.

"No suit," said Goodwin as the wind continued.

"The path will lead the way," said Agent O, its voice distorted by the thinning atmosphere, "but you must move very swiftly." He said something else in Koschite as the Valkyr scientist pushed forwards against the wind.

"Grab her," said Warden, "and let's get out of here."

Milton and Drummond moved quickly forward, grasped the surprised scientist by her arms and half-dragged, half-carried her across the windswept room.

"Get to the door," said Agent O, "and go quickly through."

The Marines surged forward, caution forgotten as the wind whipped at their heels and dragged at their suits. The Valkyr scientist shouted something but her words were snatched away by the madly venting atmosphere as it screamed through the breach in the station's hull.

<Get ready> warned Agent O cryptically as the Marines neared the doorway.

"She's turning blue," shouted Drummond, glancing from the door to the scientist.

The door opened, and the Marines stood, heads down, as they battled the renewed gale that swept through the doorway.

<Quickly> sent Agent O, <before the breach grows or I run out of atmosphere>

The Marines pushed forward, battling the gale, their power armour straining to help them progress. They pushed the scientist through the doorway and heaved themselves after her, arms linked as they fought their way out of the leaking chamber.

And then the doors shut behind them and the howling gale stopped. The abrupt silence was broken only by the hiss of gas vents as the pressure was normalised. The scientist took a few gasping breaths, her colour quickly returning to normal as she stood with her hands on her knees, shaking.

They all stood for a few seconds, recovering.

"That was too close," said Warden, looking around at his small team and the corridor in which they found themselves. "This isn't the way we came in."

<There is a room nearby with environmental suits> sent Agent O. <Please follow the path and assist Frida Skar. Then I will guide you to the docking point by the fastest route>

<Roger> acknowledged Warden.

It sounded like Agent O was reassuring Skar in Koschite, giving her instructions. She said something in reply, clearly dubious, but then allowed the Marines to escort her to the suit room.

A few minutes later she looked around at them from inside her suit.

<Thank you> she sent, and the Marines blinked in surprise as the message showed up in their public channel.

<I have enabled automatic translation and updated Frida Skar's suit to integrate with your IM system> sent Agent O. <And I have uploaded a pack of information to her suit to simplify communication>

"Useful," said Warden, nodding thoughtfully. A shudder ran through the station, bringing him back to the present. "Let's go," he said, "this place is getting dicey."

They moved out with Marine X in the lead, following the path on the floor. It took them quickly through the station until they reached a door that wouldn't open.

<Vacuum beyond> explained Agent O. <Prepare>

They had a few seconds to check their suits, then the atmosphere was sucked from the corridor. The door ahead opened, and they moved out onto the gallery under the atrium.

Or under the gap where the atrium had been. There were now gaping holes in the glass and puncture wounds in the walls. The lights were out and the cavern was lit only by the stars.

<Railgun damage> sent Goodwin, staring at the nearest hole as they passed.

But it was the trees that caught their attention. Exposed to the hard vacuum of space, they had frozen. The sudden transformation from green to frosty white was disquieting.

Warden stared around, horrified by the sudden change. Then another round of railgun fire ripped through the trees and walls, smashing trunks and filling the volume with a sprinkle of splinters and shattered leaves.

<Move!> sent Agent O as a shockwave passed through the station floor. <The remaining aggressors are attempting to leave, but I locked the door to prevent their escape. The power to the door mechanism has failed and I cannot release the lock>

<They're trapped?> replied Warden as the team ran down the gallery.

<For now, but they are increasingly desperate to leave>

There was a pause and more shudders ran through the station, almost throwing the Marines from their feet as they sprinted along the path Agent O had set for them.

<They are firing their engines to break away> sent Agent O. <I cannot release their ship. They will tear a hole in the fabric of the ring. You must h>

Then the lights failed and the path they were following winked out.

~

<*Palmerston*, are you there?> sent Warden. <We're by the door but there's no power to open it>

<Acknowledged, stand by>

"Stand by, they say," said Drummond, "as if this was some sort of jaunt."

"Quiet," snapped Milton.

The seconds dragged by, then the door to the airlock slid open. Cohen stood on the other side in power armour, waving them to hurry.

"Move," said Cohen, pulling at Skar as she stumbled into the airlock and pushing her to the far end. "Come on, hurry up."

Another shock ran through the station and threw them all from their feet. Cohen counted heads then slapped the control, closing the door to the station. The door to *Palmerston* opened almost immediately and they all bundled through.

"We're aboard," shouted Cohen running for the bridge. "Get us away, Corn."

Warden and Skar followed, arriving as Corn disengaged the docking clamps and eased *Palmerston* away from the stricken station.

"You're safe now," Warden said to Skar, hoping it was true. "We'll take you to *Child of Starlight*." He removed his helmet and adjusted his HUD so that it sat more comfortably on his head. Then he frowned at Skar. "Were you truly the only person aboard *Ornament*?"

Skar took off her own helmet. She had collected a tiny HUD of her own from the stores on *Ornament* and now she fitted this before replying.

"Yes."

"Good," said Warden, leaning against the wall and staring up at the main displays. The view was changing as *Palmerston* slipped slowly back, but even from here the damage was obvious. As they watched, an explosion tore open the wheel and sent debris spinning out into space. "It doesn't look like the station will survive much longer."

"What?" snapped Skar. "But what about *Ornament*?"

Warden shrugged. "Sorry, she's taking too much damage."

"Bring us above the wheel, Corn. Let's take a look at this pirate ship," ordered Cohen, settling into the command chair.

"Aye, sir," said Corn, fingers on the controls.

"Arm weapons, Mr MacCaibe. Prepare to fire on the pirates. Railguns only."

"Railguns it is, sir," said MacCaibe. "*Palmerston* has only two, more's the pity, but they'll make short work of these pirates, so they will."

A crack appeared in the fabric of the station as *Palmerston* shifted and the pirates' vessel came into view. They had broken free, but a huge piece of *Ornament* trailed from the outside of the ship, firmly attached to the docking mechanism.

"We're being targeted as well, sir," said MacCaibe as fresh wounds were scored across *Ornament*'s flanks. "Brace for impact."

"Keep us moving, Corn," said Cohen. "And fire now, Mr MacCaibe, a sustained burst."

"Aye, sir."

Palmerston's attitude thrusters fired as a stream of railgun rounds raked the ship. MacCaibe's hands flashed across the triggers and *Palmerston*'s railguns returned fire, punching a neat line of holes across the pirate ship's hull. The ship seemed to jump, and some of its thrusters fired frantically as it began to tumble.

"She's struggling to bring weapons to bear, but she's still trying," said MacCaibe.

"Another burst then," said Cohen. MacCaibe obliged, stitching another row of holes near the first. The thrusters stopped, and the ship's lights went out. It drifted alongside *Ornament*, tumbling gently. Then a series of explosions tore through the ship, one after another, shaking and battering it until one last blast ripped it to shreds.

"That'll do nicely," said Cohen, nodding to MacCaibe. "Take us back to *Child of Starlight*, Ms Corn."

"No, wait," said Skar, her words translated automatically by her HUD. "What about Ornament? Must be recovered."

Cohen looked round at the scientist, annoyed, then pointed to a display that still showed the station.

"*Ornament* is finished," said Cohen as another hole appeared in the station and a crack, kilometres long, ran down the edge of the wheel. "I'm sorry, there's nothing we can do."

"Not the station," said Skar in angry frustration. She pushed MacCaibe from the console, ignoring his complaints, and punched at the controls until the view shifted to show the station's hub. "Ornament," said Skar, pointing at the hub. "Must recover Ornament."

Cohen frowned, unsure what was being asked.

"Oh, shit," said Warden as realisation dawned. He looked at Skar then at Cohen. "The AI. She's talking about the station's AI."

"Yes, AI," said Skar. "Research citizen Ornament, there, in hub. We must recover."

"We can open a channel," said Cohen, shaking his head dismissively, "download the AI and take it back to *Child of Starlight* that way, if you like?"

"You have quantum neuro-processors and two thousand yottabytes of storage?" snapped Skar.

Cohen looked blank for a moment, then raised his eyebrows at MacCaibe.

"Not even close, sir," said the weapons officer.

"Go to hub, recover Ornament before station and irreplaceable citizen lost," said Skar.

"An AI?" asked Cohen incredulously. "You want me to risk the ship and everything on it to rescue an AI?"

"Ornament more valuable, more useful, more important, than everyone on this ship," snarled Skar, clearly angry and, to Warden's mind, unused to being denied.

Cohen stared at her.

"Can't leave anyone behind, sir," said Marine X quietly from the back of the bridge. "Can't fail the mission."

Cohen rounded on the penal Marine, teeth bared in anger at the interruption, but Marine X's grim expression made him pause. Then he nodded.

"Of course," he said. "Turn us towards the hub, Corn."

"Aye, sir."

"And Skar. Can you put us in touch with Ornament? Prepare it for collection?"

"Maybe," said Skar. "Normal channels down, but maybe emergency channel." She moved to another console, allowing MacCaibe to resume his station, and stared at the controls for a few seconds. Then she began to make changes, brow furrowed as she worked at the unfamiliar keyboard.

A minute later, as *Palmerston* nudged accelerated towards the hub, a message flashed onto the screen.

<Hello *Palmerston*, this is Agent O. It's good to talk again>

Skar gave a tiny grin of relief as her HUD translated the message. Then she turned to Cohen.

"Ornament," she said.

"Right, let's give this a go," said Cohen, tapping at his slate.

<Greetings Agent O, this is *Palmerston*. We're coming to get you>

An hour later, *Palmerston* had backed off to a position three thousand kilometres from *Ornament* station. The crew, the Marines, Skar and Agent O all watched the camera feed as *Ornament* bucked and shook under the force of the explosions that continued to wrack the station. Then the lines that held the hub in place failed. There was one last crack, and *Ornament* was sundered at its seams.

"I'm sorry we couldn't do more," said Warden, breaking the silence.

Skar nodded, then left the bridge. Cohen watched her go then gave the order to make the jump back to the asteroid.

<Thank you for collecting me, Commander> sent Agent O from its temporary home in *Palmerston*'s small loading bay. The AI was housed in a hardened shell three metres long, one metre wide and one and a half metres tall. <It would have been lonely out here, waiting for my power systems to fail and my consciousness to drift away like dust in the wind>

<Let's get you back to *Child of Starlight*> sent Cohen. <We can celebrate when we're all safe>

<A sentiment I can readily endorse, Commander>

15

"The handover went smoothly, sir?" asked White as Cohen walked back into *Ascendant*'s command suite. White poured a cup of coffee and pushed it forwards as Cohen sank into a chair. He grabbed at the cup and took a deep sip.

"It did," said Cohen, putting the cup back down and pulling out his slate. "You're not going to believe the scale of *Child of Starlight*." He flicked at his slate, then pushed some images to the main display.

"They gave you a guided tour?" said White, watching a video recording by *Palmerston*'s forward monitors as it was led into *Child of Starlight*'s dock.

Cohen snorted. "Not even close. See this?" He pointed at the screen as *Palmerston* drew close to the rocky face of *Child of Starlight*. "Everything's hidden. Even when you know it's there, you can't find the door without assistance because it's in a darkened tunnel. There's nothing – *absolutely* nothing – on the outside of this bloody rock that might lead anyone to suspect it was occupied."

Now it was White's turn to be sceptical. "I know our sensors are a bit buggered, but surely we'd have spotted *Starlight* if we'd been fully operational?"

"*Palmerston* didn't," Cohen pointed out, "not even when we were right on top of the bloody doors. There are no antennae, solar arrays, weapons, ports, windows or hatches. Nothing." He paused as the display showed *Palmerston* slowing almost to a halt relative to *Child of Starlight*, then twisting through ninety degrees to enter a huge canyon that led into an equally vast cavern.

The screen went dark as the camera flew into shadow. Then the rock face appeared as the forward thrusters flared to slow *Palmerston's* approach still further and turn the ship as it flew more deeply into the cavern.

The thrusters flared again to bring *Palmerston* to a dead stop, then the display went blank.

"Total darkness. A spot utterly invisible to the outside, shielded by miles of rock in all directions. Then they just reached out and pulled us into their bay," said Cohen, miming a hand reaching up to seize *Palmerston* and drag her down into the heart of the asteroid.

"Seriously?" asked White, eyebrows raised.

"Seriously. Something reached up, took hold of *Palmerston*, and pulled us down into a bay that was twenty kilometres long and ten wide. Watch."

White watched, incredulous, as the video showed *Palmerston* sinking through a rock tunnel to emerge into a volume the size of a large city.

"Are those clouds?" he asked, squinting at the display.

"And trees. A full forest, in fact, at the far end of the bay. Behind some sort of glass wall, apparently. *Palmerston's* passive sensors recorded everything, but the active sensors were glitched and got nothing, so all we know about *Child of Starlight* is what we could see in this bay."

"Glitched?" asked White, frowning. "That seems," he paused, searching for the right word before settling on, "implausible."

"Quite," agreed Cohen, "especially as they started working again as soon as we were clear of the approach canyon. Something screwed with our active sensors, and it can only have been the Valkyr."

He sat back for a few moments, watching the display as the Valkyr went about their daily lives in front of *Palmerston's* cameras.

"We need to get off this rock," he said eventually, "or get a message back to HQ. The longer we're here, the more risk there is that the Deathless will take advantage of the fleet's destruction, if they haven't already." White nodded his agreement. It was a conversation they'd had several times, but there was a limit to the speed that Mantle could work, even with the Valkyr delivering tons of processed materials every thirty hours.

"And I really don't like the fact that we're sitting on top of a technologically advanced civilisation of unknown power and scale."

"There's always *Palmerston*, sir," said White. This was another conversation they'd already had.

"A very last resort if we can't put *Ascendant* back together. Until then, no," said Cohen. *Palmerston* could make the voyage, but that would mean leaving *Ascendant* and at least half the crew amongst the Valkyr.

He pulled up images of *Ornament* and flicked through them, both the ones *Palmerston* had shot from the outside and the video that the Marines had recorded as they raced through the station.

"This station was huge, and it had two crew. It could have housed millions, but they were running some sort of experiment that needed total isolation and security."

"Any idea what they were doing?" asked White as the images flashed by.

"No, but let's get Mantle up here, and Mueller, and see if they can shed some light."

White nodded and summoned the two offices, then he and Cohen watched the video of the trees under the atrium on *Ornament*.

"You wanted to see us, sir?" said Mantle, coming into the command suite with Science Office Mueller.

"Take a seat," said Cohen, "and then take a look at this. It's the video from our mission to *Ornament*, the Valkyr research station. I want to know what you think."

Mueller and Mantle watched the video in near silence. Mueller seemed particularly interested in the exterior shots, and took them to his slate for a more detailed examination.

"There are no people," he observed, "no inhabitants except for this scientist, Skar?"

"And an AI that identified itself as 'Agent O'," confirmed Cohen.

"But it's huge," said Mantle. "You could house millions – tens of millions, probably – in a structure that size. Why would anyone build such a thing without populating it?"

"Research, apparently," said Cohen, "but that's all they'd say. Any ideas, Mr Mueller?"

The science officer was quiet for a long time. He sat with his chin resting in his hand, staring at his slate and flicking through the images of *Ornament*.

"Mr Mueller?" prompted White eventually.

"Hmm, what? Yes, sorry. Well, it's a ring, and if it is all devoted to research, then I would have to be thinking about high-energy physics, specifically a giant particle accelerator." He shrugged. "But if that were right, it would be the largest ever built by a very long way."

"Really? I thought all particle accelerators were vast," said Cohen.

"All? No, not at all. Many are very small, but it depends what you wish to investigate. But even the largest in the Commonwealth would be a fraction of the size of this monster." He fell silent and went back to reviewing the images on his slate.

"So, is it a particle accelerator?" Cohen pressed, when it became clear that Mueller wasn't going to say anything else. "Or is it something else?"

Mantle shrugged. "Not my area, but I'd have said it was a habitat if we didn't already know it was a research station."

"Yes, research," said Mueller. "A very high energy particle accelerator. Look, these parts here are similar to what you would see on a more normally scaled version. The power requirements would be stupendous."

"And what would the Valkyr learn from this facility, if it was operating?"

Mueller shook his head. "I have absolutely no idea whatsoever, sorry. But my guess is that it was uninhabited either because its research was virtually complete or because there was some degree of risk. Or both, of course."

Cohen sat back and stared at the main display. He replayed the video of *Palmerston*'s entry to *Child of Starlight* and the four of them marvelled again at the vast scale of the Valkyr's civil engineering.

"It's like they just don't know when to stop," muttered Mantle.

"I don't think we're going to learn anything more here," said Cohen after an hour, putting away his slate. He stood up and made for the exit, with Mantle and White following.

"Oh," said Mueller as Cohen neared the door. Cohen turned back with a sense of foreboding. Mueller's face was as white as a sheet and his eyes darted around as if he suddenly feared being overheard.

"Mueller?" said Cohen softly, walking over to where the scientist still sat at the table. "What is it?"

"Well, it's obvious, when you think about it," said Mueller quietly. He glanced around at the other officers. "You may need to sit to hear this."

Cohen, now thoroughly spooked, settled himself back into his chair and leant forward to listen.

"There's a branch of physics – the name is unimportant – concerning the focussed twisting of spacetime and the near light speed transmission of highly compressed, super-heated matter." He paused to take a swig from a long-abandoned cup of cold coffee. "It's hinted at in the theory, but nobody has ever been able to demonstrate the principles or achieve the practical effects in the real world, although plenty of people have tried.

"The Navy itself tried, for a while, but the costs were astronomic, even by the scale of the Commonwealth's multi-planetary operations, and they never made any progress."

He flicked at his slate, pulling up an image of *Ornament* and pushing it to the main display.

"But what if you're a super-concentrated, technically advanced civilisation with essentially unlimited resources? What if you had access to enough energy and mass to build whatever you want, and you had a stable society with a long-term, unified outlook on life and access to genuine, multi-purpose, artificial intelligences?

"What if, in other words, your civilisation had no practical limits on the research projects it could undertake?"

Cohen frowned. "I don't see where you're going with this."

"Let's take this further," Mueller continued. "What if you have an aggressive and potentially unstable near neighbour – the Deathless – whose resources are even more vast but whose outlook on life not only precludes the necessary long-term effort, but also pushes them simply to focus their attention on other aspects of life? Might the threat posed by a potentially aggressive neighbour persuade even the most peaceful of societies to turn their attention to matters of defence?"

And now Cohen was getting seriously worried, even though Mueller hadn't actually done more than describe a string of poorly-evidenced hypotheses.

"But what does this all mean, Mueller? What were they doing on *Ornament*?"

Mueller looked up from his slate. "A weapon, Commander. A most dreadful weapon, one whose research costs and experimental risks have always prevented anyone from building it. That's what they were doing. They were conducting research into particle beam weapons."

He dropped his slate onto the table and flopped back in his chair, staring at the ceiling.

"Are you sure?" asked White. "What if they were just looking for new fundamental particles?"

"Pah!" said Mueller dismissively, sitting back up again. "That avenue of research was completed decades ago. No, the only reason for building an accelerator this large is to conduct tests into the manipulation of energy and matter for the creation of a beam weapon."

Cohen shook his head, relieved. "Okay, I don't think we need to worry about this too much. Any weapon system that's four hundred kilometres across isn't going to be hugely mobile, so I don't think it's going to be a threat."

"But *Ornament* isn't the weapon." Mueller cast a disgusted glance at Cohen. "Once you have the experimental results, the station would be redundant. At that point, you could work anywhere, as long as you had a powerful AI, some smart researchers, a huge team of engineers and a sophisticated manufacturing plant. No, Commander, I'm afraid *Ornament* was never a direct threat, but the product of its research might very well be."

"Shit," muttered Cohen. "Is that as bad as I think it might be?"

"Worst-case scenario," said Mueller, "would be a weapon system capable of delivering a cutting beam at near light speed to targets ships or stations across multiple light seconds of space. An unavoidable attack of devastating power."

"We need to notify HQ," said Cohen. "If there's even the slightest chance that the Deathless might obtain a weapon like this, we have to plan to handle it."

"How big would it be, Mueller?" asked Mantle, her engineer's mind running through issues of heat dissipation and power consumption.

"Big, certainly," said Mueller, "with similarly vast power requirements. I can't imagine *Ascendant* being large enough to house one, or the generators. It would need a very large craft indeed, but definitely within the capability of the Navy's current ship-building facilities."

"Right," said Cohen decisively, "I've heard enough. How long till *Ascendant* is able to return home?"

"Another two weeks at least, after the last round of damage," said Mantle, "and ideally six to eight to give time for full engine tests and bedding-in of new systems."

"Too long," said Cohen, shaking his head. "What about the wormhole communicator? Anything we can do there?"

There was a long silence as Mantle looked at her slate.

"No," she said finally, although her tone was strange.

"No?" asked Cohen, frowning. "Or is that code for 'yes, but I don't want to do it'?"

"It's not repaired yet, but we have restored the power supplies and control systems. We still need to rework the primary ring generator, and we don't have enough of the right materials. Without them..." she shrugged. Without them, they all knew the wormhole communicator would never make a connection.

"But why don't you just force one open using the hyperspace engines?" asked Mueller, frowning at the engineer. "Hyperspace engines are fundamentally similar to wormhole communicators, they just work on a different scale. The fusion generators are fully operational, so if we reconfigure the hyperspace engine and push in enough power, it would be perfectly possible to create a wormhole that was stable enough to send whatever message you wanted." Mueller beamed at his audience as if he had just completed a trick of astounding complexity.

Mantle shook her head. "In the first place, that's hugely risky. If it went wrong, it would cause a cascade failure that might rupture the hyperspace engine, destroy the fusion generators and shred the engines, which would create an explosion that would obliterate *Ascendant* and kill everything in *Child of Starlight*, regardless of the level of shielding they have in place.

"And second, even if it worked and we didn't suffer a catastrophic failure, it risks burning out the hyperspace engine and stranding us here. So no, it's not an option."

Mueller's shoulders slumped, and he frowned down at his slate. "Then I guess you'll just have to ask the Valkyr for the materials you need to fix the WC."

"Absolutely not," said Cohen, shaking his head. "Even if they agreed, we'd have to explain our reasons and I don't trust the Valkyr, not even a little bit. They're too close to the Deathless, whatever they claim. Next?"

Mantle shook her head. "That's it, I have no other suggestions."

"Then we go with Mueller's idea," said Cohen firmly. "No, I don't want to hear it," he said as Mantle opened her mouth to object. "The risk is worth taking if it allows us to pass the information to HQ and notify them of a new player in the game." He stood up to make it clear that the meeting was over. "Lieutenant White will pull together a package of information to transmit, and I want you two to solve the problems and make this work, understood?"

"I don't like this," complained Mantle for the tenth time in an hour. She and Mueller were checking everything – again – before they reported back to Commander Cohen that their work was complete.

"We've allowed for every variable, and we've planned for every contingency," said Mueller confidently. "Even if something were to go wrong, we can shut it all down before anything catastrophic happens."

Mantle grunted. They had argued about this for hours as they made the preparations, she pointing out the impossibility of planning for every eventuality, he reminding her that science was predictable and that they had taken a logical approach.

"Like that's supposed to make me feel better," Mantle had murmured. Logic was great, but her gut was telling her that they'd missed something, and she feared the consequences would be dire.

"But if you can't tell me what we've missed or provide evidence to support your fears, why should we take any notice of them?" Mueller had asked.

Then they had moved on to the next set of problems and continued to work their way down the long checklist they'd pulled together after the idea had first been suggested.

And now they were at the end of that checklist, again.

"That's it," said Mueller, "everything checks out. The controls are in place and tested, the reconfiguration work on the hyperspace engine is solid, the fusion reactors are ready to feed us all the power we need. There's nothing more to do."

But it turned out, when they briefed Command Cohen, that there was at least one more thing to do.

"Evacuate?" asked Mueller, frowning. "Well, yes, I suppose it would be a sensible precaution, but I'm sure it's not necessary."

"I'll put myself at risk, and I'll mandate risk for the ship, but that doesn't mean I want to jeopardise the entire crew," Cohen said. "So we'll put everyone who isn't required for the operation on *Palmerston* and move them far enough away that they'll be safe, just in case."

That had taken an hour, but now Mueller, Mantle and Cohen were alone on the huge ship. Walking down the long corridors was strangely eerie when there was nobody else on board, and they congregated in the engineering team's command room to be close to the control systems.

"Are you sure about this, sir?" asked Mantle, one last time.

Cohen nodded. "Yes." Then he grinned. "And if it all goes wrong, we just pull the emergency cut-out, right?"

"Yes, sir," nodded Mantle wearily. It had been a very long day.

"Anything else from your side, Mueller?"

"No, sir," said the science officer, "although now we are at this point, I must admit to feeling a little anxious. It's not as if anyone has ever done this before."

"Wait, what?" snapped Cohen, turning to glare at the science officer. "I thought it was risky, not cutting-edge risky."

Mueller shrugged. "There's a first time for everything. And as you said, it's not like we have an alternative."

Cohen swore under his breath and turned back to the command console. White's package of information – everything they had seen, gathered and deduced since leaving New Bristol – sat tidily in the communicator's queue, waiting for a connection to be made. It would be sent automatically, they just needed to create the pathway home.

"Right, let's do this," he said before he had a chance to change his mind.

Mantle took a deep breath then triggered the script that would step through the process and ensure everything happened at the right time. She peered at the main display, which now showed the script's progress. Her hand hovered above the abort button.

"Spinning up the fusion reactors," she said, eyes darting around as she tried to monitor every system's readout. "Power chains looking good." The display went green as another step of the process ended.

"First stage preparation of the hyperspace engine, thirty seconds to go."

Mantle provided a running commentary as the script executed the process's steps. Mueller sat on the edge of his seat, practically bouncing up and down as he flicked his attention between his slate and the main display.

"Second stage hyperspace engine prep complete." She blew out a long breath to try to calm her nerves.

Cohen had a sudden vision of an exploding starship, the remnant of a long-forgotten lecture on interstellar travel engineering. Had that been a cascading failure in an engine? His mouth was dry. He couldn't remember.

"Firing now, get ready," said Mantle. She hit the final confirmation button and peered at the hyperspace engine dashboard. "Green, holding steady," she murmured. "Looks like everything is okay."

"Hmm," said Mueller, frowning. "It's running a bit hot."

"What?" snapped Mantle, her calm vanishing.

"Very hot," said Mueller. A warning klaxon sounded in the depths of the ship. "Oh, that's not good. Looks like a cooling line in the lower engine bay has come free." He switched to a feed showing the bay, where a line could be seen spraying coolant all over the floor.

Mantle switched to the same feed and zoomed in, peering closely. "That's got to be a secondary failure, those lines don't just come loose. Something else must have gone wrong."

Mueller looked up, fear spreading across his face. "But that could only mean..." His hands flashed as he searched for a feed in the right part of the engine bay. "Look."

"Shit," said Mantle, "there shouldn't be liquid there; the drive containment system is leaking. Must have dripped on the hose and burned it free."

"But how is that possible?" said Mueller, his voice rising in fear and anger. "You checked that system – it passed its tests."

"Barely," said Mantle through gritted teeth, "and this is hardly a situation within the system's design parameters." She shook her head. "No good. I'm pulling the plug."

"Wait!" shouted Cohen. "The wormhole hasn't formed yet. We're not done."

"It's too late," snapped Mantle. "If the engine overheats, the containment system will fail completely, and we'll have a catastrophic cascade that'll destroy the ship and everyone on *Child of Starlight*, just like we warned."

"Another few seconds, then we're done."

"We're done now," said Mantle, slamming her hand on the emergency kill button.

Cohen looked ready to scream with frustration, but Mantle just stared at the dashboard, then punched the kill button again. And again.

"What's wrong?" asked Cohen.

"It's not powering down the system, something must have failed." Mantle looked at Cohen, fear in her eyes. "We can't turn it off."

"So what do we do?" yelled Cohen, his calm washed away by the screaming terror of the disaster unfolding before his eyes. "Tell me what to do!"

"Quiet," said Mantle, gripping her head with her hands. "Let me think." She stood for six interminable seconds, then her hands flew across the console as she pulled up the feed from the engine bay again. "There, the secondary cutoff. A physical switch in the engine bay."

"How long?" asked Cohen, gauging the distance.

"Maybe a couple of minutes," said Mantle.

"I'll go. You two get to the escape pods."

"I'm coming with you, you'll never find it without me," shouted Mantle, "and he's staying here to power down all the other systems, right?"

Mueller nodded dumbly.

"Well bloody well get on with it," Mantle yelled. Then she grabbed Cohen's arm and set off down the corridor. "It's this way."

They sprinted through a ship transformed from a quiet sanctuary to a strobing hell of noise of klaxons screeching continuously in every room and corridor.

"Down here," shouted Mantle, pulling up a half-hidden hatch at the side of a corridor. Cohen had run straight past it. "It's a shortcut but – argh, fuck!" She reeled away from the hatch as noxious fumes poured out.

Cohen appeared at her side and pulled her upright. "You okay?" he shouted. She nodded, but she was obviously not okay. "We'll find another way through."

"There isn't one, it has to be this way."

Cohen peered towards the hatch. The stream of gas had lessened but it was still venting into the corridor. "I'll go," he said, pushing her away from the hatch and reaching for an emergency hood from a nearby rack. "Which way?"

She seemed on the verge of carrying on, but then she sat back down on the floor, dazed and confused by the fumes.

"Mantle, which way?" he repeated in desperation.

"Down to bottom, left through crawl space, hundred metres," she managed, then she passed out and flowed onto the floor.

"Shit," said Cohen, pulling her away from the hatch and the worst of the gas. "Mueller, you there? Mantle's unconscious. I'm going on, but you'll need to give me directions."

"I don't know the way, Commander," whined Mueller over the HUD as Cohen struggled into the emergency hood.

"Then fucking well find it," snapped Cohen, settling the hood and easing back to the hatch. "You've got thirty seconds to figure it out."

Then he clambered through the hatchway, pulling the hatch closed behind him. The gas made things difficult, even with the emergency hood and the toughened Deathless Rupert clone. He struggled down the ladder, moving as quickly as he could to escape the effects of the gas, until he reached the bottom. At least the air was free of toxic gas down here. He pulled off the emergency hood and dropped it on the floor, then checked his HUD was securely in place.

"Left, left, left," he muttered to himself, turning around and trying to work out which way was left. There were three passages leading from the ladder. Had Mantle meant left as he faced the ladder, or left from where she had been sitting on the floor of the corridor?

"Fuck," said Cohen quietly. "It's got to be this way," he muttered, bending down to push himself into one of the crawl spaces. It was dark down here – those spaces weren't lit unless they were being worked in, and hadn't been lit at all since the ambush – but the lamp on his HUD was bright enough to give him a glimpse of his destination.

"Are you there, Commander?" came Mueller's voice over the HUD.

"Of course," snapped Cohen, gritting his teeth.

"I have you on the plan. Mantle's right – this route is faster than going through the main corridors, but you must hurry."

"Just give me the next direction," Cohen breathed as he pushed his way forwards, his hands and knees scuffing at the grating that formed the floor of the crawl space. The tunnel closed in around him, as if threatening to squeeze the air from his lungs.

"Another fifty metres, then right."

Cohen muttered and cursed his way through the next fifty metres then turned right into an even narrower space.

"It's pretty bloody tight down here," said Cohen.

"Ten metres, then through a hatch on the left. That'll put you in the engine bay. The secondary cutoff will be fifteen metres ahead on the right."

Cohen forced himself down the narrow space, trying desperately to ignore the voices that warned what would happen if he got stuck.

"I'm at the hatch," he reported, "opening it now." He pushed it open and looked out into the engine bay. "Fuck," he said in shock, "the floor's ten metres down. How am I supposed to do this, eh?" He edged across the threshold and peered around at the neat, smooth walls on either side of the hatch.

"Hurry, Commander, we have only moments left."

"Fuck it," hissed Cohen, heaving himself out of the hatch until he dangled by his fingertips. He took a deep breath and let go, clutching hopelessly at the wall as it flashed past him, then bending his knees in a vain attempt to absorb the shock of impact.

"Argh," he said as he rolled across the floor. He lay, stunned, for a moment, alive but barely conscious. Then the pain flowed in and he snapped awake as Mueller yelled at him to close the lever. He glanced down at his legs, afraid to look, then heaved himself cautiously upright. Nothing broken, it seemed, and he staggered across the huge bay towards the secondary cutoff lever.

"We're almost out of time, Commander," said Mueller, seemingly resigned to his fate. "I guess we'll catch up after the next deployment."

Cohen forced himself forwards, ignoring the terrible pain in his legs, eyes focussed only on the lever. He caught his foot on something and fell, yelling as his knees protested, but he dragged himself on, stretching out his hand until it closed on the lever.

He pulled it down and it slid easily, breaking the power line to the hyperspace engine. Then he passed out and collapsed on the floor.

16

"How much longer will the repairs to the ship take, Captain Cohen?"

The captain glanced off screen, perhaps checking his notes.

"We're still looking at several weeks, I'm afraid, Prime Minister."

"Captain Cohen, please, I have told you that the Valkyr do not use formal titles except where strictly necessary to identify people. You may call me Haukland, or Miriam in a social setting," Haukland replied.

"My apologies, er, Haukland. I will try to remember, but years of protocol training from the Navy are hard to overcome. Is there anything else we need to discuss?"

"No, the duration of your stay is the most pressing issue. I think we have covered everything else for the time being, Captain Cohen. Goodbye."

"Goodbye, Prime Minister," Cohen said.

Haukland ended the call, shaking her head. It seemed that Cohen was remarkably uncomfortable addressing her by her name, and she didn't understand why that should be. How strange the people of Sol were. From her studies of the materials they had supplied, it seemed the societal structure on Sol had remained remarkably static since her own forebearers had left in the Ark ship *Koschei*.

Then again, the Children of Freyja – the Valkyr – had diverged from Koschite society many centuries before to pursue their own vision of the future. They, too, had developed their own social mores and societal structure, and there were significant differences between them and the bulk of Koschite society. Haukland recognised her own bias in thinking about her people, and she strove to understand, rather than to judge.

Perhaps in some distant future, humanity would come together again and develop an improved society based upon the hundreds of variants that were even now being tested across the galaxy, on colonies large and small. She liked to think the future for humankind was bright, and improvement was always possible, but did that mean there were many ways to be civilised, or would all societies tend towards a single, perfect outcome?

She made a note on her data slate to pose this as a question at the next session of the Folketing. It would make an excellent debate topic for the Valkyr parliament, and then later a subject for academics to investigate and draft innumerable theses upon. Now that they were beginning to re-establish contact with the governments of Sol, they would be able to gather data from across the galaxy, from both the British Commonwealth and the other spacefaring nations and collectives. Of course, as isolated as the Valkyr and the Koschite were, she wasn't sure what other factions and countries might still exist on Earth. They definitely needed to get more information and as soon as possible, if their work on *Child of Starlight* was not to be wasted.

She made a note on her government console to that effect. She had another eighteen months before the next election, and she was but one of many prime ministers empowered to lead the colonies of the Valkyr and serve their people to the best of their abilities. The interstellar Folketing would need to know everything she could find out through her new contacts.

But this vicious war that the Koschites had launched now posed a serious threat to the advancements the Valkyr had envisaged, strived towards, and planned over the decades. There were always changes, of course, but usually to restore the group vision, which had remained essentially unchanged since the schism from Koschite society. With violence spreading across this sector of the galaxy, it was becoming harder for her to see the path they had all agreed to follow.

Change is coming, she thought, *and with it the potential for life-threatening disruption.*

Her train of thought was interrupted by the Deputy Prime Minister, Ove Berdahl, who burst unannounced into her office. His face was flushed, though whether from anger or exertion she wasn't immediately sure.

Ove passed her a data slate then perched on the high stool opposite her standing desk to recover his breath. She looked at him for a moment, shaken by her deputy's unusual demeanour.

"An attack on a mining colony?" she asked, shaking the report. "What is this?"

"It's unbelievable, is what it is!" blurted Ove.

"I mean, who did this? Pirates from Sol? But surely not in such a remote system?"

"I know, it's inconceivable. I don't think it can be pirates from Sol's colonies, though. They are too far away."

"Yet who else would come out here to attack one of our mining facilities?"

Ove looked uncomfortable at the question. "I think it's the Koschites."

"The Koschites?" Haukland almost laughed. The suggestion was ludicrous. The relationship between the Valkyr and Koschite governments had stabilised shortly after the schism. There had been a tense decade or two, but that was ancient history.

Their respective governments and societies might have their differences, but they still kept communications open and there was a continuous exchange of both trade goods and scientific research. Travel between the two civilisations was common, and people often visited or spoke to their distant relatives. Freedom of movement was highly prized by both communities, although the right to leave the asteroid colonies of the Valkyr and become a Koschite citizen was rarely exercised.

The stern look on Ove's face gave Haukland pause. He was not laughing. Surely the man could not be serious?

"This is preposterous, Ove! The idea our sisters in the Koschite government would invade one of our colonies is simply not worth considering. What would even be the point? What do we have that they would want to take by force?"

"Rare elements and minerals for the war effort. You know as well as I that they have been building their military at an ever faster rate. They need materials to build ships and munitions. Why build your own mine when you can steal one that belongs to someone else? They are serious about winning this war, and now they have brought it to our doorstep. What are we going to do?"

"We will contact their government and ask what is going on, I suppose," muttered Haukland, flicking through the report again.

Ove snorted dismissively. "Miriam, they've barely responded to our communiqués over the past few months. In the current climate, we're lucky to get an acknowledgement, let alone a considered response. Things have changed. I'm not the only one to have noticed, am I?"

In truth, he wasn't, but Haukland hadn't wanted it to be true. Was she really presiding over the final days of the Valkyr's peaceful existence? Would they have to fight the Koschites to retain their independence? It was unthinkable.

"Nonetheless, we must ask for help and comment," she said firmly. "If we are to survive this war, the Koschites must not become our enemies. We must be allies, even if our worldviews are different. The Children of Freyja must not become alienated from the Koschites."

"What about these people from Sol?"

"We have to help them, too, and learn all that we can about them. Such knowledge is a valuable bargaining chip, should we need it. The time is right for us to re-establish contact with Earth. We have much to offer them in exchange for their assistance with the problems that our society will face as we follow this path," Haukland replied.

"Now you sound like a politician," Ove observed quietly. He sighed. "Very well. What do we do about the mining colony?"

"What does any man do when his house is on fire?"

Ove shrugged. "He asks his neighbour for help."

"Precisely," said Miriam. "Send a request through the usual channels. Let's see what the Koschite government has to say."

"If you insist," said Ove sceptically.

"Ove, you look more than usually distressed. Our guests arrive soon. Spit it out, whatever it is," Haukland asked, hoping that her deputy would not have discovered anything truly worth getting worked up over.

Berdahl flicked at his data slate in response and gestured helplessly at the viewscreen that formed one wall of Haukland's office. The screen had been displaying a live feed of the river that ran through the rainforest biome and on towards the sub-tropical cavern. Now the pleasant view was replaced by information dashboards that surrounded a video of a communications intelligence officer.

"The following video message is from Giacomo Khan, head of GK Industries. Identification and authenticity of the message have been verified with the usual methods. Personal ident encryption also confirmed. We conclude that the message is a genuine communication from Giacomo Khan."

The officer disappeared, and a GKI logo came spinning into the foreground from the depths of a starfield. The image was picked out in bright gold and showed a mounted archer, bow drawn and ready to shoot above the letters GKI. Miriam snorted. The man was well known and had embraced his nickname wholeheartedly, even referencing it in his company's brand.

"To whomever it may concern among the outcast group known as 'The Children of Freyja', good evening. I am Giacomo Khan, and it is my duty to inform you that my company's security teams have, in the past few hours, launched a daring operation to reclaim one of our asteroids from the hands of a group of pirates. These individuals had banded together to mine a valuable asteroid to which we hold the mineral rights, as granted by the Koschite government. A number of these renegades were captured during the operation, but others regrettably chose to attack our personnel. Our teams were forced to defend themselves with lethal force. These barbaric pirates also killed a number of their own people as they resisted our attempts to reclaim our property."

Haukland stared in disbelief as Khan's smug, self-righteous face was replaced with a video of an improvised holding pen containing a couple of dozen people.

"These criminals all claim to be members of the Children of Freyja outcast group. Having no means to secure them on our property long term, and no wish to have to enforce the standard punishment for piracy, to wit, body death. And so we turn to you, in the hope that you will take them off our hands. Names and details of the prisoners are provided along with this communiqué. Please respond quickly to confirm that you wish to accept responsibility for these miscreants and collect them, to do with as you will. If no response is forthcoming within twenty-four hours, we will be forced to try them as pirates and eject them into space. We have attached our request for reparations.

"If, as they claim, these bandits are your citizens, you will, of course, need to compensate us when making your collection. The compensation will cover both the damage they have caused to our mining claim, and the very considerable investment in the mission to reclaim our property, the costs of which are too great to be ignored," Khan stated, as calmly as if he was talking about trading grain for credits, rather than the lives of people for an extortion payment.

"Hear me well," said Khan, leaning into the camera. "Simply admit your citizens' guilt and deliver the reparations package, then you are free to collect the prisoners. But our patience is not unlimited. Take too long, and I cannot guarantee supplies of food will last."

Haukland stared at the screen in disbelief. "That fucking bastard!" she said after a moment's consideration.

She turned to Ove, who said nothing. Haukland flung an accusatory finger at Khan's paused image. "This is blackmail, Ove. He's attacked and plundered our colony, and now he wants to ransom our people and have us compensate him for the damage his troops did to our station!"

Ove nodded. "Yes," he said quietly. "It's a blatant attempt to extort resources from us on the pretext of a flimsy claim to ownership of the asteroid. We have had that system under our purview for decades. If the Koschite government have really given a mineral claim to GKI, it must have been a mistake." He flicked at his tablet, opening new files. "I checked, and our treaties cover all the star systems we have claimed. The Koschite government have never disputed any of the claims or attempted to renegotiate the treaties. Once the claims have been agreed, they've respected our rights and vice versa. There's never been a need for argument, considering we can trade for anything the other has in any case. I do not dispute these facts. What would you like to do about it? I see no other option but to pay their ransom with good grace and pretend it's legitimate."

"Pah. With that attitude, Ove, you'll never be able to become prime minister."

Ove nodded. "No, but then I didn't want to be deputy prime minister, either. I was happy at the university. I recall you telling me that it would be fun. That it would be an adventure. That we'd be able to make *Child of Starlight* a better place. I recall you daring me to do it, and when I still refused, you said you'd tell my girlfriend that I was dodging my responsibility to the colony."

Haukland waved her hand dismissively. "Yes, yes. You married her, didn't you? And now you can implement all the policies you want. And we are making the colony a better place," she pointed out.

"We are," he agreed somewhat reluctantly, "but still, this was further than I ever wanted to go with politics. I don't have the passion for it that you do, Miriam, and if you weren't running that side of things, I would be completely out of my depth. So please, tell me, what is it that you intend to do, so that I can play my part and help our people get home?"

She smiled at him. He was always about the practicalities, never interested in the political manoeuvring. That's why she had chosen him as her deputy. He might not have the ambition to match his intellect, but he was damned good at civil planning and strategy. Haukland provided the vision; he carried it out. They worked well together as a team, and if she'd been interested in him romantically, life might have been different for both of them. She wasn't jealous of Ove's wife though; she was utterly content with her role in life. Until the past few months, things had been going very well indeed for her.

Haukland steepled her fingers and said cryptically, "You'll know the answer to that very soon, Ove. Very soon indeed."

17

Berdahl jumped out of his chair like a startled mandrill when Haukland's personal assistant thrust open the door to the prime minister's office and ushered in Captain Cohen and Captain Warden. He smiled at them and awkwardly shook hands as Haukland stood up to greet them.

"Welcome, gentlemen, thank you for coming. Would you like a drink?" asked Haukland, gesturing for them to sit.

"No, thank you, prime minister, we're pressed for time, I'm afraid," Captain Cohen said as he parked himself in one of the offered chairs.

"Tea if you have it, ma'am, coffee if not," Warden responded, earning a flicker of disapproval from Cohen. The ship's captain seemed like a tightly coiled spring being forced into the chair, while Captain Warden, his Marine colleague, was far more relaxed. "Never refuse a hot wet, Captain Cohen. You never know when it might be your last in the field."

Haukland bustled at the bar while Berdahl sat in his chair, drumming his fingers on the arm.

"Your colleagues are taking the tour?" Berdahl asked, as the conversational pause lengthened uncomfortably.

"They are, yes," said Cohen. "We brought a few of the off-duty crew and Marines. They've earned a little relaxation time, but the work on *Ascendant* is not going well and I really need to get back as soon as possible to oversee it."

"We understand, Captain, but we have a pressing matter that cannot wait, and we think you might be able to help. We very much appreciate this chance to – what is your phrase? A chance to poke your brains."

Cohen nodded politely as the translations rolled across his HUD.

"We are happy to help," said Cohen. "Please feel free to poke our brains as much as you want."

Haukland turned back from the bar and placed a mug of tea on the desk in front of Warden.

"The situation is delicate," said Haukland. "Our ability to act is limited, and so we come to you in the hope that you might be able to help." She glanced at Berdahl, who took up the story.

"One of our mining colonies has been attacked," he said, flicking an image of an asteroid mining facility to the large screen on the office wall. "Pirates, we thought originally, but then we received a demand for compensation from GK Industries, a Koschite conglomerate with links to factions within their government and broad freedom to act."

"GKI's mercenaries stormed the facility and killed a number of residents. They have taken the rest hostage and demand 'compensation' for their release. They expect us to collect our people and leave the station in their control. I won't prevaricate," said Haukland. "We would like you to deliver the ransom payment – a cargo of metals – in HMS *Palmerston* and retrieve the hostages."

Cohen blinked in surprise, then frowned.

"I'm sure we can help, Prime Minister," he said slowly, "but is this not something your own people should handle?"

Haukland shook her head. "This is a peaceful colony, Captain. We have no military personnel, vessels or equipment. A straightforward ransom delivery is possible, of course, but..."

"But you're worried that something might go wrong," said Cohen, finishing the sentence for her. "Yes, I can see why you might like our help."

"How many hostages are there?" Warden asked, turning to the practicalities of the exercise.

"Twenty-six, Captain Warden."

"And what sort of force does GKI command? Are these sorts of attacks common?"

"We don't know that, I'm afraid. My guess would be only one ship and a small number of mercenaries. The miners have a habitable station, but they don't have a military presence, so an assault would be simple and easy. I simply don't have any information to confirm either way. To answer your second question, no, attacks like this are unheard of in Valkyr space."

"Then why attack, ma'am? They must be pretty confident if they're willing to demand a ransom and hold on to the mining station to boot," Cohen asked.

"They have reason to be. Perhaps my translation is obscuring matters. Let me show you the ransom demand from the aggressors," said the Prime Minister, tapping her console to replay the video message from Giacomo Khan.

The military men watched in grim silence as the video played out. Haukland stole glances, and their reaction to the translated message was plainly written on their faces. When it finished, they turned back to face her.

"So this is a private company that claims to have rights over the asteroid, and on the back of that claim they have attacked the station and taken the miners hostage? Is that about it?"

"Yes," said Berdahl. "This is all we know so far. We have not been able to contact our people on the station directly, which is obviously a bad sign."

"I take it that you believe the Valkyr have the rights to this asteroid?"

"Yes, we have treaties with the Koschite government regarding all our systems. Settlement and exploitation rights are clearly laid out and we don't share any systems with them, or vice versa. Since we are primarily interested in systems like this," said Haukland, gesturing around her, "which lack habitable planets, there are rarely disputes, but those are negotiated in any case."

"If there's no dispute, why are they so keen on this particular asteroid?" Cohen asked. "Interstellar travel for mining is a bit of an oddity, from our perspective."

"This asteroid, and others in the system, contain substantial quantities of rare elements in reasonably accessible forms. We mine asteroids on a large scale, accumulating resources from systems that are otherwise unusable, and then transport them to where they can be used," said Berdahl. "GKI does something similar, but on the basis of private enterprise."

"But, why?" persisted Cohen. "I don't understand why anyone, let alone someone from another system, would go to the effort of attacking an asteroid. How can their gains possibly make the risk and effort worthwhile?"

"I wonder if you may have misunderstood the scale of our colony," said the prime minister, "or the scale of asteroid habitation in general, perhaps because you are more used to thinking about planets where only the surface is occupied. Maybe the translation system is not helping."

She stood and moved to the viewscreen wall, banishing the face of Giacomo Khan with a gesture and bringing up a live feed of the desert biome. The camera showed a river running through a rocky desert landscape that stretched into the distance. The cavern was lit as if by a star. Vultures could be seen circling over something in the background. In the foreground, a group of figures sat around a viewscreen. Warden let out a long whistle of appreciation.

"How big is this place?" he breathed, staring at the vultures.

"*Child of Starlight* is a dwarf planet, Captain Warden," Haukland said. "To all intents and purposes, we have as much space as we want to have. The swimming pool you see in the compound is a hundred metres long, if that helps you get a sense of scale."

"You've built a desert, inside an asteroid, complete with vultures and presumably other life, so you can run what looks like a class for primary school children?" asked Warden, incredulous.

Haukland gave a thin smile. "Would that be such a bad idea?" she asked rhetorically. "But no, it's not just a teaching facility. We can run simulations on a grand scale in this biome. We can try new technologies and see how they affect the desert. Once built, can we push it back and turn empty brush into fertile forest? We can terraform here, test our ideas and improve methods so that we can, one day, speed up the process of bringing life to dead planets. We can also make more palatable environments for our citizens. One day, humanity may need to inhabit places like this simply to survive as the stars are extinguished one by one."

"Yes, but that sort of need is billions of years away," Cohen said.

"True," said Berdahl, "but we believe in being well prepared, and the terraforming technologies are of much more immediate benefit. We also use these biomes for leisure and entertainment purposes. The techniques and technologies required to build and maintain such things have many applications."

"And all of this requires a great deal of material to build, and it must be precisely the right material of course. *Child of Starlight* provides us some of what we need but the rest we get from asteroid mining and other resource gathering techniques," said Haukland.

"Wait, you said other biomes?" asked Cohen.

"Yes, of course. The artificial river you see runs in a continuous loop through many biome caverns that allow us to experience life as you would on a planet and to run experiments." The Prime Minister flicked at her slate, changing the display to briefly show an arctic zone, which was beautiful in a stark kind of way, followed by a temperate zone where a huge deciduous forest ran up to one bank of the river and the other side was green fields of pasture and crops.

Then she came back to one of her favourite zones, the tropical rainforest that she'd had on in the background earlier. First she showed them the view along the river, then she switched to another camera.

"Ah, and here we can see the tour group for your personnel."

The small group of Marines and naval personnel was being shown around by a couple of Valkyr guides. A series of treehouse homes and other buildings could be seen on the ground, behind a stockade fence. One figure could be seen striding toward the gate, a guide behind him gesturing wildly and shouting. A large monkey with an orange ruff, long blue cheeks and a scarlet nose appeared between the gates and the man walked straight up to it. They appeared to be talking to each other.

"What on earth is going on? Is that one of your Marines talking to a monkey, Tom?" Cohen asked.

Warden let out a resigned sigh. "Yes, that'll be Marine X."

"How exactly is he talking to a monkey, though? It looks like they're having a conversation."

"I did tell you he'd encountered space monkeys, but you seemed to think I was winding you up."

"The mandrills were bio-engineered by our ancestors, so they have certain improvements," explained Haukland. "They're larger than their cousins on Earth, a little more intelligent, and perfectly capable of conducting a conversation. Their vocal chords aren't entirely suited to speaking our language, but they wear throat microphones that translate for them. It prevents them from getting a sore throat. They have the same problem you would have if you tried to put on a scary growling voice to tell a story to a child. Our languages are just a bit hard on them, but that was easily solved. You say this man has met mandrills before, Captain?"

"Yes, on one of the Koschite planets we, err... visited," Warden confirmed.

"Then I'm sure he will be fine. Our mandrills are similar to theirs, though ours have the same voting rights as any other resident of *Child of Starlight*," said Haukland, watching as this Marine X was escorted into the mandrill village and up the steps to the foreman's office.

"Voting rights?" Cohen asked. "I thought you said they were only engineered to be a little more intelligent."

"Of course," said Haukland, frowning. "Out of interest, how intelligent do you think the monkeys of Earth are in comparison to us? Do you restrict voting rights to people who can't understand quadratic equations or who don't like reading? Is that how Sol runs their societies now?"

They watched as the guide approached the gates and another mandrill appeared to block his entry to the village. They spoke, then the tour guide nodded and went back to his group. Curious. The mandrills didn't invite strangers into their villages, not even Valkyr, but they had taken Marine X. Haukland made a mental note to find out about this Marine X and discover how he had persuaded the mandrills to forego their usual practice of meeting people outside the stockade. She had never heard of anyone being invited so quickly into a mandrill village.

Warden answered for Cohen, who appeared entirely flummoxed. "No, ma'am. Every government in Sol space is democratic, in one form or another, and although there are some that have experimented with alternative voting methods, they're still fundamentally democratic. We don't have any non-human voters, that's all. Captain Cohen is merely surprised by this news. It's a bit of a revelation to me too, to be honest, and I already knew about the mandrills."

"My apologies. I shouldn't be judgemental, there was no way you could have known this. We have been out of touch with Sol for a very long time." Haukland glanced at the screen, still showing Khan's frozen image.

Captain Warden said, "Getting back to the matter at hand, you want us to deliver the requested ransom, recover the hostages and return them to *Child of Starlight*? You don't want us to assault the asteroid, deal with the mercenaries, and liberate the hostages?"

The Prime Minister shook her head as Warden's words were translated.

"That approach has obvious advantages," she said carefully, "but I absolutely cannot ask you to put yourselves at risk, and we have no military resources to contribute to such an operation."

There was a pause, and it was clear that she was considering her words carefully. "I do fear that paying the ransom will embolden Khan and weaken our position, but all I can ask is that you help us carry out the exchange. It is a serious blow to lose the asteroid, but we don't have the capability to free it through military means, and our first duty is to the miners and their families."

"Hold on, there are families on board that station?" asked Cohen.

"Yes, it's a significant installation," said Berdahl. "Once the first asteroid is mined out, there will be considerable space for living quarters and as our survey drones identify similarly suitable asteroids, we'll look to mine those too. Typically, we establish an initial colony on any sizeable asteroids or dwarf planets, like *Child of Starlight,* and then use that as a base to process more asteroids. Only during the very earliest stages of a new build do we restrict families from travelling together."

"This station had plentiful facilities before the first children were allowed to live there, I assure you," said Haukland. "It's one of the reasons we're so loathe to relinquish control."

"I suppose it shouldn't surprise me," said Cohen bitterly. "The Koschites attacked New Bristol, and there are children there, too."

"That is deeply regrettable. I am unable to explain why they would attack you or allow their companies to attack us. We have recently had problems communicating through our normal channels, and I am not hopeful that we will get a response on this issue before Khan's deadline expires." She paused and looked calmly at Warden and Cohen. "Are you able to help us, Captain Cohen?"

Cohen turned over the request in his mind. *What would Admiral Staines do?* he wondered. Then he dismissed the thought. Trying to second-guess the admiral wasn't helpful.

"I will have to see information about what exactly is required," he said. "*Palmerston* isn't a big ship, and there's a limit to what she can carry."

"As soon as my technical people can confirm the requirements, I'll send the information to you, and you can let me know your decision. You'll have the coordinates of the asteroid, plans of the station, and the details of the ransom within the hour," she said.

"Understood. We'll take our leave and await further information.

If you wouldn't mind telling the guide the tour is over, we'll meet our personnel at the docking bay."

Haukland nodded and showed them out of her office, where they were escorted down to their transport ship.

"You'll take care of the details, Ove?"

"Of course, Prime Minister," said Berdahl, flicking at his slate.

"Good. Do you think they'll agree?"

Berdahl's hand hovered over his slate. Then he looked up at the prime minister.

"Yes," he said. "I think they will."

Haukland nodded, relieved, and Berdahl left to ensure that everything was in motion. Their scans of *Palmerston* had confirmed that the ship could carry the cargo and that she had space for the hostages during the cramped, but brief, return flight to *Child of Starlight*.

Then she relaxed into her chair and turned on the massage feature. For a while she lay there, letting the vibrations soothe her body while her mind mulled over the meeting.

Would Cohen understand her unspoken request?

18

Warden followed Lieutenant Commander Cohen into his conference room and headed straight for the tea. He wasn't quite sure what Haukland had served him, but it wasn't from any tea plant he recognised, and he needed something to wash away the lingering taste.

"I'll be mother, shall I?" he asked, choosing to interpret the grunt he got in response as 'Why yes, Captain Warden, I would love a cup of tea. My usual two sugars and plenty of milk, please.'

"What do you want us to do about these GKI people? Get stuck in, root them out, and free the hostages?" he asked as he slid a mug of tea across the desk toward Cohen.

The captain looked up at him and the sense of relief was palpable. "Yes, that's exactly what I want to do. These people are bloody barbarians. Attacking a space station with children on it, over a bunch of rock. It's despicable."

"Rare rock, but yes, I couldn't agree more. You don't have any objections to me planning to switch out the cargo for an assault team, then?"

"Actually, I do have some reservations. Prime Minister Haukland clearly had no idea of the military strength of these mercenaries, what kind of ship, or even ships, GKI have sent to deliver the troops or how many people have occupied the station. For all we know, we might turn up and find a thousand GKI personnel aboard the station with three light cruisers in support. Yes, I want to actually liberate the mining station, not just rescue the hostages. But we may simply be outmatched."

Cohen paused to take a sip of his tea.

"So we take the ransom with us and pay it if necessary. You'll have to work around the space problems to come up with an assault plan that we can then execute only if the situation allows it. If there aren't too many combatants there, and you think we can succeed, and the ships are something we can handle, we'll do that. If not, we play it cool, pay the ransom and live to fight another day," Cohen said. "Any major disagreement with that?"

Warden sipped his tea for a moment while he considered their options.

"No. I can't spot a problem, much though it pains me to admit we might not be able to do what we'd prefer. If we have to bring back that many hostages, we'll only be able to take a small team of Marines, and that means we can't reasonably expect to deal with large numbers of GKI mercenaries, especially when they have the advantage of home ground."

"Good, then let's see if we can work out the details while we wait for the information from the Prime Minister, hmm?" Cohen said, tapping at his slate until a projection of *Palmerston* appeared.

<C aptain Warden, I think I may be of some assistance here> Agent O transmitted.

Warden blinked. *What the hell?*

<Agent O, how are you getting through to us?>

<I am simply transmitting using your standard HUD protocols, Captain Warden. Is something wrong?>

<We're in hyperspace. You're not supposed to be able to do that>

<I'm sorry, Captain Warden. What do you mean you're not supposed to be able to do that?>

<You're not supposed to be able to communicate with us whilst we're in hyperspace> sent Warden.

<There is nothing at all unusual about what I am doing, Captain. It is quite simple to send a message on the HUD system whether or not the ship is in hyperspace>

Warden pondered that for a moment before he started to become suspicious.

<Agent O, are you on HMS *Palmerston*?>

<Yes, Captain Warden, of course I am. It would not be possible for me to communicate with you if you were in hyperspace and I was still on *Child of Starlight*>

Warden rubbed his temples.

<How did you manage to get aboard, Agent O?> Warden asked.

<We commandeered a shuttle from *Child of Starlight* and cracked into your ship's computer to alter the cargo manifest so that the loading bay crew would find a valid authorisation to take my pod aboard when we docked with your ship>

<When you say 'we', Agent O, you mean...?>

<Why, Frida Skar, of course, Captain Warden. I should have thought that was obvious>

Warden pulled open the maglock drawer on the tiny desk in his cabin and pulled out a couple of painkillers, knocking them back with a dose of good strong water. That was as exotic as drinks got on *Palmerston*. There was no space for anything that smacked of luxury.

<Are you still in the loading bay?>

<Yes, Captain. My pod is still in the loading bay, although I am not confined to it, of course>

Not confined to it? He wasn't sure he wanted to know what Agent O meant by that, but he was pretty confident it would go down like a ton of bricks with Cohen.

<I'm on my way down to see you both> Warden replied.

Before he went down to the loading bay, he stopped in at the small bridge that perched atop the great barrel of the rail cannon.

Going up and down levels in *Palmerston* was mostly achieved with ladders to minimise space requirements. It was quite the most uncomfortable ship he had ever been on.

Warden went straight to Cohen's side and whispered in his ear, starting with a pre-emptive warning that the captain shouldn't get angry. It didn't work. Cohen leapt to his feet.

"Midshipman Robinson, you have the con," he announced.

On *Ascendant*, Warden would have had trouble keeping up with Cohen, but you couldn't get far on *Palmerston* before you had to change direction and they soon had to slide down a ladder to reach the mess hall, such as it was.

Inside they found the Valkyr scientist, Frida Skar, eating a sandwich and poring over her data slate.

Cohen coughed to announce his presence when she didn't look up. She seemed lost in her own world, barely paying attention to her half-eaten meal but scrolling up and down her screen and muttering to herself. Cohen coughed again.

"If you are ill, Captain," said Skar in Koschite without looking up, "then I would appreciate it if you would see a medic and not cough all over me. I am an extremely important scientist and the Valkyr can ill afford to lose me to some primitive virus you have brought from Sol."

Warden bit his lip as the translation scrolled across his HUD. Lieutenant Commander Cohen was technically his superior and certainly not in the mood for laughter after finding a stowaway on his ship, but Warden struggled to contain himself.

"Miss Skar, I am not ill–" he began.

"Then why are you coughing? This is not logical; we cough when something is affecting our throat or lungs. If you are not carrying some kind of virus or bacteria, have you perhaps inhaled a large quantity of particulates? If so, you should still see a medic because that could easily damage your respiratory system."

Warden held back a laugh as his superior grew red. "I was coughing to get your attention," Cohen said, "not because I am ill and not because I have inhaled something I shouldn't!"

"That is silly and inefficient. And anyway, I don't want to give you my attention. I have far more important things to be doing."

Cohen was growing visibly angrier. Probably not a good idea to ask him for anything for the rest of the day.

Then the captain reached out and pulled the data slate from Skar's hands. She looked up in horror.

"Give that back this instant, Captain Cohen! That research belongs to me!" she spat with venom, the most emotion Warden had yet heard from her.

"Shan't," came the rejoinder from Cohen. "Not until you tell me what the bloody hell you're doing aboard my ship!"

"I'm doing research, obviously. I'm a research scientist. What else would I be doing?"

Exasperated, Cohen turned to Warden for support, but his eyes narrowed suspiciously when he saw the look on the Marine's face. He turned back to Skar.

"How did you board my ship? Why did you board my ship? Are you a spy?"

Skar laughed. "Why would I want to spy on you, Captain? Are you a physicist?"

"Not you, madam, your government. I repeat, why did you sneak aboard?"

She cocked her head. "I didn't sneak aboard. I presented my credentials and your crew accepted them and welcomed me aboard. A nice young lady showed me where the cafeteria was."

"Your authorisation was the result of breaking into our computer systems, Miss Skar," Cohen fumed.

"I didn't break into them."

"Then who did?"

"Ornament, of course. I don't know anything about cracking into computers, but for Ornament it was apparently a 'breeze'. That was the word it used. Does that make sense?"

It made sense to Warden, though it wasn't entirely comforting to know the AI had described their security that way.

<Yes, it was a breeze. Your security systems are hopeless, Captain>

"What in the name of the stars possessed you to come aboard the ship without permission?" Cohen asked.

Skar stared at Cohen in puzzlement. "We came to save the hostages, of course."

"Save the hostages?" Cohen spluttered.

"Yes. Why else would I be here? My research is impaired by being in this environment. I would only place myself in this situation if it were of the utmost moral imperative."

"To save the hostages?" Cohen asked helplessly.

"Yes, to save the hostages. Must I repeat myself so often? It is tedious, and I have work to do, you know. Even without a laboratory, I have notes to collate, data to interpret and hypotheses to test."

Cohen's shoulders sagged and he turned to Warden and mouthed something at him. Whether it was an imprecation or a silent plea for help, Warden wasn't quite sure, but he thought he'd give it a go.

"Frida, how are you going to help free the hostages?"

"I would have thought that was obvious, Captain Warden," she said.

He nodded along. "Sure, sure. But perhaps not quite as obvious to us as to a genius like yourself. Would you mind explaining how you'll help, and while you're at it, it would be really nice to know what made you think you should try?"

Skar sighed. "The hostages are citizens of the Children of Freyja. It was explained to me in some detail that it is our responsibility to do everything we can to rescue them without further harm. So I came with Ornament to assist you with the liberation of the mining colony. Ornament can help you plan your assault and provide intelligence as you carry it out, much as it did on the research facility."

<It? It? I'm not a box of nuts and bolts, you know>

"You *are* a thing, Ornament. You don't have gender, or biological life, so 'it' is the correct pronoun," Skar responded verbally, though Warden, and Cohen by the look of him, had seen the message too. *How had Skar, though?* Warden wondered. She wasn't wearing a HUD visor. These Valkyr had an air of mystery about them. Did she have an audio feed perhaps?

<But I have children!>

"No, you have forks. And this is not the time to revisit that particular philosophical discussion, Ornament."

<At least call me Agent O>

Skar sniffed. "I refuse to do that. It's childish."

<It's fun!>

Skar rolled her eyes at Cohen and Warden, throwing her hands in the air as if to say, 'See what I have to deal with?'

"So, gentlemen, we are several days from the colony by my calendar, and I have a lot of work to do. Since I am here primarily to bring Ornament onboard and monitor how well *it* processes the tasks that you will have for it, perhaps you might leave me to my work? If you have any questions of a tactical or military nature, I'm sure Ornament will be more than happy to answer them. At length. In great detail."

<Agent O!> Ornament protested.

Cohen gave up in exasperation and stormed from the room. Warden smiled lopsidedly and waved over his shoulder as he followed.

19

<C aptain, it is time to fire your weapon!>

"Yes, thank you, Agent O, we're well aware of that. Midshipman Elson, fire when ready."

"Package away, sir. Impact in T minus forty-five seconds."

They watched the feed in the rail cannon bay as the skeleton crew reloaded the weapon with another sabot. This one was a shining tube of metal, with a pointed end and an interior filled with dense rock. With a mass impact driver, you didn't need an elegant sabot, merely a mass that would hold together until it hit the target.

Cohen glanced at the second feed, which showed the progress of the first shot.

"How are you doing in there, Captain Warden?"

"Hnnggh!" came the strangled reply. Vital signs were good, though a couple of the marines had passed out from the g-force. Cohen glanced across at Parks, who was monitoring their trajectory and checking to see they hadn't been killed outright by the rapid acceleration. Parks held out her hand and wiggled it from side to side.

"You're doing splendidly, Captain. Everything is absolutely fine. You're on target and the boarding pod will have you there in no time.

Just a few seconds more," he said encouragingly, grinning at the Marines' discomfort.

"Second shot away, sir. Impact in T minus twenty-five," said Elson as he fired the rail cannon again, this time with a rather deadlier cargo.

"Any sign of a response?"

"No, sir, enemy ship's status is unchanged," Midshipman Shepherd said.

"T minus fifteen seconds on the drop pod," Parks confirmed.

"Robinson, follow that sabot. I want to make sure the threat from the GKI ship has been removed."

"Aye aye, sir. Engines full ahead," Robinson acknowledged.

"Railguns targeted on the enemy vessel and ready on your order, sir."

"Hold until we know it's necessary, Elson," Cohen said.

"T minus five seconds on the drop pod," Parks said.

"Enemy vessel is emitting chatter, sir. She's firing thrusters," Shepherd said.

"Drop pad retro rockets firing."

"Drop pod engaged with target. All troops safely delivered," Parks confirmed.

Cohen smiled grimly at the completion of the first phase of their plan. Now he just had to finish off the GKI vessel so it couldn't cause problems. "Elson, will our shot connect?" he asked.

"Thrust and mass parameters of enemy vessel unknown, sir. It's going to be close."

"Stand by to fire railguns."

"Aye, sir."

<This is exciting, isn't it? The Marines are already attacking>

Cohen ignored the AI, grateful that it was using text and not a voice, which he was sure would be giddy with excitement.

"Three, two, one. Impact!" Elson said.

"Damage assessment, Mr Elson. Quick as you can, please."

Elson turned to face him. "Not a direct strike I'm afraid, sir. We hit the fore section and appear to have taken out their comms array, but the ship was moving and hasn't been crippled. Damage to the enemy vessel is substantial but not critical."

"She's moving, Captain!" Robinson called out.

"Then let's pursue her, Midshipman."

He sent a message to the assault team as he gave orders, <Pursuing enemy vessel. Stand by for update>

<Roger that. Happy hunting>

"Elson, fire railguns at will. Robinson, don't lose them. These GKI privateers are going to learn that the Royal Navy doesn't tolerate piracy."

20

"Fletcher, Drummond, take point. Colour Milton and I are your support. Goodwin, get me drone coverage of the areas that have gone dark. Ten?"

"Yes, sir?"

"You've seen the footage of the GKI attack. These people kill women and children for sport. They deserve a taste of their own medicine, wouldn't you agree?"

"My sentiments exactly, Captain."

"Teach them what it means to be hunted by a Royal Marine, Ten," Warden ordered.

Ten snapped a quick salute and then pushed off with his legs, jumping with the assistance of his power armour up through the remnants of the bio-dome roof. The bundles of artificial muscle fibre, combined with the low gravity of the asteroid, allowed him to leap like a cricket. He thrust out one hand and a grapnel fired out over the surface of the station, pulling him quickly from sight.

Warden didn't know exactly where he was going, but Agent O had cracked the station's security and accessed archived and current video feeds throughout Oldervik. Ten was receiving updates as quickly as they came and, guided by the near omniscient Agent O, he would take care of any GKI troopers while Warden and Milton led the rest of the team directly to the hostages.

He waited for Goodwin to finish launching drones and follow Colour Milton into the station before he moved. The frozen trees were a harrowing reminder of the video Agent O had extracted from the station shortly after *Palmerston's* arrival.

They had watched the attack from the perspective of cameras inside the bio-dome. Watched as the GKI boarding pod crashed through the alloy and glass lattice. Watched as atmosphere, plants and people alike were sucked into space. Watched as the GKI mercs, heedless of the carnage, had tramped past the dead and opened the doors into the rest of the station.

Warden rolled his shoulders, checked his rifle and headed after Goodwin, who was moving through the first door. He wanted to be calm, rational, in control. But deep down he knew there was another part of him that wanted revenge, that wanted to punish the attackers for what they'd done.

"You okay, boss?" Milton asked as he closed the door behind them, as if she sensed something wasn't quite right.

"Yeah, I'm fine. Let's get this done and get these people their station back so they can rebuild their lives."

"Roger that. You heard the captain. Let's get in position before Ten makes himself known," Milton said, gesturing with her left hand for Fletcher and Drummond, in their hulking ogre clones, to move out.

<A ny chance you're going to say anything useful?>
      <I'm sorry, Marine X, I thought I had been>
<I mean, useful to the current problem. Not useful if I wanted to know the primary uses for rhodium>
<Which problem is that, Marine X?>
<The entry hatchway's location>
<I already told you that when we were planning the mission on HMS *Palmerston*, Marine X>

Ten sighed. <Yes, I know that. But now that I'm here, in the dark, it turns out that secondary airlock fourteen isn't actually marked by a big red ring and the word ENTRY. Can you put a wireframe in my HUD to make things a bit more obvious?>

<Yes, I can do that. Will that do?>

Green and red lines appeared beneath his feet, tracing the corridors and rooms of the station interior as he looked around him. Red indicated an airlock or doorway. A fat yellow arrow floated at the bottom of his view, pointing off to his left.

Turning, Ten saw that the hatchway he had been looking for was a hundred metres away or more. He reached it with a few leaping steps. In gravity as low as this, you had to develop a new way of moving if you wanted to make speed. You couldn't just run as you would on a normal-sized planet, you had to turn each stride into a long bounce, loping across the surface almost as if it were a gigantic trampoline. It took a lot of practice, and it had been years since Ten had tried.

Caution being the better part of valour, he took his time. He didn't want to risk a stride that would bounce him far into the void before bringing him crashing back down somewhere he hadn't intended, like onto an observation window, for instance.

<Almost at the hatch> he sent to Captain Warden, receiving a brief confirmation blip in acknowledgement.

<Have you got any internal footage of this area?> he asked Agent O. He hated relying on the AI. Its personality seemed flaky at best, but its information so far had been first rate. If it went on the fritz in the middle of a mission when he was relying on it, though, he'd be in serious trouble.

<No, this hatch is a blind spot. Technically, there could be a GKI mercenary guarding the inside, but if so, they haven't moved in the last thirty-four minutes while we've been approaching Oldervik>

Ten considered that for a moment. Was it likely there was an enemy merc standing in just the right spot to guard this particular entrance without showing on a camera? They had assessed dozens of entry points while planning the assault, but this one had seemed to

Ten to be the most likely to be useful. It wasn't particularly special, so it shouldn't be guarded.

See? he thought. *That's exactly the sort of sloppy over reliance you need to avoid.* If he hadn't been looking for guidance from the AI, he would have breached the airlock already and found out for himself if it was guarded, dealing with it on the fly. Now he had wasted valuable time just thinking about it.

He tapped in an engineering code the Valkyr had supplied and, sure enough, it overrode the airlock's protocols and allowed him to open the external hatch. Ten dropped down into the wide tube below, pulling the hatch shut above him. Gas flooded the chamber and the lighting scheme inside changed from a wan red to a lurid green. He span the wheel on the door opposite him and pushed it open, weapon raised.

Ten checked left and right. The corridor was empty.

<Any hints, Agent O or am I going to have to find these bastards the old-fashioned way?>

<If you turn around, and head toward the red dot on your map, you can reach a viable target within one hundred and sixty-three metres, Marine X. Here is a camera feed>

Ten moved off immediately. He had a lot of work to do, and very little time to do it.

<Thanks. Is the target alone?> he asked. The GKI goon was sitting on a sofa in someone's quarters, watching something on the viewscreen while munching on snacks. He wasn't wearing power armour, and it looked like he believed himself to be safe.

<Negative. The target has a hostage in the bedroom of the apartment, restrained to the bed>

Ten stopped as the rage rose, struggling for calm. He needed to be in control, not let his personal feelings get in the way. This portion of the station was living quarters and had functioning artificial gravity, allowing him to run toward the target.

<Can you open that door for me?>

<Yes. It will take one third of a second for it to open fully>

<Time it so it's open by the time I run through it, okay?>

<Certainly, Marine X>

<Call me Ten> he sent as he rounded the corner and saw the door outlined in red. Off centre a red wireframe figure was seated in the first room. He sprinted for the door.

<The target is beginning to react to the sound of your footsteps. Impact in three, two – opening door> Agent O sent, updating Ten even though he could see the wireframe figure rising and reaching for a long arm of some description.

It didn't do him any good. Ten flew through the open door and hit the figure like a maglev, ramming his armoured shoulder into the animal's gut, punching him from his feet and leaving him winded, gasping desperately for air.

"*Dobryy nochnoy tovarishch,*" he said as his fist hammered into the man's face.

<Agent O, where's the nearest airlock? My friend and I need to have a word outside>

<Out of the apartment and to the left>

Ten grabbed the semi-conscious man by the scruff of his neck and dragged him from the room.

Sergeant Grigory Sokolov blinked against the spots in his eyes. Dammit, his head was killing him. What had he drunk? That bitch had had some strong stuff in her liquor cabinet, but he didn't remember drinking that much. His mouth tasted acrid, like vomit and blood. He drew his hand up to wipe his mouth and it clanked against the visor of his helmet. Wait, when had he put on an environment suit?

A voice came through his helmet speakers.

"Wakey, wakey, sunshine." He had no idea what that meant.

He tried to look around but he could barely move. Then the voice came back. This time he could understand the language.

"You think you're a soldier, don't you, boy? A big hard man? Running around, doing the dirty work for this Khan fella."

Sokolov swallowed blood and spit. There was an armoured figure in front of him with rank and company markings he didn't recognise. Who was this man? He wasn't wearing Valkyr power armour, not that they really had a military force.

"Not a talker, eh? Your type rarely are, I've found. No problem, I can talk the hind leg off a donkey, but strictly speaking, this is a diversion, and as special as you are, I'm going to have to work extra hard to catch up. Normally, I'd take the time to explain my point of view about your particular activities, but instead I thought a practical demonstration would make my point far more quickly," Ten said, hammering the control to open the airlock they were stood in.

Atmosphere vented rapidly and Sokolov felt the familiar change in pressure on his suit.

"Who are you?" he spat through his bloodied lips, struggling to stand up.

"Me? I'm justice, son," said Ten said, reaching out and ripping away a patchwork of duct tape.

For Sokolov, the agony was immediate. His suit began to blare alarms at him, flashing warnings of depressurisation. All he could think about was the intense pain from his crotch as the coldness of vacuum did its work.

"That's my first point, you vicious bastard. Don't think you'll be feeling hard any time soon. Not in the usual sense, anyway. You're probably feeling really hard in the literal one, eh? No? Not even a courtesy laugh? Well, I dunno, a man lays his hand on a woman, a civilian woman, claiming to be a soldier. Forces himself on her. Then he loses all sense of honour. You're barely a man at all," said Ten, hauling him to his feet.

"Didn't anyone ever tell you not to lay hands on a woman without her permission? No? Perhaps there's something special about yours that makes you think you can grab anyone you please, eh? Let's see them then," Ten said, pulling the gloves of the environment suit from Sokolov's hands. The gloves hadn't been attached properly and they came away easily.

Sokolov howled as the cold gripped his hands. He could feel his blood freeze and he thrashed about but Ten held him firmly.

"Bit nippy is it? Your hands don't look special to me," Ten said, pulling up one of Sokolov's hands by the wrist. He wiggled the index finger and it snapped off at the joint, frozen solid. Sokolov felt an urge to puke as he looked at his abruptly truncated digit.

"You know. I don't think many women will want you to touch them with these. Why don't you go and have a look and see if you can find some to ask, eh?"

Sokolov found himself hurled out of the airlock, onto the surface of Oldervik. He stumbled back towards the airlock. The door slid closed before he could get there.

The sudden loneliness – the vast silence of the void – was unbearable. A long-forgotten fear of the dark arose again in Sokolov, and he wailed out his despair and terror.

The power armoured enemy stood on the inside, watching through the window, his eyes pitiless. Sokolov banged his hand on the door, and it snapped off at the wrist.

The man inside turned away from the airlock, and Sokolov fell to his knees as his body began to freeze.

21

< Ten, do you intend to deal with every target in the same manner? If so, I fear you may run out of time>

<No. That seemed like a special case>

<Would you like the location of the next target?>

<Give me all the targets you can find>

A small flurry of red dots appeared on the tactical map in his HUD. Ten began to move, heading down the corridor then up a staircase.

<Ten, that is not the most direct route to the nearest target>

<I know, but I have an idea. You control all the doors in this place, right?>

<Yes, Ten>

Ten ringed a large circular room on the tactical map.

<See how close they are to this room? Can you open the doors nearest them and close them again so they notice, and keep doing it until they come and investigate that room?>

<You wish to lure several targets to one spot for efficiency of elimination?>

Ten pounded up several flights of stairs. The Valkyr artificial intelligence was pretty quick on the uptake. It didn't get everything, but it had told him it had studied a wide range of the classic military texts as well as basic training manuals. It didn't have access to anything that had been done after the Ark ship *Koschei* left Sol, though.

<Got it in one. A door moving on its own should make them suspicious>

<There are other methods I could use to lure them. Would you like me to try them?>

<Improvise, adapt, overcome. Go right ahead>

<I will do as you request. Do you wish them all in one group?>

Ten climbed into an engineering lift and slapped the up arrow.

<No, better if they're spread out throughout the room, not on the same level of the space. Understood?>

<Yes, Ten, I understand. You wish them to be proximate to one another but not in the same place, so you can target them individually and quickly move to the next target>

<Yup>

<I will let you know when my pawns are in place>

Ten chuckled as he exited the lift, climbing out onto the gantry of a huge cylindrical atrium that plunged deep into the asteroid below. Above was a geodesic dome with a view out into space. Below him was a multi-purpose room, much of which was devoted to hydroponic units. Other areas were used for storage space or even picnic tables. This was probably a good place to eat your lunch, especially if you really liked fresh salad.

Not all the plants would be edible; some were likely to be efficient processors of atmosphere. Somehow the air smelled better when filtered through plants rather than carbon-nano filters – although, theoretically, it shouldn't make any difference. Ten's personal belief was that the plants added pollutants of their own, introducing a smell associated with freshness.

Ten checked the tactical map, flipping it to an isometric projection so he could more easily distinguish the different levels of the room. Sure enough, whatever Agent O had been doing, the GKI bastards were heading in the right direction. Once he knew where they were heading, he moved down to meet the one who would be highest up the structure.

The man walked through a door moments later, looking around as if he'd lost something. He reached up and pressed a button on the side of his HUD mount. Probably rebooting it, confused at whatever false information Agent O was feeding him.

Ten appeared behind him. A pale amber glow rose up between them and a soft hum could be heard. With a sizzle, the Deathless vibro-knife slid home through the mercenary's spine and into his heart. For good measure, Ten had clamped his hand over the condemned's mouth to stifle his cries, however unlikely that was. He levered the knife forward, slicing through more of the chest as he freed it. Then he took his thumb off the button and wiped the now static knife on the trooper's uniform.

With both hands free and the use of his power armoured strength, Ten lifted the corpse clear off the ground and walked it over to a nearby seating area, laying it gently on a couch near some coffee tables.

"Nothing of any use," he muttered as he frisked the body.

Then he checked the map. One level below him another target was about to enter. He looked down at the floor and then upended a vase from one of the coffee tables, letting the water drip through the grill to the solid floor below. He took the cut flowers and dropped a couple on the dead merc, then scattered the rest down the flight of stairs nearby.

Ten blended into the shadows and waited. It wasn't long before the red dot on his HUD reached the dribbled water. There was some kind of profane exclamation, then the sound of hurried footsteps as the trooper climbed the first flight of stairs. They slowed when they reached the first flowers, and more cursing followed.

The red dot, a woman as it transpired, reached the top of the stairs and looked about, taking a few seconds to spot the prone figure on the couch. She hissed something at him as she approached. There was enough time for her to pull aside the blanket, revealing the bloodstained chest, then her hand flew to her belt.

Ten didn't give her time to draw her sidearm. He snapped her neck, a mercifully quick death that she probably didn't deserve, but easily and cleanly accomplished in power armour against an unarmoured foe. In his youth, following the example set by numerous holovids, he had tried snapping necks with his bare hands, but he'd soon realised he should stick to the tried and trusted methods taught by the unarmed combat instructors during commando training. The first and most important of which was, of course, don't ever be caught unarmed.

His HUD showed his third and fourth targets had met up three levels below, so he dropped the body on the couch with her friend and padded down the stairs. Apparently the Valkyr liked a little luxury in their facilities as the treads were actually carpeted. Not real carpet, of course, but some close approximation that was considerably better than bare metal for his purposes. He was wearing Commando class stealth armour, complete with soft-soled armoured boots.

Ten was still a little vexed that he hadn't been able to try out an ogre clone yet. Honestly, it was starting to feel like someone in authority was denying him the chance to test one out. He couldn't remember pissing off any generals, at least not recently, so maybe it was simply bad luck.

On the plus side, the standard marine clone and light power armour he was using were familiar and comfortable, like a well-worn pair of jeans. He could slip into them and immediately have full control. That was what allowed him to stalk a pair of GKI men and open both of their throats with his vibro-knife before they had registered his presence.

He finished them swiftly with a thrust to the heart, cutting off the bubbling gasps as they tried to suck down air, even while their blood pumped from their necks. Mercy wasn't on the cards tonight, but he didn't need them thrashing about and making a noise to warn or interrupt his next kill.

Wiping the knife quickly, because getting dried blood out of a sheath was always fiddly, he stood up and moved to the railing overlooking the atrium. His HUD overlaid the positions of the enemies that Agent O had identified. The next was three storeys down. He checked the mission timer.

Too fucking long, he thought, cursing himself for being self-indulgent with his earlier punishment work.

A thought occurred to him and he grinned wickedly in his helmet.

<Agent O, can you shut down the artificial gravity in this section? >

<Yes. Would you like me to do so? I do not understand why? Won't it alert the targets that something is wrong?>

<Probably. Are any of them in power armour?>

<No>

<Be ready to cut the gravity on my go, then>

<Yes, sir!>

<Don't call me sir, I'm not an officer, Agent O. I'm a mere Penal Marine trying to serve out his time> he sent as he pulled a small table over to the railing and used it as a step to stand on top of the railing, steadying himself with one hand on a nearby pillar.

<Are you sure? Your files suggest that you have had your sentence increased on a number of occasions for infractions that could have been avoided>

<I don't know what you mean – and stop reading our files, they're supposed to be classified> Ten replied as he shot his grapnel line over a cross strut above him, then swiftly set it to pay out the correct length of line.

<Ready?> he asked.

<Yes. It will take two seconds for the gravity to switch off once I deactivate it>

<Do it now> sent Ten, a moment before he dove head first into the shaft.

As he plummeted through the atrium, he calmly released the mag lock that kept his suppressed carbine attached to his breastplate and pointed it toward the enemy. He was one storey above the level of the next target when the gravity dropped to a fraction of Earth normal and his acceleration slowed dramatically. The target was looking about in surprise when Ten slowly dropped past him and pumped a burst into his head.

Ten continued to drop, the line from the grapnel slowing his descent just enough to give him thinking time. Five more targets in total in this space. All of them surprised to find themselves without standard gravity. The next two were on opposite sides of the same level and he had to shoot the first from above as he fell, then wrench his body wildly to turn and shoot the second before he dropped below their level and they vanished from view.

Only now he was spinning good and fast. It was starting to make him dizzy, and he didn't need to be disoriented right now. Fighting drunk in a bar was one thing; fighting the urge to puke inside a helmet while despatching three combatants was quite another.

He pressed a button on his grapnel and released the line, hoping that he'd remembered the depth of the atrium correctly. Without the grapnel to slow him, he would begin to accelerate again, even in this low gravity. Looking down, he could see the last three gathering near the ground floor. They were about to look up.

Ten snatched a small object from his belt and threw hard, sending it streaking towards the ground below. He tried to aim the throw, but there was still a little spinning going on, either in his head or because he was actually rotating. No time to think.

The flashbang went off and the Deathless trio floated away from the detonation, hands covering their ears. Ten hit the ground and bounced, bringing his left fist down on the skull of one as he hit the deck.

Bone splintered, and Ten winced as realised he'd have to wash the armour later. You only had to put away gore-spattered power armour once to appreciate the lesson about showering after combat.

He dropped to one knee to absorb his momentum. The remaining two GKI troopers turned to look at him in amazement, twisting in the air.

That's right, look at me, the big damned hero, landing right among you, he thought.

Then he struck, and when it was over, he looked in dismay at his gauntlets. Drenched in gore.

<There are towels and a jet wash in a cleaning station behind you; the botanists use it for washing up after potting> Agent O.

Bloody hell, thought Ten. *That was damn close to reading my mind.*

It didn't stop him pushing off to float across to the cleaning station, though. He rinsed quickly, wiping himself clean while he plotted his next move.

"Warning. Artificial gravity loss in atrium core. Manual reset required. Recommend immediate action to prevent loss of food supplies. Please use the nearest station panel to confirm acknowledgement. This message repeats in three minutes."

<Ten, sitrep> sent Captain Warden.

<Just cleaning up> Ten replied, bracing against the wall as the water sprayed across his armour.

<You're done?>

<More or less> Ten checked the tactical map. <There's a few stragglers, but only one hostage that I've seen. Do you want me to pick them off or come to you for the assault?>

<We're good here. Agent O has got us video of the enemy. Only a few guarding the hostages, but we'll have to make it through their colleagues first. There are alterations to the original plans the Valkyr supplied, so we can't make entry the way we planned. They're not moving, so you get the stragglers and we'll go if we have to>

<Roger that. Omw>

<C aptain. Can you hold for about six more minutes?>
            <No idea, Ten. Colour Milton had to scrag some guy they sent out to investigate the atrium. They might come looking for him any minute>

<I think I can get to the room they're holding the hostages in. Agent O has found a route. Permission to risk life and limb in the interest of saving civilians?>

22

Warden considered for a moment. They'd arrived a day earlier than the ransom required, thanks to some prompt action and hard work by Captain Cohen and his crew, but surely even these low-level scum would soon notice they were missing people. Then again, Agent O's video showed a lot of drinking amongst the GKI troopers. Maybe they were just too distracted.

<Permission granted> Warden sent. There was a long pause with no response. <Ten? Problem?>

<No. No problem. I was just hoping you'd say no. The access isn't what you'd call welcoming>

<But it will work!> Agent O chimed in.

<Easy for you to say> Ten replied.

<Can you do it or not, Ten?> Warden asked.

<Yeah, I can do it. But someone owes me a beer after this. And a shower. No, make that three showers, with industrial cleaning solvent>

<Then get on with it. Can't be worse than the assault course, can it?>

<Ha. Ha. Ha. Wanna bet, Captain?> Ten sent <Effecting entry now, updates before breach. Suggest simultaneous entry upon breach>

<Roger that>

Warden turned to Colour Milton who shrugged. What the hell was Ten having to do? Every entry they'd examined while he'd been clearing out the stragglers had been dismissed. The GKI troops had booby-trapped a couple of doors and some of the station's plans had been superseded by later modifications. They could blow a hole through the wall, but their goal was to get through the mission without civilian casualties, and that would be hard enough without using explosives.

<Everyone get ready to breach on the first sign of trouble> Warden sent to the rest of the team.

The Marines were huddled inside corridors and alcoves, clustered around the rec room where the GKI mercenaries had holed up.

~

Ten wriggled in the tight space which Agent O had so kindly found for him. It wasn't designed for humans, though thankfully there had been an access hatch in a maintenance room that let him get into the conduit in the first place. Still, he'd had to ditch his armour, and even with the lean muscle of a Marine clone, this was a tight squeeze.

Compounding the tightness of the space was the thick layer of greasy effluent running down it. The hostages were being held in the kitchen, and this pipe led to the system for disposing of cooking oil and food scraps. Ten wondered idly if it would smell worse in an omnivorous kitchen rather than one that prepared only the vegetable-based diet of the Valkyr.

Another wriggle and he made it a few centimetres further up the tube. He took a deep breath and tried to avoid the urge to puke. Then another wriggle, and another. Ten was beginning to regret raising this option with the captain.

Was it the stench, the claustrophobic confines, the grease that made it hard to move, or the lack of weaponry and armour that was bothering him? Just about the only plus was that his small handheld lamp was so covered in filth that he couldn't see most of what he was more or less sliding through.

Five metres to go. Ten fought to keep from slipping backwards down the pipe as he made each shuffling move forwards. It wasn't steep, just inclined enough to keep the waste flowing down to the lower level for recycling. It was the oil that made it particularly hard. Why was he doing this, again? For people he didn't know. As soon as he had the thought, he felt guilty.

He was doing it because of the woman crying in her bathroom. He was doing it because of the mother and child he'd seen torn out into the vacuum of space by the breach made by the GKI troops. He was doing it for the same damned reasons he'd fought in every filthy skirmish, uprising and combat zone across the Commonwealth since he was a young man, oh so long ago. Ten didn't like bullies.

Correction, he thought. *I fucking hate bullies, and there's some of them in the room up ahead. Just a little further and you can teach them some manners.* All above board; not just justice, but legal justice.

Ten renewed his efforts, concentrating on developing a skill that he would almost certainly never use again in his life. Definitely not if he did something else better, like find some other poor bastard to do this sort of thing for him. That was the downside of not being in command. As a Marine, you got ordered about. Officers didn't do this sort of stuff, or take this sort of risk. Except sometimes killing officers, like Atticus and Warden.

They were good kids, and Warden needed him to do this. He'd seen the look on the lad's face when the AI had shown them the archive footage. His own face had remained blank, but he thought Warden had been close to tears. Ten had looked away, giving him his privacy. There was no shame in it, but he didn't have time to offer counselling in the middle of combat, and not everyone responded to tough love.

<I'm at the grate, Agent O. Anyone near me?>

<No, they are on the other side of the kitchen. There is a rubberised matting on the floor, so you can slide the grate out onto it without making too much noise. It's designed to be lifted for cleaning and isn't bolted down>

<Thanks. Very informative. Remind me to take you with me next time I have to crawl through a sewer>

<It's not a sewer. If you remember, you refused to use the sewer even though it has a much larger pipe and an easier approach>

<Yes, because a) it would smell of actual shit, which for some reason I thought would smell worse and which I'm now willing to admit I may have been mistaken about, and b) because I'd have had to smash my way through the toilet as well>

<I don't know why you are complaining. I found you goggles from that bedroom, didn't I?>

<True, true. I'm not convinced about the pinkness and the glitter in them, though. It's almost as if you deliberately found a little girl's goggles instead of her brother's>

<If I did do that, would it not be an excellent practical joke?>

<Yes, yes it would> Ten conceded as he slowly lifted the grate.

<Good. I will tell Frida. She maintains I am not capable of a sense of humour. I maintain that she is not. This will be a feather in my cap. Also, her brother's goggles were on the other side of the room. Ha. Ha>

Ten rolled his eyes and slid up into the room, looking about for what he needed most to deal with the GKI in the room. Yes, there it was. In a crouch, he moved forward and reached out, taking hold of a kitchen towel and carefully rubbing his face clean, or as clean as he could, before pulling the goggles up. He blinked a couple of times to make sure nothing had run into his eyes, then he wiped his HUD clean and slipped it back on.

Instantly the red outlines of three GKI mercenaries and the green outlines for the hostages appeared in the overlaid wireframe view of the room. Two were seated eating a meal. A double tap to the head with his suppressed pistol dealt with them. The one he shot from behind slumped forward into his food. The other just slumped.

Ten was moving to the third man, who was standing nearer the hostages as they huddled at one end of the room, near the pantries and cold storage. There were only women there, and for a moment he thought the GKI troops might have murdered the men and children, but his HUD showed them locked away in the large storage rooms that supplied the kitchen. They were alive.

The third man turned to face him, dropping his weapon so that it dangled from his neck by a strap as his mouth opened in a silent protest. Ten raised his pistol.

"Niet! Niet!"

Ten paused, lifting the barrel as he advanced and aiming it just to the side of the GKI man's head. "Why shouldn't I shoot you, hmm?"

"Niet! Niet!"

Ten switched his HUD to auto-translate. This was as good a time as any to give the head shed's work a field test.

"What's your name?" he said. The HUD offered him a translation into Koschite, all neatly laid out in phonetic English, but clearly the man's own HUD was giving him a translation. Ten watched as the man frowned at his HUD, then he started babbling.

"Specialist Popov," the snivelling man said, then sneezed. He looked startled. "Please, I have the fever of the hay. They grow many plants here."

Translation isn't quite right, thought Ten, *but it'll do for now.*

"Why shouldn't I shoot you?" Ten asked again.

"I am soldier just like you! I don't want to be here, they made me come. GKI force me to do bad things for them. I do not wish. I just want to go home. I did not want to do this."

"Oh really? Someone made you do it, did they? Someone made you kill women and children? Who was that, then?"

The man dropped to his knees, tears streaming from his eyes. Ten was pretty sure that wasn't the hay fever.

"It was Captain Petrovna. I didn't want to hit the bio-dome, but she made me guide the pod there. She killed them."

The slight delay for translation and the reading of the text made for a somewhat surreal interrogation.

"Did she now? I don't see any bruises on you, mate. Did you put up much of a struggle or just do as you were told?"

"She would have killed me. I couldn't prevent her. I would have died."

Ten shook his head sadly. "Son, if you were really a soldier, you would have told her to fuck off anyway." He put a comforting hand on the man's shoulder and saw the hopeful look bloom in his eyes. "Your mother still alive, son? Any sisters?"

Popov nodded. "Mother is home, she doesn't know what GKI make me do. My sisters are still in school."

"If Petrovna ordered you to shoot your sisters, would you do it, or would you try and stop her?"

Popov snivelled. "I would try and stop her, but she would kill me."

Ten patted his shoulder. "This is a clone body, yes? If you die, you get redeployed in a new one, safe at home, right?"

Popov nodded miserably.

"Then what the fuck did you have to lose, eh? We just don't do it, son. It's the job. You take a bullet for your mate, you take one for a woman, you sure as fuck take one for a child. 'Bad men need nothing more to compass their ends, than that good men should look on and do nothing.' You heard that one? John Stuart Mill. It means evil men aren't the problem, it's the good men who surround them but are too cowardly to act who are the problem." Ten poked him in the chest. "You're the good man, Popov."

"I would have died," Popov sobbed between breaths.

"Yeah. With your conscience clean." Ten reached down and

pulled the rifle up over Popov's head, passing it to one of the older women behind him, and placing a finger over his lips for silence.

\<Captain. Hostages are secure\>

\<Roger that, Marine X. Let us know when you're ready to breach\>

Ten glanced at the room beyond the kitchen. Another six red outlines showed the GKI troops in there. No hostages. He brought up the internal camera feeds. No friendlies. He pulled something from Popov's belt and stopped by the two he'd shot to resupply.

\<Breaching in two\> he sent to Warden.

\<No! We need a countdown, Ten!\> Warden sent. Ten could picture him swearing and gesturing wildly at the team. He grinned.

Ten swapped his pistol to his left hand and looked to the left of the door, where a red outline sat on a barstool on the other side of the wall. He squeezed the trigger repeatedly and then opened the door. He didn't kick it in or shout. He simply stepped through into the room and threw the flashbang he'd pulled from Popov's webbing to the right, where the GKI captain seemed to be with her cronies.

Then he executed. Five, four, three and his clip was empty.

"Who the fuck are you?" roared the last man standing in Koschite, grabbing a vicious looking vibro-sword and advancing to protect his captain.

Ten could hear Warden and the rest of the team bursting into the room; he felt bad that they'd waited to do their part and he'd left them nothing but potential scraps. He just wasn't in the mood for sharing.

"I'm a Commando. Who are you? Just another walking, talking turd? Or are you someone important?"

"I am Sergeant Pichugin Filippovich and I am going to kill you, little man!"

"Okay, well, I'm Penal Marine X and when we next meet, I'll kill you twice over. Alright?"

Filippovich didn't seem to appreciate Ten's disrespectful attitude, and he charged with a roar. He screamed briefly when his sword arm split from his body, and gurgled when Ten drove the sergeant's own vibro-sword through his chest, and casually tripped him, pinning him to the floor with his own weapon.

"Bloody hell. You're still alive, Sergeant Filippovich. It's almost as if I miraculously missed all your vital organs, except your spine. It'll probably take ages for you to die like this. I'd help, but I have places to be, murderesses to kill, that sort of thing."

Captain Petrovna snarled at him.

"What? You want to grandstand too?" Ten barked at her.

"No, I am going to kill you," she said, raising her pistol.

"With a gun? Bit impersonal, isn't it? Don't fancy doing your killing up close and personal then? I understand. If he was your best fighter, you've no hope," said Ten.

"Hah. You think you can beat me with bare hands?"

"No idea. But I'm damn sure as mustard I could kill you with this grenade if I drop it before putting the pin back in. So. Would you like to find out? If you win you'll go to jail, but you'll have one up on me, if that helps," Ten said, unfurling his hand to show the grenade nestled in it, the pin dangling from his index finger. Petrovna nodded and tossed away her pistol.

Marine X reciprocated, putting the pin back in the grenade and kicking it to the far end of the room, just in case. He laid his knife on a table.

Petrovna didn't wait for him to get ready. She pounced, reaching out to grapple him and take him down before he'd even made a move. Ten grinned and let her wrap her arms around his grease-covered body. She struggled, trying to get a grip on him, but soon her hands where slippery and she couldn't get a purchase.

Ten's smile widened, and he butted her in the face, hearing a satisfying crunch as her nose broke.

"You're not a soldier, Petrovna. You're a thug." Ten slammed his head forward again. Petrovna released him and staggered back. "A petty criminal, given big guns by a weaselly little shit who thinks he's above the law," said Ten, delivering swift strikes to her torso.

She screamed in rage and flung herself at him again, flailing and kicking as she came on.

"You think you can play at soldier, but you're not one," Ten repeated, sweeping Petrovna's legs from under her. He allowed her to stand and come on again. "You're certainly not a Marine. You kill because it gets you off, some twisted part of your brain enjoys the sadism of it." He flung her away again, but she was surprisingly tough and she bounced right back.

"For me, it's usually not that enjoyable. But in your case, I must admit, I'm taking great pleasure in seeing the fear build in your eyes. That's what you like, isn't it? To watch them die in terror. You know why?"

"You talk too much, Marine," she said spitting blood at him. She couldn't help following up, though. The open loop gets them every time. "Why do you think?"

Ten shrugged. "Buggered if I know. You're probably just a garden-variety sociopath. A serial killer working for a company. Either way, the only death you don't enjoy is your own."

She let forth a guttural scream and grabbed Ten's vibro-knife from the table he'd been watching her edge toward. Ten could see the triumph in her eyes as she swung the deadly blade at him. He watched that gleam die as he stepped quickly into her reach, grabbing her wrist in one hand and wrenching it hard until she dropped the knife, even as he punched viciously at her throat, once, twice, three times.

The knife clattered to the floor, and Ten took a step back as Petrovna dropped to her knees, gasping for air. It would do her no good; he'd crushed her throat. He watched her, slowly removing his knuckledusters as she turned a different shade.

"Bloody hell – I've got to help her, Captain," said Goodwin.

Ten whirled and stepped between her and the GKI leader. He shook his head. "Don't, Goodwin. You'll only prolong it, and if you help her, you'll probably get a broken arm for your troubles."

Goodwin reeled back in shock and Ten winced.

"Ten, stand down!" roared Milton.

"I'm sorry, Goodwin. I didn't mean that. But don't help her. She's not a soldier, she's a terrorist."

Goodwin nodded. "Yeah. I know, Ten. Sometimes, though, you're almost as much of a bastard as they are." The tech specialist turned on her heel and walked back out of the room.

Ten sighed and knelt down by Petrovna who was still sucking in painful gasps of air.

"This is better than you deserve. I won't go so easy on you next time we meet, so I suggest you resign, because any time I see this company badge from now on, I'm going to kill the wearer as slow as I can." The mercenary stared at him but couldn't speak. Ten slammed his vibro-knife into the mercenary's skull to deliver the coup de grace. Then he stood up, calmly collected his pistol and slapped in a fresh magazine.

He came back from the kitchen, grabbed Popov by the scruff of the neck, and marched him over to where he could see the captain. "She's dead now, son. She can't order you to kill kids anymore."

"Oh, thank you, thank you. I am free. Thank you."

Ten shook his head. "You're not free, Popov. You still did it, you have to pay for your crimes. In any case, I need you to deliver a message. You tell him I'm coming for him."

Popov looked confused, "Tell him? Who?"

"You tell Giacomo Khan, that..." Ten paused racking his brain. "Baba Yaga is coming for him. Tell him that I did this. His entire team. Okay, except for the one Milton got. The rest was all me, and I'm just one Royal Marine. Tell him I know he ordered this. Tell him I'm a criminal, a Penal Marine. Tell him I'm a ghost, and I'm not for hire like this arsehole," he said, toeing Petrovna's corpse.

"He can't find me. He can't stop me. He can't run from me. Frankly, he should just kill himself now and save me the bother. He won't believe you. He won't take it seriously." Ten leaned in close to watch Popov's eyes skim across the text in his HUD. "But you believe me, don't you, Popov? You know I'm coming for him, don't you?"

Popov nodded. "I want to go home to my mother," he whispered.

"You can go home to your mum, Popov. But first, you deliver my message. Understood?"

Popov nodded miserably, confused until Ten raised his pistol. Then he understood.

<Agent O, push a backup for Popov, would you?>

<He is fully backed up, Ten>

Ten fired and Popov went home to his mother, via GKI regional headquarters.

Warden's head whipped round at the sound and he strode over as the Penal Marie began stowing his kit.

"What the hell, Ten?"

"Look, Captain, if it bothers you that much, just put it in the report and they'll add some years to my sentence. I'm not going to apologise for offing those bastards. Not even Popov, the naive idiot."

Warden stared at him for a long time. "I don't think our HUDs have been backing this up properly, I'm afraid," he said. "They've been on the fritz for the last five or ten minutes, I think. Can't prove you did anything untoward, especially with no eyewitnesses. Anyone else see any unprofessional conduct enacted against these child-murdering scum?" he asked to a resounding silence. "There you go then, no case to answer."

Ten gave a wan smile.

Warden moved to stand in front of Marine X then leaned in close, so only Ten could hear.

"Reign it in, Marine," he hissed, "before the darkness consumes you."

Ten blinked, not quite believing his ears.

Then Warden straightened up and turned away.

"No, what I am surprised about, Ten, is seeing you wear pink goggles with glitter in them and what appear to be unicorns on the strap. I wouldn't believe my own eyes, but fortunately my HUD has started working again and I've got it saved in glorious high resolution, so we can all see it." Warden grinned.

<Agent O, would you mind directing Ten to the nearest shower? He smells of... well, I don't know what the hell it is, but one of us is bound to puke if he stays in the room much longer. Cohen won't take him back aboard *Palmerston* smelling like this>

The rest of the team moved off to speak to the hostages, leaving Ten to attend to his personal hygiene.

<Agent O, no tricks this time> sent Ten. <Find me some quarters with something clean to wear. These young Marines will be horrified if I go back to the pod in my birthday suit. They're prudish about that sort of thing>

<Of course, Ten. It's in your HUD now>

Ten nodded, following the directions.

<And then you'd better find me a clean route back to my armour> sent Ten. <Can't be leaving it behind, after all>

23

"Come on, people, where did they go?" Cohen sat on *Palmerston*'s cramped bridge, scanning the displays.

"I'm sorry, sir, we've lost them," Midshipman Parks replied.

"How the hell did that happen? We hit them with a rail cannon and went straight after them with our railguns when they left dock with Oldervik," Cohen fumed.

"I'm sorry, sir, it's my fault. I took my eye off the ball when we were manoeuvring to evade their missiles. They released decoy drones to create false signals and by the time I realised what was going on, they'd slipped into the asteroid belt proper. I think they've released more drones because I'm getting pings from all over the place."

The railguns fired again.

"What are you doing, Elson?" Cohen asked his weapons officer.

"Attempting to clear the drones away, sir. Six down in that burst, but this might take a while."

"There are at least ninety drones out there, sir," Parks added.

"Cease fire, Elson. We aren't going to get rid of them all without going into that asteroid belt. If we do that, they could pop up from behind any mid-sized asteroid and strike us. Even damaged, they outclass us. We can't match them head-on," said Cohen.

He stood up and paced about the bridge, considering their options.

"We need to leave before they manage to find a firing solution and we end up venting atmosphere. Discretion is the better part of valour and all that. Elson, deploy mines to cover our retreat. Robinson, get us back to Oldervik."

Elson blinked and looked at Parks.

Cohen closed his eyes. "What is it, Midshipman?" he said, dreading the no doubt upsetting answer.

"Sorry, sir, it's just that *Palmerston* doesn't have a minelayer or weaponised drones. We have basic chaff for missile defence. The old girl's not supposed to do much but bombard static targets," said Elson.

"Buggery bollocks. Do we have anything defensive? Anything better than chaff," Cohen asked. "Anyone? Any ideas at all? Fine. Robinson, let's just about face and present our rump then, shall we?"

"Er," said Elson.

"Bloody hell, Elson, if you have something to say just spit it out, man!"

"We do have one thing. It's not defensive, though."

"What are you talking about?"

"The rail cannon, sir. I have an idea I'm not sure you'll like," Elson said, looking quite apologetic. "We can shoot it at maximum power at one of the larger asteroids. If we pick the right one, it will give us time to escape the area and get back to Oldervik."

"There are thousands of the bloody things. How do we pick the one that the GKI ship is hiding behind?"

"Oh no, sir, I didn't mean that. We just pick the largest one that the rail cannon can shatter into a million pieces of shrapnel. It should obliterate any of the enemy drones within a sizeable radius."

Not a bad idea, thought Cohen, *and definitely worth a try*.

"Do it. Straightaway, please. Parks, if this works, make sure you have a course solution for Robinson to get us out of here and back to Oldervik to retrieve our team as fast as possible. We aren't staying here to be shot at a moment longer than necessary."

"I've identified a suitable target, sir, firing solution is confirmed, the asteroid is in the area where we lost track of the GKI ship, so it should have the desired effect. I have the railguns primed and ready in case we get lucky and reacquire their signal."

"Then have at it, Mr Elson."

"Launching projectile now, sir. T minus one minute to impact,"

Cohen flicked a button and raised the loading bay. "Sub-Lieutenant Corn, get us reloaded as soon as possible, please. The rail cannon is our strongest weapon if the GKI ship is reacquired."

"Already reloading, sir. We'll have her ready to shoot again in a moment."

"Elson, any targets?"

"Scanning, sir, but I'm not finding anything."

"Damn and blast," Cohen said. "Pick another target, Elson, and get the next round underway. Robinson, I want to be out of here before it strikes. If it's close, they'll have to move. If not, they might come after us. I want us underway before they can pursue."

"Roger that, Captain. Plotting firing solution on the next target now."

Cohen opened a comms channel to the Marines. "Captain Warden, are you ready for a pick-up anytime soon? We may not have time for prolonged goodbyes. Was your mission a success?"

"Yes, Captain Cohen. We're done here; the Valkyr are back in control of Oldervik. We can leave when you're ready."

"Projectile launched, Captain."

"Midshipman Robinson, get us out of here," Cohen ordered.

Robinson nodded, and the ship turned.

"Projectile impact, sir," Elson said.

"Show me," Cohen said, and Elson sent the view of the second shattered asteroid to a viewscreen.

"Sir, I think I've got a solid ping!" Parks cried out.

"Firing, sir!" Elson confirmed.

"They're coming at us hard and fast, sir!" Parks added.

"Robinson, you'd better be doing everything you can to get us out of here."

"Working on it, sir."

"They're firing railguns, sir," Shepherd said.

"Don't let them hit my ship, Robinson. I won't hesitate to dock it from your wages."

"Doing my best, sir."

An asteroid ahead lit up with impacts from the GKI railguns, as Robinson dodged around it.

"Elson, is the rail cannon primed?"

"Yes, sir, but I don't see why it matters, it only shoots forward."

"Robinson, give the engine everything she's got and head for that asteroid there," Cohen said, ringing one on the viewscreen. It was a massive spinning oblong several times larger than *Palmerston*, tumbling through space.

"Sir?" Robinson asked, her question's meaning clear despite the brevity.

"Elson, fire when we're as close to it as possible and, Robinson, when I say close, I want us to be able to put our hand out a window and stroke it as we pass, got it?"

"Not really, sir."

"Corn, find some junk you can blow out of an airlock. Anything you have that will make it look like we've been hit."

"Roger that, Captain," Corn replied.

"What are you planning, sir?" Parks asked.

"That GKI ship has, what, six railguns?"

"Ten, sir," Elson confirmed.

"Right, ten railguns against our puny complement. With her astern of us, we'll be ripped to pieces as soon as Robinson picks the wrong direction to jink the ship."

"What's that got to do with shooting another asteroid, sir?" Parks asked.

"We're not shooting it to blow it up, we're shooting it to make it look like we tried to use it for cover and Robinson fucked up. That and the rubbish Corn is throwing out, it'll look a lot like we clipped the asteroid as we flew by and, Robinson, we'd better not clip it, you hear me?"

"Yes, sir!"

"Robinson, when you dodge past that asteroid, I want the ship to look like it's tumbling after a collision, understand?"

Robinson took a moment to reply. "You want to trick them to come in for the kill while we flip the ship over and line up for a shot of our own?"

"Exactly. Get on with it, everyone," said Cohen.

There was a chorus of confirmations from around the small bridge.

"You'd better all have adjusted your crash webbing properly – this is going to be rough," Robinson warned.

"Ready on your mark, Robinson," Elson advised.

"Brace for high-G manoeuvres," Cohen broadcast throughout the ship.

"Elson, fire on three... two... mark!" Robinson said.

"Projectile away," Elson confirmed.

Cohen expected Robinson to do something dramatic, but she just tweaked her controls with the lightest of touches, sending *Palmerston* skipping over the asteroid. She used every trick she knew to reduce their velocity and send them tumbling at the same time, as if they'd hit the rock.

Then the rail cannon round hit the asteroid and it splintered into half a dozen large chunks, as *Palmerston* pinwheeled over it, her crew pressed against their seats by the deceleration.

"Elson, stand by," Cohen shouted as he saw two crewmen in environment suits sail past the viewscreen as the ship rotated. He cursed.

"Corn, are you hit down there?" he asked.

"No sir, why?"

"There's bodies outside!"

"You said to make it look realistic, sir! I thought a couple of spaced crewmen would be really convincing, so I got rid of Stent and Yards and killed two birds with one stone," Corn replied.

Parks sniggered, and Cohen would have bitten his head off, but he wasn't the only one.

"Their sacrifice will be noted in the action report," Cohen replied.

"Firing solution locked in, sir," Elson confirmed, rather spoiling the moment.

"Fire at will," Cohen ordered with a wolfish grin.

The GKI ship closed in for the kill, unaware that Elson was caressing his trigger figure, waiting for the perfect moment. The bridge crew cheered as he showed them their mistake.

Immediately, Robinson stopped their rolling, which was physically uncomfortable but allowed Elson to follow up with more sustained bursts of railgun strikes. Impacts blossomed across the hull of the GKI ship.

"Enemy railguns damaged, sir," Parks reported.

"Let's close in for the kill, Robinson – no straight lines, please, just in case," Cohen said, leaning forward in his chair.

"Aye aye, Captain!"

"Shit, Captain, I think they're trying to ram us!" Shepherd said.

"Evasive manoeuvres!"

Robinson didn't really need telling. Elson tried another burst but missed. *Palmerston* went one way and the GKI ship went the other, passing straight over them, almost grazing *Palmerston*'s hull.

Immediately *Palmerston* fought to turn, but the viewscreen shifted to show the GKI ship powering away from them at top speed. Then it vanished.

"We got it!" Shepherd said.

Elson shook his head. "No, Shepherd. She went into hyperspace."

Shepherd said something unseemly.

"Oldervik – now, Robinson. I want us out of here and back to *Child of Starlight* as soon as possible."

"Aye aye, Captain!" Robinson confirmed.

Palmerston swung around and shot towards the asteroid miners, but Cohen couldn't shake a nagging doubt that the escaped GKI ship hadn't gone far.

24

"Coming out of hyperspace in three, two, one," said Midshipman Robinson at the helm. The main display flicked from a simple status report and a countdown timer to show instead the real view of space ahead.

"*Child of Starlight* is dead ahead, sir," said Robinson with satisfaction.

"One hundred thousand kilometres, a flight time of a little over three hours, sir," said Parks.

"Good," said Cohen, nodding with satisfaction. The mission had been challenging, but the voyage back to Folkvangr, *Child of Starlight*'s home system, had gone as well as could be hoped. "I will leave this with you, Corn," he said, standing up.

"Thank you, sir. We should be able to take it from here."

Cohen settled into the small command suite behind the bridge and opened a comms channel to *Ascendant*. Lieutenant White took the call.

"Welcome back, sir," he said. "Good to see you're still in one piece."

"A walk in the park, Lieutenant, a walk in the park. And how is *Ascendant*?"

"Coming along, sir. The forward weapons arrays are operational, as are the engines. Mantle's team have been working around the clock. The hyperspace drive is in good shape but not yet working, and obviously the wormhole communicator is still offline."

"The Valkyr are still delivering supplies?"

"Like clockwork," said White. Then he grinned. "It's almost as if they wanted to get rid of us."

"Yes, well. As soon as *Ascendant* is ready to fly, they'll get their wish. We can't waste any more time out here on the edge of nothing doing minor good deeds."

"Couldn't agree more, sir. And as for flying, we're actually off *Child of Starlight* and tracking alongside under our own steam. I wouldn't want to push her too hard, but *Ascendant* hasn't broken apart yet. In fact, you took so long that we were going to come looking for you as soon as the hyperspace engine was in working order. So you've saved us a trip."

"The day hasn't been a complete waste, then," muttered Cohen. "I need to speak to Haukland. We'll be with you in a few hours."

"Acknowledged, *Ascendant* out."

Cohen gathered his thoughts then opened a channel to Haukland, who answered almost immediately.

"Commander Cohen," she said. "You have news?"

"Yes, Prime Minister. I am pleased to report that the hostages have been rescued and are now safely aboard *Palmerston*." He watched as her eyes flicked offscreen, checking the translation. "We will arrive at *Child of Starlight* in around three hours."

"Good," said Haukland, nodding. "A navigation path has been prepared for you, please follow it."

"As you wish. Cohen out." He cut the channel and sat back for a moment. From here, everything should be simple. It was merely a matter of completing the repairs to *Ascendant's* hyperspace engine, verifying her readiness for space flight and making a decision to leave for home.

"What could possibly go wrong?" Cohen muttered to himself.

Then a warning klaxon sounded and, just like that, everything went wrong.

~

"What's going on, Corn?" said Cohen as he strode back onto the bridge and took his seat.

"The GKI battlecruiser, sir," said Corn, turning in her seat. "It followed us through hyperspace and now she's on a path to intercept us well before we reach *Child of Starlight*."

Cohen frowned as he peered at the main display, which showed a schematic diagram of their flight path and the route that the battlecruiser was taking.

"How did they follow us?" he said to himself. Then he shook his head. It didn't really matter how. The problem was why.

"*Child of Starlight* is the nearest logical destination, given the hostages' origin, sir," said Corn, which at least explained the 'how'.

"That we know of, at least," agreed Cohen. "Take us to Action Stations, Ms Elson, and let's get our guests safely stowed away."

"Aye, sir," said Midshipman Elson, triggering the warning klaxon.

"This is the captain," said Cohen, triggering the ship-wide announcement system. "Prepare for evasive manoeuvres." He clicked off the channel and turned his attention to the main display.

"Weapons ready, sir," said Elson.

"Crew and passengers are locked down, sir," said Sub Lieutenant Corn, who had been monitoring the internal feeds.

Cohen was silent for a moment, thinking. Then he nodded to himself. "Right. A little burst of speed, please, Ms Robinson, just to get things started."

"Aye, sir. Thirty second burn at one hundred per cent, starting in three, two, one–" Midshipman Robinson punched the button when her countdown reached zero.

Palmerston's engines fired, pushing crew and passengers alike into their chairs.

"We can't outrun them, sir," said Corn as the burn came to an end.

The main display changed to show *Palmerston*'s revised flight time, but the enemy ship was already adjusting.

"Cruiser is firing her main engines," reported Elson. "Looks like she's still aiming to intercept us before we reach *Starlight*."

Cohen nodded, not taking his eyes from the display, a faint grin on his face as he ran through the plan that was forming in his mind.

"It's not about getting away from the hunter, Sub Lieutenant, it's about enticing them in, leading them on so they think they're winning."

"Sir?" said Corn, frowning. "They are winning. They're bigger, faster, better armed and they have more armour."

"And yet, even now, they rush forward to meet the inevitable. Let's see if we can hurry them up a little more. Another thirty seconds on the main engines, please, Ms Robinson."

"Aye, sir," said Robinson.

"And let's open a channel to *Ascendant*, Mr Curtis."

"Aye, sir," said Curtis. "Channel open."

"What ho, *Ascendant*!" said Cohen, his tone almost playful. "Are you ready to party?"

At the side of the main display, Mr White appeared, sitting in the command chair on *Ascendant*'s bridge.

"The shakedown has found a number of problems, sir, if I'm honest. Mantle and her team are racing around fixing them at the moment, and she's looking as grim as she ever looks when things aren't going well," said White. Then he leaned forward a little. "Between you and me, I think she's enjoying herself."

"That's excellent news, Mr White, but I'm rather hoping you can help us with another problem. We seem to have picked up a most unwelcome admirer, and we need a little help discouraging them."

"Ah," said White, his tone turning serious. "We do have some operational issues that might make combat somewhat dicey."

Cohen shook his head. "This should be easy. No strenuous manoeuvres, I just need you at the right point in space at the right time. Let me send you the flight plans." He flicked at his slate, sending a package of information to *Ascendant*.

"Understood, sir," said White a few moments later, grinning as he reviewed the plans. "We should reach the intercept point just in time."

"Make sure you do," warned Cohen, "or this will be the briefest of brief encounters."

"Aye, sir. *Ascendant* out."

On the main display, a new line appeared to represent *Ascendant* as she moved out from the shadow of *Child of Starlight* and headed towards the intercept point.

"Another sixty seconds on the main engines, please," said Cohen. "Let's see how fast this thing can go."

"Aye, sir," said Robinson, although her tone was sceptical.

"Is this wise, sir?" asked Corn quietly, her tone suggesting that she thought it really very unwise indeed. "*Palmerston*'s not built for high speed, she doesn't have the shielding. If we hit anything bigger than a grain of sand, we risk taking damage."

"If we're caught out here by that cruiser, we'll be hit by things a whole lot more dangerous than sand, Corn," replied Cohen.

Corn subsided back into her chair, but it was clear she wasn't at all happy.

"What's the smallest mass you can deliver with any degree of accuracy through your main cannon?" asked Cohen.

"Smallest? There isn't a minimum, so any correctly manufactured projectile would work. But the cannon is really only effective when used with high mass projectiles."

Cohen pulled the test projectile from his pocket and stared at it thoughtfully.

"How quickly can you make, say, a few hundred of these?" he asked, holding up the small ceramic ball.

"The test projectiles?" asked Corn, frowning in surprise. "They take about ten seconds each, sir, so in an hour you could have over three hundred. But they're far too small to do any damage even if they didn't burn up in the atmosphere."

"It's not all about size," he said, nodding sagely. "Get the fabricators running. I want to have at least fifty ready to go in ten minutes,

and another fifty ten minutes after that." He gave Corn a conspirato-
rial grin. "And then we'll see if you can hit anything smaller than a
planet."

Twenty minutes later, Corn announced that the fabricators had
constructed one hundred and sixteen of the tiny projectiles
and were still churning them out. Only thirty-four millimetres in
diameter, they weighed about a hundred and fifty grams each.

"Keep the fabs running, Ms Corn. We're going to use everything
we can."

"I still don't see what you're hoping to achieve, sir." She had one of
the sample projectiles in her hand. A small ball of rock covered in an
opaque ferro-ceramic shell. "These will just bounce off that cruiser.
They won't even feel them. The mass driver can shift big masses, but
it's designed to get them started on a precise trajectory so that they
accelerate under gravity. It's a delivery system, not a railgun."

"I understand the theory," said Cohen, taking the projectile from
her hand and weighing it thoughtfully. "But we're not going to throw
these at their hull, we're going to disperse them like caltrops and let
them stumble across them in their haste."

"Sir?" said an evidently confused Corn.

"Look it up later. For now, I want you to put these in front of our
eager suitor."

"I'm not sure I follow, sir."

"The mass driver is a precision instrument. We know how fast our
friend is going and where they're going, so I want you to put a cloud
of these little things," he tossed the projectile back to Corn, "in their
path. A big cloud. They might only hit a few, but at the speed they're
going, these'll be a lot more effective than grains of sand."

Corn grinned as realisation dawned. "Understood. Tricky, but we
can do it. Let me get to work."

She briefed Elson, the weapons officer, then they spent the next fifteen minutes working it out and running simulations on the targeting computers.

"It's going to be close," Corn said eventually, "and if they spot what we're doing, it'll all be for nothing, but I think we have a solution." She and Elson walked through the plan and described the manoeuvres they would need to execute.

"That's the risky bit," said Corn, "because there's only a small amount of adjustment built into the cannon itself. We basically have to point the ship in the direction we want to fire. If they're watching closely, they'll see, and there's no way to disguise it." She nodded at Elson.

"But what if we screw up?" said Midshipman Elson. "If we put a full-sized projectile across their bows, close enough for them to see but far enough away that they'll think we've missed, they won't change their approach because they'll just think we've missed." She looked expectantly at Cohen, who nodded appreciatively.

"They'll see the big shot because it's three metres across and made of iron," said Cohen slowly, thinking it through, "but they'll track its trajectory and know it's off target. They'll think we've missed and that our cunning plan has gone wrong."

"Exactly, and they'll be so busy tracking the big missile that they'll never see all the little ones," said Elson.

"Very good, Midshipman, very good indeed." He looked at the simulation once more then nodded. "How far behind are they now?"

"Ten thousand four hundred kilometres, sir, and they're closing at about forty kilometres a second," said Robinson.

"So they're about two hundred and sixty seconds out. Time to get moving, people. You have command, Sub Lieutenant Corn. Make this plan work."

"Aye, sir," said Corn with renewed snap in her voice. "Ms Robinson, spin us around by one hundred and sixty-nine degrees and bring us ten degrees to starboard."

"One hundred and sixty-nine by ten to starboard, aye," said Robinson, laying in the change. "Attitudinal thrusters firing in three, two, one." There was a gentle kick from the thrusters as the ship changed orientation. "Manoeuvre complete, ma'am."

"Prime the cannon, Ms Elson. Let's get the big one away."

"Ready to fire. The firing computer has control, projectile away in three, two, one... Missile away. Looking good. Should miss the enemy by a few hundred metres if they hold their current course."

"Time for the cloud – everything the fabricators have made. As soon as firing is complete, spin us around, Ms Robinson."

"Aye, ma'am, ready to go," said Robinson.

"Reloading complete, automated firing sequence beginning now – sixteen bursts of twenty projectiles, half a second apart." There was a pause. "Done," said Elson, waving at Robinson.

"Firing attitudinal thrusters now," she said, triggering the control.

"Thirty seconds till the first missile crosses their path," said Elson. "No sign of a change to their trajectory."

The bridge fell silent as all eyes watched the countdowns on the main display.

"Zero," announced Elson. "First missile passed two hundred and seventy-three metres beneath their hull. Ten seconds to first cloud impact."

"Get ready to spin us around, Ms Robinson," said Cohen, "and cut our velocity by fifty per cent."

"Aye, sir, course laid in."

"Contact," said Elson, "direct hit."

"Now, Ms Robinson," said Cohen calmly. He couldn't help feeling a little sorry for the enemy. But only a little.

"Aye, sir, firing now."

"Last cloud impact now," said Elson.

"Main engines firing, ninety second burn at fifty per cent power."

"Any sign of damage to the enemy?" asked Corn.

"Nothing obvious, ma'am," said Elson, "but they're still on their original course. No indication they've reacted to our change."

Then a message flashed onto the screen.

<*Ascendant* in position. Enemy vessel approaching at high velocity. Engagement range in six minutes. Orders?>

The enemy vessel ploughed on towards *Ascendant*.

<Fire as opportunity allows, *Ascendant*> sent Cohen.

<Acknowledged. Out>

"Lay in a course to *Child of Starlight*," he told his crew. "Let's take our rescued people home."

"Main engine burn complete," reported Robinson. "Setting course for *Child of Starlight*."

On the display, the enemy ship hurtled relentlessly on, flashing past *Palmerston* and disappearing on towards *Ascendant* and *Child of Starlight*.

"No weapon discharge detected, sir," reported Elson as they watched their enemy dwindle into the distance.

Cohen nodded, attention glued to the display.

<Ten seconds to impact> sent *Ascendant*.

The seconds ticked by, agonisingly slow.

Then the enemy vessel, at the very limit of *Palmerston*'s monitors, seemed to shake and shudder before an explosion tore through the ship, ripping it open from bow to stern and transforming it into a fast-moving and rapidly expanding cloud of debris.

<Hit> reported *Ascendant*, as if there was any chance that *Palmerston*'s crew might not have noticed.

<Acknowledged> sent Cohen. <Thank you for your assistance, *Ascendant*. Will rendezvous as soon as we've delivered our passengers. *Palmerston* out>

25

C ohen stepped out onto the floor of *Ascendant*'s main bay and looked back at *Palmerston*.

"That's a solid ship, Sub Lieutenant Corn," he said. "And a good crew."

"Thank you, sir. She'll be even better once we've redeployed the rest of the crew and completed our repairs."

"I think you're due a refit when you get home," said Cohen as Warden and the Marines trudged down the ramp carrying their kit. "Get her resupplied. I want her ready to fly again as soon as possible."

"Aye, sir," said Corn saluting. "We'll be ready when you need us." She turned back to *Palmerston* and disappeared into her ship.

"Captain, a word, if you please," said Cohen, leading Warden to one side. They watched the Marines leave as *Palmerston*'s small crew began a visual check of the ship's exterior.

"Good work today," said Cohen, more gruffly than he might have liked. "I'll catch up with Mantle, but I think *Ascendant* is close to being ready. We'll be out of here soon. Can't see anything else keeping us here."

Warden nodded wearily. It had been a long day. "A little downtime might be good," he said. "It's been non-stop since we arrived at New Bristol."

"But, er," began Cohen. He sighed and looked at Warden.

"Yes, sir, we'll get everything pulled together, just in case," said Warden. Then he picked up his pack and followed the Marines across the bay floor towards the mess.

"Mantle," said Cohen when he caught up with her outside the engineering command room. "What's left to be done?"

Mantle turned to face him. She looked exhausted. "The main engines are working, life support and fabricators are running well, and the weapon systems are operational."

"As we saw. Your intervention was most timely."

"Timely?" snorted Mantle. "I'm pretty sure that cruiser was already dead, she just hadn't stopped moving."

"Maybe," conceded Cohen. "I notice you didn't mention the hyperspace drive."

Mantle's face hardened. "That little 'shortcut' did more damage than we thought, sir. It'll take a while to unpick the work, and then longer to repair and make everything ready."

"A while?" said Cohen, focussing on Mantle's vagueness.

"Several weeks, maybe more. To be honest, we've been working on the other systems. The hyperspace engine's going to be a big job."

"Hmm," said Cohen, not entirely happy.

"I need to get back…"

"Of course," muttered Cohen, lost in his own thoughts. "Give me an update in twelve hours."

"Aye, sir," said Mantle before she vanished into the engineering command room. Cohen headed the other way, making for the bridge.

"Welcome back, sir," said White as Cohen stepped onto the bridge.

"Good to be home," said Cohen as he settled into his chair. "I've spoken to Mantle. I'd hoped for more progress."

"Sorry, sir," said White, "maybe we can ask Prime Minister Haukland for manufactured parts instead of raw resources? That might speed things along."

"No," said Cohen firmly, shaking his head. "We make it ourselves or manage without. I don't want to rely on them, and I don't trust Haukland any more than I trust the Deathless."

"Very good, sir. They've offered to let us dock at one of their facilities to simplify the transfer of resources and allow our teams to have a little shore leave."

Cohen thought about it for a moment. "That seems like a fair offer." Then he frowned. "I didn't think they had externally accessible docking points?"

"A hidden dock with a high-speed transit system connecting it to the habitable parts of the station, from what they would tell us. We have the directions. All we need to do is get into position and they'll take it from there, apparently."

"Fine," said Cohen, too tired to worry about it any further. "Put us alongside *Child of Starlight*, get us docked, and wake me if anything happens." Then he stood up and headed for his cabin before he could fall asleep in his chair.

~

A formal reception was the very last thing that Cohen had wanted, but the Valkyr had spared no effort. Mantle had found some 'emergency' that required her immediate attention, so Cohen, White and Warden accepted the invitation and brought with them *Palmerston*'s crew and the Marines who had taken part in the hostage release mission.

The paucity of resources on *Ascendant* meant they were all wearing everyday flight uniforms rather than anything more formal, and Warden felt distinctly underdressed amongst the celebrating Valkyr.

"They haven't held back with their dress," he murmured to White as the two men hovered at the edge of the room near a bar.

They gazed out across a sea of brightly coloured outfits, no two the same, that filled the hall. Unlike the Deathless, the Valkyr didn't seem to pursue ostentatious body modifications, and they had no need for the more extreme military clones, like the ogre or harpy models. Instead, they pursued an ideal of human form, melding genetic engineering and exotic micro-electronics to give themselves abilities beyond the obvious. Next to the high-end beauty of the Valkyr, Warden and White's workmanlike clones were obviously low-end and functional.

"What the hell?" muttered White, nudging Warden and turning his attention to the Marines who had just entered. Milton and Goodwin wore clean versions of their everyday uniforms, but the same could not be said of Marine X.

"What is he wearing?" said Warden, shaking his head in amazement.

"And where did he get it?" replied White. "I'm damned sure Mantle's fabricator schedule didn't include tailoring dress uniforms."

Marine X looked resplendent in a fresh white shirt, dark trousers and a dark blue coat with tails. A long sword hung from his waist and on his chest he wore a single ribbon. He waved at the officers and sauntered over, escorted by Milton and Goodwin.

"Evening, sirs," said Marine X, collecting glasses from the bar and passing them around. He looked the two officers up and down, taking in their drab, workmanlike clothes, and shook his head sadly. "It's tragic when standards are allowed to slip, don't you think?"

Warden was momentarily lost for words, but White suffered no such problem.

"Where did you come across an outfit like that, Marine X?" asked White, sipping at his drink.

"It's not so much what you know, sir," said Marine X cryptically with a sly grin, "and more about who you know and how persuasive you can be."

"The ribbon, Marine X," said Warden as he felt White gearing up to ask another question about the uniform. "I don't recognise the ribbon. Is it for a campaign?"

"Long service, sir, very long. I'm not supposed to wear my medals, not till my time's served," he paused and shrugged. "But if I cared too much about the rules, I'd never have made it this far, eh, sir?"

"We've already asked these questions, sir," said Milton, "and he gave us much the same answers. Inscrutable, that's our Marine X. Can't get a straight answer out of him."

"Maybe Goodwin can dig something out of the files," said Warden, grinning. "I hear she's pretty talented when it comes to ferreting out secret information."

Marine X's grin vanished immediately. As he shifted his stance, the friendly atmosphere evaporated, becoming altogether darker and more threatening. "Can't say I'd recommend that course of action, sir," he said quietly, leaning slightly forwards. He gave Warden a stern glare, and for a moment it seemed like a cloud had covered the small group.

Then Marine X grinned again and relaxed. "More drinks," he said, emptying his own glass. "That's what we need." He busied himself at the bar, handing out more glasses like the station's best-dressed waiter.

Then there was a gentle chiming noise and all eyes turned to the podium, where Prime Minister Haukland now stood ready to address the gathering.

"Friends," she said in Koschite, relying on the guests' HUDs to provide translations. "Welcome. Tonight we thank Commander Cohen, the crews of *Ascendant* and *Palmerston*, and Captain Warden's Marines for securing the release of our fellow citizens." She waved at Cohen to step forward, then she turned to an aide and lifted something from a cushion.

"We have no tradition of military medals or awards, but please accept this as a token of our appreciation and of our friendship."

Cohen stepped forward and Haukland passed over a scale model of *Ascendant* mounted on a slab of rock.

"Thank you, Prime Minister," said Cohen with a polite bow of his head. "You have been both gracious and generous during our unexpected visit, and it has been a pleasure to offer what limited aid we could during our stay."

He gave her another nod then backed away as a polite ripple of applause rolled around the chamber.

"Trygstad told me they plan to add defences to some of their facilities," said White quietly after Marine X had left in search of food, Milton and Goodwin trailing after him like an honour guard. "They're not at all pleased about the situation, or the need for change, from what I gather."

"Defences?" asked Warden.

"Automated gun emplacements and some sort of semi-autonomous drone weapons platform system, specialised AIs to monitor for hostile vessels and coordinate a response, emergency beacons and escape vessels, extra shielding and engines. That sort of thing."

Warden raised an eyebrow. "She told you all that? Bit indiscreet, wasn't it?"

White grinned widely.

"Ah," said Warden, grinning. "That sort of conversation, was it? Didn't realise you'd been pumping her for information."

"That's not–" began White before quietening as Cohen walked up, still clutching his model ship.

"Glad to see you two are enjoying yourselves," said Cohen, setting the award down on the bar and picking up a glass. He took a sip, grimaced, and put the glass back down again.

"Did you get anything else from the Prime Minister?" asked White.

"They want us gone, but we knew that already. Other than that, just disappointment at the actions of their erstwhile allies, I think. And they're still bitter about the loss of *Ornament*. They had big plans for that station."

"Nice model," said Warden, inspecting Cohen's award. "Why is *Ascendant* resting on her side? Is that normal?"

"Something's up, sir," said Marine X, appearing like a well-dressed ghost at Warden's side. "Haukland's vanished and her aides have gone with her."

"Marine X," said Cohen with evident distaste. "Shouldn't you be on *Ascendant*?" Cohen looked from Marine X to Warden.

"I'm only here to offer my support, sir," said Marine X quietly. "I'll take the troops home," he said, turning to Warden, "and make sure they're prepped, just in case."

Cohen opened his mouth to object but Warden, with longer experience of Marine X's hunches, nodded. "Best to be prepared," agreed Warden. The Penal Marine disappeared into the crowd, pinging Milton and the others as he went.

"You're concerned?" asked Cohen, frowning hard.

"It's probably nothing, sir," said Warden, "but he has a fine sense for these things."

Cohen nodded thoughtfully. Then he leaned in towards White. "Get the team ready, Lieutenant. We don't want to be caught unawares if there really is something going on." White blinked in surprise then nodded when he saw that Cohen wasn't joking. He followed Marine X, leaving Warden and Cohen alone.

"We'll look like a right pair of paranoid idiots if he's wrong," muttered Cohen.

Then a Valkyr aide appeared.

"Prime Minister Haukland would like to speak to you," he said. "If you would be so good as to follow me."

～

"Admiral Tomsk," acknowledged Giacomo Khan, the eponymous CEO of GK Industries. "It is good to see you in such fine form."

"Cut the small talk, Khan," snarled Tomsk. "What the hell is going on?"

Khan raised an eyebrow mildly and lowered his hand to rest it on the head of Vlad, his mandrill bodyguard and butler. "Going on, Admiral? Mine is a grand enterprise. There is so much going on it's difficult to keep track of it all. You will have to be more specific."

"Don't fuck around," snapped Tomsk. "The Valkyr splitters are screaming about some rock, making all sorts of noise and fuss."

"Ah, that," said Khan, a little of his blustering confidence leaking away. He rubbed his hands together. "How much do you know?"

"Not enough," said Tomsk angrily.

"The Valkyr stole an asteroid, a large one with a high concentration of rare and heavy elements. Our troops took back control. There was a fight; some of the Valkyr died." He shrugged.

"But that's not the whole story, is it?" said Tomsk. "You don't have rights over anything in that system. I checked. So what the hell is going on?"

Khan narrowed his eyes. He didn't like the way this interview was going.

"There was a disagreement, and then a raid," he admitted. "We dealt with it, but the Valkyr had help from some external party. The raiders were pursued by our frigate, *Hostile Takeover*. A Commonwealth ship, identified by our people as the stolen Koschite vessel *Varpulis*, intervened, and *Takeover* was lost with all hands. After that, things are confused."

"*Varpulis*?" hissed Tomsk. "You found *Varpulis*, and I hear of this only now?"

"We're dealing with it," said Khan dismissively. "It isn't going to be a problem for much longer."

"Where is *Varpulis* now?" asked Tomsk, leaning forward, his teeth bared. "No, don't try to lie," he snarled, "just tell me where she is."

"*Varpulis* is in the vicinity of the Valkyr facility, *Child of Starlight*," said Khan, "but our forces are already preparing to–"

"You have already failed once, Khan," snarled Tomsk. "I will deal with this personally. *Varpulis* will be recovered and her villainous crew brought to justice."

"But–" began Khan.

"Don't get in my way, or you will feel my anger directly. I will let you know when this situation has been resolved."

The connection ended, and Khan was suddenly alone in his office.

Then Vlad appeared carrying a small silver tray upon which rested a diamond-glass shot of vodka. Khan stared at it briefly as condensation froze on its super-cooled surface. Then he snatched it up and threw it back.

"Tomsk is becoming a problem," he muttered, replacing the glass on the tray.

~

Cohen and Warden followed the aide into what was unmistakably a briefing chamber of some sort. The oval room wasn't crowded, but only because it was large and elegantly furnished. Maybe twenty Valkyr were already seated in a horseshoe shape, with a huge display at the end of the room.

"Still worried we might be paranoid?" whispered Warden as the aide led them to a pair of vacant chairs at the end of the line.

Cohen grunted a response as he fiddled with the data slate built into the arm of the chair.

Then the Valkyr all stood as a door opened and two people came in. Prime Minister Haukland with her deputy, Ove Berdahl. Cohen and Warden stood as well, then sank back into their chairs when Haukland waved everyone to sit.

"I'll get right to the point," said Haukland as the chatter died away. "We have received a video message from a representative of the Koschite armed forces." She nodded to an aide and the lights dimmed. A face appeared on the room's main display.

"For those of you who may not know, this is Admiral Tomsk. It appears that he is a member of the Progenitor faction within the Koschite Government, as is the CEO of GKI, the organisation that attacked our asteroid mining facility at Oldervik."

There was a murmur of disquiet around the chamber. It was clear that Admiral Tomsk was infamous amongst the Valkyr.

"Admiral Tomsk sent us a recorded message, part of which I will now play for you."

She sat down and nodded at her aide. The display changed briefly to show a dark logo of some sort, then Tomsk's face returned.

"You have made a grave error by hiring mercenaries to attack legitimate GKI facilities. This cannot stand! I will not let it stand! Aggression will not be tolerated. You will surrender your illegally occupied facility and compensate GKI for the loss of their equipment and personnel. You will return the stolen vessel *Varpulis* and the criminals who crew her. *Child of Starlight* will be garrisoned with Koschite troops to ensure your continued adherence to the rule of law. You will commit to having no further contact with mercenaries or the fanatical scum from Earth. You will make good all the damage you have inflicted on our peaceful and lawful enterprises, or you will suffer the consequences!"

Haukland paused the video.

"There is more, but after this, his threats become repetitive and ever more elaborate."

"This is intolerable," said someone from the far end of the chamber. "We cannot possibly accept this!"

There was a rumble of angry murmuring and agreement until Haukland held up her hand for silence.

"Of course not," she said firmly. "Tomsk is deluded if he thinks we will agree to any of this. But he has the power to force us to comply and make good on his threats, and the rest of his message makes it clear he is already en route to enforce his demands. We have reached out to our usual contacts in the Koschite government, but communication with them has been patchy at best in recent months and it may be some time before we receive a response."

More grumbling, and no small amount of shouted anger. Enlightened and liberal the Valkyr might be, but in meetings, they behaved pretty much like everyone else.

"Do you have a plan?" asked someone at the end of the table. Warden looked around and blinked in surprise when he recognised the physicist, Skar. "I see our friends are here," she said, gesturing in the Cohen's and Warden's direction, "and I assume that we do not plan to hand them over."

"We do not," said Haukland firmly. "Admiral Tomsk's statement is wrong in every significant respect, and in any case, he has no mandate to operate in our volume. This is a disagreement between us and the Progenitors, as represented by Admiral Tomsk. Our

Commonwealth friends, and in fact the larger Koschite government, are not to be drawn into it."

"With respect, Prime Minister," said Cohen, leaning forward and raising his hand. "I think we're already involved. These battles are only part of a larger conflict between the Commonwealth and the Koschite government."

"But you need not be drawn further into *our* argument, Commander," said Haukland. "Instead, we prefer that you continue your repairs and leave the system as soon as possible. We will handle Admiral Tomsk."

"Again, with the greatest respect, I don't see how you will manage that given the current state of your military readiness," said Cohen. "And it will be some time – weeks, in all likelihood – before *Ascendant* is fit to flee, so I'm afraid our paths are linked for at least a little longer."

Haukland frowned at Cohen.

"Then what do you suggest, Commander?"

Cohen looked slowly around the chamber before glancing at Warden.

"You have friends within the Koschite government?"

Haukland nodded.

"If I have understood the situation, you need time for the government to bring Admiral Tomsk under control. We'll buy you that time, and keep the admiral from making good on his threats to *Child of Starlight*."

"But how, Commander? How will you do all this?" asked Haukland.

Cohen glanced again at Warden, who nodded his support.

"I have an idea, Prime Minister, but we'll need a little time to develop it."

26

"The update for this shift, sir," said Mantle, slipping into the room to deliver her report to Command Cohen. They were in *Ascendant's* command suite, from where Cohen had been coordinating the ship's continuing repair efforts since the Valkyr council meeting three days before.

"Anything surprising, Sub Lieutenant?" he asked, not looking up from his review of the schedule for the next phase of work, which would finally see the hyperspace engine returned to full service.

"No, sir," said Mantle. "We've restored the main sensors arrays, so you should have solid visibility across a wide angle. And the final tests on the upgrades to the forward railgun array are complete. The system is about twenty per cent more effective, giving you faster projectiles and increased fire rate."

"Excellent, thank you."

"The downside is that the barrels will wear out more quickly," she continued, ignoring Cohen's praise, "so we'll need downtime to replace them every four or five hundred rounds."

Cohen nodded. "For every gain..." he muttered. But this was a price worth paying. Battles were so infrequent that replacing the barrels after every encounter with the enemy wouldn't be a problem.

"We've completed the initial work on the counter-measures systems, but the fabricators aren't yet working correctly. We *think* we're making progress," said Mantle, but the doubt in her voice was palpable.

"You 'think'? You mean we have an operational weapon system but without the required ammunition?"

Mantle nodded unhappily.

"When will it be fixed?"

"I don't know. I'm working on it. It's a fiddly, one-person job, and it'll take as long as it takes."

"So that clears all the other teams to work on the hyperspace engine?" asked Cohen, although he already knew the answer.

"Yes, sir, but we've only patched many systems. They're held together with spit and string. A strong wind might cause them to fail, and if we push too hard, I can't be sure which will go first."

"I understand, Sub Lieutenant, just do what you can to keep things ticking over. And get the hyperspace engine working."

"Aye, sir, I'll see what–" she began. Then a klaxon wailed.

Cohen closed his slate and double-timed it to the bridge with Mantle a half-step behind.

"What do we have?" he asked, standing behind his chair with his hands resting on its back.

"Proximity warning, sir," said Midshipman Susie Martin at the helm, the only member of the team currently on the bridge. "Two large Deathless vessels have just exited hyperspace, approximately three hundred thousand kilometres away."

"Very good, Ms Martin," said Cohen. "Go to action stations and let's disembark our friends from *Child of Starlight.*"

"Aye, sir," said Martin, flipping up the safety cover and pressing the button that set the battle condition across the ship.

Red lights flicked on around the bridge, or at least half of them did. A second later, an automated message rang out, "Action stations! Action stations!" There was no change on the bridge, but elsewhere on the ship the crew would be packing up non-essential work and hurrying to their combat stations.

The plan that Cohen had thrashed out with Trygstad called for all Valkyr personnel to leave *Ascendant* within fifteen minutes.

"We must be ready for action with all possible haste," Cohen had said, overriding Trygstad's concerns. "Your people must know how to get off the ship if Admiral Tomsk arrives unexpectedly." Given that they had no idea where the admiral was coming from, an unexpected arrival was about the only type anyone could reasonably imagine.

The rest of the bridge crew arrived at a run, heading quickly to their seats as a timer on the main display ticked steadily upwards.

"Four minutes and counting," muttered White as he took his own seat. "Not too bad. The Valkyr personnel are clearing out, all except Trygstad, who has chosen to stay on board."

"No surprise," said Cohen, shaking his head. "Just as long as she knows when to stay out of the way and when to do what she's told."

White snorted. "She could teach a class on how to be stubborn," he said, "but she's not daft. I think she'll do what she needs to do."

"Channel request from *Child of Starlight*, sir," reported Wood at the communications desk.

"On the main screen, please, Mr Wood," said Cohen, directing his attention to the display as a Prime Minister Haukland's image appeared.

"Yes, Prime Minister. We are evacuating your people from *Ascendant*, and we will be de-coupling from *Child of Starlight* in the next few minutes."

"And you are set on this course of action?" Haukland spoke Koschite, but her words appeared in English as subtitles.

"I am," said Cohen. "We'll update you as soon as we have news."

Haukland was silent for a few seconds as if considering a final plea. Her lips creased in a tight smile and she gave a short nod.

"Good luck, Commander," she said in heavily accented English. Then the link was broken.

~

Twelve minutes later, *Ascendant* was free of *Child of Starlight* and powering towards the incoming Deathless fleet with *Palmerston* safely stowed in her main bay.

"Take us five degrees above their trajectory, Mr Jackson," said Cohen. Above the bridge, the main display showed the tactical view, with all the ships picked out in different colours and their current flight paths shown as dotted lines. "We're hoping to scare them off, not ram them."

"Aye, sir," said Jackson. "Laying in the course now."

"Course looks good," said Martin at the helm. "Attitudinal thrusters firing first, then a thirty-second burn on the main engine at thirty per cent."

Cohen nodded his approval. Mantle's instructions regarding the engine were clear: keep the power down, keep the burns short and don't be surprised if the whole thing blows up and kills everyone on board.

"Incoming communication, sir," said Wood. "I think it's Admiral Tomsk."

"Interesting," said Cohen, straightening a little in his chair. "Very well, let's see what the admiral has to say. On the main viewscreen, please."

There was a brief flicker as the two comms systems established a connection at the protocol layer, then a Deathless face appeared on the screen. For a few long seconds, the two men stared at each other.

"You are Cohen?" The translated words popped up beneath the speaker.

"Lieutenant Commander Cohen, Royal Navy, at your disposal, sir," said Cohen formally. "How may we be of assistance?"

"You are a war criminal, soon to experience the full weight of Koschite justice. Your vessel, *Varpulis*, is stolen and you will heave to and prepare to be boarded."

"Are you Admiral Tamsak? I don't believe we have met, and it's so important to be clear on these things."

"I am Grand Admiral Tomsk," corrected the Deathless officer

haughtily, "commander of the fourteenth fleet. You are a pirate charged with the most heinous war crimes. Surrender immediately, and submit to judgment and punishment."

"I'm sorry, Admiral, our translation system is still somewhat flawed. Did you say that you wished to surrender? We are of course happy to accept," asked Cohen with an expression of mild surprise. Tomsk ignored the question.

"Your ship is in no state to fight. Your bravado fools nobody. Power down your systems and prepare to be boarded," snarled Tomsk.

"Tempting," admitted Cohen. "Let me put you on hold while I discuss this with my senior officers." He nodded to Wood, who blanked the comms channel so that it showed a 'holding' message under a gently spinning RN logo. A jaunty version of 'Drunken Sailor' played over the image. Cohen smiled. Whoever had added that, it was a nice touch.

"Does anyone wish to surrender themselves to Admiral Tomsk?" The room was silent. "Good. Then let's make this count. Mr White, please be so good as to put things in motion."

"Very good, sir," said White, rising from his seat to leave the bridge.

"Mr MacCaibe, what's your assessment on the two enemy ships?"

"They're big, sir, but the closer one is more heavily armed. It's a carrier if I'm any judge. The other one looks," he hesitated, scrutinising his display as he struggled for the right words, "it looks like a converted passenger liner. It has weapon systems, but they're strapped to the hull, like warts on a maiden's arse."

"A troop carrier, then?" mused Cohen, skipping past MacCaibe's colourful metaphor.

"Aye, sir, that would seem to be the size of it."

"The closer ship is *Target One*, our primary; the other is *Target Two*," announced Cohen. "Focus on *Target One* and ignore *Target Two* for now. When I give the nod, send them everything we have for as long as we can manage it, understood?"

"That might leave us nothing left for *Target Two*," cautioned MacCaibe.

"Understood, Midshipman. Set the target, if you please."

"Aye, sir, targeting now."

"And let's take the admiral off hold, Mr Wood."

There was a momentary pause, then Tomsk's face reappeared.

"Admiral," said Cohen with a friendly grin, "we have considered your generous offer but find ourselves unable to accept at this time."

"You refuse?" spluttered Tomsk.

"You are hardly the first Koschite to threaten us, Admiral, and yours will be the fourth vessel we've destroyed in recent weeks. What is that you're flying? Some sort of converted freighter? If your crew is as incompetent as all the others we've faced," he glanced at the time, "then I think this'll all be over well before tea time." He leaned forward. "Are you ready for your lesson, Admiral?" he asked, giving the most disrespectful grin he could manage and watching as Tomsk's expression tightened.

"You boast of your crimes, but you will pay the price today," promised Tomsk.

Cohen cleared the grin from his face, coldly serious.

"You have made threats against us and our peaceful friends, the Valkyr. You have attacked our planets and colonies, our ships and our people, our stations and our outposts. And now you wish us to surrender to your 'justice'? I'm sorry, Admiral, but today ends only with the destruction of your fleet and the safe delivery of our friends from harm."

"You will regret your insults, Cohen. Your name will be a byword for fear and cowardice across the universe. Your punishment will last a thousand years. I, Admiral Tomsk of the fourteenth fleet, promise this in the name of the Koschite Republic!"

"At least I won't be a bore, Admiral," said Cohen, forcing back a yawn.

"Your insolence is beyond belief," snapped Tomsk. "Make your preparations, Commander."

Cohen leant back and grinned at the display. "We're ready," he said calmly. Then he beckoned towards the screen. "Bring it."

Tomsk snarled, and the channel closed.

"First time I've negotiated with the commander of an enemy fleet," he muttered to himself. "Could have gone worse."

It took an hour of tense and tedious travel to bring the enemy ships within the effective range of their weapons. *Ascendant* jinked marginally a couple of times, but both sides needed to close the distance if they were to exchange fire, and there weren't many options except to charge in and hope for the best.

"Is there any chance we could have missed a third ship? They came in much larger numbers at Akbar, and he is an admiral," White pointed out.

Cohen replayed the ambush at the Battle of Akbar in his mind. The constant stream of Deathless vessels dropping out of hyperspace and launching into a coordinated, and deadly assault. He had no idea if Tomsk was involved there, but this time he didn't have the same sense of trepidation. Nor did he have Admiral Morgan giving orders to hold back.

"This doesn't have the same feel," Cohen said after a few seconds of consideration. Tomsk seemed confident to him, and well he should be with that monster of a flagship against *Ascendant*. "I think two is all they have."

And so they flew on, watching as the distance slowly shrank. *Target Two*, the troop carrier, had fallen behind, letting Tomsk forge ahead to meet *Ascendant*. Now *Target Two* had turned towards *Child of Starlight* and had set an intercepting course.

"Two hundred and fifty seconds to firing range," said MacCaibe, although in the airless void of space, 'firing range' was a variable distance based on the closing speed and the enemy vessel's perceived manoeuvrability rather than a maximum engagement range.

"Sound the klaxon for imminent action, Mr Wood," said White, who was monitoring the internal systems. The crew, such as it was, were still at action stations, all waiting for something to happen.

"*Target One* is reconfiguring their forward hull-plating, sir, the wee jessies," reported MacCaibe, hands flicking at the controls as he pushed composite images from the forward sensor array to the main display.

"What the hell...?" murmured Cohen, leaning forward to examine the picture more closely. The slab-fronted ship had changed utterly. Now, instead of a flying wall of metal, *Target One* presented a sloping, curved face.

"Angled to deflect railgun rounds and as welcome as a maggot in your neeps," said MacCaibe, somewhat awed by the vast panels that *Target One* had deployed.

Cohen was silent for a moment, nodding gently.

"Let's send this to *Target One*, Mr Wood: Your current path suggests hostile intent. Reverse your course immediately, or we will deploy lethal force to defend ourselves and *Child of Starlight*."

"Done, sir," said Wood.

"Looks like they're deploying gun turrets, sir," said MacCaibe, highlighting on the main display two large sections of *Target One* that had been raised above the ship's sleek exterior.

"I guess they're proceeding with hostilities," muttered Cohen. He opened a ship-wide channel. "This is Cohen. Prepare for imminent action."

"Thirty seconds," said MacCaibe.

"Send a short burst of railgun fire into that shielding, Mr MacCaibe, to test it," said Cohen. "I'd like to see what it can do. Then everything else into the flanks as we sweep past."

"Aye, sir, locking in the programme now."

Cohen watched the numbers count down to zero, then waited another ten long seconds.

"Fire now, Mr MacCaibe."

"Aye, sir, firing now." The midshipman triggered the firing programme and pushed the weapons dashboards to the main display. "Number two gun has failed," he reported as the status indicator flashed red, "some sort of mechanical problem. And numbers four and five are overheating."

"Keep firing until they fail," said Cohen. MacCaibe nodded and moved his fingers away from the button that would have paused the firing.

"Incoming fire from *Target One*," reported MacCaibe, "deploying counter-measures." MacCaibe frowned and punched at the buttons again. "No response from the countermeasure launch system, sir," he said, continuing to press at the buttons.

"Mantle," barked Cohen, opening a channel to the engineering command suite. "What's going on with our counter-measures?"

"We're on it," snapped Mantle. "Looks like something shook loose."

"How long?"

"I don't know – a few minutes, maybe more."

Cohen looked questioningly at MacCaibe, who shook his head.

"We don't have that long, Mantle."

"So stop distracting me," she said, closing the channel.

"*Target One* is deploying counter-measures, sir," reported MacCaibe, "analysing the pattern. And they're firing again. Railguns and rocket-propelled missiles of some sort."

"Twist us around, Ms Martin," ordered Cohen. "Ten degrees down and main engine for thirty seconds at maximum burn."

"Aye, sir, laying that in," said Martin, working her controls. "Attitudinal thrusters firing, ten-second burst."

"*Target One*'s countermeasures look about ninety-five per cent effective, sir," reported MacCaibe sourly. "Railgun three has suffered some sort of failure and is firing randomly. Railgun's four and five have overheated like middens in summer."

"Manoeuvring complete," said Martin, "main engine burn in three, two, one." The engine fired, but instead of a solid kick of acceleration there was a far more modest nudge, as if *Ascendant* had been given a friendly prod.

"What happened to the engines, Ms Martin?"

"Don't know, sir, they're running at maybe four per cent." She called up a diagnostic and threw it to the main display. "Looks like something might have failed in the main power generator."

There was a ping and a channel opened from the engineering

suite. Mantle's face appeared on Cohen's slate, her expression angry and stressed. "Can't fix the countermeasure system," she shouted over a blare of klaxons and other background noise, "and the safety coupling at the primary generator has tripped, so there's only a trickle of power to the engines."

"I had noticed," said Cohen with Herculean calm. "Can you fix it?"

"Can't hear you," replied Mantle, "but we can't fix this quickly. Needs a week of work to be sure. We're just trying to hold things together down here. Out." She closed the channel and a red warning flashed across Cohen's slate.

"Shit," he whispered. Doubt assailed him, and no small amount of fear, as he watched *Target One* firing again. Victory was beginning to look more than a little unlikely.

"Thirty seconds to first impacts," reported MacCaibe.

"Twist us around, Ms Martin, let's take it head on," said Cohen, resignedly.

"Aye, sir, attitudinal thrusters firing in three, two, one."

Nothing happened.

Martin punched at her controls again. "Sorry, sir, looks like they're dead as well."

"Five seconds, brace for impact," said MacCaibe, sound the ship-wide alarm.

Then *Ascendant* shuddered as a flurry of railgun rounds chewed through her armoured hull and ripped into her innards.

27

The bridge was a confused mess of tumbling debris and lower power emergency lighting. The railgun rounds had torn at *Ascendant*, stitching ragged holes along her flank and punching out her core systems. Then the missiles had arrived, and it was only by luck that they had not destroyed the ship outright.

"What's the picture?" asked Cohen, forcing his feet back against the floor. The artificial gravity had failed and anything that hadn't been glued to a surface was now floating around the bridge, shaken loose by the pummelling the ship had taken.

"Like a Saturday night in Inverness, sir," said MacCaibe, still tethered to his station. "The computer logged forty-two railgun strikes before it went offline. There's nae telling how many more after that." He shook his head, flicked at his controls again, then he gave up in disgust. "Dead as a doornail, sir."

"Come on, people," said Cohen, clapping his hands together. "Give me some good news."

"Internal comms seem to be working," said Midshipman Wood, "and we have power to some other internal systems."

"Helm's dead," said Martin.

"It looks like external comms are still working," said Wood in surprise. "Can't say I'd expected that," he added under his breath.

"A welcome piece of good news," said Cohen, although he was buggered if he could see how they would talk their way to victory.

"Navigation offline, life support inoperative," said Jackson.

"Weapons had mostly failed before they hit us," said MacCaibe morosely, "and they're no better now. Sensor arrays and processors are non-responsive."

The main door to the bridge opened and Mantle floated in, already wearing a full environmental suit. She activated the external speaker.

"Everything's dead in engineering except the primary power generator, which is still running at maybe ten per cent. Enough to power the emergency systems, but that's about it."

"Can you fix it?" asked Cohen, without any real hope.

"Sure," shrugged Mantle, "but it'll take weeks and we'll need help." She glanced around the bridge at the dead displays. "I don't think we have that long."

"No," agreed Cohen. "An hour, maybe less, for *Target One* to turn around and come back within range."

They looked at each other for a moment.

"The comms system is working. I think it's time to see if they're ready to accept our surrender," said Cohen.

Mantle frowned at him through her faceplate, and Cohen could feel the rest of the bridge crew staring at him as well. He looked around behind him at the now dark bank of viewscreens against the wall.

"Sub Lieutenant Mantle, can you please smash those screens?"

"Smash?" asked Mantle, staring at Cohen as if he had gone mad. "Why?" But Cohen had already turned away and was composing himself. Mantle shook her head and floated across the bridge. She wedged her feet against the floor, then wrenched at one of the viewscreens until the case failed and the screen shattered. Fragments of plastic and silicon filled the air as she took out her frustration on the other screens, bashing them to pieces.

"I think that'll do," said Cohen, glancing around. Mantle nodded, breathing hard, and pushed herself away towards the remains of the weapons desk where MacCaibe was still trying to boot his console. "Open a channel to Admiral Tomsk, Mr Wood. Let's see how badly he needs to gloat."

"Aye, sir, making the request now."

For several long seconds, nothing happened. Then Admiral Tomsk's face appeared on a corner of the main display. *Ascendant's* crew watched as the admiral peered over Cohen's shoulder, taking in the destruction wrought on the bridge.

"So, Commander," said Tomsk, smirking, "do you now wish to surrender? Will you give yourself up to Koschite justice?"

"I do, Admiral, and I will," said Cohen through gritted teeth. He gestured around him, "The state of *Ascendant* hardly allows me to do anything more."

"The state of *Varpulis* is testament to your supreme incompetence, Commander. Your reputation was greatly exaggerated," replied Tomsk, triumph seeping from every pore. "Heave to, insofar as you are able, and prepare to be boarded. We will be alongside in," he glanced at something off-camera, "forty minutes, and I expect to find your docking ports unlocked and ready."

The channel went blank.

Cohen slumped back and blew out a long breath. Then he released his straps to float clear of the command chair.

"All hands on deck," he said firmly, giving the order every commander hoped they would never have to use. "Mr White, get everyone aboard *Palmerston* and ready her for flight."

"We're not surrendering?" asked White, frowning with confusion.

"We are not. Get to *Palmerston,* then send Sub Lieutenant Corn to the mess hall. She'll need a full power suit. Mantle, you're with me."

"We're not leaving?" asked Mantle, her own confusion evident from within her helmet as the siren signalled all hands on deck and the bridge team began to move.

Cohen looked at Mantle and gave a sudden manic grin. "One last card to play and I'll need your help. Meet me in engineering in ten minutes. I need to speak to Captain Warden."

~

"Captain Warden," said Cohen as he floated into the mess hall where the remaining Marines had congregated. All wore full combat power armour and they were armed to the teeth, kitted out with every piece of offensive equipment that *Ascendant* carried.

"Sir," nodded Captain Warden, the face plate of his helmet open, eyes gleaming in the dull red light. "We're ready to go. What's the next step?"

Cohen grinned grimly. "Tomsk's coming alongside for a boarding action. Thirty-five minutes, or thereabouts."

"Alongside? He told you that? He's going to dock with *Ascendant*?"

"So it seems."

"Good," said Warden, nodding. "We can set up on the inside of the airlocks and really make them pay."

"That's one option," agreed Cohen, "but I was thinking you might prefer something more direct. We'll take *Palmerston* and distract Tomsk, while you and your merry band take a walk to *Target One* and do something nasty to her innards."

"A walk?" asked Warden dubiously. Then Cohen grinned, and suddenly Warden got it. "Oh, a 'walk'. Yes, that might work." He looked around at the assembled commandos, working out who to take. "Tricky job. Never been done before, as far as I know, but it's something we've trained for. I'll pick a small team; the rest can come with you."

"Good," said Cohen, glancing at the timer in the corner of his HUD. "You've got about thirty minutes to prepare. You'll need to steal a shuttle of some sort and rendezvous with *Palmerston* once everything's done and dusted."

"That's a risky plan, sir," said Warden, stating the blindingly obvious.

"I'm open to suggestions," said Cohen, "but only ones that can be put into action in a little over thirty minutes."

Warden was silent for a few long seconds, then he shook his head. "Nothing springs to mind, sir, so I suppose we'd better make this plan work."

"Good man. Brief your team and get them to the airlocks. We'll coordinate by HUD from here on." He held out his hand and Warden gave it a firm shake. "Good luck, Captain. See you on the other side."

"And good luck to you too, sir."

arden watched him go then turned to his company. The numbers were much reduced, but he still had eighty-four bodies to work with.

"More than enough," he muttered. "Too many, in fact." This was a risky mission and there was too much at stake to attempt the job with anyone who wasn't fully trained for the work at hand. He cleared his throat and waited for quiet.

"Commander Cohen's given us a mission, but it requires specialist skills. Everyone who's done the spacewalk and zero-G combat training, over on that side. Everyone else, over there," he said pointing across the room.

There was a short period of confusion while the Marines sorted themselves out, and about four-fifths of the company ended up on the right-hand side of the room. "Anyone who's still carrying an injury, over to the right," Warden went on, waving a few more people away from the smaller team.

"Good," he said, staring at the fourteen Marines who were left. He turned to the others. "You don't have the right training, so you're sitting this one out. Get to *Palmerston* in the main bay, report to Lieutenant White, and keep yourselves out of trouble." There was an undercurrent of grumbling – nobody liked missing a critical mission – but the Marines cleared out, leaving only the smaller team behind.

"Here's the news," said Warden. "A short spacewalk, forced entry to an enemy vessel, maximum sabotage within said vessel, then steal a shuttle and escape." He paused to look around. "Questions?"

"We'll need a pilot," said someone at the back of the crowd, "and can it be anyone but Ten?"

"I think that's where I come in," said Sub Lieutenant Corn as she floated into the hall. She was wearing power armour and carrying a magnetic grapple. "Someone lend me a gun?"

Ten passed her a massive combat shotgun. "Not a gun, never a gun. It's a weapon. You're an engineer, you should know better. You see any Deathless, you shoot them. No hesitation. Got it?" he said, not waiting for an answer before he took a replacement weapon from a nearby rack.

Ten turned back to the rest of the troop. "Outside of an exercise, have any of you ever done a ship to ship assault with exo-suits before?"

Nobody responded in the affirmative, and Ten sighed.

"Here's a top tip. Under no account should you miss the target spaceship. If you do, you are in space. You will not stop going. Ever. In a modern suit, air and water are recycled efficiently. You will die of starvation, which is pretty unpleasant. Secondly, do you all know the procedure to follow if you do miss?" he asked.

Again, nobody seemed to have an idea. Ten mimed placing a gun under his chin.

"You place your rifle like this, and you pull the trigger firmly."

"Tomsk will be alongside in twenty minutes or less," said Cohen as he pushed his way into the engineering department. Cohen nodded at the console Mantle and Mueller had rigged for their aborted attempt at opening a wormhole using the hyperspace engine. "Is that thing still working?"

"We haven't dismantled it, if that's what you mean," said Mantle, "but it didn't work, remember?" Then she narrowed his eyes as she realised the implications of his question. "You want to use it to destroy the ship?"

"Got it in one," said Cohen, positioning himself in front of the console. Then he looked up at Mantle. "Well?"

She raised her eyebrows, then gave a quick nod. "We didn't fix the damage, or the flaw," she said, "so if you activate the system, it'll go critical in a few minutes, then explode. Goodbye, *Ascendant*."

"What?" asked Cohen, looking up from the console.

"The emergency cut-off lever needs to be reset, down in the engine bay, or it won't start up."

"Seriously?" said Cohen, incredulous. "I thought you'd fixed all that stuff."

"Why would you think that?" snapped Mantle. "You saw the work schedules. Did you think we were sneaking back to do a bit more instead of sleeping?"

"Right, fine," said Cohen. "Here's the plan. You make sure everything's working up here, while I go down and sort out the emergency cut-off. Once you're happy, get to *Palmerston*. I'll trigger the sequence remotely then join you in the main bay. Got it?"

Mantle nodded slowly. "That should work."

"Good," said Cohen. "Keep your HUD on. I'll ping you when I'm done."

"You remember the way?" she asked as he headed for the door.

"Yeah, no problem. Should be easier without the gravity."

Except it wasn't, not really. Where he could have run, he had to pull himself along the corridor and bounce off the walls, continually correcting his course. And where he could have dropped, he had to climb instead. Even squeezing through the narrow crawl space was made more difficult.

"Nothing's ever bloody easy," he muttered as he heaved himself out into the engine bay. At least he didn't have to contend with a ten-metre drop to the floor this time. He pushed off from the wall and floated across the bay to land neatly by the cut-off lever.

<I'm at the lever> he sent to Mantle. <Ready?>

<Ready> came the reply.

"Fingers crossed," muttered Cohen as he heaved on the lever, pulling it back into the 'on' position.

<Looking good> sent Mantle. <Power is flowing. Simulation suggests ten minutes from trigger to catastrophic systems failure>

<On my way> sent Cohen, pushing off to head back the way he'd come. <Get to *Palmerston*>

<Roger>

But when he finally reached engineering, Mantle was still there, in front of the console where he'd left her ten minutes before.

"Why are you still here?" Cohen snapped angrily. "Get to *Palmerston*, now!"

"The remote trigger isn't going to work," she snapped back, "not unless you're here so I can rig it."

"Right, so I'm here now. Patch the controls through to my HUD," said Cohen.

"Working on it," she muttered, fiddling with the console. "See anything?"

"A big red button just popped into my HUD," said Cohen. "Is that it?"

"No, it's the in-flight entertainment system," Mantle snarled. "Of course that's it! You'll have about ten minutes from activating the trigger to detonation."

"Good. What's the safe distance?"

"Safe? From an exploding starship? I have no bloody idea," shouted Mantle, "but at least a hundred kilometres."

"Got it," said Cohen. "Now go, and make sure *Palmerston*'s ready to leave as soon as I arrive."

She stared at him for a moment, suddenly suspicious, then she nodded and pushed her way to the door, disappearing quickly into the corridor.

Cohen sat for thirty seconds or so, listening sadly to the great ship's last moments.

"That's enough moping around," he muttered, shaking his head as if to free himself of his melancholy. Then he heaved himself around and opened the engineering store, searching quickly in the dim red light until he found the engineering environmental suit and accessories he was looking for.

"That'll do nicely," he murmured, squeezing himself into the suit. As he fastened the helmet and triggered the diagnostic suite, a message appeared in his HUD.

<We're ready to rock and roll> sent Warden.

<Good. I'm on my way to the bridge>

There was a pause, then, <That wasn't the plan. Has something gone wrong?>

<We need to draw Tomsk in and make sure he takes the bait, or this will all have been for nothing>

There was another pause, then *Palmerston* joined the conference.

<I concur with Warden> sent White from *Palmerston*'s bridge. <This isn't what we planned>

<It's what I planned> replied Cohen. <How long till *Target One* docks?> he asked, changing the subject.

<About five minutes> sent White. <Looks like she's coming in on the port side>

<As soon as she docks, open the starboard doors and head for *Child of Starlight*. That's an order>

There was a pause, then, <Acknowledged, but I don't like it>

Tough, thought Cohen, shaking his head, *sometimes these things don't go the way we hope.*

<Captain Warden> sent Cohen, <launch your attack as soon as the boarding party from *Target One* gains entry to *Ascendant*>

<Acknowledged> sent Warden.

<Until later, gentlemen. Good luck. Cohen out>

28

"That's it," said Midshipman Shepherd from the comms desk on *Palmerston*. "Docking is complete, *Target One* is now locked to *Ascendant*."

"Very good, Mr Shepherd," said Lieutenant White from the command chair on *Palmerston*'s small bridge. "And what's our status?"

"Crowded, sir," said Midshipman Parks from the navigation desk. "Every room is pretty much full. *Palmerston* doesn't have enough acceleration couches for everyone, not even close, so it might be a bit uncomfortable."

That was an understatement. Without an acceleration couch to support the body, any high-G manoeuvres were likely to cause injuries amongst the passengers. Fatalities were not impossible, especially if anyone was caught by surprise.

"Can't be helped," muttered White. "It's not like we can leave anyone behind."

"*Target One*'s assault team has cracked the doors, sir. They're entering *Ascendant* now," said Shepherd.

"Let's see the action, Mr Shepherd," said White.

"Aye, sir," said Shepherd, pushing the feed from *Ascendant*'s internal cameras to *Palmerston*'s main display. The bridge team watched in silence as a Deathless assault force floated onto *Ascendant* and began to make their way along the corridors. They were wearing standard Deathless power armour and carrying a selection of low calibre arms suitable for combat aboard ship.

"That's our signal, Ms Robinson," said White grimly. "Open the main doors, let's get out of here while we still can."

"Aye, sir," said Robinson, "triggering *Ascendant*'s starboard doors now."

"Plot a course to get us outside but keep us hidden beneath *Ascendant* for now, Ms Parks," said White, leaning forward slightly as he watched the tactical view update. Half the main display now showed the inside of *Ascendant*'s main bay with the starboard doors sliding gently open. Beyond, only the stars could be seen.

"Slowly does it, Ms Robinson. Just put us on the outside for now."

"Aye, sir, taking us forward on attitudinal thrusters only." The view shifted as *Palmerston* nudged forward, turning slightly before heading slowly through the doors. Behind them, the bulk of *Ascendant* rose up, dwarfing the gunboat and curving away out of sight.

"Let's bring the weapons online, Ms Elson," said White, "and sound the warning klaxon."

"Aye, sir," said Elson, triggering the klaxon. It blared – three loud blasts – then fell silent. Nobody made a sound as *Palmerston* turned slowly under the gentle puffs from the attitudinal thrusters.

On the main display, the view switched as Shepherd worked the cameras, following the Deathless assault team.

"Is that the admiral?" asked Elson as a figure in more ornate armour with obvious, if unrecognised, rank markings floated past a camera.

Then a proximity warning cut through the quiet and the view from inside *Ascendant* vanished. An external view flashed up on the screen in its place and there, in the centre of the display and highlighted with a glowing red ring, was *Target Two*, Tomsk's troop carrier.

"Well that's less than ideal," muttered White to himself. He watched the screen for a few seconds, then made a decision. "Can't leave her sitting there like that."

<*Target Two*'s come looking for us> he sent to Cohen and Warden. <Dealing>

<Acknowledged> came the response from Warden. <Best of luck>

"Spin us around, Ms Robinson. Point us towards *Target Two*, five degrees above her current plane, then take us in," said White. "Let's see if we can bag another of these Deathless bastards."

~

C ohen whistled as he made his way to the bridge. He'd collected a sack of supplies as he passed the armoury, and now he was busy mining his own ship.

"The indignity of the thing," he murmured to himself, pressing another strip of high explosive into the joint on the inside of the hull. He added a detonator, keyed it to his HUD, then flicked across to check the progress of the Deathless assault team.

Slow and cautious, unlike their previous attacks, he observed, but that suited his purpose. He pressed on, hoping that he'd remembered how this was done, then he pushed away from the wall to admire his handy work.

"Sloppy," he muttered, "very sloppy, but it'll have to do."

He added one more charge – larger, and in a new area – then pushed his way to a chair on the far side of the bridge, pulled up the feed of the camera that watched the corridor outside and settled down to wait.

But not for long, as it turned out. The Deathless, having established that the ship was empty, moved more rapidly, taking the most direct route from the airlock to the bridge. There were about thirty of them, all told, and one had insignia across his armour that suggested high rank.

"Welcome aboard, Admiral Tomsk," whispered Cohen, grinning from within his own suit.

As the first of the Deathless troopers reached the bridge door, Cohen checked the icons in his HUD and ran through his plan again. Simple, straightforward and very, very risky.

A message popped suddenly into his HUD from *Palmerston*.

<*Target Two*'s come looking for us. Dealing>

Cohen stared at the message, then he flicked through his HUD until he found a feed from *Palmerston*'s viewpoint. He watched for a few seconds as *Palmerston* manoeuvred to engage *Target Two*, then he pushed the feed to the last working part of *Ascendant*'s main display and resumed his wait.

The door opened and the first of the Deathless assault team floated onto the bridge. There was a ripple of excitement when they noticed him, but nothing more. They were quick and confident, clearly familiar with zero-G work. In moments, the room was filled with enemy soldiers, all pointing their weapons at him.

One last figure floated onto the bridge before the door closed. Even allowing for his more cumbersome, or at least more ornately decorated, armour, Admiral Tomsk was clearly less nimble in zero-G. He pulled himself across the bridge, looked around, glanced at the main display, then saw Cohen sitting in the corner and came to a halt, holding uncomfortably to a handle on the ceiling.

"You are Cohen?" said Tomsk. "I had not expected to find your ship so bereft of crew. Where are they?"

Cohen read the translation and steeled himself for the endgame.

"They were keen to meet you, Admiral, but I'm afraid I had to send them away."

"Away?" asked Tomsk, immediately suspicious. "What do you mean 'away'?"

"Let me ask you something, sir," said Cohen, ignoring Tomsk's question. "Does your government know what you're doing out here? Do they know you're working as a low-rate privateer, that your ships are attacking the Valkyr's facilities and stealing their resources?"

Tomsk said nothing, and Cohen couldn't see his face through the Deathless admiral's opaque helmet.

"What else have you got up to, Admiral? Do you still follow orders, or are you operating entirely outside the Koschite command structure?"

"My actions are of no concern to a war criminal like yourself,

Cohen. You should be more worried about your own fate, now that you are to experience justice for the crimes you have committed."

"Allegedly," corrected Cohen.

"What?"

"The phrase is 'allegedly committed', Admiral. Unless you've already decided I'm guilty, of course, but then the concept of justice wouldn't have much meaning, would it?"

"You will have plenty of time to learn the meaning of 'justice', Cohen, and what it means to lose."

"To lose, Admiral? I'm sorry, but that's not on my list of things to do today," said Cohen, putting into his tone all the insolence he could muster. He stretched in his chair, careful not to push himself free, and grinned as the Deathless troopers adjusted their positions to keep their weapons pointed at him.

"Would you like to join me for today's entertainment?" asked Cohen, raising a finger to point to the main display. "I think you might find it diverting."

29

"A spacewalk," muttered Warden as he floated across the void. "Daft idea."

He gave Fletcher an extra few seconds to get clear of the assault tether before detaching himself. He glanced over his shoulder at *Ascendant*, a hundred metres away along the taut line that extended from a winch next to the airlock hatch. Ahead of him, separated from the personnel by a few metres with a safety stop, was a simple drone to pull the line out and keep it taught.

This equipment was normally used to inspect the outside of a ship. The drone pulled a spacewalk tether taut and allowed anyone in an exo-suit to go directly along its length, which saved a lot of human guesswork and skill with suit thrusters.

Fletcher was ten metres out in free space, heading toward Tomsk's flagship, at the rear of a line of power armoured Marine and Navy personnel. He'd been concerned about Sub Lieutenant Corn coming on the mission, but her engineering and flight experience meant that this portion of the mission profile was at least something she was familiar with. She probably had more practice in this environment than any of the Marines.

He checked his angle of approach, gently engaged his thrusters to check they were pushing him in the correct direction, then disengaged from the tether. Warden gently floated after Fletcher. The drone registered his exit and after a few seconds, started its return to the capsule by the airlock that it lived in. He was on his own.

Around him, the stars of the Milky Way provided a beautiful backdrop to this dangerous stunt. Untethered spacewalks were dangerous at the best of times, but as the prelude to a combat assault it was near suicidal. The view would be something to be thankful for, if it weren't spoiled by Tomsk's enormous flagship. There was nowhere better to see the stars than from the cold hard vacuum of space.

Ahead of him, the first of group had reached the enemy ship, and the rest were steadily catching up. Everything was going remarkably well, but he couldn't stop glancing at the railguns that festooned the ship. They were intended to deal with assault craft and torpedoes, but they'd do a person in an exo-suit a serious power of no good. Even the Marine Commando suits weren't going to resist shipboard weapon fire.

"Fletcher, are you drifting?" he asked, suddenly concerned. Everyone ahead of him was in a straight line, like a series of fence posts. Fletcher was out of synch with everyone else.

She didn't respond. "Fletcher? Fletcher, respond. Are you okay?" Warden demanded.

He gave his thrusters a short extra burst. *Gently does it*, he thought. *Remember your training. Panicked bursts send you far off course, really quickly.*

"Is there a problem, Captain Warden?" asked Sub Lieutenant Corn.

"Fletcher is drifting off course and not responding."

"Roger that. Checking."

"Negative, Corn. I'm following."

"This is my skillset, Captain. Leave it with me. I'll retrieve Fletcher; you proceed as planned."

Warden was about to say something else but he stopped himself.

She was right. Comparatively, she was expendable, and in any case, she did have more exo-suit experience than he.

"Don't put yourself at risk, Corn. We still need you to get us off this thing and Fletcher won't thank you for dying whilst trying to retrieve her dead clone."

"Understood," Corn replied. As Warden worked to adjust his angle of approach back toward the group, Corn turned on the spot and manoeuvred to neatly intercept Fletcher.

"I'm on the ship and beginning to crack the door panel, sir," said Goodwin.

Warden looked back as he zipped past Fletcher, who was at least a hundred metres off course, and passed Corn going the other way. The Royal Navy officer waved at him as she passed, completely relaxed about the risks she was taking.

Warden shook his head in bemusement.

It takes all sorts, he thought.

Royal Navy personnel were often seen as people who liked the luxury of conducting war through a viewscreen, but that didn't mean they lacked bravery, and using exo-suit thrusters to pursue a potentially dead colleague adrift in space was about as brave an action as Warden could think of. If it went wrong, Corn had little chance of being rescued. She would likely have to resort to the method Ten had demonstrated earlier.

"Captain, are you slowing down at all or shall we just order you some painkillers from your med-suite now?" Milton asked.

Warden blinked back to life from his reverie and stared at the fast-approaching ship.

"I'll be slowing down, Colour, just trying to get this over with quickly," he lied, adjusting his velocity with a short burst of his thrusters.

"As long as you're not trying to pull a sickie by breaking your arms, it's fine by me," Milton replied.

"Hang on, you mean to tell me if I'd broken my arms, I wouldn't have had to do this?"

"Pretty much."

"Well, bugger. That makes me peevish, you know."

"Yup. I suggest taking it out on the Deathless. It's all their fault, remember?"

Seconds later, Warden's feet touched down on the surface of the target and he pulled himself around to grip the ship. It was strangely comforting to have something to hold onto.

"Can I open her up now, Captain?"

"One moment, Goodwin," he said, turning back toward space.

"How goes it, Corn?"

"I've got her Captain. It looks like her suit was holed by a micro-meteorite or some other piece of junk floating out here. She seems to be unconscious; I'll be catching up with you soon. You should get inside and kill everything you find. If I need to give her medical atten- tion it'd be helpful not to have any Deathless bothering me."

"Roger that, we're going in," Warden said, signalling for Goodwin to do the honours. The airlock door slid open silently, and they stepped inside.

W arden pulled the trigger and stepped forward into the room, putting a hand on the chest of Deathless crew member who'd tried to shoot him. His gauntlet slapped into wet flesh as he pushed the corpse aside.

There it was. The airlock that led back to *Ascendant*. He strode forward to the controls, dropping the technician with a double tap to the head. He peered at the controls as his HUD provided translation. Then he tapped away, locking the docking tube so it couldn't be disengaged.

Goodwin busied herself at the actual tube, setting up a simple booby trap in case anyone forced their way through the doors and tried to regain access to *Target One* manually.

<Ten, how are you and Fletcher doing?> he asked, mostly to kill time while he booby-trapped the console.

Fletcher had recovered quickly once Corn had rescued her. Her ogre clone was tough, but when her suit began to lose pressure, it shut off non-essential functions like communications to preserve power, focussing instead on heating the area around the hole to prevent freezing.

As it was, Fletcher had a wound she wouldn't be able to ignore if she weren't drugged to the eyeballs on combat sims and painkillers, but Corn had patched the massive power armour she wore, and her vital signs were good.

<Not doing too badly> sent Ten. <We just found an armoury and Fletcher is using her Deathless disguise to requisition equipment for us. The bluff seems to be going well. No, wait a minute. She may have been rumbled>

<How do you know?>

<She's decapitated the armourer. Hang on>

Warden began walking from the room, checking the HUD to see the targets Goodwin's drones had identified.

<Yeah, no witnesses. We might be able to have some fun here. They have lots of toys>

<I hope you're going to share>

<Most of these toys are single-use only, but you should be able to enjoy the view from afar>

<We've secured the docking tube, and laid charges along our entire route. We're heading through the crew compartments looking for intelligence, then on to the hangar to try and steal a ride> Warden sent, pinging their locations on the tactical map.

<Okay, we're going to try and take out some major systems to cripple the ship. We'll be underway in a minute or two>

<Keep it brief, Ten, we don't have time for diversions>

<Pity, I was hoping to pick up gifts for the kiddies>

30

"What do you reckon, Ten? This way?" asked Fletcher, gesturing towards a pair of blast doors to the right.

"Why not through here?" Ten said, pointing at a set of double height, double width airlock doors to the left. "It's a more direct path to the auxiliary generator. According to Agent O's information about starships of this class, anyway."

"I dunno. There's just something about it that puts me off. Perhaps it's the oversized doors, or the huge yellow and black warning lines on them, or that angry red triangle with the big exclamation point in it. Perhaps it's the HUD translating the warning signs restricting it to authorised personnel that's putting me off."

"Bah. No sense of adventure. Look, we're on the capital ship of the admiral of the fleet. What could possibly be in here that you'd have to worry about, dressed like that?" he said, gesturing at her current clone and the bulky power armour. The ogre towered over Ten's RMSC clone. It was massive, hence the nickname, and the power armour the Deathless used turned it into a true behemoth.

"Fine. But you go first. And if this turns out to be the spaceship equivalent of a shark pit in a volcano base, you're the one getting eaten by mutated crocodiles bred for war," said Fletcher, slapping a blood-splattered access card she'd picked up earlier on the access panel.

The doors opened with a whoosh. "Umm. That was a very vivid image, Fletcher. Perhaps we should talk about you staying up late reading comics and eating cheese, hmm?" Ten suggested as he headed into the cavernous space. He received a two-finger salute for his trouble, and it wasn't the polite sign for victory.

Fletcher ducked into the room. With her current height, even the larger doors on the Deathless ships still felt a little low. She found herself on a wide metal gantry overlooking a room that was three or four stories tall. It was hard to see the floor through the jungle below.

"What the fuck is this?"

Ten shrugged. "Maybe you weren't wrong about the crocodile monsters?"

"Let's just try and get across here as quickly as possible, eh? Good-ers, you still got a drone near us?" she asked over comms.

"A micro-drone, set to keep pace with you. We're in the middle of a firefight, so be quick. What's up?"

"We've just hit a huge room and need to know if there's a quick way to cross it. It's our most direct route to the auxiliary power systems. Any chance you can map the room for us?" Fletcher asked as she peered over the edge of the railing that was all that stood between them and a fall into the steamy darkness below.

The room was amazing. It reminded her of a huge tropical hothouse she'd visited with her school to see the pretty butterflies and unusual plants and parrots. Only that one wasn't on a spaceship dozens of jumps from Sol space. She couldn't see the far wall, and could only see one of the adjacent walls. A biome area mixing hydroponics and oxygen-generating plants wasn't uncommon among capital class ships, but they were usually more like formal gardens than forest, let alone jungle.

"No problem. Give me a second," Goodwin replied. There was gunfire in the background and Fletcher could see Ten getting fidgety. His fingers twitching to the beat of the weapons in frustrated sympathy. A micro-drone appeared in front of Fletcher, did a loop and flew out into the room. "Done. It'll map the layout, then return to follow mode."

"Thanks, Goodwin. Fletcher out."

Fletcher watched her tactical map as the drone's scanning filled it in, the gangways appeared, and it looked like they could cross the whole room on them.

"See? What did I tell you," Ten said as he set off after her.

"I'm not going to the ground floor."

"Fletcher, they don't have crocodiles in here."

"Says you," Fletcher said as they jogged through the jungle canopy.

"Yeah, they probably have something else in here. Like giant robo-snakes!"

"Not just space monkeys then?"

"Hey, I wasn't lying about the space monkeys, was I?"

Fletcher had to admit that he hadn't been, preposterous though it had sounded at first. No-one had believed him until they had seen the monkeys on *Child of Starlight*. If anything weird or spectacular was going on, Ten always seemed to be at the heart of it.

"No, you weren't. Is that what this place is? A space monkey habitat?" she asked.

"Probably. Might just be a hot, sweaty, pungent rest and relaxation garden. Admiral's prerogative, maybe?" Ten replied as they passed the halfway line to the other side of the immense chamber.

"Maybe it's worth it to keep them happy. I heard they work for the Deathless, right?"

"Yeah, all sorts of jobs."

"How many are on this ship, do you think?"

Ten pulled up short. "Fletcher, I don't know, okay? I'm not a bloody expert on space monkeys."

She stopped as well. "Okay, no need to get touchy. I'm just making conversation, right? A big ship, with a jungle only for the space monkeys, my mind naturally wonders how many there might be on board." Fletcher held up her enormous hands. "But if you don't want to talk about it, let's just go and find that auxiliary power thing and blow it up, eh?"

"Yeah. Right. Yeah," said Ten hesitating.

Fletcher put her hands on her hips.

"What's up now, Ten? We're short of time!"

"You're right, Fletcher," said Ten, waving his hand around the room. "There must be dozens, maybe hundreds of them on this ship, and we've come to kill them."

"Them and the Deathless. Nothing they wouldn't do to us."

"Yeah, but the mandrills don't even know about the war. They don't know what's going on Fletcher. They're innocent in all this," said Ten.

"Shit. You want to save them, don't you?"

Ten shrugged again. "I've got to try and find them, and at least give them a fighting chance. But you get on, Fletcher. You complete the mission, I'll catch up with you. Trust me, you don't want to get court-martialled and end up like me."

"Ten, I don't think I'll ever meet anyone like you again. Promise me you'll catch up? Don't bugger about."

"Don't worry. If I can't find them soon, I'll be out of this place faster than a scalded cat. Go Fletcher, and give 'em hell."

Fletcher found herself in a large, long room, flanked on either side by auxiliary power systems, just as Agent O had described. The generators and converters towered above her, stretching towards the distant ceiling and making even her ogre clone seem small.

She looked for the weakness that Agent O had identified, not that having access to the internal systems of a ship was really much of a weakness. If you couldn't destroy a ship from the inside, you were a pretty piss-poor commando. Every ship was vulnerable to sabotage, especially if the crew kindly allowed you to wander around unimpeded.

Then she saw it – a confluence of pipes and vents in the rafters of the room. Fletcher had been told the room would have multiple power generation, storage and recovery facilities. It was like a central clearing house for power on the ship. In normal practice, the fusion reactors would power everything on board the ship, from lighting, to wormhole generators and life support.

The Deathless had redundancies for everything and they used much more efficient ship designs than the Royal Navy. It was in their nature, as descendants of an Ark ship culture where everything – air, water, even people – was recycled to keep the ship going. Shutting down the main generators wouldn't even slow them down.

Captain Cohen had suggested they blow the fusion generators, but Sub Lieutenant Mantle had advised that the resulting detonation would destroy *Ascendant*, *Palmerston* and any chance of escaping the battle. Instead, they had planted charges to cut the power coming from the fusion generators, and now they were going to cut backups as well, since Agent O had supplied a way to do it from the inside.

There wasn't time to do a circuit of the room and climb several flights of stairs to reach her goal. Instead, Fletcher sprinted along the gantry, planted her foot on the railing at the end, and jumped into space, thirty metres above the artificial gravity systems in the floor of the room.

Her hand snaked out as she fell, pointing towards the cluster of pipes that met in a central column that fell from the ceiling. Her magnetic grapnel sailed across the space and clamped onto the top of the column. Then the motor began to wind in the tether, pulling her up towards the ceiling of the vast chamber. The power armour took the brunt of it, taking the strain so that her arm wasn't wrenched from its socket.

She heard shouting from below. Someone had seen her. She looked down and saw that weapons were being raised. Nothing that could penetrate her armour, as far as she could see, but the tether was another matter. A third of the way to go, and now she was swinging back to the middle of her arc. Soon she would be going directly upward and then she'd been an easy target.

Fletcher reached into her webbing and began dropping things

from it. Then she pulled out her massive hand cannon, the brutal automatic pistol the ogre clones were equipped with, the version for their power armour.

The grenades detonated, drowning out the bangs and zings of the gunfire in the roar and flash of explosions. She holstered the pistol as she completed her arc, stretched out her arm and caught the lip of the gantry. Then she pulled herself up and squatted down, trying to make herself a smaller target.

Below, a barrage of smoke and dust billowed. She threw in a flash-bang for good measure then turned to the job at hand. Nobody down there would be bothering her for a few seconds.

Fletcher looked at her target, an air intake not much more than two metres across. Ten had suggested a missile launcher from the armoury, but even a bullseye would have been risky. Her armoured fingers gripped the maintenance hatch and she tore it from its hinges. She threw in a pack she had prepped in the armoury, slapped a relay device on the side of the tube to ensure the detonation signal could be received, then turned to leave.

But coming along the gantry her were two ogre clones, both in power armour. Bugger. At times like this, it was helpful to have Ten nearby. The Deathless ogres had their helmets off, and were both grinning at her, joking and laughing with each other as they advanced.

They were friendly with each other, but they weren't going to give her a warm welcome, despite the fact she was wearing one of their clones. If swinging over them on a grapnel line hadn't made it obvious she wasn't a friendly, responding with grenades to their gunfire would have done the trick.

Backing up, Fletcher moved to the end of the gantry. The two Deathless troopers drew their swords and the massive vibro-blades hummed to life with a bright orange glow. They waved them about in a threatening manner, demonstrating their skill with the weapons.

Bloody poseurs, thought Fletcher.

She drew her pistol as they began to advance, and they laughed, taunting her. She stuck two fingers up at them and fired at the gantry's support bolts. Fletcher blew them a kiss, then she stamped down hard on the end of the gantry. The Deathless saw what she was doing and began sprinting toward her, yelling.

She grabbed part of the railing on the central section of the gantry and slammed her foot down again and again as the Deathless ogres charged ever closer.

Then, with an awful screech of tortured metal, the bolts sheared. The gantry slipped, bouncing crazily as it swung from its supporting cables. Fletcher emptied the magazine into the ceiling where the cables were anchored and then, with the Deathless ogres mere metres away, the gantry failed.

Fletcher waved as the Deathless ogres fell screaming to their deaths.

<Captain, are you ready to rendezvous?>

<We're on our way to shuttle bay MA-R5 now. The RV is flagged. Are you and Ten done?>

Fletcher looked around. Ten hadn't caught up yet.

<The primary fusion generators are offline; the backups are rigged. Looking for new targets>

<Negative> sent Warden. <Get your arse to MA-R5, Fletcher!>

<Roger. On our way!>

31

M ilton ducked back into cover as a burst of fire rattled down the corridor.

"Fletcher, glad you could join us," she said as Fletcher caught up with the rest of the Marines. "Thought we'd lost you for a moment."

"Happy to be here, Colour. Need a hand?"

"Yes, we're a bit pinned down here. I don't suppose you found a route to flank them, did you?"

"Don't think so, Colour," Fletcher replied, firing off a shot with her enormous pistol.

"Pity, I'd really like to get in that bay, and these bastards have had us on the back foot for a while now."

"What's behind their position? Anything we need?"

"Yeah, the corridor that leads to the docking bay."

"So nothing dangerous or valuable for about a hundred meters until the door to the bay?"

"Yes, why?"

"I've got something that might help," Fletcher said, holstering her pistol and flicking the release on a strap that ran across her breastplate. She unslung a large backpack and began opening fasteners.

Milton fired another burst toward the other side of the room. "What have you got there, Fletcher?"

"Confiscated enemy weapon, Colour. Shall I give it a go?"

"Have at it. We'll back you up."

Fletcher hefted the brutal multi-barrelled weapon and grinned. Then she leapt from cover and charged down the corridor, holding down the trigger as she went. Gouts of flame shot from the barrels as each fired in turn, spraying huge numbers of rounds at the enemy position.

"For fuck's sake Fletcher! I didn't mean that!" Milton shouted, as she fired her own weapon at the enemy position.

"Die you bastards!" came a scream from somewhere behind Milton. She turned to see, to her astonishment, Sub Lieutenant Corn charging after Fletcher, her shotgun firing wildly.

"Corn, get your head down!" Captain Warden yelled.

Fletcher bounded over an enemy barricade and despatched the Deathless crew who had been firing over it.

Oh balls. Those stupid bastards will get themselves killed on their own, thought Milton.

Milton piled over the crates she'd been sheltering behind and swapped in a fresh magazine as she pelted after the suicidal pair.

"What the bloody hell are we doing?" she heard Captain Warden shout as he joined the charge.

Corn was sprinting full tilt, directly for a cluster of enemies huddling behind an armoured position. The Deathless behind it were firing wildly, not even bothering to aim as they cowered back. Milton lobbed a flashbang then pummelled them with fire. The enemy troops ducked, and Corn leapt over their shield, howling like a banshee.

"Die you bastard, die!" she screamed as she smashed an unfortunate trooper's helmet with the heavy butt of her shotgun, over and over.

The rest of the Deathless scrambled away from the lunatic who'd descended on them. Milton dashed to the shielding and dropped to one knee, firing short, controlled bursts into the fleeing enemy, cutting them down one by one. Warden joined her, and they made quick work of the remaining enemy.

"Corn, he's dead," said Warden, laying a hand on her shoulder to gently pull her back. "It's over."

Corn looked up and stepped back, breathing hard. Then she looked around, clearly slightly confused.

"Goodwin, get that door open," said Milton. "Everyone else, stand by in case there's any resistance on the other side."

<Marine X, where are you?> sent Warden.

<Incoming. ETA to MA-R5 about three minutes at this rate>

<Roger. Don't be any longer than that>

"Fletcher, is the auxiliary power down?" Warden asked.

"Not yet, Captain. I wanted to make sure we were all clear," Fletcher replied.

"The tactical map confirms we are – blow it now," Warden ordered.

Goodwin whirled, shouting, "No! I haven't got the door open and we need power to open the bay door as well, or we can't get the shuttle out."

Warden mulled over that for a moment, nodding.

"Good point. Fletcher, blow the power when Goodwin gives you the nod, okay? We don't want to be trapped on *Target One* when *Ascendant* goes pop."

He turned to Milton and grinned as she rolled her eyes in exasperation.

The doors dilated into the bulkheads with a pronounced hiss, and the hangar beyond was revealed, along with a handful of the Deathless crew determined to defend it. The Marines dropped below the captured security barriers that they'd turned around and brought close to the entrance, while Goodwin hacked the lock.

Projectiles clanged off the thick plating, ricocheting down the corridor above their heads.

Warden wagged a finger at Corn and Fletcher. "Don't even think about it, you two."

"What now?" Milton grumbled.

"We could try another suicidal charge?"

"I'd rather not," Milton remarked as she lobbed a grenade in the enemy's general direction.

Warden popped up, fired an extended burst and ducked back down under a hail of return fire. "I'm not keen either."

"Should I have a go at them, sir?" Fletcher asked, firing her hand cannon blind over the barrier.

"No! No more heroics. Everyone, check magazines, we're going to give them a concerted barrage on the count of three. Three, two, fire!" Warden finished, popping up again and firing methodical bursts downrange. The others all discharged a variety of weapons at the same time. Shotgun blasts, carbines, rifles and a couple of grenades. Then they ducked again.

The enemy fire started up again, pinning them behind their purloined security barrier.

"We can't keep this up, sir," said Milton. "We'll probably run out of ammo before they do."

"Yes, but what else we can do?"

"We could close the door and try another shuttle bay?" Goodwin asked.

Warden checked the timer in his HUD, then he shook his head. "The nearest is too far, and it might be just as heavily guarded."

"How about closing the door and trying to find another way into this one so we can flank them?" Fletcher suggested.

"Goodwin's drone shows the only other entrance is on the far side of the bay. It'd take too long," said Milton.

The Marines looked at each other, then back at their captain.

"Charge?" they all suggested to him simultaneously.

Warden sighed. "Right. If we're going to do this, let's have some discipline. A round of flashbangs before we move, then bounding overwatch to the next cover, then a final rush to overwhelm them. Try not to get shot. Everyone got it?"

Everyone nodded at him. "Good, then on my mark."

Warden shouted "Charge!" as he rose to his feet and began to sprint into the bay.

He slowed after a few paces. The enemy didn't shoot at him. Warden watched as a lone figure reached down, elbow rising and falling, a glowing knife in its fist. Once, twice, three times for good measure, then the figure stood.

"Everyone ready to leave?" Ten asked, the pistol in his other hand coughing quietly. There was the distinctive thud of a body sagging to the floor.

Warden stared for a moment, not quite sure exactly what had happened. He rallied magnificently, pushing away his confusion.

"Goodwin," he snapped, "get us into that shuttle, pronto. Everyone else, police the bodies, grab any last-minute intel, then get on the bloody shuttle. We're out of here."

Minutes later they were all crammed into the tight confines of the smallest shuttle they could find. Warden flopped down into the co-pilot's chair and buckled himself in. He reached out and clapped their pilot on the shoulder as the shuttle dropped through the access doors of the bay into open space.

"Sub Lieutenant Corn."

"Yes, sir?"

"Nice and easy does it, we don't want the bastards rumbling us. Make it look like we belong, okay?"

"Yes, sir. Slow and steady it is."

"Permission to detonate charges?" Fletcher called out, waggling her detonator. Ten and Milton held up more.

"Do it," Warden confirmed, flipping views of *Ascendant* and *Target*

One to screens around the small cabin. They watched as a series of small explosions rocked the enemy vessel. It was like a firework display. *Target One* was still very much intact, but atmosphere was venting in multiple locations, and the crew would have a lot to worry about right about now.

Warden grinned, and wondered how Cohen was getting on.

32

"Let's do this clean and fast, people," said Lieutenant White from the command chair. "We get one pass, let's make it count, and remember *Target One* is behind us. She might be clamped to *Ascendant,* but she'll have a clear view of our arse as soon as we move out from *Ascendant*'s shadow."

There was a murmur of quiet determination from around the bridge.

"Right. Sound the warning for high-G manoeuvres, Ms Parks, then maximum burn on the main engines for as long as we can take."

"But the crew, sir," protested Parks. "They'll take a dreadful punishment if we –"

"Can't be helped, Parks," said White. "Either we deal with *Target Two*, or she deals with us. We can't stay here and hope to get a better opportunity. Sound the warning."

"Aye, sir," said Parks. The alarm sounded, and White could imagine the effect it was having on the passengers. He gave it another few seconds.

"That's all we can spare," he muttered to himself. "Give it everything, Ms Robinson."

"Aye, sir," said Robinson, triggering the main burn. The bridge crew were rammed back in their seats as *Palmerston* rocketed away from the safety of *Ascendant*'s sheltering bulk.

"Get the railguns warmed up, Ms Elson," said White. "I want a nice neat line stitched right down the centre of that troop carrier. Let's see if she's as lightly armoured as she appears to be."

"Aye, sir," said Elson, hands flashing across the console. "You know we only have one pair of railguns, sir? The mass driver is our primary weapon."

"I know, Ms Elson, but I don't think that'll be much use to us today. Lay in the programme, you have, er–" he looked up at the main display, where a counter showed the rapidly reducing distance to *Target Two* as *Palmerston* continued to accelerate.

"About fifteen seconds, sir," said Robinson, "then another ten seconds before we're past."

"Work fast, Ms Elson," said White, "work fast."

Elson's hands flew as she set the firing lines for the railguns.

"Five seconds," said Robinson.

"Done and ready, sir," said Elson.

"Fire," said White simply, relaxing back into his seat as the acceleration continued.

"Firing, both guns, continuous stream," said Elson.

The bridge crew watched as the projectiles appeared on the tactical display. A neat row of yellow dots superimposed on the background stars, all following a line linking *Palmerston* and *Target Two*.

"Attitudinal thrusters firing on *Target Two*," said Parks. "Looks like they're preparing to run or trying to bring their weapons to bear."

"Six seconds to first impact," said Elson. "Still firing."

"No sign of incoming fire from *Target Two*."

"Nothing from *Target One* either. Not sure they've realised what's happening, yet."

"First impact, direct hit," reported Elson. Then, "Multiple impacts, still firing, no response yet from *Target Two*."

The bridge crew fell silent as *Palmerston* completed her pass unchallenged. *Target Two*'s thrusters spluttered and failed, the first sign that damage had been done. Then there was some sort of explosive event near the centre of the ship and a hole appeared in the hull. Debris floated out into space as *Palmerston*'s display switched cameras to keep the view focussed on *Target Two*.

"Firing has ended," reported Elson. "Ammunition at fifteen per cent, beginning automated replenishment."

"Main engine burn complete in three, two, one," said Robinson.

The end of the acceleration was a relief, but White couldn't help thinking that they had been tested and found wanting.

"Damage assessment, Ms Elson. Did we actually achieve anything more than a few minor hull breaches?"

"Reviewing the images now, sir," she replied. "Looks like we achieved greater than ninety per cent hit rate." She frowned, suddenly mistrusting her own figures. "That can't be right," she muttered, triggering a recount and forcing the AI to repeat its work.

"Ninety-six per cent," she breathed in astonishment. Then she grinned, nodding in satisfaction.

"Well done, Midshipman," said White, "that's excellent, but did we actually do any significant damage, or is she now going to blow us out of the sky?"

"Er, checking, sir," said Elson, reining in her celebrations. "Looks like multiple hull breaches along the length of Target Two. Suggests little to no armour, sir. High probability of major casualties and internal damage, but we'll need to go back and check to know for certain."

"Bugger that for a game of soldiers," muttered White. Poking the suspected corpse or a large vessel like *Target Two* was a good way to get yourself killed, no matter how many holes it had taken. "We'll wait, and see what–"

There was a flash on the main display.

"What the fuck was that?" said White, leaning forward to stare. A new hole had appeared near the rear of *Target Two* and gas could clearly be seen venting into space. "Come on," whispered White, daring the ship to do more than puff like a damp firework.

Then a further series of explosions ripped through the ship before one last, enormous blast shattered *Target Two*'s corpse and blew it to pieces. When the flash died away, there was nothing left but an expanding cloud of rapidly cooling debris.

"That's more like it," muttered White, nodding to himself. "Good work, team. Now let's check on our passengers and get this thing turned around. We're not out of the woods yet."

$\sim$

Tomsk turned to *Ascendant*'s main display and stared at the feed from *Palmerston*. The display went dark for a moment, and when it returned, it showed the tactical view from *Palmerston*.

"Sorry, our systems took some damage and aren't all working as they should," said Cohen, waving his arm around the bridge. "This view might be a little clearer."

They watched for a few seconds as *Palmerston* shot towards *Target Two*. Then Tomsk began waving his arms around. Cohen couldn't hear, but it looked very much like the admiral was having a violent argument with whoever was still aboard *Target One*. He grinned to himself and sat back to enjoy the show, with rather more insouciance than he really felt.

"Oops, that'll be the firing line from *Palmerston*. She's a gunboat, you know," said Cohen conversationally. "Originally designed for bombarding planets or other things that sit at the wrong end of a deep gravity well."

Tomsk was still waving his arms around gesturing at the display and generally making a fuss.

"Apart from the mass driver, which is pretty useless against something like that," said Cohen, nodding at *Target Two*, "I'm afraid *Palmerston*'s armaments are very light indeed. I must confess, that paucity of weapons has proven to be something of a hindrance, but I think we've managed to overcome the most serious of issues, wouldn't you say, Admiral?"

Tomsk whipped his head around to stare at Cohen. He flipped up his faceplate.

"What have you done?" he snarled in Koschite. Cohen waited for the translation then shrugged and gave the admiral an insolent grin.

"It's not my job to lose, Admiral, or to make things easy for you," he said. "I offered to accept your surrender, or to let you leave unmolested, but you chose to attack."

The admiral yelled something in Koschite that the translation system didn't catch, then he gestured angrily at his soldiers.

Cohen watched, wondering just how far he could push.

"If you surrender now, maybe we can still settle this peacefully." Tomsk stared at him, and Cohen had to work to keep the grin from his face. Death might be close at hand, but for the first time, Cohen thought he understood what drove the Marines, what led them to seek out dangerous solutions to difficult problems and to strive for victory even while everything seemed hopeless. Here, on the very edge of death, there was joy to be found in the simple things.

"Ah, look," said Cohen, working hard to keep his tone light and friendly. "*Palmerston* has opened fire."

Admiral Tomsk turned back to stare at the main display, mouth open in appalled horror as the feed showed *Palmerston* spitting untold numbers of railgun rounds at the troop carrier.

"Yes, you can follow the trajectory of the rounds on the tactical overview," Cohen went on. "It looks like your ship's going to take a bit of a pounding. Why isn't she firing back, or taking some other step to defend herself? Don't you think she ought to?"

Tomsk shouted in Koschite again and Cohen watched the translation as it rolled up in his HUD.

"Don't be too hard on them," he said sympathetically. "They're amateurs, after all."

"This is your doing, Cohen," said Tomsk angrily, rounding on the lieutenant commander and flailing angrily towards him.

"Yes," admitted Cohen, "although your crew's incompetence is certainly making things easier."

On the display, the feed had switched from showing the tactical overview to a close-up of the troop carrier as it floated serenely through space. All looked normal, except for the flashes of railgun rounds puncturing the hull and the spurts of gas as the penetrated chambers vented their contents into space.

"It's still not too late to surrender, sir," said Cohen, "if that's what you want. I would be happy to–" He stopped as an explosion punched a hole in the troop carrier's hull. "Ah, no. Maybe it is too late."

All eyes turned to the screen. Gas was blasting from a hole near the rear of the troop carrier. Then they saw several more explosions shudder along the length of the ship before one final blast shredded what was left. The Deathless watched in mute horror as the feed showed the remains of the troop carrier drifting through space. Then the feed ended, to be replaced by a slowly spinning Royal Navy logo.

"And that is my cue to leave, ladies and gentlemen," said Cohen, triggering the first of the explosive charges. There was a loud bang and then the atmosphere began to vent quickly from a small hole on the far side of the bridge.

Tomsk screamed something as the faceplate on his helmet closed, but Cohen couldn't make it out. He triggered the door control, over-riding the safety mechanism to force it to open even as the ship's atmosphere leaked from the bridge. Then he punched the icon to run the script that would overload the hyperspace engine and trigger *Ascendant*'s destruction.

<Ten-minute warning> he sent to Warden and White. Then he flicked the final icon on his HUD and the detonators in his hastily rigged device fired, igniting the plastic explosive. There was a bright fizzing flash accompanied by a weirdly quiet bang, and for a moment nothing more happened.

Then a large piece of the hull blew out of the side of the ship, taking the remaining atmosphere from the bridge and turning the breeze from the open corridor into a howling gale. Cohen watched as Tomsk clutched at the bridge furniture while around him his troops were blown or knocked through the gaping hole.

Cohen waited till he was sure Tomsk was looking at him. Then he gave a friendly salute and pushed himself into the stream of gas. In seconds, he was gone, snatched away by the wind and blown outside the ship. The stars flashed before his eyes as he spun end over end. Then the suit's automated systems took over, firing manoeuvring thrusters to stabilise him and stop his tumble.

"That seemed to work," muttered Cohen. Then he took control of the suit and set a course that would take him back to *Ascendant*.

33

Corn's hands flew over the shuttle's controls as she guided it along the underside of *Target One,* using the bulk of the capital ship to shield them from detection until they were ready to make a break for it.

Unlike the interstellar ships, the shuttle had transparent ports in her nose, offering a panoramic view of the way ahead. Designed for short range ship to ship transfers, the shuttle lacked the heavy shielding that made high-speed travel possible in an environment where even grains of sand were dangerous.

It also lacked both space and compartments, so as Corn flew, the Marines were crowded in behind her watching every move. It was like sitting every flying test she'd ever taken, all at the same time.

"Nicely done," said Warden as Corn guided the shuttle clear of *Target One*'s bulk. "Where is *Palmerston*?" he asked, looking around.

"Should be waiting for us over there," said Corn as the shuttle span, "nice and safe behind *Ascendant*." Then the great ship came into view, sliding upwards as the shuttles came down.

"Last round of charges firing now, Captain," said Marine X from the back of the shuttle. He was peering out of the rear viewing ports, taking in the undeniable majesty of Tomsk's flagship as the shuttle slid slowly past.

"Any sign of action?" asked Warden nervously. The shuttle was completely unarmoured. A railgun round would go right through the tiny ship and out the other side, and that would mark an ignominious end to an otherwise successful venture.

"Not a sausage, sir," said Ten happily. "Looks like they're busy with other problems." As well they should be. The Marines had torn through *Target One* using every demo pack they could carry and leaving behind a trail of high explosive charges. A few they had triggered as they went, others were waiting to be detonated remotely, and a few were on timers; all were placed against sensitive or delicate parts of the ship.

Corn brought the shuttle over the lip of *Ascendant*'s hull into the relative safety of her shadow and relaxed a little. Then she frowned as she looked around.

"She's not here," Corn said quietly as the shuttle came to a halt relative to *Ascendant*. "That's going to make things a bit tricky."

"They said they were dealing with *Target Two*," said Warden, "but shouldn't they be back by now to collect us? And where is *Target Two* anyway?"

"Can't tell," said Corn slowly. The shuttle's sensors were limited, however, and wherever *Palmerston* and *Target Two* had gone to play, they were out of range. "Or destroyed," muttered Corn under her breath.

"We'll be next if *Palmerston*'s been destroyed," said Warden quietly. It was a grim thought, especially so far from home.

Then a message popped up on Corn's HUD.

<Still breathing, Corn? This is *Palmerston*. Stand ready, we'll swing by and pick you up>

"Oh, thank fuck for that," murmured Corn, dragging Warden into the channel.

<Acknowledged, *Palmerston*. ETA?>

<About five hundred seconds, give or take>

Corn and Warden exchanged a glance.

<That's a bit close to the wire, sir> sent Warden.

<Can't be helped> sent White. <We're breaking bones as it is, can't get there any sooner>

Warden frowned at Corn.

"He means they're accelerating too fast for safety and taking injuries," she explained.

"Shit," said Warden.

<Flight plan to follow. Be there, or get left behind> sent White.

A package of data unfolded into Corn's HUD.

<Flight plan acknowledged. We'll be there. Out>

"This is going to be tricky," she said as she worked to translate the flight plan into the unfamiliar Deathless navigation system. It took a minute, then a blue line appeared on the main screen showing a suggested route to the rendezvous.

"Okay, we can work with that," said Corn. "They're coming in close and braking hard. Difficult, but we can get most of the way there in *Ascendant*'s shadow."

"And the rest?" asked Warden with a frown.

"If you wanted safe," said Corn with a shrug, "you should have stayed on New Bristol."

Warden looked at her for a moment then nodded. "I'll brief my team."

Corn guided the shuttle along *Ascendant*'s flank, staying close to the hull and moving so slowly she could see every gouge, puncture and tear in the great ship.

"Strange, the damage doesn't look so bad from out here," she said as *Ascendant*'s hull floated past. Then she passed a gaping hole almost big enough for the shuttle to land in, and she quickly revised her opinion.

<Sub Lieutenant Corn, is that you in the shuttle?>

The message floated across her HUD attached to Cohen's avatar.

<Any chance you could pick me up? The locale is becoming a tad dangerous for my taste>

She stared at the messages, open-mouthed, then she grinned.

"Cohen's alive," she yelled to Warden and the Marines.

<Aye, sir, every chance. Where are you?>

<On the outside of the hull, near the bridge>

"On the outside," she said quietly, her grin fading.

<We don't have an airlock, sir. If we open the doors to let you in...>

<Understood> Cohen replied. <But I'm in a suit. Maybe I could just hold on to the hull?>

Corn shook her head. It was insane. People travelled inside ships for a damned good reason. But she didn't have a better plan.

"We're going back for Cohen," she yelled to the Marines. "Hang on to something."

She flipped the shuttle around and mashed the accelerator, pushing the shuttle's tiny engine to burn as hard as it could. There was a chorus of disgruntled protests as the Marines were tossed and bounced around the inside of the shuttle, but even going flat out ,the little ship wasn't much faster than an old-fashioned bus.

"Quit your whining," she yelled over her shoulder as Warden heaved himself into the co-pilot's chair.

"Where is he?" Warden asked as the shuttle raced along only metres above *Ascendant*'s hull. The guidance computer pinged and beeped for attention, continuously re-plotting their route as Corn took the shuttle further and further from the rendezvous point.

"Up there near the bridge, somewhere," said Corn, waving her hands vaguely. "Keep your eyes open."

"There," said Warden, pointing excitedly. A small figure was standing on the outside of the hull, waving at the shuttle and flashing a weak light.

<We see you, sir> sent Corn. <Stand by>

<Valuable advice>

"Here we go," muttered Corn, hands hovering over the console as she judged the distance.

"Wait, you're doing this by eye?" asked an incredulous Warden.

"No time for anything else," shouted Corn. "Hold on!"

Then she killed the main engine, fired the thrusters to flip the shuttle through a hundred and eighty degrees, and rammed the engine back to full power. It screamed, and the Marines were thrown around like dolls on the inside of the shuttle.

Corn flicked up a feed from the rear cameras and watched as the image of Cohen grew rapidly. He threw himself flat against *Ascendant's* hull at the last minute as the shuttle came to a halt above the hole in the bridge's wall.

In the forward windows, Corn, Warden and the Marines watched as Cohen, only a few metres away, levered himself upright.

Then he pushed away from *Ascendant* to float across the gap and land on the outside of the shuttle. There were four distinct clangs as the magnets in his suit's gloves and boots engaged, clamping him to the shuttle's hull.

<The engineer has landed> sent Cohen.

<Welcome aboard, sir. Now hang on, we're a little behind schedule>

Corn fired the shuttle's thrusters, angling the tiny ship along the path the computer was showing, then she triggered the main engine and pushed it to maximum. There was another round of groaning complaints from the Marines as the shuttle shot forward.

<Thirty seconds to rendezvous> sent White from *Palmerston*. <Ready?>

<Working on it> replied Corn as the shuttle's engine propelled the craft back along *Ascendant's* hull and the timer on Cohen's improvised self-destruct mechanism hit the thirty-second mark.

"This is going to be very close," Corn muttered, teeth gritted.

Then the shuttle shot out from the protection of *Ascendant's* shadow and streaked across open space.

"Come on, come on," muttered Corn, almost bouncing in her seat. She glanced at the rear monitors as *Target One's* bulk came quickly into view before receding slowly into the distance.

"Is that turret moving?" asked Warden, zooming the image to focus on a small section of *Target One's* hull.

"Oh, shit," murmured Corn, glancing at the monitor as the gun swung slowly in their direction.

<Critical overload in fifteen seconds> sent Cohen.

<We see you, Corn> came a message from White. <Looks like you're still accelerating?>

<Only way to get there in time, *Palmerston*>

<Ten seconds, kill your engines>

Corn slapped at the controls and the engines died. The change in acceleration was a relief to the Marines, but it didn't stop them grumbling.

"Where the hell is *Palmerston*?" hissed Warden as *Target One*'s gun came to bear.

"There," said Corn, pointing out of the window as the engines of the gunboat flared brightly against the stars. "Bloody close," said Corn in a tight voice as she gripped the arms of her chair.

<Critical overload in three seconds>

There was an awful moment when Corn thought they might have overshot and missed *Palmerston* entirely. Then there was a flash of dark grey hull and the shuttle was suddenly inside the gunboat's bay. There was a terrible shudder as the shuttle touched down and then the most appalling juddering as she scraped across the floor of the bay, twisting to run backwards into the wall.

Corn had one last look at *Ascendant* and *Target One*, still locked together, then the bay doors closed, and *Palmerston* escaped into hyperspace.

~

Admiral Tomsk watched in disbelief as Cohen escaped through the hole he had blasted in the wall of the bridge.

"Get him," he screamed, although it was obvious that none of his boarding party were in any state to obey his order. It was all they could do to hang on to the furniture to avoid following those of their comrades who had already made the ultimate sacrifice.

Then the wind finally died away as the last remnants of *Ascendant*'s atmosphere were vented into space. No longer fighting against the wind, the Deathless recovered their poise and looked again to Admiral Tomsk for orders.

"Back to the ship," yelled Tomsk, pushing away from the console to which he had been clinging, and heading for the door. He bullied his way past his troops and into the corridor, but where previously their passage had been eased by the open doors, now they found every door closed against them.

"Get them open," commanded Tomsk, gesturing wildly. The troopers struggled to obey, eventually resorting to cranking open each of the heavy doors manually. By the time the party reached the inner airlock that led to the flagship, they were exhausted.

Tomsk cycled quickly through the airlock and across the tube to his flagship, but things were hardly better here. Emergency sirens wailed and red warning lamps flashed everywhere, but at least the ship's gravity still worked. There was nobody to greet him – an appalling breach of protocol – and a series of updates, alerts and dire warnings scrolled through his helmet's display. He silenced the feed and walked quickly towards the bridge.

"What the hell is going on?" he yelled as he strode onto the bridge.

The ship's commander, Captain Smirnov, glanced over, then straightened and saluted.

"We've been boarded, sir," he said in a tone of mild panic.

"Boarded?" hissed Tomsk, outraged. He removed his helmet and tossed it onto the floor. "What do you mean?"

"A hundred at least, maybe more. They opened an airlock and forced entry, then made an assault against our systems."

On a screen behind Smirnov, a feed from a corridor played, showing enemy troops moving quickly through the ship into the main shuttle bay.

"Sir, something's wrong with *Varpulis*," said Junior Lieutenant Kuznetsov, pointing at his monitor. "The radiation readings are spiking and there's a strong heat signature from the hyperspace engine."

"What?" snapped Smirnov. "Show me."

He crossed the bridge to look closely at Kuznetsov's screen.

"Shuttle bay doors have opened," reported Orlov quietly. Nobody took any notice.

"Hyperspace engine overload," breathed Kuznetsov. He turned to look at Admiral Tomsk. "They've rigged the ship to blow, sir. It'll take us with it."

"Get someone over there, right now, and fix it!" instructed Tomsk.

"Yes, sir," said Smirnov, relaying instructions to the science and maintenance teams.

"And move us away from *Varpulis*," snapped Tomsk, "immediately!"

"We can't detach, sir," said Smirnov. "The mechanisms are locked."

Tomsk stares at him. "Don't give me 'can't', you worm. Fire the engines, move us away from *Varpulis*."

"Engines are offline, sir," said Junior Lieutenant Ivanov, hands shaking as they rested on his console. Tomsk whirled around. "Something cut the power supply, sir," said the hapless helmsman quietly.

"How long till *Varpulis* becomes critical?" shouted Smirnov.

Kuznetsov looked around, shaking his head, fear etched into his face. "I don't know, sir."

"Then find out!" screamed Tomsk. "And get us away from *Varpulis*."

The bridge crew worked feverishly, shouting instructions to maintenance teams or just trying to reboot their own consoles. The damage to the ship blocked everything they tried.

"It's no good, sir, there's nothing we can do!" said Smirnov.

"What is that?" snarled Tomsk at a comms message in the corner of the display.

"The mandrills, sir," said Kuznetzov. "They're abandoning us."

A mandrill waved at the admiral, then the comms link was cut.

"They've gone to hyperspace, sir."

Then a feed on the main display showed a shuttle emerging from behind *Varpulis* and heading into space. The movement caught Tomsk's eye and he stared at it for a moment, distracted from the mandrill and captivated by the craft's slow progress.

"Kill them!" he yelled suddenly, pointing manically at the screen, eyes blazing. "Kill them, kill them, kill them!" He leapt across to the weapons control desk, shoving the operator out of the way to take direct control.

"Argh! Does nothing work?" he screamed in frustration, cycling through the weapon systems to try to find one that hadn't been disabled. "Hah, now I have you!"

The screen flipped to show a targeting display for the ship's only working railgun. Tomsk hissed as the weapon slowly turned, gradually coming to bear on the fleeing shuttle.

"Die, you bastards," he yelled in triumph.

But in the instant victory, a second ship flashed into view and the shuttle disappeared into its bay. Tomsk stared, open-mouthed, unable to believe what he was seeing as the railgun churned slowly into position.

The ship's doors closed, there was a sudden burst of light, and both shuttle and rescuer disappeared into hyperspace.

"No!" screamed Tomsk, punching the controls and sending railgun rounds spewing harmlessly across the void.

Then *Ascendant*'s hyperspace engine exploded. A ripple of blue light seared along the length of the ship, tearing it apart before cutting into Tomsk's flagship and slicing it to pieces. Further explosions followed, ripping open both ships and atomising Tomsk and his remaining crew.

34

Palmerston dropped out of hyperspace mere seconds after entering, appearing only a few hundred kilometres from *Child of Starlight*. An hour later, Palmerston touched down in *Child of Starlight*'s main bay to be met by a flood of medical personnel.

Cohen, White and Warden stood by as the injured were triaged and taken for further treatment.

"There wasn't anything we could do," said White quietly as the Valkyr worked. "*Target Two* diverted from their course."

"You did the right thing, Tim," said Cohen. "The Deathless would have wrought havoc on *Child of Starlight*. We're lucky they turned back."

"And you couldn't have left then unchallenged, sir," said Warden, adding his support. "One way or another, they had to be dealt with."

White looked at them both, then nodded his acceptance, although it was clear the parade of injured crew and Marines was taking its toll.

"That's everyone, sir," said Corn eventually. "And I've been over *Palmerston*. She's still going to need that refit, but she'll be fine to fly once we've refuelled and resupplied."

"Good work, Corn," said Cohen. "And thank you for your efforts. This day would have been a lot worse without your skills as a pilot."

Corn nodded her appreciation and was about to say more when one of the Prime Minister's aides appeared.

"Please," she said with a slight bow of her head, "Prime Minister Haukland would like to see you, if you are available?"

"Of course," said Cohen, although his face suggested that he really didn't want to attend another diplomatic function.

"She has promised to keep it short, Commander," said the aide, perhaps noticing Cohen's reluctance, "and you need not come alone. Please, follow me."

Cohen nodded. "Right," he said quietly, "you three with me, and let's keep things tight."

The aide led them to a light rail station where an empty carriage waited for them.

"It is not far," explained the aide, gesturing for them to board, "but it would be a long walk."

The train whisked them away, disappearing quickly into a tunnel and accelerating rapidly before slowing to stop at an enclosed station a few minutes later. A short walk through the station and a ride in an elevator brought them to a large chamber that looked out over *Child of Starlight*'s main bay.

"Commander Cohen, Lieutenant White, Captain Warden and Sub Lieutenant Corn," said Prime Minister Haukland in heavily accented English, striding forward to greet them with a warm smile on her face. "You have done great service. Thank you." She gave them a polite bow and led them to the huge windows that looked out across the rainforest that filled this end of the bay.

"English is still a foreign tongue," she said, slipping apologetically back to Koschite and reactivating her throat mic and automatic translation system. "But we hope to learn more and to build the friendship between our two nations."

"Thank you, Prime Minister," said Cohen, dipping his head. "It has been an honour to make your acquaintance and to get to know your people."

Haukland nodded and looked out over the forest. "This is why we live out here," she said, gesturing at the trees. "The freedom to build, to grow and to live as we see fit. Only here, amongst the asteroids, can we build like this. This is a special place, Commander, and it would not have survived the attentions of Admiral Tomsk."

"It is breathtaking," said Cohen, shaking his head in admiration as he surveyed the forest and the bay beyond. "But I'm afraid Tomsk is not a man to be easily dissuaded. I feel sure he will return, sooner or later."

"Of course," agreed Haukland. "Such men are not easily stopped, but our friends within the Koschite government are now alerted to Tomsk's obsessions and will act to calm the situation. More sober heads will prevail, Commander."

A small flock of green parakeets squawked noisily across the tree canopy in front of the viewing platform.

"And although it pains me to admit it, we too will now take measures to ensure our safety. The admiral will not find us ill-prepared again, should he return."

Cohen nodded.

"I think it is time for you to take some rest, Commander," said Haukland. "I see the weariness on you and, I think, the grief at the loss of *Ascendant* and your colleagues, even though they may be only temporarily absent."

Cohen nodded again, too tired to do much more.

"Since you cannot return to *Ascendant,* and *Palmerston* is too small to hold you all, we have prepared apartments for you and your people. Ramberg will take you to them and ensure that you have all you need, including the very best medical care we can offer. Tomorrow, or maybe the day after that, we will meet again."

"Thank you, Prime Minister," said Cohen.

"Please, this way," said Ramberg. "The apartments are nearby, and those of your crew who require no further treatment are already there."

∾

The next day, somewhat restored by a solid night's sleep, Cohen summoned his team to the communal area at the centre of the suite of apartments that the Valkyr had provided. One part of the elegantly proportioned space was laid out as a conference or meeting room, and Cohen waited at the front while his people filed in and found seats.

"Firstly, I'd like to thank you all for your efforts. Not just yesterday, but ever since we left New Bristol. This has been a difficult period for us all, and your professionalism and commitment have been outstanding. We may have lost *Ascendant*, but we have gained new allies, disrupted a dangerous faction within the Koschite government, and done great damage to the Deathless cause."

"More damage than that prick Morgan," said Ten, inserting his comment neatly into Cohen's pause and just loud enough that everyone could hear.

"*Palmerston* has done sterling service," Cohen continued, sliding past Ten's remark, "but she is too small to carry us all safely home, even in our reduced state. So I propose that some of our party remain on *Child of Starlight* for a short period while the rest travel home. We will then return with a larger ship, and maybe a party of diplomats, retrieve the rest of the party and establish proper relationships with the Valkyr."

"I'll stay," offered Ten.

"If the Valkyr agree, and I do not think they will object, then I propose to leave behind the wounded and ask for volunteers from amongst the crew and the Marines. I will then nominate an officer to command. Questions?" He looked around at the team.

"We could refit *Palmerston*'s bay, strip out her armament fabricators and dump her missile mass, sir," said Corn. "That might let us get everyone home in one trip."

"No," said Cohen, shaking his head. "I did consider that, but it would take time we really cannot spare. As soon our hosts agree, and *Palmerston* is ready, we leave."

There was a chorus of murmured assent, but nobody had any

further questions, so Cohen closed the meeting and sent them back to their rest.

～

"Commander, welcome," said Prime Minister Haukland as Cohen was shown into her office. "You look much recovered."

"Thank you, Prime Minister. The apartments are very comfortable, and I'm well rested after the, er, excitement of the last few days."

"And your crew? They too are rested?"

"Yes, Prime Minister, thank you."

"Good. Then I suspect you will want to be on your way," she said. "Not that I am trying to get rid of you, you understand. You are more than welcome to stay as long as you need, but I suspect you have duties that require your return."

"Indeed," said Cohen. "I have much to report and although you have been most generous hosts, we do need to get back."

"I understand that *Palmerston* is ready to fly. Have you decided when you will leave?"

"Within the hour, ideally," said Cohen, "but we have a problem with numbers, and I need to make one further request."

"You wish to leave part of your crew here with us while you return home? Yes, we anticipated that need. *Palmerston*'s size would be uncomfortable for such a large number of people."

"Exactly so, Prime Minister. And yes, we would like to leave around half our people, if you would be able to accommodate them."

"Of course, Commander, that is entirely possible. Indeed, we were thinking that the entire suite of apartments your people are currently using might be permanently assigned to a diplomatic mission, if your government would consider such an effort to be desirable."

"That is most generous, Prime Minister, thank you. I can't speak for my government, but I imagine they would be very interested in taking up your offer and in establishing a consulate of some sort."

"Good. We can take care of the details later," said the Prime Minister. "But this is an offer you can accept without needing to leave behind you people," Haukland went on. Cohen frowned, confused. "We have discussed this issue at length, and we feel that it is time for the Valkyr to reconnect with the people of Sol."

Cohen nodded thoughtfully but said nothing as he waited for Prime Minister Haukland to elaborate.

"Isolation suited us for a long time, but things change, and the Valkyr must change with them or risk being swept away. Recent events have demonstrated just how great those risks truly are."

Cohen nodded again, unsure what Haukland was proposing.

"So we will send a trade and diplomatic mission with you when you return. A vessel is being prepared," she said, gesturing towards a display on the wall that showed a view of the main bay, where a sleek white ship like a sculpted oval gleamed beneath *Child of Starlight*'s lamps.

"She's beautiful," said Cohen appreciatively, running his eyes over the ship's smooth lines.

"And brand new, the first of a new family of vessels. A fleet, I suppose you might say. Her crew is boarding as we speak, and *Brisingamen* has room for everyone from your crew who will not have a berth on *Palmerston*. In fact," Haukland went on with a touch of humour, "I think the passengers on *Brisingamen* will be rather more comfortable than the crew on *Palmerston*."

"Thank you, Prime Minister," said Cohen, "that is extremely generous of you."

"Well, all things come with a price, Commander," said Haukland with a wry smile. "We have a small cargo of goods, a selection of technical information and engineering samples that we wish to trade, and a personnel request."

Cohen hesitated, unsure where this was going. "Personnel?"

"Yes. Three of our people have asked to join your crew."

"I'm not sure that'll be possible," said Cohen sceptically and with a little shake of his head. "*Palmerston* is a fighting ship–"

Haukland held up her hand and Cohen nodded. "My apologies, Prime Minister. Please, continue."

"I must admit that I was surprised, but Frida Skar has always been something of an enigma. Brilliant, of course, but she can be a little difficult."

Cohen nodded, unsure what to say.

"And where Skar goes, Ornament – Agent O – follows."

Cohen was gobsmacked.

"Your research AI? You would let it travel with a foreign force?"

"Agent O is a citizen, Commander," she said with a tone of mild rebuke after reading the translation, "not a slave. It is free to choose its friends and make its own decisions. And as you found earlier, neither Skar nor Agent O are easily denied when they have set their minds to something."

"But the hardware..." murmured Cohen, not quite able to wrap his mind around the idea of an AI that was free to act of its own volition.

"Mere atoms, easily replaced," said Haukland, sweeping aside Cohen's concerns. "Indeed, we already have a dozen other similar hardware systems in *Child of Starlight*, with more being fabricated as we speak. Agent O will remain here as well, of course, as a fork of its software, albeit with some changes to its personality to maintain a degree of individuality."

"Two instances of Agent O would present a challenge to any leader," observed Cohen drily.

"Quite," agreed Haukland with feeling, "and this way it and its forks – there are several already – can play other roles."

"I understand," said Cohen, "and we would be happy to have Skar and Agent O aboard." What Admiral Staines would say was anyone's guess, but that was a problem for another day. "And the third person?"

"Trygstad," said Haukland, somewhat less amused. "We might have sent her with *Brisingamen* in any case, but she has asked to join Skar and Agent O aboard *Palmerston*."

Cohen raised his eyebrows, but having accepted Skar and Agent O, he could hardly refuse Trygstad. "We would be honoured," he said.

"Then that's settled," said Haukland. "*Brisingamen* will accompany you when you leave and will carry as many of your people as necessary. Skar, Agent O and Trygstad will join you on *Palmerston*, and we will set aside the apartment facility for use by your government." She stood up and offered her hand. "Thank you again Commander, and I wish you a safe journey home."

"Thank you, Prime Minister," said Cohen, hoping he had made the right decision.

35

C ohen opened a channel to Vice Admiral Staines as soon as *Palmerston* dropped out of hyperspace near New Bristol.

"Captain Cohen," said Staines from what looked like his private suite on HMS *Iron Duke*. "This is a most welcome surprise."

"Good day, sir. I thought it best to report as soon as possible, given the circumstances."

"After we lost contact with the fleet, we feared the worst." Then he frowned at something offscreen. "Wait a minute, HMS *Palmerston*? What happened to *Ascendant*?"

"Scuttled, sir," said Cohen grimly. This was the conversation he had been fearing throughout the return from Folkvangr. He went on, determined to get it done as quickly as possible. "In the face of over-whelming enemy aggression, I took the decision to preserve the mission and achieve a victory. The Deathless loss was greater than ours."

Staines was silent for a moment, but his expression was dark.

"Everything's in my report, sir," said Cohen, struggling on under the growing weight of Staines's obvious disappointment. He triggered the despatch of the files and watched as they were transmitted.

"And where is the rest of the fleet?" asked Staines quietly, in a tone Cohen recognised as one the admiral used only when he was exceptionally angry.

"Destroyed, sir. Utterly destroyed, during the Battle of Akbar."

Staines's expression darkened further, until it seemed he might simply disappear into the shadows.

"Destroyed?" he hissed.

"Ambushed, sir, by the Deathless, and cut to pieces." Cohen paused. "*Ascendant* and *Palmerston* retreated with heavy damage. All other ships were lost."

Staines leaned back, and his hand slid to his face, covering his eyes for a moment before he spoke.

"You're sure? What about Admiral Morgan and HMS *Duke of Norfolk*?"

"Yes, sir, certain. We were ordered to the reserve at the rear of the fleet. *Palmerston* docked with us by the skin of their teeth before we escaped to hyperspace. But we saw *Duke of Norfolk* destroyed before we left. Escape pods were launched prior to the explosion but none bore the transponder of Admiral Morgan. I assume he went down with his ship."

Staines rubbed his eyes. "At least we can redeploy Admiral Morgan while we wait for the Akbar system to be surveyed for intact escape pods. I'm sure if he had been in a fit state to leave, he would have been in his personal escape pod." said Staines. "We will debrief in person when you reach New Bristol. Is there anything else you should tell me now? Any good news? Perhaps some useful intelligence from the battle?"

"We have new allies, sir. The Children of Freyja who are known, informally, as the Valkyr. They live in asteroid colonies in the systems the Deathless don't want."

"And what makes you think they might be useful allies?"

"They're an offshoot of Koschite society, sir, a peaceful people without a military force but they are technologically advanced. They split decades ago, maybe a century or more." Cohen took a deep breath. "They gave us aid when we needed it, and my decision to sacrifice *Ascendant* took place during our successful efforts to protect their people from Deathless aggression."

"Sacrifice?" asked Staines, his expression now as grim as Cohen had ever seen.

"Diplomatic outreach, sir. A hearts and minds campaign."

"A hearts and minds campaign, led by a junior lieutenant commander in the Royal Navy, acting outside the chain of command and with no orders to that effect," Staines stated flatly.

"Sir." Cohen played his last card. "Standing orders are to render all possible assistance to allied nations. On discovering they were not part of the Koschite government, I determined that cooperation was vital to the survival of my crew, as well as to win the trust and material support of the Valkyr. It's all laid out in my report, sir."

"You scuttled an irreplaceable vessel of significant importance to our war effort to aid a foreign power," summarised Staines. "There will have to be a Board of Inquiry, and I do hope, for your sake, Captain, that your report appropriately justifies all your actions." Staines muted his microphone and spoke to someone off camera. "I've given orders for Admiral Morgan to be redeployed. His crews will have to wait until we have checked for survivors in escape pods."

"Sir? I know the protocol is to revisit the site of the battle, but it hasn't been used for decades. Surely the Admiralty won't risk another fleet going to Akbar just for this?"

Staines frowned. "And if you were the one stuck in an escape pod with dwindling supplies, Captain? Would you be so worried about the risk if it were you in a pod? I know this isn't something the Navy has had to do for a long time, but I would no more leave our personnel to starve to death in deep space than I would redeploy them and risk creating concurrent duplicates because we hadn't checked their status. We don't have ships for the crew who've died in any case, so we don't need to redeploy them yet, but rest assured, we will rescue any survivors, Captain."

"Yes, sir, of course. My apologies. I didn't mean to imply we should abandon them. I will happily volunteer to lead the mission to rescue them sir."

"If you had a ship of your own, I would take you up on that. I will read your report fully and call you back. You can take me through it all, from the beginning."

"Captain Cohen," said Rear Admiral Harper, "it is the judgement of this Board of Inquiry that your actions following the Battle of Akbar were in line with the standards required by the Royal Navy. The Valkyr were deftly handled, and you displayed the initiative we expect of every commanding officer. We therefore clear you to return to active duty and your record will reflect that your conduct was not at fault."

"Despite the loss of *Ascendant*," said the recently redeployed Admiral Morgan, glowering sternly at Cohen.

"And you will be mentioned in despatches," said Staines, casting an annoyed glance at Morgan, "for your actions in the face of overwhelming odds."

Cohen snapped a salute.

"But your immediate future," said Morgan, leaning back in his seat, "is more complicated." Cohen sat perfectly still, his face coldly neutral as his heart raced with sudden unease at the admiral's tone. "Our nose was bloodied in the ambush at Akbar."

A masterful understatement, thought Cohen, given the loss of all but two ships.

"Our focus is recovery. Full mobilisation of all fleets is underway and new ships have been commissioned, but those already have full complements of bridge officers," said Morgan.

Cohen gritted his teeth. He could see what was coming. He would have to serve as general staff to a senior officer until a new ship was completed. That could be months, or even years from now.

Morgan stabbed his finger at his data slate until a wireframe image appeared on the viewscreens around the conference room.

Cohen's eyes widened before his face settled into a confused frown. The ship was familiar, but he couldn't place it.

"This is the first available vessel that lacks a commander," said Morgan, gesturing at the hulking ship on the screen.

"I don't think I know her, sir. Is she still under construction?"

"No, Lieutenant Commander," scoffed Morgan, "she is not."

"Maybe the academy should step up their silhouette recognition tests, hmm?" quipped Harper, earning himself a frown from Staines.

"She's undergoing a partial refit en route to New Bristol. Headquarters brought her out of mothballs, along with anything else that will hold an atmosphere."

"She's part of the ghost fleet?" Cohen said incredulously.

"Perhaps this will help," said Harper, flicking a file from his slate to the display. The rotating wireframe was replaced by high definition video of a ship in orbit around a mid-sized moon.

It did help. There wasn't a schoolchild across the Commonwealth who wouldn't recognise that ship, or this particular video.

Cohen knew that in a few minutes, a light cargo freighter would come into view and instead of pulling up alongside the mothballed ship, it would ram her amidships. The explosion would result in hundreds of casualties, including several parties of schoolchildren visiting from settlements across the system.

One of the mightiest symbols of Commonwealth bravery and strength, she had been targeted by terrorists upset by some minor local issue. The bombing of HMS *Dreadnought* had horrified the Commonwealth, fuelling the interstellar news channels for weeks.

Cohen had done a project on the ship in school. Several, actually, now he came to think about it. The first had involved glue, bottles and cereal boxes. Later, he'd written essays about the attack and then, at the academy, he had studied *Dreadnought*'s military campaigns, the real meat of her century-old story.

HMS *Dreadnought* had been the first of her class, a technological marvel when she was first constructed. But now she was a museum piece, used for decades as a tourist attraction. That was why so many people had been aboard when the separatists had attacked. As they saw it, she was a symbol of the regime of the Sol governments which they saw as oppressive. It was utter nonsense of course.

In truth, she was a derelict. A discarded remnant mothballed as part of a ghost fleet distributed across the Commonwealth. The official argument was that such ships could be brought online in the event of large-scale conflict, but, unofficially, Cohen knew that the expense of safely deconstructing them was higher than mining new materials from asteroids. Ships as large as *Dreadnought* were rarely scrapped; they were dumped into orbit somewhere out of the way.

And now *Dreadnought* was his. A junior officer moving from a captured enemy cruiser to a battleship should be a huge promotion. But mothballed ships were stripped before retirement, downgraded and forgotten. *Dreadnought* wouldn't have weapons or manufactories, creature comforts or up-to-date equipment of any kind. The only reason it still had engines and power was to keep her safely in orbit. She was, in every respect, utterly outclassed by modern vessels and hopelessly decrepit. A flying antique.

But it was a command, and a capital ship at that. A second chance. He would still be the captain of a vessel, and he would see her returned to glory if he had to sweat blood to do it.

Cohen stiffened his back and took a deep breath.

"Thank you, sir. It will be an honour to command a vessel with such a long and illustrious history."

EPILOGUE

"Admiral Morgan, please reconsider," pleaded Governor Denmead. "We cannot risk more ships and leave New Bristol defenceless. My citizens are on the front line of this war, and they're vulnerable without the Navy's protection."

"Governor..." Morgan started but didn't seem to be able to finish.

"Denmead," she said through gritted teeth.

"Yes. Denmead. Protocol requires us to return to Akbar and search for survivors. *Ascendant*'s and *Palmerston*'s records as they fled the battle show escape pods launching. There could be crew in need of assistance, and the Royal Navy does not leave people behind. Now, if you'll excuse me, I have a job to do."

With that Admiral Morgan strode off to board a shuttle to his new flagship.

Denmead turned to Atticus and Staines, her anger obvious.

"What is wrong with that man? Am I the only one who thinks this is madness? What's stopping the Deathless fleet pulling the same trick and attacking this new mission?"

Staines shrugged. "In theory nothing, but I think it's very unlikely. Regardless, it has been Royal Navy protocol since the time of the Ark

JON EVANS & JAMES EVANS

ships. Even if it weren't, Admiral Morgan has control of the Naval forces stationed around New Bristol, and the decision is his to make."

Denmead wasn't happy with his response. She looked at Lieutenant Colonel Atticus for support.

"And you? What do you think of Morgan?"

"It's not really my place to comment, Governor. I'm just a Marine," he said. But hidden from Vice Admiral Staines' view, he jerked his hand up and down in a gesture that told Denmead exactly what he thought of Admiral Morgan.

Denmead snorted. That seemed about right. Morgan struck her as a by-the-book prig.

"So we're without a defensive fleet until Lieutenant Commander Cohen's new vessel arrives," said Denmead. "If Admiral Morgan insists on his snark hunt, what can we do to bring HMS *Dreadnought* up to fighting form as soon as possible?"

"She's your ship, Cohen. How soon till she's combat ready?" asked Staines.

"It's difficult to say, sir, but I have some ideas," replied Cohen. "They, er, may be a little unorthodox."

"What do you need?" asked Denmead.

"Engineers and technicians, fabricators and equipment, resources and materials from you, Governor." He paused, looking around the small group. "And permission from Vice Admiral Staines to involve the Valkyr in the refit."

There was a chilly silence. Staines's clearly wasn't happy, but Denmead was in no mood to compromise. She glared at him, daring him to disagree, and he nodded his assent.

"You'll have everything you need," said Denmead, "and as far as I'm concerned, you can use the Valkyr however you see fit just as long as you get your ship ready to fight."

"Thank you, Governor. HMS *Dreadnought* and her crew will answer the call when it comes."

THANK YOU FOR READING

Thank you for reading Volume Two of the Royal Marine Space Commandos series, which contains Ascendant and Gunboat, Books Three and Four.

The series continues with Dreadnought (coming soon), and we hope you'll enjoy that as well the future books in the series.

You'll soon be able to get a whole new series in the RMSC universe from a new collaborator, Paul Teague. Join the Imaginary Brother mailing list to find out when that's available.

It would help us immensely if you would leave a review on Amazon or Goodreads, or even tell a friend about the books.

Or contact us on Facebook to let us know what you thought of the book. We look forward to hearing from you.

Jon & James Evans

SUBSCRIBE AND GET A FREE BOOK

Want to know about upcoming releases?

Would you like to hear about how we write our books?

Maybe you'd like a free book, Ten Tales: Journey to the West?

You can get all this and more at imaginarybrother.com where you can sign up to the newsletter for our publishing company, Imaginary Brother.

When you join, we'll send you a free copy of Journey to the West, direct to your inbox*.

There will be more short stories about Ten and his many and varied adventures, including more exclusive ones, just for our newsletter readers as a thank you for their support.

Happy reading,

Jon & James Evans

We hope you'll stay on our mailing list but if you choose not to, you can follow us on Facebook or visit our website instead.

imaginarybrother.com

* We use Bookfunnel to send out our free books. It's painless but if you need help, they'll guide you through so you can get reading.

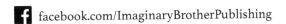 facebook.com/ImaginaryBrotherPublishing

IMAGINARY BROTHER PUBLISHING

Jon & James began writing the RMSC books in 2017 and published the first, Commando in March 2018. Three more books follow later in the year.

We formed Imaginary Brother to handle the Royal Marine Space Commando intellectual property going forward.

If you'd like to keep up with the new releases, we suggest joining the mailing list at imaginarybrother.com/journeytothewest

As a thank you, you'll get a free copy of Ten Tales: Journey to the West* and access to desktop wallpaper based on the new cover art for the books by Christian Kallias.

The fifth book, Dreadnought, will be out in early 2019 along with the audiobooks from Podium Publishing.

* We use Bookfunnel to send out our free books. It's painless but if you need help, they'll guide you through so you can get reading.

f

ABOUT THE AUTHORS JAMES EVANS

James has published the first two books of his Vensille Saga and is working on the third, as well as a number of other projects. At the same time, he is working on continuing the RMSC series with his brother Jon.

You can join James's mailing list to keep track of the upcoming releases, visit his website or follow him on social media.

jamesevansbooks.co.uk

- facebook.com/JamesEvansBooks
- twitter.com/JamesEvansBooks
- amazon.com/author/james-evans
- goodreads.com/james-evans
- bookbub.com/authors/jamesevans3

ABOUT THE AUTHORS JON EVANS

Jon is a new sci-fi author & fantasy author, whose first book, Thief-taker is awaiting its sequel. He lives and writes in Cardiff. He has some other projects waiting in the wings, once the RMSC series takes shape.

You can follow Jon's Facebook page where you'll be able to find out more about the RMSC universe. If you're a fan of Instagram, you can follow him there, and perhaps explain to him what it's for.

If you join the mailing list on the website, you'll get updates about how the new books are coming as well as information about new releases and the odd insight into the life of an author. Or insights into the life of an odd author.

jonevansbooks.com

facebook.com/jonevansauthor

amazon.com/author/jonevansbooks

goodreads.com/jonevans

bookbub.com/authors/jon-evans

instagram.com/jonevansauthor

Printed by Amazon Italia Logistica S.r.l.
Torrazza Piemonte (TO), Italy

11713958R00315